Penguin Books
SKYSHROUD

Tom Keene has worked with Thames Television and
Westward Television as both researcher and producer of
various current affairs programmes. In this capacity he has
travelled extensively in Europe, the Middle East and the
United States. He now writes full-time from his home in
Devon.

Brian Haynes spends part of the year living and working
in London making current affairs films for ITV. The rest
of the time he spends at a cottage in the Malvern Hills
flying kites and playing croquet.

Skyshroud is their second novel to be published in
Penguin, following *Spyship* which was published in 1981.

Tom Keene with Brian Haynes

SKYSHROUD

Penguin Books

Penguin Books Ltd, Harmondsworth, Middlesex, England
Penguin Books, 625 Madison Avenue, New York, New York 10022, U.S.A.
Penguin Books Australia Ltd, Ringwood, Victoria, Australia
Penguin Books Canada Ltd, 2801 John Street, Markham, Ontario, Canada L3R 1B4
Penguin Books (N.Z.) Ltd, 182-190 Wairau Road, Auckland 10, New Zealand

First published by Allen Lane 1981
Published in Penguin Books 1982

Made and printed in Great Britain by
Richard Clay (The Chaucer Press) Ltd, Bungay, Suffolk
Set in Monotype Plantin

For all those private reasons this book is for my wife,
Margy

AUTHOR'S NOTE

For thirty years an international stability – of sorts – has existed between East and West.

From behind the security of their vast nuclear arsenals, both superpowers have recognized that a nuclear attack by the missiles of one nation would be greeted by an instant retaliatory strike.

There could thus be no victors, only losers.

Acknowledging the gloomy merits of such 'Mutual Assured Destruction', the development of anti-missile systems was actually *banned* by the 1971 SALT* agreement.

In 1972 General Keegan, Head of United States Air Force Intelligence, began to suspect that the Soviet Union might be developing a charged particle beam weapon – a space-directed stream of atomic energy that would vaporize incoming American missiles should the day ever dawn when they were fired at the Soviet Union. With such a weapon, reasoned General Keegan, the Russians would be able to build an electronic shield, a missile-proof umbrella, over their vital installations.

That belief, that lone conviction, was held in the face of the intellectual arrogance of an American intelligence community that believed America had a monopoly on advanced technology, and that, since America had been unable to construct such a weapon, it could not exist.

That impasse led, ultimately, to General Keegan's resignation as Head of USAF Intelligence.

It led also, many months later, to his complete vindication.

On 1 March 1950, thirty-eight-year-old Klaus Fuchs, a

* SALT: Strategic Arms Limitation Talks.

naturalized Briton and leading atomic scientist, appeared before Lord Chief Justice Goddard at London's Central Criminal Court on two charges of 'communicating to a person or persons unknown information relating to atomic research which might be useful to an enemy'. Convicted of spying, Fuchs was sentenced to fourteen years' jail.

He received full remission for good conduct and was deported to East Germany in June 1959.

In September 1979 television cameraman Nick Downie witnessed a strange red glow in the sky, a circular, moon-shaped expansion of light, utterly unlike anything anyone had seen before in the skies above the mountain village of Shultan in the Hindu Kush of Afghanistan.

Traced back by compass bearings taken at the time by the ex-Special Air Service trooper, the strange light seemed to be coming from the Soviet anti-missile test centre at Sary Shagan, across the border.

That much, at least, is documented fact . . .

Tom Keene

SKYSHROUD

They had waited a long time for this moment.

Professor Eduard Ryabov glanced around the silent bunker at the tense, waiting faces and rubbed the palms of his hands down the soiled sleeves of his white coat. 'I will give the command. It is my responsibility.' The others nodded.

Professor Ryabov was a small, slight man in his mid-sixties. He stepped up to the observation slit, adjusted the telescope and peered carefully down range. All appeared to be ready. He stepped down, crossed to the control point and lifted the green handset that would connect him to the firing point. 'We are ready,' he said. 'At your discretion, thirty seconds from now.'

'*Da.*'

The line went dead and Ryabov replaced the receiver. 'In thirty seconds,' he repeated to the others. 'Take up your positions.'

The scientists and observers – nine men and three women – nodded and moved forward to cluster carefully around the Professor behind the thick armoured glass.

Down range there was nothing to see but a cluster of drab, low, brown buildings set into the backdrop of remote, dun-coloured mountains. The buildings were four miles away, lost in the vast hinterland of the Soviet Union.

'Masks,' ordered Ryabov. There was a rustle of cloth in the silent shelter as twelve pairs of hands adjusted the face masks with their thick, shaded lenses. Over by the door two uniformed guards turned and faced the wall, their flat features impassive. The silence became absolute as Ryabov counted off the seconds: 'Four – three – two – one . . .'

Nothing happened.

They strained forward, eyes smarting behind thick goggles.

'We should perhaps –' began one of the women at Ryabov's elbow as a flash of piercing, horizontal, blue-white light crackled blindingly across the dry, wind-blown dust-bowl at their feet.

Within moments the skies above their shelter as far as the mountain peaks beyond were shot first with a light, delicate pink which turned, even as they watched, to a bright, flaring crimson as released protons and neutrons collided savagely across the heavens in a stupefying display of nature out of balance with herself.

Long minutes passed in utter, spell-bound silence before the angry light began to fade and then vanished altogether as the scientists stepped down from the observation platform and tugged away their goggles, each aware of a profound, almost mystical sense of awe at the power they had unleashed across the desert sky.

The phone jangled at the control point and the spell was broken. Ryabov crossed to it rapidly. 'Yes, yes. That is so. Satisfactory, I think. Yes – we could see it quite clearly.' He replaced the receiver. 'Now we must wait,' he declared simply.

Four hours later a sand-coloured BTR-152 personnel carrier without the usual deck armour squealed to a halt outside the shelter's massive steel doors. The party climbed awkwardly aboard, their movements necessarily hampered now by the stiff folds of the protective suiting, by the over-boots and the heavy rubber respirators that reduced each breath to a laboured, sinister wheezing. The personnel carrier was designed for seventeen fully armed combat troops, so there was plenty of room within for the scientists and observers to stretch out more comfortably as they jolted over the harsh, arid plain towards the target, a banner of dry yellow dust dragged across the hot sky behind them.

The gun-ports were battened down against the dust, and the group jolted forward past the road blocks in hot, darkened silence, each scientist preferring the company of his own thoughts as they bumped and bounced towards the culmination of eight years' work.

Finally the vehicle halted and they climbed down into the bright sunlight, the sweat running freely down the insides of their charcoal-impregnated protective suits.

Professor Ryabov stepped to the front of his waiting, ghost-like colleagues and began walking forward cautiously, his eyes on the geiger-counter that crackled ominously as he swept it from side to side, picking his way across broken ground towards their objective.

He walked on, his breathing unnaturally loud in his own ears as he led the party forward. A hand clutched his arm and he swung around in alarm. Another of the ghostly, helmeted figures loomed forward into his restricted field of vision, and an arm was thrust forward, pointing violently for emphasis.

Ryabov stared intently through the sweat-smeared eye-pieces of his respirator.

Long disused, their target had been a cluster of steel-reinforced shelters used years ago to augment test firing of the now replaced S S-7 Saddler surface-to-surface missile. Each shelter had been designed to withstand an over-pressure of 2,500 pounds per square inch, and into these steel and concrete shelters had been led two dozen sheep, all of whom had bleated mightily as they were tethered behind the protective, four-foot-thick walls to await the test firing of Ryabov's modest little weapon.

Now Ryabov looked around with awe. Of the six reinforced shelters, only a pile of charred, broken rubble remained. No piece was larger than a grapefruit, and overall hung the not disagreeable aroma of roast mutton.

The smell was quite unmistakable, even through the protective layers of the charcoal filter. Professor Ryabov turned to scramble through the sea of broken rubble, the geiger-counter sweeping before him, its message of alarm crackling furiously as the heat of the ground beneath his feet began to beat up through the thick soles of his over-boots.

After a few paces he paused, rubbed a gloved hand across his misted lenses and peered through the billowing clouds of orange dust towards the gently sloping hillside beyond. He rubbed again, as though reluctant to acknowledge what he saw: he thought at first he was looking at the remains of some World War 1 battleground.

As far as he could see through the swirling dust, for three, four hundred metres in every direction down-range, the ground was levelled, smoking, charred to blackness, the convexity of the hill pocked here and there with the stumps of blasted trees that, even as he watched, flickered into sudden, smouldering flame.

Two hours later the locker-lined changing room at the firing point was still strangely subdued as scientists and observers shared the same silence of introspection as they stripped off their protective suits and went through the laborious procedure of decontamination before changing gratefully back into their civilian clothes. Presently only two elderly men were left to finish their dressing – a balding scientist, nearing seventy, with round black spectacles, and Professor Eduard Ryabov, who was sitting on one of the bare wooden benches, his untied shoes forgotten as he immersed himself in the stream of calculations he was jotting on the back of an envelope.

The older of the two men finished straightening his tie, reached for his jacket and glanced in the mirror at the seated Professor, whose brilliance he had been among the first to recognize and whose position he had protected behind the shield of his own awesome reputation. He studied the Professor's frown of concentration and walked slowly over to the bench, where he laid a hand gently on his protégé's thin shoulders.

'Come on now, Eduard – you should be celebrating! Are you all right?'

'What? Oh . . yes, yes. Quite all right,' replied Ryabov, his face haunted by some deep inner turmoil. 'Why do you ask?'

'You appeared worried.'

'I'm fine, fine.' He paused to wave the envelope gently between his fingers. 'It's incredible – quite incredible! Do you realize that that demonstration we have just witnessed represented merely one fortieth of the predicted power source of Skyshroud? One *fortieth*? With that minor order of magnitude we did . . . we did *that*? Did you see the extent, the scale of the devastation?'

The older man nodded silently as Ryabov plunged on, staring up at his mentor. 'Tell me, Klaus: when you and the others – when you were working on the Manhattan Project back in '42 – did you feel you were standing on the brink, on the very edge of a whole new world of discovery? Of something that would alter the very fabric and balance of the world you lived in? Did you feel that?'

The older man stifled a sigh of impatience. His wartime work for the Allies at the vast gaseous diffusion plant at Oak Ridge, Tennessee – in its day the biggest industrial undertaking ever attempted, with its hundreds of miles of welded piping and its fully automated procedures scattered over the fifty-acre site – appeared almost crude in comparison with the majestic opportunities thrown forward now by this Skyshroud project. He shrugged. 'Something like that, yes. There was a great sense of excitement, of –'

'That is what I feel too. Our work here has enormous defensive potential, Klaus – enormous! But we're not God, you and I: there must be limits to what we attempt to accomplish for those people –' he gestured vaguely towards Moscow – 'we, us – you and I, Klaus – *we* must impose those limits! In the wrong hands the nuclear balance achieved through the SALT talks between East and West could –'

'The SALT talks? You worry too much, Eduard,' scoffed the older man, his eyes suddenly flat and distant as he detected his friend's faint-heartedness. 'It's a defensive system, Eduard – a defensive system, just as you say. How could that be misused, eh?'

Ryabov said nothing. But the older Professor's full name

was Fuchs – Klaus Emil Julius Fuchs – and already, somewhere, there was a chilling answer to that question.

*

At a little after 7 p.m. on Wednesday, 27 March, Simon Blackler ruffled the soft blond hair of his sleeping daughter, kissed her on the cheek and closed the door gently behind him.

As he moved towards the front door of their apartment he could hear his wife working in the kitchen, preparing supper. She was humming to herself as he reached stealthily for his topcoat. Blackler licked dry lips and made to call a cheerful farewell but the words stuck in his throat like olives in a jar He lifted the chain off the lock, stepped outside and pulled the door closed. He stood there in the darkness looking out along the sour, crowded sprawl of downtown New York. Then he struggled into his coat and swallowed nervously. They had said no guns – they had been quite definite about that; no weapons of any kind. They wanted an accident.

And so he, Simon Blackler, was going to give them one. He was setting out to help murder a perfect stranger.

He didn't even know the man's name.

It had begun the day before yesterday, and the signal had been two pieces of orange peel on the porch step. Orange peel would be safe, they'd said: fool-proof. It would cause no comment; it would be safe both from theft and from the nosings of stray animals looking for scraps. He had pushed the meticulous reasoning to the back of his mind for many months in the hope that if he forgot about them, they might forget about him.

They hadn't.

And so, that same lunchtime, he had left the loading bay of the department store where he worked and travelled briskly north to the subway bridge in the Bronx. Stopping at the fifth girder along, he reached up and removed the flat metal box he found clipped by magnets to the girder above his head. Then he turned and hurried back to work, the box weighing a ton in his pocket.

He was late back at the bay and had to wait until mid-afternoon before he was able to slip into one of the narrow toilet stalls and slide open the flat metal box. It contained a thick wad of currency, a man's photograph and a thin sheet of coded instructions. With his trousers around his ankles and his eyes flicking often to the top of the wooden partition to ensure he was unobserved, Blackler deciphered his instructions. It was there, amid the scrawled graffiti and the raucous shouts of his workmates, that he learnt he was being reactivated.

If anything, he had done his work too well. Ordered to infiltrate the system, blend into the background, build solid cover amid his country's enemies and await instructions, he had done just that – and the inevitable had happened: despite the long weeks of ideological training at the academy on the top floor of the apartment block on Kutuzovsky Prospekt, the cracks had begun to appear in the façade of his own conviction. Imperceptibily, he had been turned around by intimate exposure to the very freedoms and values he had been trained to scorn.

Blackler turned his coat collar against the wind that cartwheeled the rubbish around his legs and his footsteps quickened.

Ferris turned the last of the keys in the metal blind on the front of his jewellery store, waved a cheerful greeting to the patrolman across the street and set off briskly towards the subway. Unlike Blackler he walked with a solid confidence, grinning to himself as he thought of the patrolman guarding his store while he went about his business. His arm brushed against the pistol under his jacket and he glanced casually up at the wedge of sky outlined against the rim of the tall buildings that flanked his progress across town. Chill, sharp and with the threat of rain – not a night for dawdling on street corners watching other people's business. That was good, thought Ferris.

*

Blackler emerged from the warmth of the subway, turned down W135ST and hurried on past the bright shop windows and the bustling, urgent, anxious-to-be-home crowds. He concentrated on wiping the fears and doubts from his mind, from his face. They mustn't show, he thought – not for an instant. He turned left again: there was a bus stop over on the right and there, standing a little apart from the others, was a tall, lean-looking man with an umbrella in the crook of his left arm. He regarded Blackler implacably as he drew nearer. 'Say, would you know where I can get some aspirin?' asked Blackler quietly. Ferris shrugged.

'The drug store around the corner closed half an hour ago.'

'That's too bad,' completed Blackler. 'My headache is getting worse.'

The other nodded, satisfied. 'OK – let's get to it. We haven't a lot of time,' he murmured, as they turned away together.

'A coffee first? While we discuss things?' suggested Blackler mildly. Ferris glanced at him sharply and noticed the dilated pupils, the pulsing Adam's apple above the buttoned collar. Nervous, he decided. Perhaps, worse than that, frightened. They were right. He would bear watching.

'I think not. Unless, of course, you want half New York to know what we're about,' decided Ferris with a grim smile. 'We'd better find somewhere outside. Come with me.'

Blackler fell into step beside the larger man. Presently 'Do you have a gun with you?' he asked quietly, after a glance behind to make sure they were not overheard.

Ferris shook his head. 'You read the orders,' he replied curtly.

Nine floors up, high above the honk and the blare of the city's traffic, Vasili Lyudin was making dinner. Dinner. A grand name for a chore he detested, cooking for one on an electric stove – and besides: this food, this pap – it was too bland. It had no taste, no bite, not like the *Zakouski*, the *borshch* and the *blini* of his homeland. Certainly, he some-times bought the food of his choice from the deli across the block, but where, truly, was the point? He could buy good food, but there would be little money left for his books and none at all for the heating; he could sit in warmth and com-fort without his books and eat, or he could read like a scholar and starve to death in the cold. He shrugged. Well, soon it would all be over. Soon, once he had talked to the American General, given his evidence, told him as much as he knew about what that ex-spy Professor Fuchs and his team of scientists were really up to, he would be wealthy – a quarter of a million dollars wealthy, and the need for such equations would be over. A brilliant scientist and Soviet mathematician, Lyudin was used to equations.

High up there above the streets, among the private intel-lectual clutter of his apartment, he had opted for a compro-mise: he ate badly in rooms that were never warm enough, and he bought his books with the care of a miser donating to charity. For the rest, it was not so bad – he had the sweaters that would keep out the cold of the winter and the friends who . . . he paused, frowning at the glutinous mass that was bubbling unhappily at the bottom of his saucepan. He had no friends, he recognized soberly as he stirred the mixture disinterestedly. Still! – he sighed with exasperation, turned down the stove and then laid the wooden spoon aside as the doorbell rang again.

He walked slowly towards the door. He stood back, the chain still on the lock, and called out in a thin, wavering voice: 'Who is it ? What do you want?'

'Mrs Kastner sent me over –' the voice seemed strangely muffled – 'from the Deli. Over on Hamilton.'

'Mrs Kastner? But I ordered no food. There must be some mistake,' called Lyudin, puzzled by the confusion. He hadn't ordered from Mrs Kastner's for a long time.

'You're Mr Lossman? Harold Lossman?' called the voice.

'That is I,' conceded Lyudin carefully. It was the name he had hidden behind since he came over.

'Then this is for you. Look, man – don't give me a hard time. Open the door will you? I've got other deliveries to make too, you know?'

Lyudin hesitated and then fumbled the chain off the lock.

There was a man in a dark blue topcoat holding out a brown paper bag from which arose steam and the aroma of fresh, savoury *pirozhki*. The man outside smiled pleasantly. 'Smells good, yeah?'

Lyudin took the paper bag and glanced inside.

'Two thirty-eight to pay,' said the man promptly. Lyudin nodded abstractedly, patted his pockets for change and then waved the man inside with a gesture of impatience. 'Come in, come inside quickly – and close the door before all the heat it escapes.'

The man stepped across the threshold as Lyudin turned to rummage in the bulging pockets of an old sports jacket hanging over the back of a chair. The stranger closed the front door and crossed soundlessly to the window. He looked down for a moment and then slid open the wider of the two panes of glass.

Lyudin heard the sudden muted hum of traffic far below and felt the draught of cold air on the back of his neck. He turned around.

'Hi!' he said sharply. 'What do you think you are doing? Please – close that window!'

'Don't you go worrying yourself about me, Professor,' said the other man, the smile now quite gone. 'I was just admiring your view. It's quite a –'

'Professor? Who told you I was a professor?' demanded Lyudin in a whisper, the fear a sudden lurch below the heart. For a man in his late fifties he then moved surprisingly quickly: he crossed to the kitchen, swept up the delicatessen delivery bag, snatched the phone off the hook and began dialling the number on the bag with feverish fingers. 'You are not from the deli, I think,' he began shrilly, wagging a bony finger at the man, who moved swiftly towards him across the lounge. 'You are from –'

The phone was wrenched from his thin fingers, the connection was broken and Lyudin was sent spinning violently across the room to fetch up against a small table that went over, scattering books and papers everywhere.

The man replaced the receiver and then crossed again to the front door, his eyes never leaving the Professor, who had thought himself safe, so stupidly safe, just because he had hidden behind a new name. Ferris opened the front door and Blackler stepped into the room.

Both men advanced slowly towards Lyudin with infinite menace. Lyudin backed away into a corner, a dark stain spreading across the crotch of his baggy trousers.

He started to scream.

Ferris moved up behind him, got a hand around his throat and jammed a teatowel into that wet, screaming hole. The man's eyes bulged as he gagged, his cries turning into a bubble of stifled pleading. Blackler broke away and darted into the kitchen, his heart pounding. He wanted to be sick; he wanted to leave; he couldn't go through with it. He couldn't! Eyes flicking around the kitchen for distraction, he saw the meal cooking in the saucepan and turned down the electric stove.

'You – quickly,' commanded Ferris. At the crack in the voice Blackler came forward hesitantly, a knuckle clenched to his mouth. There was terrible, naked pleading in the scrawny, struggling figure of the scientist as Ferris began to edge his squirming burden towards the beckoning window and that yawning drop down into the darkness.

'Come on, then – grab his other arm,' commanded Ferris impatiently as Lyudin threatened to get away.

'I . . . I can't . . .' began Blackler, the sweat gleaming on his forehead.

'Come on, damn you – do it,' snarled Ferris. Eyes starting, Blackler made a grab at the man's twisting body.

'That's it – now grab hold,' ground out Ferris. They shuffled towards the open window in a violent, grisly six-step accompanied by the muted pleadings of their terrified victim.

Ferris looked down at the terrified face. 'Traitor,' he said quietly. 'Traitor, defector. Did you really think you could escape to the Americans? Did you? You are about to die, comrade, as a lesson – a lesson to the others.'

Ferris edged up against the windowsill and, twisting aside, pushed Lyudin's thin hips up and over the sill.

'Now,' said Ferris, panting slightly from the exertion. 'Listen while I go over it again: when I say "Go" you are to push with the legs. When you do that I will pull the gag from his mouth and then push also, understood?' Ferris allowed himself a thin smile. 'I think that, at that stage, a little scream might be permitted – don't you agree? Traitor?' Lyudin, bathed in sweat, foam flecking the corners of his mouth, rolled his eyes in terror as he felt the sill work its way up his buttocks inexorably as Ferris began to wriggle him forward. Blackler clutched the man's legs, closed his eyes and began muttering under his breath.

'Go!' grunted Ferris. Blackler shoved, Ferris tore away the towel and Vasili Lyudin disappeared into the black night with that thin hideous wail that goes with dying. Ferris stuffed the sodden teatowel into a pocket and turned to Blackler as they heard the squeal of brakes far below. 'Done,' he said briskly. 'Now move! It's time we were gone.'

Fifteen minutes later Ferris turned down a side street into a dark cul-de-sac piled high with rubbish and cardboard boxes. He stopped in the gloom and waited for Blackler to catch up, the man's arrival preceded by the scuff of heels and the rasp of laboured breathing. 'OK?' asked Ferris softly. Blackler caught his breath and nodded.

'Well done,' congratulated Ferris with a smile as he laid an arm across Blackler's shoulders. 'You did OK.' Blackler shook his head and dragged a hand across his mouth to wipe away the sour bile of tension. 'I'll tell you something: I never want –'

Ferris shot him once in the exact centre of the forehead with his silenced pistol. The force of the shot lifted Blackler cleanly off his heels and sent him crashing back among a pile of cardboard boxes. The body twitched once and lay still. Ferris paused, looked carefully about him, crossed to the corpse and placed the barrel against the roof of the gaping mouth. He fired again.

'They thought you might have grown too soft,' he murmured, reaching down to pluck the man's bulging wallet from an inside pocket. 'They were right too, weren't they? Comrade.'

A truck slushed by and Ferris dodged nimbly round the puddles and across the road to push gratefully into the steamy warmth of the coffee house tucked away behind Roosevelt Hospital and W59th. The place was crowded with the usual late-night crowd of students and secretaries, couples and loners, exchanging glances and jokes, small-talk and partners. Ferris had come to exchange information.

The man he knew as Michael was sitting in a wooden booth at the back of the bar, his hands clasped firmly in front of him as he nursed a tall glass of beer. Early forties, roll-neck sweater beneath a conservative sports jacket, black hair spiked with needles of grey, he glanced up briefly as the door banged open and then resumed his study of the glass before him as Ferris ordered a cognac and moved to join him.

'Everything go OK?' asked Michael quietly. Ferris nodded curtly and tossed his coat over the back of an empty chair. He sat down abruptly, hands and fingers moving restlessly, the high of the killing still with him. Michael knew the feeling. Ferris took a swallow of cognac, replaced the glass on the table and linked the wet rim patterns with the tip of a finger. 'It was all right. No complications – the job itself, that is.'

'And your friend?'

Ferris drew another wet pattern on the table top. 'He couldn't make it. It was as you suspected –' he gave the ghost of a grin that had nothing whatever to do with humour – 'there was something wrong with his stomach.'

The man Ferris knew as Michael was in fact Major

Dmitri Muratov, Field Officer in charge of the Soviet Rezidentura's Executive Action Section (Department V) in New York. Later, alone in the high-ceilinged, sparsely furnished second-floor office, he pressed the buzzer at his elbow and crossed to the heavy metal safe set into the thick inner wall while he waited for the KGB security guard to arrive.

As he waited, his eyes ran once more over the brief report he was about to send to 'The Centre', the massive new KGB headquarters on the circumferential highway outside Moscow.

Detailing successful compliance with orders sanctioned by the Head of the First Chief Directorate himself regarding the disposal of Vasili Lyudin, and prefixed by the initials MD, the report's very existence was already a matter of solid fact known to the State. Perhaps that was because the words, freely translated, have become KGB jargon for sabotage, kidnapping and political murder – MD: *Mokrie Dela*, 'wet affairs'.

In one of the more expensive French restaurants in Washington D C the kitchen doors swung back and a waiter swept through into the dining area, a tray balanced with precarious, practised ease above his head as he picked his way between busy tables towards the party of three near the window.

The table was laid for four and there was one empty seat. Of the three middle-aged diners sitting at the table one was male, the other two women in expensive evening gowns. Now the women murmured together excitedly as the waiter reverently lowered the tray and they caught the first glimpse of the steaming *bourride*, a Provençal fish soup with garlic mayonnaise and soft flakes of bream served over a *croûte* of toasted French bread.

As the waiter began to serve, Doris Freeman glanced at her gold watch and looked about the crowded restaurant with irritation. 'I wish that once – just once, Emily – Clarke would turn up on time. I truly believe he does it just to vex me, you know? Last week it was –'

'And for you, madame?' Doris Freeman nodded curtly, and the waiter dipped the ladle once more. As he did so, Emily touched Doris lightly on the shoulder. 'Here he comes now.'

Doris turned and glanced towards the door. Her husband was moving slowly towards them between the crowded tables, a hand raised in greeting. Doris frowned. He was still in uniform. He knew how she hated that, hated the constant, all-pervading reminder of the military.

General Clarke Freeman arrived at their table and nodded pleasantly to his wife's friends. 'Emily, Dan – good to see you! Sorry I'm a little late.' He bent to peck swiftly at his wife's cheek, picking up immediately on her frown of disapproval. Emily, at least, smiled a warm welcome. She liked Clarke Freeman. Unlike Doris, she secretly enjoyed the furtive glances of association from the other tables as they took in the well-tailored dark blue uniform and the rows of medal ribbons beneath the craggy, handsome face. She thought of Clarke Freeman as strong, protective, uncompromising, and she basked, privately, in the aura of security that surrounded a man far stronger than her own rich husband.

'Did you have to come in uniform, Clarke?' whispered Doris as he bent beside her. General Freeman straightened with a sigh. 'You'd rather I went home and changed? I should make it back in time for the coffee –'

''Evening, Clarke – they keeping you back at that fun factory of yours?' beamed Dan maliciously. Clarke Freeman grunted, sat down and shook out the starched folds of his napkin. Dan always called the Pentagon that: the fun factory. The remark was typical of his shallow façade of fashionable, calculated sophistication.

'Something like that,' he offered in tones that warned that the joke was tired, the matter therefore closed.

Dan ignored the warning. 'Anyone started World War Three?' he beamed.

Emily looked up, alarmed, and laid a hand on her husband's arm. 'That's enough of that, Dan, you hear? We're celebrating Doris's birthday, not starting one of your arguments.' She smiled brilliantly across the table. General Freeman glanced up at the fat little President of Nimrod Swimwear, Inc. He smiled easily, hiding his true feelings behind a practised air of casual dismissal. It lay within his knowledge as the Head of United States Air Force Intelligence to wipe away the civilian's look of smug, protected complacency with one chilling glimpse at the intelligence report he had been compiling less than one hour ago: a report that, he believed, led him towards the inescapable conclusion that the Soviet Union was preparing to fight *and survive* a nuclear war. He smiled easily and dipped his gleaming spoon into the still surface of his soup.

'Not yet, Dan – when they do I'll ensure Nimrod Swimwear are among the –'

'Pardon, m'sieur. General Freeman?' They all glanced up at the head waiter, who had arrived soundlessly at their table. 'I have a telephone call for you. I am told it is important.'

Doris Freeman groaned aloud as her husband crumpled his napkin and rose to his feet without a word, without apology. 'I'll be just one moment.'

He turned and followed the waiter towards the telephone. 'General Freeman.'

'Major Conroy, General. Duty Intelligence.'

'Go ahead, Major.'

'Sorry to disturb you, General, but we've just heard: another of your Windjammers has gone down.'

General Freeman's knuckles whitened on the phone. 'Another? Who?'

'Lyudin, General. In New York. He died earlier this evening.'

'Accident?' demanded Freeman sharply.

'We don't think so, General –'

'OK, Major – start putting it together. I'm on my way in.'

The aircraft rose steeply into the clear night sky, its red belly light revolving a warning across the sky as it climbed on into the smoother air above Cincinnati and swung away to the east towards Washington DC.

Frank Yates unbuckled his lap strap, stretched his legs and breathed an inaudible sigh of relief. A qualified fixed-wing pilot with the US Air Force, Frank still felt nervous away from the controls, sitting back here among the passengers, helpless, his fate in the hands of others.

His fate in the hands of others: he glanced down at the lean, brown hands that lay now in repose – hands that, at the controls of his McDonnell Douglas F-4 Phantom jet, had mastered terrible skills to bring fiery death to others from the clear blue skies above the rugged and eerie Central Highlands of Vietnam. The date was eight, nine years ago –

the memory: yesterday-fresh. The hands moved now and ordered a scotch from the smiling hostess, who returned his glance with interest.

The flight was smooth, the other passengers subdued. A few were dozing. Frank finished his drink and lay back in his seat. Three weeks away and he was going home. One, two hours from now and he would turn the key in his Georgetown apartment, and soon there would be the rush of feet and the detonation of welcome from Louise, his own private whirlwind of flying blond hair and long, coltish limbs. More memories crowded in then and he frowned suddenly, twisting his head against the seat rest. Presently he dozed.

The aircraft landed at Washington an hour later. There was the squeal of rubber on concrete, the scream of reverse thrust, and Frank was walking swiftly up the terminal ramp at Washington National to the blue USAF limousine.

He dumped his bags in the boot, nodded to the driver and settled back for the short drive along Jefferson Davis Highway to the Pentagon. It was good to be back, he realized, as he watched the gleaming Potomac roll by, flanked by wide green verges and the long lines of cherry trees between which ran a cluster of late-night joggers, as much a part of the Washington landscape now as the Iwo Jima Memorial.

The limousine slid to a halt beside the nondescript interior concrete staircase that gave on to the lower level of shops, laundries and gift stalls that made up the lower floor of the five-sided building. Frank would always remember this part of the Pentagon as a place of frenzied transit between 'the world' and 'Nam' during the bad years – a place of movement orders, dumped valises and duffle bags; of sudden, boisterous reunions and of bad news grabbed on the run. Now, late at night, the place was almost deserted and he hurried away from the hall of memories, of dead young faces.

He took the elevator up to his office. With luck he could check in, pick up his mail and be home within the hour. With luck.

He had no sooner reported at the duty desk, shaken a few hands, traded a few stories, than an earnest young Lieutenant was standing at his shoulder holding out a slim blue folder. 'General Freeman's compliments, sir, and would you mind reading this before reporting to his office at 2300?' Frank groaned, signed receipt of the folder and hooked his heels over the edge of his desk. He glanced at his watch. He had an hour and a half exactly. He reached across for the phone and dialled Mrs Headley's number. He'd be home in a couple of hours – God and General Clarke T. Freeman permitting.

An hour later, changed into uniform, Frank Yates flicked shut the report, slipped it into its folder, rose from behind his desk and strode briskly along the silent corridor to the elevators, black shoes gleaming beneath the strong overhead lighting. He rode alone to the third floor, his mind busy with the report on Lyudin's death.

In his mid-thirties, fair-haired and dapper in the dark blue uniform with its cluster of medal ribbons and gleaming buttons, Frank turned past the fallout shelter indicators and the 'Panel of Heroes' exhibition and stopped outside a gleaming, walnut-panelled door upon which was set the inscription 'General Clarke T. Freeman. Head of USAF Intelligence'.

Frank glanced up at the unwinking eye of the TV monitor and then tapped out the coded entry sequence on the display panel set into the wall. The tumblers on the lock clicked back, the door swung open with a faint buzz and he stepped through into a small antechamber. An armed and uniformed Air Force Sergeant glanced down from the monitor, inspected Frank's security pass, yawned and waved him through.

Frank stode across the rich carpet, knocked on the General's door and entered.

General Freeman was leaning forward in his chair, eyes locked intently upon a TV screen showing a playback of the news digest programme transmitted coast-to-coast earlier in the evening. Freeman glanced up, smiled and waved a hand in greeting. 'Good to see you, Captain. Take a seat – I just want to catch a little more of this.' He jabbed a finger towards the screen as the presenter's voice filled the office: '. . . US dependence upon what has become known as the Strategic Triad: that is, the three different strategic delivery systems currently at our disposal.'

The TV showed a rocket rising from its underground silo flanked by two diagonal spurts of flame. The voice went on: 'The three components of that Triad are: silo-based Minuteman and Titan; submarine-launched Polaris, to be replaced by Trident Is and IIs once submarine construction delays have been overcome; and short-range attack missiles – SRAMS – carried some way towards their target by B-52 bombers long overdue for replacement. However –' film cut back to studio and the concerned, professional gravity of the presenter in close-up – 'with the increased throw-weight of Soviet ICBMs* there's now a growing concern on the Hill over the survivability of our existing static silos, which, though hardened to withstand attack, have in recent years become increasingly vulnerable to counterforce assault by missiles which grow more powerful with each passing year as CEPs† diminish. It is to counter *this* threat that the Pentagon now pins its hopes on a revolutionary concept of *mobile* missiles buried beneath a thin crust of desert on a hidden trackway. Sounds incredible? Mike Conrad has that story –'

General Freeman snapped off the set angrily from his desk. 'Jesus,' he growled in exasperation. 'What do those mothers think they're doing? They cancel the Rockwell B-1, cut the balls out of the Cruise programme until it's damn' near restricted in range to theatre operations, and then start sounding off about the MX system like it's the answer to some kinda rain-prayer –'

He dragged a hand through short grey hair and glanced up suddenly, the weathered face breaking into a tired smile.

* ICBM: Intercontinental Ballistic Missile.
† CEP Circular Error Probability – the area in which there is a fifty-fifty chance of target strike.

'Better rope me down, Frank. Your General's off on that old hobby-horse of his.'

General Freeman's lone stand – shared by not one of his career-minded superiors within the service – was already legend within the Air Force. He stood alone in his belief that the basic concept of US national security contained a single, fatal flaw:

Thirty years of peace – if not actual stability – had been built upon the belief that a surprise nuclear attack – on America by the Soviet Union, on the Soviet Union by America – would be an act of national suicide and self-immolation because it would result in immediate, devastating retaliation even as the first missiles lifted from their silos. Tit for tat – in megatons, blast, fallout and charred dead that you could count in millions.

Someone had even dreamed up a label for such a God-defying concept: Mutual Assured Destruction. There was a curious comfort in that, somewhere.

But General Freeman believed the Russians were quietly removing the 'Mutual' from MAD.

They were doing it, he believed, by directing their efforts towards a fearsome, top-secret breakthrough in space-directed high-energy technology.

While the West chattered on shrilly about SALT, détente and MAD.

Now the General cast a critical eye at Frank's lean figure and shook his head in mock exasperation. 'You're looking a bit paunchy, Captain: all that good living, all those fine meals out there in Sin City . . .'

Frank smiled wryly. General Freeman didn't change. 'Only good living I saw out there, General, had a couple of lubber grasshoppers for openers and a Mexican free-tailed bat for main course.' He had spent the last three weeks on surveillance detachment with the 64th Fighter Weapons Squadron on the Escape and Evasion phase of the Red Flag programme run out of the Nellis Air Force Base in the Nevada desert outside Las Vegas.

'Any problems on that?'

Frank shook his head emphatically. 'Not a one. I'll be recommending suspension of that senior Lieutenant. The other two are clear. It'll all be in my report.'

Freeman nodded and pointed abruptly at the folder on Frank's lap. 'You've read that piece from New York?'

'On Lyudin's death? Yes, sir. New York Police think they're dealing with someone called Lossman. Harold Lossman. Straightforward suicide,' replied Frank obliquely. Freeman nodded impatiently.

'I know that, damn it! I want to know what you think, Frank.' He reached forward into the lamplight and pressed the intercom.

'General?' came the instant reply from the Sergeant outside.

'Sergeant – think you can rustle up some coffee? Two cups.' Frank sat back, conscious once again of the easy, privileged relationship he enjoyed with his commanding officer, a relationship which, like much else, had its origins in Vietnam. Now, while they waited for the coffee to arrive, Frank studied the man sitting in the lamplight behind the wide, curved desk.

Others, he knew, had made the mistake of underestimating General Clarke Tobias Freeman, and it was a mistake which had cost them dear. Seeing no further than the wide smile, the gruff manner and the ready handshake, they had dismissed the man from their minds as transitory, unimportant – yet that veneer hid the very qualities that had carried him, at fifty-four, to this position of prominence within the US Air Force. It was not hard for Frank to glimpse the steel that had kept Freeman in that seat as the Head of Air Force Intelligence for the last three years: the jaw was still firm, the eyes – above the tailored uniform with its glittering collection of medals, clasps and ribbons beneath the coveted silver pilot's wings – were still sharp, shrewd, calculating.

The man was impressive, would be so even in his pyjamas, and the props that surrounded him in this traditional setting did him no less than justice: the unfurled flag of their nation standing sentinel behind the desk, the signed photograph of the President looking down upon one of his Generals, the battery of coloured telephones, the silver model of the wartime P-38, that single untarnished reminder of the incumbent's time-in-trade, his opening subscription paid long ago to this exclusive club of high office.

The Sergeant arrived with the coffee. After they had helped themselves, 'Well?' demanded Freeman, watching Frank Yates closely over the rim of his cup.

'No,' said Frank finally. 'I don't believe it. There's no way Lyudin would have killed himself, General. As the man says – he didn't jump, he was pushed.'

Freeman nodded. He appeared almost relieved. 'Any doubts?'

Frank shook his head. 'I wasn't there, General, but I'm as near as can be. When I saw him four weeks ago he was looking forward to the trip to Washington, joking about how he'd spend the dough on books and good food. Christ –' Frank tapped the report dismissively – 'If these yo-yos are to be believed, he jumped halfway through fixing dinner. No one's that bad a cook.'

Freeman grunted, rose from behind his desk and crossed to a heavy metal filing cabinet decorated with security tumblers. He opened a drawer and pulled out a thick file.

'OK, Frank – I'll buy that: Lyudin was murdered to stop him giving his piece to the Scientific Advisory Committee. My next question –'

Frank held up a hand. 'I know what it's gonna be, General.'

Freeman looked up sternly and then gave a slight smile. 'So tell me.'

'You're going to ask if I think his death has anything to do with Hammer.' Project Hammer and his Soviet scientific defectors, his Windjammers, were General Freeman's over-riding obsession. Hammer rumours, Hammer details, Hammer theories – all would bring General Freeman to the phone or to his desk without a grumble, day or night, round the clock.

33 :

'Right, Frank,' admitted Freeman quietly.

Frank shrugged. 'Sure, it's possible. Anything's possible, General, although –'

'Because if it does – if it does tie in with Hammer – then it'll be the third, Captain. The third in nine months.' Freeman tapped the heavy file with the back of a powerful hand. 'We're losing them, Frank – we're losing them like flies.'

Hammer.

It had begun with a routine USAF Intelligence report identifying inexplicable amounts of gaseous hydrogen with traces of tritium vented in the upper atmosphere that had been back-tracked to the Soviet secret faculty at Semipalatinsk, Central Asia. Four months later and a high-flying SR-71 spyplane had returned with air samples of the same substance picked up over the eastern Mediterranean. When it too was back-traced, its source of origin was the same: Semipalatinsk.

The germ of an idea discarded as impractical twenty years earlier had begun to stir in a dusty cupboard of the General's mind. The next step had been simple: routine reports featuring this new place, Semipalatinsk, were to be forwarded directly to his desk. The General even gave the nagging worry a codename: Project Hammer – something solid, something tangible, among the half-formed straws.

The months rolled by, and slowly those straws began to cling together: another venting sample; a Soviet scientist's indiscretion at an international seminar on electron accelerators; a series of infra-red satellite reconnaissance photographs that revealed the beginnings of major earth-moving activity – to the General's straining eyes at least, the haystack of Soviet nuclear intent began to emerge from the mists of implausibility.

In the last nine months those thoughts had hardened into beliefs which had taken on the gleaming edge of conviction. General Clarke Freeman now believed he *knew* what the Russians were up to in Semipalatinsk, behind the deceptive façade of détente and SALT and positively aided by a weak American President whose ingenuous refusal to heed his intelligence gatherers truly frightened the General. His lack of proof was awkward but not something that threw his own convictions into the slightest doubt. The files in his safe, the photographs – most importantly, the feeling that reached out and gripped him in the guts – all these spelt out what to him was unmistakable: the Soviet Union was ploughing massive resources into the development of a weapon of such awesome potential that it would make America's ICBM system as obsolete as the bow and arrow. By hosing a beam of atomic and subatomic particles up into the atmospheric re-entry window of incoming American missiles, the Russians would be able to build an impenetrable shield over their major installations against which the most sophisticated missiles in the world would simply . . . vaporize. They would be neutered, made harmless – and America, in her turn, would be laid bare. Naked, vulnerable.

His country.

Now General Freeman opened the file, prised out a single sheet of paper and read aloud: 'Viklov, Boris. 15 August 1977 in Joliet, Illinois – automobile accident. Osipov, Vadim. Not three months ago in Tampa, Florida – heart attack on the stairs leading to his apartment. Except that we found traces of prussic acid on his cheeks. They'd got him with a facial spray.'

Frank nodded. He too had read the reports. Now Freeman advanced towards him, waving the folder for emphasis. 'Both were top defectors, Frank. Both leading Soviet scientists – and both are now dead. Removed.'

'And now Lyudin,' supplied Frank.

'And now Lyudin.'

'How much went out to the public? About their deaths?'

Freeman shook his head. 'Not a word. Not a word about their deaths, not a word when they come across. Only defectors the public gets to hear about are the ballet dancers, the ice skaters, the guys who drift across the Iron Curtain on hot-air balloons and Christ knows what. The others – the ones of real importance – we keep to ourselves.'

'So these guys – Viklov, Lyudin and the other one – any ideas how they were picked up?'

Freeman shrugged and sipped his coffee. 'We don't know. Maybe they just got careless, started leaving tracks, sticking to habits. Whatever it was, it was enough.' He paused, thinking deeply, then 'Lyudin was in on Hammer, Frank, I'm convinced of it.'

'He told you that himself?'

'Not in so many words, but –'

'You debriefed him personally –'

'He was holding something back. He was quite candid about it – he admitted it. A last card – something to bargain with against his own safety.'

'– and to push the price up.'

Freeman nodded soberly. 'We'd settled on a quarter of a million, Frank. A quarter of a fucking million.'

Frank paused, then 'What about the woman, General? What about Prolev?'

General Freeman closed his eyes briefly as though in prayer. 'Still on ice. On ice and undetected. Thank God.'

*

It was after 3 a.m. when Frank climbed the few steps to his home on Dumbarton Street NW Georgetown, eased open the front door, dumped his bag in the hall and switched on the lights. Silence greeted his return.

He had steeled himself for that, braced himself, yet even through his tiredness it came as a shock. Even now, after all these months. He stood there in the hall, listening to it. Nothing but the tick of the clock and the silence that spelt empty.

Frank moved through to the lounge, shedding tie, jacket and shoes. He turned off all the lights save the one on his desk, sank down on to the settee and linked his hands behind his head. He sat there quietly for long moments, staring in the almost darkness at the happy photograph on his desk: a photograph in a silver frame that showed a handsome young Air Force officer in flying gear standing proudly in front of an F-4 Phantom jet. Between man and machine, her arm around the pilot's waist, stood a beautiful woman brushing a strand of fair hair out of her eyes.

Man, woman and machine – the things of his youth, the things he had valued most.

And now, only the man was left.

*

Professor Eduard Ryabov wrestled his suitcase on to the wooden rack above his head and settled into the compartment's far corner, his thick coat pulled around him to shield his thin body from the icy draughts that swirled around this remote, desolate station.

Remote, desolate. He sighed. Only a madman – or, he supposed, a scientist – would be stuck out here at Tyuratam, Central Asia, miles from anywhere on the banks of the still frozen Syrdar'ya.

It was now almost six months since that first successful testing of the Professor's new weapon in the dry, arid foothills to the east of Tyuratam at a place called Sary Shagan on the western edge of Lake Balkhash, and although much progress had been made since those first tentative steps to the very brink of success, Ryabov bitterly resented each and every distraction that dragged him away, however briefly, from the safe, secure world of his desk and the few close companions who shared his field of specialized technology.

Ryabov was a nuclear scientist. Were he to live in the West, that of itself would be sufficient professional identification, but here, inside the Soviet Union, rather more was necessary in order to qualify for the position he held within the complex machinery of the State. Ryabov was a high-energy physicist, a civilian whose military training had ended amid the swamps and dark forests of Malinka in 1944. The muscles and skills he had used then as a partisan had long fallen into disuse, yet the military still controlled his brain, his intellect.

The end of the Great Patriotic War saw the Soviet

Union with no cohesive policy of homeland defence. In the years that followed, there was little the Soviet Union could have done against a determined attack by America's Strategic Air Command. So they blustered, they blustered and built with a cold urgency born out of a nation's defencelessness. Effort had its reward, and such vulnerability did not last: MIG-15 interceptors were soon joined by the first surface-to-air missiles, and, on 1 May 1960, America's impudent domination of the skies high above a foreign land were brought to a sudden and flaming halt when Gary Powers' Lockheed U-2 spyplane was clawed out of the sky at 60,000 feet by a Soviet missile.

Much else changed at that time along with American perceptions of Soviet abilities as Eduard Ryabov's brilliant mind pushed him into the scientific forefront of a nation that, learning the lesson of history, placed the defence of the homeland at the very top of its list of national priorities. He was one of three scientists whisked to Schonefeld in East Germany to take part in the debriefing of Klaus Fuchs after his expulsion from Great Britain. Fuchs then sank from sight, yet behind the scenes Ryabov returned with him to the Yefremov Institute in Leningrad early the following year. Many still believe it was this work with Ryabov, together with Fuchs' own revelations about the gaseous diffusion process at Oak Ridge, Tennessee, that led, on 13 December 1971, to Fuchs being awarded the East German Order of Merit of the Fatherland in gold by East Germany's Party Chairman Herr Ulbricht.

As Ryabov and his team worked quietly in the background on the weapons they believed would bring their country a more secure future, PVO STRANY, the Soviet Air Defence Command, itself underwent further change: ranking third in national importance behind Strategic Rocket Forces and Soviet Ground Forces, the service already had a Commander-in-chief responsible directly to the Ministry of Defence; now, when all the sums had been done, more than 500,000 radar, anti-aircraft artillery and anti-aircraft missile troops were placed under the direct command of Vladimir Gladky.

By the late 1960s Ryabov found his time divided between the secret faculty at Semipalatinsk and the Nuclear Physics Institute at Novosibirsk directly to the north – trips like this one to Tyuratam had become the exception, not the rule – and even that had been brought to an abrupt halt by the summons that was responsible for his being here, now, on this frozen, immobile train on the way to Moscow, armed with a special pass to see him through the innumerable checkpoints.

Eduard Ryabov tugged his coat tighter around his shoulders and huddled down into his collar. No wonder the airport was frozen in. He shivered. It was the cold, he told himself – just the cold.

But it wasn't just the cold.

It was also the memory of the last time he had been called before the dour members of Protivokozmicheskaya Oborona. Like everything else he dealt with, PKO was concerned primarily with the defence of the Soviet homeland against space weapons and with the monitoring of intelligence and reconnaissance space vehicles. PKO was thus watching Ryabov's progress closely, and that was to be expected. Indeed it caused the Professor little worry – alone in the rarefied air at the lofty peak of his chosen profession, Ryabov could lose those who came panting in his footsteps with almost childlike ease. What he could not control – and thus feared – was the activity of those ordered to ensure that he and his colleagues worked in total, shroud-like secrecy.

Weeks after his last summons to appear before PKO in Moscow, the first ugly rumours had begun to seep through. It was only then, with a sense of dawning horror, that Professor Ryabov began to suspect it might have been *his* innocently given testimony of their involvement with his work that had sent a handful of his former colleagues to their deaths. Viklov. Osipov. Lyudin, perhaps. He sighed. He wasn't certain, of course. One never was. Not any more. About anything.

The train lurched forward and began to grind slowly over the frozen points. Moscow lay thirteen hundred snow-clad miles to the north-west. Presently Ryabov tried to forget his worries as he tugged out a pack of playing cards and began to play patience.

As the train shouldered aside the first drifts of snow and Professor Ryabov settled down for the long, cold journey to Moscow, a 227-foot-long gleaming metal cylinder began its long, cold journey from Underground Storage and Assembly to Pre-Check Staging Area Two some four miles north of the complex research laboratories that had been the object of Professor Ryabov's visit to Tyuratam these last few days.

Ryabov's work had kept him wholly occupied in the acres of laboratories and experimental sheds well to the south of the underground assembly area whose walls echoed now to the throb of the diesel transporter as the rocket moved slowly forward, flanked by the men who had built her, the high priests of technology who walked slowly, silently beside their charge, their white coats and soft white over-boots adding an air of brooding, celibate menace to the brilliantly lit procession as it inched its way up the smooth concrete ramp that led towards the dim daylight.

If whim had suddenly taken the Professor and he had decided to walk around, to poke a friendly and inquisitive nose into activities elsewhere in the space complex, he would have found his wanderings rigidly, abruptly pro-scribed. But he was busy, tired and in no mood for sub-zero sightseeing. Which was perhaps just as well.

The very existence of Proton-Soyuz 9, a three-stage manned rocket with 5.4 thousand metric tons of thrust and the ability to lift a payload of 50,000 kilograms into space was a closely guarded secret, and of all the people who were required to know nothing at all about the construction and ultimate destiny of Proton-Soyuz 9, Professor Eduard Ryabov came very near the top of the list.

It had taken General Clarke Freeman forty-five minutes to drive back along Indian Head Highway from the Pentagon to his modern, split-level home on Beachside Landing on the banks of the Potomac.

He went downstairs into the basement study, placed his papers on the desk and returned upstairs to make himself a sandwich. He trod softly out of habit – Doris was sleeping heavily in the bedroom next door: he could hear the monotony of her breathing recede as he retraced his steps downstairs. He closed the study door softly and glanced at his watch. It would soon be dawn, the time he enjoyed most – a private time of assessment and reflection, a time that brought back the smell of high-octane fuel, of aircraft on a dozen different landing strips – of the days of his youth, of history, when issues seemed clearer and the sense of national purpose among those around him less elusive.

He pulled an old pine rocking chair over to the window, unbuttoned his uniform jacket and laid it carefully aside, the garment heavy with the stars and decorations of high rank. He went upstairs once more, poured strong black coffee into a thick enamel mug and returned downstairs to sit there in his chair, rocking gently, gazing out of the window and nursing the warmth in his hands.

Often he would use these moments of privacy to reflect upon a dozen different facets of his life, but today, at this quiet hour, his thoughts were dominated by one single, disturbing question:

Why now?

Every instinct, every nuance of professional training told him that such overt action as the liquidation of these three Soviet scientists contradicted the behavioural code long recognized by both superpowers, a code that permitted both the United States and the Soviet Union to fight the bloodless battles of the Intelligence war without drawing restrictive public attention to their activities.

Yet now the pace was hotting up: three deaths in the last nineteen months – two in the last ten weeks. Why were they shutting doors, removing voices?

Freeman sat back in his chair, gazed out of the window at the lightening darkness and reviewed the common ground each victim had shared with the others. Once again, he had no need of notes:

Viklov had been working at Tyuratam, the Kennedy Space Center of the Soviet Union in Kazakhstan. He had defected during a scientific exchange to the Lawrence Livermore Laboratory. Osipov – he had been lecturing to East German university students in Berlin on pulse-power generation until he had wandered over to share his experiences with the Americans on a more permanent basis – and Lyudin, Vasili Lyudin, Lecturer at the Kurchatov Institute of Atomic Energy, Moscow, until he had claimed asylum during an official visit to Stockholm.

And now they were gone.

Of Freeman's private stable of defectors, leading Soviet scientists able to point the way to the breakthroughs in Soviet thinking, three were gone.

One was left. Lydia Prolev.

And Lydia Prolev had worked as a scientist at the Soviet nuclear faculty at Semipalatinsk, Central Asia.

And Lydia Prolev was saying nothing. Not a word.

Time and again the General banged up against that same stubborn wall of silence. That she had crucial information he did not doubt. He was equally convinced she would keep that information to herself just as long as her ten-year-old son remained trapped inside the Soviet Union.

Stalemate.

And, meanwhile, that fragile goldmine of information had to be guarded, protected. Freeman got up from his rocker and paced the study restlessly as he recalled the elaborate care with which his own service had arranged the protection of the others. It hadn't been enough, he acknowledged bleakly. They had failed them, failed them all.

He opened a locked drawer in his heavy oak desk and flicked through his leather-bound diary to a single, cryptic notation written in ink at the top of a page four and a half months ago.

Four and a half months ago. It was too long.

Dawn was now washing over the lawn but the General missed it. Animated by a sudden sense of urgent, gloom-laden foreboding, he plucked the phone off its cradle. He punched the buttons impatiently and got through to the Duty Operations Officer. Freeman rattled off his own clearance sequence, followed that by the code of the day and then gave the man the single, enciphered command that would initiate an immediate change in Safe House Location.

The DOO had been enjoying a quiet shift. An hour more and it would all be somebody else's problem. Now the sudden order out of the blue and the immediate mountain of extra work that came with it made him a trifle petulant. 'It's 04.45, General. Perhaps it would be better if –'

'Jesus!' General Freeman smashed a heavy fist down on his desk. 'I didn't call you up for a time check, Major,' he snarled. 'If you want to hold that position this time tomorrow, get on it! I want a full status report advising completion on my desk in three hours' time, understood?'

'Whatever you say, General,' replied the Major hastily. Old Iron Balls was on his charger again.

'You bet your goddam life!' Freeman slammed down the receiver and fumed back in his chair, his mood of introverted reflection burnt off with the morning mist. Did even his *subordinates* consider his views, his beliefs, his *convictions*, amusingly obsessive?

He pushed the leather-bound diary to one side and swung round to read once more the framed and faded Western Union Telegraph flimsy that had given him strength throughout the stormy crises of his life. It was addressed to his mother:

MRS JUNE FREEMAN 1001 NORTHWEST HEIGHTS
PHOENIX ARIZ. WITH DEEPEST REGRET INFORM YOU
YOUR SON LT FREEMAN CLARKE T 24146113 US ARMY
AIR CORPS REPORTED MISSING PRESUMED KILLED
FOLLOWING AIR ACTION PACIFIC THEATER OPERA-
TIONS FEBRUARY 12 1945. LETTER FOLLOWS.
                         ADJUTANT GENERAL
                  UNITED STATES ARMY AIR CORPS

Yeah, well, they'd been wrong that time too: his superiors, his subordinates, all of them. He'd been bobbing about
in the Pacific on a half-inflated liferaft getting the kind of
all-over tan that put him into a naval sickbay for close on a
month. The Executive had been wrong about him then,
and they were wrong about him now. Wrong about his
motives, about the soundness of his judgements, about
Hammer. He was out of the liferaft now but he was still
swimming against the tide, fighting a different battle for
survival.

As General Freeman sat on alone in his study, Lydia
Prolev, the Soviet defector who was the cause of much of
his concern, shifted awkwardly behind the wheel of Pligin's
battered sedan and resumed her sightless staring down from
the flyover at the line of red tail-lights that swept past below
on the Inter-State Highway. Going somewhere.
   She had been sitting out here for hours, tired beyond
sleep, cold beyond realization, gazing down at the cars and
trucks of this strange, bewildering, extravagant country
ever since she had woken suddenly in the nondescript
'safe house' that had been her refuge these last four and a
half months. She had dressed on impulse, listened outside
Pligin's door for the ragged rise and fall of his snoring,
pocketed his keys and slipped downstairs to the car. To
drive anywhere. To drive, drive, drive.
   She looked down with sad eyes as the fast-moving stream
of purposeful, faceless Americans hurried by – a spectator
caught in the no-man's land between the cultures of East
and West, lost in a private world of depression and rootless

loneliness so vast, so huge, she would not have dreamed it existed.

Dawn began to lighten the sky. She snapped open her plastic handbag and drew out a worn, creased photograph of her son. She studied the picture minutely for a moment, the tears running unchecked down her smooth cheeks. Then she pressed the picture to her lips, closed the handbag with a snap and reached forward for the ignition. She would have to hurry if she was to find her way back to Hagerstown before Pligin awoke and realized she was missing.

Three hours later a fragment of General Freeman's previous good nature had been restored. He had grabbed some sleep on the couch in the study, and now, as he shaved briskly in front of the bathroom mirror, he caught the fragrant smell of bacon, French toast and fresh coffee. Doris had the radio on in the kitchen and he walked through to join her, fastening the sleeve buttons on a crisp, fresh shirt. 'Morning, Doris. You all have a good time last night?' he asked with a glance at the cloud base through the kitchen window. Doris, hair in curlers and wrapped in a mauve housecoat like some strange domestic caterpillar, offered a few words in reply and proffered the side of her cheek in morning ritual. It sometimes seemed to General Freeman that he was actually married to two women at once – the one with the private, lined face devoid of make-up and the bright, brittle woman behind the public mask that clicked into place behind a locked door shortly after breakfast each morning. Now the General kissed the undressed cheek automatically. Then he poured himself a glass of Florida orange juice and went through to the hall for the papers, his polished black shoes biting crisply on the floor.

'Did you get any sleep at all, Clarke? I waited up for you, you know,' admonished Doris sternly. Freeman glanced at the dumpy figure and thought unkind thoughts.

'I grabbed a couple of hours,' he grunted at last. 'I'm fine, Doris.'

They ate together in silence broken only by the turning of newspaper pages at each end of the dining table.

Suddenly Doris sighed in vexation. Her husband glanced up. 'What's the matter?'

'Well, honestly,' declared Doris. 'There's a man here – a boy, really – he's given two years for breaking into a hardware store over on Pennsylvania! I mean – *two years*, Clarke? It's . . . it's unreasonable! It's so . . . so unfair! If it was anywhere else –'

'Hurrumph.' Penal Reform, Legal Aid, Citizens' Advice and the Cause of the Underdog – Doris Freeman had room for them all in her ample bosom. She ran coffee mornings, she held committee meetings. Dressed to kill, mask clipped into place, she sallied forth on missions of 'good works' among the under-privileged. In recent months the General had returned home once or twice to discover committee meetings in full swing, here in his own home – and there had been mighty rows afterwards as he detected that Doris considered his sudden appearance in military uniform an untimely and embarrassing intrusion into the important events of her social calendar.

'Well, Clarke, really,' she was saying now, 'I do think that for someone who's supposed to be –'

The phone began to ring. General Freeman laid his newspaper aside with some relief. 'I'll get it.'

It was the Duty Operations Officer. With one brush with the General behind him, he sounded nervous.

'Er . . . we've some bad news, General, regarding that Secondary Position you mentioned. I think you'd better come in. Right away, sir, if it's OK with you.'

'Give me ten minutes,' replied the General.

Frank Yates' late-night mood of depression and loneliness had given way to one of pleasurable anticipation: he was going to see Louise.

He had shaved, showered and changed, unpacked his bags and thrown open the apartment's long-closed windows. Then he had gone for a stroll among the shops and boutiques of his old neighbourhood.

Away from the early morning snarl of traffic on Wisconsin Avenue, the Georgetown streets – his streets – were some of the finest and quietest in the city. He revelled, as he always did, in the old, uneven, cobbled sidewalks, in the lines of still bare cherry trees and the proud, dignified ramble of weather-boarded houses that once belonged to Washington's earliest merchants and statesmen.

Once or twice he was recognized, greeted, stopped in the streets by traders and old friends – and that made him feel best of all. It was good to be home.

He returned to the apartment, his arms laden with flowers and pointless, extravagant gifts he had ceased bothering to justify. He became suddenly busy with duster and vacuum cleaner, taking pleasure in the chores of male domesticity after three weeks in the sterile, military environment of a front-line Air Force Base.

He arranged the gifts he had brought Louise in the bedroom and sat down in an armchair to flick impatiently through a magazine. Twice he got up to pace to the window and glance out at the passing traffic. Finally a car pulled up outside, there was the murmur of voices – one raised high in excitement – and then a furious ringing on the door bell.

Frank strode to the hallway and threw open the door.

'Daddy, Daddy!' Louise, sole heiress to Frank's emotional millions, was just six years old.

Arms, legs, blond hair flying every which way, Louise hurled herself across the porch and launched herself at her crouching father. Thin arms curled around his neck and a child's eager wet lips crushed against his cheek as she burrowed into the security of his shoulder.

Frank closed his eyes, hugged her fiercely to him and felt the pain strike into him like a hot knife. He rose, twirled round swiftly once, twice and then lifted the girl high in his arms. She shrieked with delight and laughed down into his face with shining eyes. Her mother's eyes. He placed her gently on the ground as he became aware of the other woman watching them fondly from the door. 'Mrs Headley – come along in. She been behaving herself?'

47 :

Mrs Headley smiled her pleasure. 'She's been just no trouble, Frank – no trouble at all. Why, only –'

'Daddy, Daddy – Mrs Headley says this dress is too short, but it's the one you like best, isn't it? Isn't it, Daddy?' she demanded, hopping agitatedly from one foot to another.

Frank squatted down and regarded her gravely. The dress was one he and Carole had chosen together no more than a week before the sailing trip from which he had returned alone. It *was* too short; it drew unnecessary attention to pale, scuffed knees that looked suddenly very vulnerable. Frank rubbed his nose vigorously and got to his feet. 'I think it looks just fine,' he pronounced quietly, watching the little face light up like a lantern. 'But if you take a peak inside your bedroom –' the voice dropped to a whisper and Louise leant forward excitely – 'you'll maybe find something that'll make you the prettiest princess for miles around.'

Louise scampered away happily as Frank exchanged glances with Mrs Headley. 'Those cheques been coming through OK?' he asked quietly.

Mrs Headley nodded. 'Week by week, Frank – regular as clockwork, thank you. Never missed.'

Frank nodded, relieved. 'How's she been?'

'No trouble, no trouble at all, Frank – I'd tell you if she had, believe me.' She grasped his arm. 'My three have taken to that child, well, like she was one of the family.' She smiled fondly. The cheques had made a big difference to her family, too.

Frank hesitated, suddenly awkward unsure how to go on. 'I . . . I meant really herself, Mrs Headley In herself. Ever since, ever since her mother died, it hasn't been . . .'

Mrs Headley cast a glance over her shoulder to ensure they were still alone. 'Well, now.' She considered. 'That's not so easy to tell, you know? I mean, she *seems* perfectly happy, but then, sometimes, I don't know . . . sometimes I'll catch a faraway look, and – she needs you, Frank, she needs her family around her, that's the up and the down of it. Especially now – not just with gifts and surprises and fancy dresses and sudden, exciting things like that –' she saw the hurt and was quick to comfort him – 'there's nothing wrong, nothing *wrong* with any of that – but it isn't enough: it'll never be enough, Frank, you know what I'm saying? Especially –'

There was the scamper of feet as Louise burst back into the room wearing the new dress her father had bought her.

As the phone began to ring.

Frank's lips were compressed into a thin line of anger. 'Yes, sir. I understand – 1400. Yes, I'll be there.' He replaced the receiver and turned with great reluctance to confront two long faces. The older of the two looked merely disappointed – the younger, as though her entire world had just caved in around her ears.

'You're going away. You're going away again, aren't you?' she accused, the tears starting to run down the smooth cheeks. Without waiting for a reply the little girl turned to run from the lounge. Frank turned to Mrs Headley and spread his hands helplessly.

'What can I tell her? I'll be back later this evening.'

'It does seem a bit hard, Frank. You've hardly had a chance to unpack. Don't they give you guys furlough any more?'

'Guess not,' muttered Frank as he walked through to Louise's bedroom. The door was shut but he could hear muffled sobs from within. He knocked softly. There was no reply. He opened the door and stepped quietly into the bedroom.

'Go away. I hate you,' she said unconvincingly, her voice muffled by the quilting.

Frank sat down on the edge of the bed. 'I haven't got to go away until this afternoon. We can have the rest of the morning together – and we can go somewhere special for lunch if you like. Sort of early celebration. You choose, OK?' Dimly he was aware of the empty inadequacy of such provision as Mrs Headley's words rang in his ears.

The girl sat up and regarded him gravely. 'You promise?'

Frank placed a hand on his heart and tried to look pious. 'Promise. Cross my heart.' He smiled and felt a twinge of guilt as he saw the beginnings of an answering smile tug at the corners of her mouth. How easy to turn on the sunshine. The smile broke through and he pulled away to place both hands firmly on her shoulders. 'Now. No more tears. Tidy up in here, put your things away and we'll go out. Then I'll drop you back at Mrs Headley's and in an hour or so we can start our holiday all over again – deal?' He held out his hand.

'Deal.' His daughter placed her hand in his and they shook gravely like business partners, the small bones fragile as glass beneath his strong fingers.

In Moscow that same morning the ancient lift rose, creaking ponderously, to stop at the fifth floor of the huge, grey-stone building that, until the summer of 1972, had been the headquarters of Komitet Gosudarstvennoy Bezopasnosti, the Committee for State Security – the KGB.

'The Centre', as it is known, moved to the new, purpose-built five-storey building on the outskirts of Moscow in that year and the infamous building adjoining Lubianka prison became partly vacant. Only partly, because the KGB did not move out completely: Directorate T of the First Chief Directorate remained behind to spread out into less cramped quarters and to work in convenient proximity to the organizational 'tail' of PVO STRANY, the National Air Defence Command.

The metal lift clattered open violently and the portly figure of First Deputy Mikhail Kostikov squeezed out of the lift cage and began walking down the corridor to his office, his heels clipping importantly on the parquet flooring.

Although the day had hardly started, Kostikov had been in the building since just after 8 a.m. His arrival at such an hour owed more to greed, however, than to any sense of weighty duty. The explanation was simple: the basement of the building was given over to the KGB restaurant and food store. Here, senior officials were able to buy at nominal cost the goods and services denied their fellow citizens on the open market. Now, fortified as usual by an excellent cooked breakfast of bacon, sausages and eggs washed down with real coffee, Kostikov was returning to his desk, a packet of American cigarettes in his pocket, his arms full of prestigous western groceries.

He was hurrying for two reasons: first, because the fewer comrades who were reminded that the People's Paradise treated some rather more equally than others the better, and, secondly, because ahead lay another full day. He would attend a committee meeting of PVO STRANY's department PKO and he hoped he might be able to go there armed with good news.

He turned now into his office and almost collided with Genik, his diminutive aide. The man's eyes were flashing excitedly behind his thick round spectacles, and he was waving a message. 'It's here, Comrade Deputy,' he breathed excitedly. 'It's arrived!' Kostikov frowned his annoyance at the man's habitual excitement and walked through to his office. He closed the frosted glass door, placed his groceries aside and slipped behind his wooden desk. He snapped his fingers.

'Show me,' he commanded. Genik placed the message in front of him as though it was part of the Dead Sea scrolls. Kostikov waved Genik away, crossed to his safe, removed the cipher books and bent over the signal with impatience. Now, indeed, they would know.

The message, beamed from New York, had been flashed through internal 'burst' circuits from headquarters to the communications centre on the sixth floor above his head. Coded for his personal attention, the signal's stamp of origin was Executive Action Department V.

The KGB arose out of the infamous Cheka, an investigative agency spawned by the Revolution of October 1917. It is the eyes, the ears and the vicious right arm, not of the State, but of the Party. It serves the Central Committee of the Communist Party of the Soviet Union, the CPSU, and employs 90,000 staff officers and a further 400,000 clerks, guards, informers and special troops.

The KGB infiltrates every facet of Soviet life, both civil and military. It consists of four main Chief Directorates, seven Independent Directorates and no fewer than six Independent Departments. Although nominally responsible to the Council of Ministers appointed by the Supreme Soviet, it is accountable in fact only to the Communist Party's Politburo itself. The most important of the four Chief Directorates is the First because it is responsible for all foreign operations. Action against the United States, Britain and West Germany stems from the First Chief Directorate, which in turn is made up of various departments and branches responsible for different aspects of clandestine activity abroad: Directorate S (Illegals), for example, selects, trains and employs all Soviet agents who live abroad under false identities; Directorate T (Scientific and Technical) was created to intensify the theft and monitoring of western data relating to nuclear, missile and space research, the strategic sciences, cybernetics and industrial processes. Directorate T also has a loud voice within GNTK, the State Scientific and Technical Committee that alone decides which Soviet scientists can be trusted to return from international conferences abroad.

Kostikov now completed deciphering the brief signal from Muratov in the Soviet Rezidentura in New York, replaced the cipher books and sat back with a satisfied smile. He would be able to take good news to PKO after all: Vasili Lyudin had ceased to represent a problem.

The Commander-in-Chief of the National Air Defence Forces, Vladimir Gladky, laced his fingers together and peered over bushy eyebrows at the row of heavy faces on either side of the wide table on the fifth floor of the former KGB headquarters. Comrade Kostikov looked remarkably pleased with himself, thought Gladky. No doubt they would discover why a little later in the meeting.

If Marshal Gladky's presence at the head of the table

puzzled any of the PKO committee members, they had the political good sense not to show it. However, it *was* puzzling; officially, there was no obvious reason why Gladky should choose to attend this particular meeting, although, in any event, the Commander-in-Chief was past giving reasons for his actions.

In fact, the reason was quite compelling. It had to do with the report that lay before him now. Stamped 'Top Secret. For Your Eyes Only', it had been compiled by Professor Klaus Fuchs.

Marshal Gladky was sitting at the head of the table with the other nine members of PKO ranged down either side. They sat beneath the bulbous, opaque glass lamps that hung on ornate chains from the vaulted ceiling high above. The room basked in the winter sunshine streaming through the high windows overlooking the square itself; motes of dust floated slowly in the bolts of sunlight that turned Gladky's reading glasses into brief flashing mirrors as he glanced from one committee member to another, the line of brown bemedalled uniforms broken here and there by the dark suits and the tiny blood-red lapel badges of the CPSU.

Gladky referred to his notes and glanced up. 'Comrades, Professor Ryabov is waiting outside. I propose that we ask him to join us.'

The high, inlaid doors were opened, Ryabov was summoned and he entered shyly to a polite smattering of applause. He looked about him in some confusion, a small man in a huge room. Presently the applause ceased, Gladky gestured him to a chair and Ryabov sat down cautiously, thoroughly alarmed to see Gladky at the head of the table. He waited in silence, acutely conscious of the committee's careful scrutiny.

'Congratulations, Comrade Professor – our sincere congratulations,' beamed Gladky to a ripple of agreement from the others as he indicated the report Ryabov had submitted to PKO a few days earlier. 'A most remarkable achievement.'

'Thank you, Comrade Marshal,' bobbed Ryabov

awkwardly, vowing as he scanned the sea of heavy, seamed faces that this time he would not be drawn into a position where he might be forced to implicate former colleagues. This time he –

'But tell me, Professor –' one of the Generals at the far end of the table hunched forward over his hands with an audible chink of medals – 'your first ground tests centred around that bunker complex were successfully completed more than six months ago. Why is it only now that you feel able to report your conclusions? I find that a little curious. It would –'

'Your point, Comrade General, is well meant, I am sure,' interrupted Mikhail Kostikov silkily from the far side of the table as Professor Ryabov licked dry lips. 'However, I feel it is not for us to monitor the timetable of one of our leading scientists as though he were some first-year student at Armavir. Professor Eduard Ryabov has our complete confidence.'

Was there just a tiny edge of sarcasm behind that last remark? Ryabov had been unable to see who was speaking, his view hidden by a uniformed shoulder. Now, as the speaker leant forward, sound and vision confirmed the beginnings of suspicion. It *was* the same man, the same civilian who, at his last summons before the committee, had pried so closely, so deeply into the knowledge he personally had passed to those Soviet scientists who had later defected to the West.

And who had later died.

Now Professor Ryabov clenched his fists in his lap, nails biting into the palms of his hands with dull, welcome pain. It would not happen again . . .

Marshal Gladky heaved his bulk forward and piled his hands on the green blotter before him. 'Tell me, Professor: now that the first stage of your tests is satisfactorily concluded – how long would it take before this weapon of yours could be converted for . . . offensive deployment?' He detected the beginnings of the Professor's frown of annoyance and added hurriedly with a bland smile: 'Purely as a hypothetical exercise, of course, Professor. But how long? How long would it take?'

There was a hunching forward, a stirring of interest as every eye turned first to Gladky and then to the Professor with an intensity that disturbed him.

Mikhail Kostikov studied the Professor closely. There was tension in the hunched shoulders, in the arms held tightly into the sides, in the clench of white knuckles in the man's lap. A natural, commendable nervousness before so august a committee – or something else entirely? The beginnings, perhaps, of anger, of objection, of rebellion, even? The last time, Kostikov recalled, Ryabov had been most co-operative; thanks to the Professor he had been able to present Department V with a list of names for disposal in the United States within twenty-four hours. But now? Something had changed, he was sure of it . . .

Professo Ryabov shrugged. 'It is hard to say – almost impossible. It would depend upon the core-hardening of the –'

Gladky interrupted: 'I don't want the fine print, Professor – just tell me: how long would it take you to ready your system for conversion, for offensive deployment? One month? Two? A whole year?'

Ryabov shifted impatiently, deeply worried. The thing was a nonsense. 'I do not see that I can answer the Comrade Marshal,' he said finally. 'The system is *defensive*. That is its purpose; its role – that is how it has always been planned. Tomorrow we will commence over-the-horizon radar testing from our faculty in Gomel. If that is successful, we will then be in a position –'

'*How long?*' insisted Gladky sharply.

Ryabov's fingers played nervously with a thread of loose cotton. 'If I must consider such a . . . such a foolish possibility –' he picked the words with care and watched the rows of heads stiffen into offended silence; he could almost hear the pen of damnation scratch across his page in Party records – 'I should say three or four months. At the very least. But, as I said just now –' Professor Ryabov talked on. Gladky nodded, satisfied. It fitted.

When this meeting was over he would talk once more with Defence Minister Voskoboy. Then he would present Voskoboy with what he believed were compelling, strategic reasons for a fundamental expansion of the whole Sky-shroud concept – an alteration from defensive to offensive usage. He would press for the earliest possible deployment of a space-based battle-station, a Skyshroud weapon platform that, once tests had been completed, would radically and irreversibly alter the balance of power between America and the Soviet Union.

By demonstrating impregnable, first-strike target capa-bility against America's thinly defended missile silos, the Soviet Union would be able to impose her political will once and for all on the decadent western world.

Gladky smiled.

Such a threat would, truly, be the final end-game on the world's nuclear chess-board; the ultimate, ultimate deter-rent . . .

'That is not so very long,' observed Marshal Gladky quietly as Professor Ryabov fell silent. 'Thank you, Pro-fessor Ryabov – that will be all. And again – our warmest congratulations, comrade.'

The heavy doors closed behind the Professor and there was a moment's silence, then: 'Tell me –' Gladky turned towards Mikhail Kostikov – 'I recall the Centre was worried regarding the security of the Skyshroud project. There was the question of names, I recall?'

Kostikov nodded and took out the signal he had received earlier that morning from the Soviet Rezidentura in New York. 'You are about to steal my thunder, Comrade Marshal.' He smiled thinly. 'You are perfectly correct: four names were initially the cause of some concern.' He brought his hands together and began playing with a ring on his little finger. 'Vasili Lyudin – a name doubtless familiar to you all for his work towards megagauss fields?' There was a nodding of recollection from around the table. 'It is my duty to report that Vasili Lyudin died in unfortunate circumstances just yesterday. In New York. Some kind of domestic accident, so I am given to understand.' There were no smiles, just a chilling, sober nodding of interest. It was to be expected. The man was a traitor.

'You said there were other names?' prompted Gladky gently.

Kostikov nodded. 'Only remaining is the woman – the woman Prolev. You will recall she is related to Professor Ryabov? It has been decided that she too must be ... discouraged.'

Two hours later, the PKO meeting concluded, Marshal Gladky knocked quietly on the door of Defence Minister Voskoboy.

As he did so, Mikhail Kostikov pushed his typewriter away with relief, arranged in order the numbered pages of his report and called for the dispatch rider who would take his papers across town to 'The Centre' on the outskirts of Moscow. There they would be placed before his own superior, the Head of the KGB's First Chief Directorate Igor Bayev.

Kostikov sat back, a pencil drumming against his teeth. He wondered idly what Bayev would make of the suggestion contained within the last page of his report: that the brilliant Professor Ryabov might possibly benefit from a short, sharp reminder of where duty and loyalty lay. Just a reminder.

Frank Yates turned into Beachside Landing and cruised slowly past the crescent of manicured lawns and ornamental fountains looking for the General's mail-box. Among a dozen houses set back from the street, hidden among the trees and well groomed shrubbery, he recognized the General's licence plate jutting from a garage beneath a split-level home. He crunched to a halt on the gravel, picked his way between half a dozen badly parked cars nearby, crossed the sweep of green lawn and rang the door-bell.

Melodious chimes echoed within. Frank adjusted his civilian tie and waited. Then the door was flung back and the General greeted him warmly: 'Frank! Good of you to come by.' He grasped his arm and led the way through the hall. Frank was aware of the murmur of voices behind opaque glass doors and the sudden ripple of light, frivolous laughter. The General turned and winced visibly. 'My wife's got another of her meetings going on in there. Civic Guard Against Injustice. We'll go down to my study, Frank, and get right to it. Guess there's a whole raft of things waiting for you back home.'

'Damn right,' mouthed Frank at the General's retreating back as he followed the broad, uniformed shoulders down the stairs and into the study.

Freeman pointed him to a low couch and dropped into a chair over by the window. He regarded Frank steadily for a moment, then: 'Louise all right, Frank? Glad to have you back?' Frank was startled. The man had always bothered with details, it was part of the legend, part of his strength, part of his domination of those that surrounded him. But Frank too was skilled in the art of interrogation, and he recognized the ploy for what it was – a gesture of kindness, to be sure, but a ploy nonetheless. First the sugar and then . . .

'She's fine, thank you, General. Just fine.' He waited. Freeman nodded slowly, considering. A burst of laughter drifted down from upstairs.

'OK, then.' The General sighed and leaned forward. 'I know I've called you out at a bad time, Frank. What with Carole's death and the girl and all – well, you've earned that leave.' Frank's eyes narrowed as the General stepped on to very dangerous ground. 'I'm sorry. But I know you also realize I wouldn't have done it without good reason. I called you to my home because, in view of Lyudin's elimination, it is my belief SOPs * for the protection of Windjammer personnel have become insecure. Remember last night we were talking about Prolev? Lydia Prolev? The one defector, the one trump card we've still got up our sleeve?'

'I remember.'

'After you left I came back here and I got to thinking: maybe it was time to move her on, you follow me? Another safe house, new ID, new locale? I ordered just such a move.' Freeman paused, hands grasping the back of a chair. 'Then, three hours later, I got the word from Operations: that secondary position – her alternative safe house – it's gone cold. Backed out. As at this moment in time there is no secondary position – we've run out of prepared options.'

There was silence. Each option, Frank knew, took weeks to prepare.

'I want her moved, Frank,' said Freeman quietly. 'She must be moved, and she must be moved now. Today. She's been static four and a half months. Longer than anyone else. Longer than she should be even under the most secure conditions –'

'General, surely –?'

'I want her moved, Frank, and I want you to do it.' He held up a hand as Frank looked up, astounded. 'Purely as a

* SOP: Standard Operating Procedure.

temporary measure – a couple of days at the most. I want you to move her and I want you to be the one that hides her, You and no one else. No one else in Intelligence will know.'

'*Hide* her, General? Where am I supposed to –?'

'At home. With you.'

'With me? At home? In my *apartment*?' Frank's eyebrows crashed through the roof. 'Look, General – with the greatest of respect – I'm the last guy in the world –'

'You're the only guy in the world, Captain. There is no one else. There is no *where* else, believe me.' General Freeman spoke with quiet, calm insistency: 'Purely as a temporary measure –'

'Why the hell use me, one of our own people? Get her away to a motel somewhere! Jesus – we're supposed to work in with the other agencies on matters of this nature. Rope *them* in on this – they've got the resources, the budget, the manpower –'

'Those monumental whores?' growled Freeman. 'I wouldn't trust them with a list of groceries.' His conflict with the Central Intelligence Agency, specifically, was also near-legend within the Air Force.

'Then why not go to the NIB – the Nuclear Intelligence Board? It's their problem too,' Frank ended, harsh anger overcoming his exasperation. 'Why me? Why me to move her and – doubly why – why me to hide her away?'

Another thought suddenly occurred to Frank and he proffered it eagerly, almost with relief, for surely this was unassailable. 'What about Louise, General? What about my daughter? I can't involve her in this – it's out of the question!'

He sat back among the cushions breathing heavily. Jesus! What had gotten into the man? If General Freeman ever invited him out to his home again, he'd drop the phone and take off running . . .

'You think I should go to the NIB? The Sam Tollands of this world? You can tar those fat cats with the same brush as the Agency. As far as both Agency and NIB are concerned,

Hammer is just the latest obsession of Iron Balls Freeman –
not that they know a whole heap of shit about it in the first
place: there's no *proof*, no *evidence*, nothing to suggest
Hammer is anything more than the latest figment of my
imagination.' He shook his head in disgust. 'Proof? I'll
give those mothers proof! All they've –'

'But the photographs? What about satellite reconnaissance – those BigBird missions?'

General Freeman shook his head emphatically. 'Not
conclusive. As at last Wednesday's meeting of the co-
ordinating committee between CIA, NIB and ourselves,
Semipalatinsk is still listed merely as PNUTS – Possible
Nuclear Underground Testing Site. *Possible*.' He made a
disgusted gesture of dismissal.

'If Lydia Prolev decided to talk we'd be out of the woods:
home free.' There was a silence during which Freeman
studied Frank shrewdly. His words were striking through,
he was sure of it. 'I'll tell you another reason it's got to be
you, Frank: you're out of it – you're not tainted with the
politicking that's been going on in there. You've been away
– in New York, in Nellis. Before that it was Mildenhall,
Suffolk – before that, Turkey. You're on the outside up
here – people hardly know where you fit in. You do this for
me and it'll just be between you and me. No one else – it
won't even go through the Department. That way I'll *know*
it's clean, secure. Only for a few days, Frank, I promise.'

'Where is she now?' The words were out before he
realized what he was saying. But Freeman was too wise, too
seasoned a campaigner to exploit such an advantage by even
a smile.

'Forty, fifty miles up State. Staying with a guy called
Pligin. Airline steward, came over in 69/70. He's in our
debt up to his armpits. He's been keeping her under wraps
in a place called Hagerstown, not two hours' drive from
where we are now.' Freeman got up, crossed to his desk and
stood there for a long moment weighing a leather-bound
diary in his hand. Finally 'I'm not a man who makes deals,
Frank, but I'll tell you this: I know you've been having a

rough time travelling up and down the country with a six-year-old daughter you've hardly seen farmed out to child care every time you go away. Expensive, too. Well, here's my offer: you look after Prolov for a few days and those travelling days will be over. Finished – if that's what you want. You'll be Washington-based from here on in. You have my word. That's my offer.'

There was silence while Frank sat back and closed his eyes.

'Only a few days?'

General Freeman nodded. 'Money, round-the-clock protection – you name it, you've got it.'

'And no one else will know?'

'You have my word.'

Frank hauled himself slowly to his feet. 'Then you've got yourself a deal, General.'

'Thanks, Frank. I won't forget it.'

'Neither will I,' warned Frank.

He was heading north now, north towards Hagerstown and the woman called Lydia Prolov, his mind on the deal he had struck with General Freeman.

Up ahead, lights turned red and he slipped the car into neutral and eased to a halt. He waited, fingers drumming idly on the steering wheel as, unbidden, the words Louise had spoken at lunchtime returned to haunt his mind. As her straw slurped at the bottom of her huge milk-shake: 'Chocolate is my favourite, Daddy. It was Mummy's favourite too, wasn't it? When she was alive, I mean.'

Slurp, slurp.

When she was alive – just like that, with a six-year-old's natural, unconscious acceptance of change. Frank reached out and brushed his fingers against the pair of miniature pink ballet slippers dangling from the rearview mirror. He had placed them there as a joke really, two, three years ago, when Carole had been attending classes two nights a week. The shoes danced and quivered at his touch. He watched them until the blast of a horn shook him out of his memories and he slipped the car into gear.

Masochistically, he worked it out: Carole Yates had been killed thirteen months ago. Thirteen months, two weeks, four days and – he looked at the clock on the dashboard – two hours.

They had been married seven years. Seven. As marriages went with his generation, it had been something of a record. They didn't think so. They were going to go on for ever.

Carole had been working in the Pentagon's Civil Aide programme – nothing brilliant, nothing brainy – except that she had turned the head of every warm-bodied male for blocks around with a tall, liquid figure and a glossy mane of blond hair that shimmered and flowed as she laughed and tossed her head with that warmth and youthful spontaneity.

And he had killed her.

That wasn't what the coroner's report said, of course – but that only made it worse. In his heart, in the depths of his soul, Frank knew that he had killed her. He and he alone. By stupidity, carelessness, conceit and inadequacy.

Louise had been five, five and a bit. Frank had just come back from Sheppard AFB. A day or so later they'd parked Louise with friends for the weekend, loaded up the station-wagon with sleeping bags, food and cold beer, and rushed down to the marina early that Friday afternoon, Carole laughing beside him, hugging his arm, her hair blowing a ragged banner of gold as the station-wagon bucketed down the freeway.

Frank and Carole had sailed often before. They hired their usual twenty-four-foot sloop, crammed everything on board, slipped their moorings and used the engine to put half a dozen miles behind them before anchoring in a secluded, deserted, sand-washed cove a million miles away from Washington.

They'd kedged out the spare anchor, reefed down and stowed the sails and then rowed ashore, the inflatable dangerously low in the water beneath its load of beer, food, sleeping bags and happiness.

They'd built a driftwood fire while Frank clowned about in the dusk, splashing through the shallows as he tried to cool the beer, dig a sandpit and organize the provisions all at the same time It had been balmy and hot, then deceptively still, but Frank had ignored the warning.

They were miles from anywhere, alone in a private world of softly growling surf and warm sand. As the sun tipped into the west, Carole and Frank swam close together, naked, their supper baking in the glowing embers of bleached driftwood given up by a thousand different tides. They left the water laughing, dripping, glowing naked in the warmth of the fire, Carole's large, firm breasts gleaming softly in the flicker-glow of firelight as she leant forward and used a twisted stick to hook their supper from the ashes.

Later they loved together, locked on the warmth of their sleeping bags. For long moments after he had come deep within her, Carole held him to her, stroking his temples. Then she fondled back a curl of damp hair and whispered: 'Guess what, darling? I felt it. We just started a little friend for Louise, I know we did.' And, such was his love for the girl-child that had become his wife, Frank did not doubt it.

They woke to wind; to heavy, dark, brooding cloud.

Ignoring the warnings, the radio, the rising sea and Carole's cautious questions, Frank had insisted they scramble back to the boat, weigh anchor and pull away to the north, determined to race the storm to the sanctuary of the next harbour.

The storm caught them four miles short, two miles from land with sixty feet of angry water beneath their keel.

The sea rose to flash and curl around the fibre glass shell of their vessel. Inevitably, ten minutes later, the engine packed up.

Frank had been in the cockpit, hanging on the tiller, judging the seas, fighting to keep head to wind.

Clipped into her safety harness, wet hair flogging wildly around her shoulders, he had sent Carole for'ard to take in sail. As she threw him a brave, frightened grin and began to move forward, a huge wave hunched threateningly over the bows of the little vessel. Carole didn't even see it coming. Frank shouted a warning, the words lost in the moan and rip of wind in steel halyards. As Carole released the shackle at the apex of leech and luff on the foresail and reached both hands to gather in the wet, billowing nylon, the wave struck.

Frank watched powerless from the cockpit as his wife vanished in a crashing welter of dark water as the boat heeled venomously. When she rolled sluggishly clear, throwing the seas off her narrow decks, Carole had gone, the safety harness ripped from its clips.

Not a sight, not a sound. It was as if she had never existed.

Four hours later Frank limped into harbour. Haggard, haunted by grief, changed for ever.

And Louise had been waiting. For Daddy and Mummy.

Frank pulled his battered station-wagon in to the kerb, killed the engine and stretched behind the wheel. It had taken two and a half hours to drive to this tree-lined street in Hagerstown, and he was tired.

Number 49 was across the street, top floor. He settled a little deeper in his seat and began a minute examination of the approaches. Lower-middle-class area. Private, detached houses run to seed, interspersed with shops and, over there, a red-tiled church with a high, pointed steeple. Access? Access from the main street via a steep interior staircase that began just beyond the wooden door with the peeling green paint beside the car port.

A blind was drawn half-way down one of the front windows and telephone wires trailed into the building in a lazy loop from the sidewalk.

Frank tugged Freeman's letter of introduction from an inside pocket, smoothed out the envelope and pushed open the car door. He crossed the street and rang the doorbell. He could hear no answering chimes from within, so he banged on the door for good measure.

There was silence. He glanced up and saw the blind move in the window above. Presently steps dropped down the stairs towards him, heavy with suspicion. The door opened a crack. It was retained by a stout chain.

'Yes?'

'I've a message,' announced Frank simply. He thrust the crumpled envelope through the crack and it disappeared, the door closed and there was another lengthy silence. Finally it opened again.

'You are alone?'

'I'm alone.'

The chain came off the door and the man stood aside abruptly. 'Come inside. Quickly.' The man's nervousness was contagious and Frank did as he was bid. The chain went back on the door and the man stepped back to regard him with hostility. Aged about forty-five, he was in his shirt-sleeves, and his trousers were held up by braces. He looked tired, strained. As he reached past Frank to replace the poker on the shelf above the door Frank noticed the stale breath, the dark wet patches under each armpit. He was scared, too.

'Come.' He turned and led the way upstairs. Frank followed. The stairs gave on to a small living room with doors off it that led to a kitchen, bathroom and bedrooms. The man gestured his visitor to a chair. To Frank's surprise the apartment was clean and tidy. Books were stacked neatly in a bookshelf and there was a vase of flowers on a table. Only the man's appearance, his demeanour, struck the eye as dishevelled, unkempt.

Pligin regarded Frank in silence, a finger drumming nervously against one knee. 'You come from the General?' he demanded finally, beady eyes peering forward intently. 'I shall check, of course.'

Frank gestured at the letter flapping nervously in the other's hand. 'Go right ahead – call him on that number. He's expecting your call.'

The man came out of the chair in an explosion of nervous movement and crossed to the phone. Presently he was talking into the receiver with one eye on the General's handwritten instructions. Then, satisfied, he replaced the receiver.

'OK?' said Frank.

The man swallowed and sat down hurriedly. He nodded.

'He says I am to do exactly what you say. I am to place myself entirely in your hands.'

Frank nodded and there was a pause as he glanced about him, waiting. When nothing happened 'Where is she?' he asked. 'I would like to see her. The Prolev woman.'

Pligin held up a hand. 'In a little while. Your General Freeman says only that I am to cooperate, to do what you tell me. But he does not tell me what you want, why you come here. So now I ask: why do you come?'

'I'm taking her away, Mr Pligin. To another place. Somewhere safer.' Frank saw the hurt leap into his eyes and realized he was resented not simply because he was a stranger to a man for whom all strangers were synonymous with fear, detection and betrayal, but because he was a rival.

'Where are you taking her?' he demanded.

'I can't tell you that.'

'And myself? Am I also to be moved?'

There was silence.

'My orders only concern Lydia Prolev,' said Frank finally.

Pligin got up and began to pace the room nervously. 'But . . . but if it is dangerous for her, then it is dangerous for me also, no? Am I to be left out in the open like . . . like –'

'Like the goat that is tied out for the tiger?' added a new voice.

Frank spun round.

One of the bedroom doors was ajar and a woman stood in the doorway, a bread knife held down by her side. She was in her mid-thirties, medium height, medium build, with a head of rich dark hair dragged back and tied simply at the nape of her neck. Large brown eyes flashed dangerously as Pligin moved impulsively towards her. 'Lydia! You should not –'

Frank interrupted: 'I have a message for you from the General. General Freeman.'

'I hear what you say to Viktor.' She nodded sharply, hostility in every line of her body. 'About "the Prolev woman". Well, I am here. In the bedroom.' She placed the bread knife back in a drawer and pushed it shut violently. She turned to face Frank. 'So – that General of yours: what does he want?'

'You are to move. It is no longer safe for you to stay where you are. I am to escort you to a new place.'

Lydia Prolev gestured towards the man standing between them. 'And Viktor? Does he come to this "safer" place? What does the good General plan for him?'

'He is to remain here.'

'Why, then, must I move? If it is safe for one Soviet defector to remain it is safe for another.'

Frank shrugged. 'My orders concern you and you alone. There may well be other plans for your friend here, but those plans are not my concern.' She made a good point. By the simple passage of time, Pligin had become a pawn of little value.

'Why is such a move considered necessary? It is quiet here – it is safe. We see no one, we are seen by no one.' Frank said nothing as the large brown eyes regarded him shrewdly, then 'Something has happened,' she said slowly. 'And so now your General Freeman is worried. Yes? Yes – it must be so,' she decided emphatically.

Frank maintained a silence that in itself was eloquent enough.

'There has been another death, yes? Another killing? Am I not correct?'

Despite himself, Frank nodded.

'Who?'

'I can't divulge –'

'Who?' she demanded, the single word slashing across the room like a knife thrown in anger. 'If I am to place my life in the hands of this wonderful –' the word was heavy with scorn – 'Intelligence Service of yours, then I demand that you tell me. And besides –' the shoulders drooped into an eloquent piece of punctuation – 'Viktor and I – who are we going to tell?'

'A man in New York. Lyudin. Vasili Lyudin.'

The pain flashed into the eyes, and Lydia Prolev drew in her breath with a quiet hiss. 'Vasili! We were friends. A long time ago. We work together.'

'I am sorry,' murmured Frank.

'Sorry!' She shook her head angrily. 'Sorry? We come to you in faith for safety, for protection – we take the risks; we come to the great United States of America and – we are killed! We are killed because here, in your own country, you cannot keep us safe. And you, you say you are "sorry"!' she ended angrily.

'You are to be moved to a new place. A safer place,' repeated Frank patiently. It was time to move things on. His car had been outside long enough. 'Mrs Prolev – you are to pack your things. Get ready to move, now. I will drive you to this new place. But we must move soon. Please, be as quick as you can.' He crossed to the window, peered through the blind and examined the street below. It was clear.

Lydia Prolev and Viktor Pligin exchanged glances. The woman made to move towards one of the bedrooms but stopped on Frank's voice: 'Do you have a headscarf? Dark glasses? Something like that?'

Lydia Prolev placed her hands on her hips and gave a low laugh that carried little humour. 'Ah, Mr American Secret Agent – headscarfs and dark glasses! What a marvellous idea!'

'Lady,' snapped Frank, patience running through his fingers, 'I'm carrying out my instructions. I don't much care if you want to go out of here looking like Davy Crockett. What I do know is that we're leaving in –' he glanced at his watch – 'fifteen minutes, and right now you're wasting time.' The woman glowered at him silently, but the hands came down off the hips and presently a bedroom door slammed shut behind her.

Half an hour elapsed before the final farewells had been exchanged upstairs between the two Russians. Now Hagerstown was twelve miles behind them, and the silence in the old car had grown to the size of a house. A mile after that it began to get dark, and then the rain came on. Tired windscreen wipers flogged noisily across the windscreen, and a little after that Frank pulled in at a McDonalds, left the woman in the car and splashed across the puddles to buy hamburgers and hot coffee for them both.

The move was calculated. It is difficult to maintain a dignified silence while battling with the practical difficulties of hamburger, dressings, onion rings, French fries and hot coffee.

Frank dropped his onion rings on his lap for the second time, swore briefly and glanced suspiciously out of the corner of his eye. Two large brown eyes regarded him with the beginnings of amusement.

'You are all fingers,' she said, unfurling the flag of truce with caution.

'Thumbs,' corrected Frank, truce honoured. 'All thumbs.'

The wealthy, middle-aged woman in the fur coat appeared unable to make up her mind. It was one of the few privileges of widowed wealth.

'It does look kinda small,' she said doubtfully. Ferris stifled his annoyance behind a bland smile, reached into the black velvet display tray and removed another ring with great delicacy. The single diamond glittered brilliantly in the store lighting.

'How about this one here, madam? Claw set, eighteen carat, white gold solitaire. A truly beautiful piece.'

'May I try it?'

'Most certainly you may.'

The woman held out a fat finger with inelegant haste. Assuming an air of almost papal dignity, Ferris squeezed the ring on to her finger as one of the junior assistants glided quietly up to his shoulder. 'Telephone call for you, Mr Ferris.'

Ferris nodded, replaced the display tray in the cabinet and made his excuses. He moved to the back of the store.

'Ferris.'

'Michael. That movement order is now confirmed. There is a ticket awaiting collection in the usual place in the name of Thomas E. Mason . . .' Michael spelt out the details rapidly. Washington until further notice: Lydia Prolev was to be found and liquidated. As far as his professional colleagues were concerned, he had been called away on an important and highly secret buying trip.

'Understood.'

The line went dead and Ferris returned to the lady with the fat fingers.

As Frank Yates moved Lydia Prolev slowly southwards back towards Washington, something very strange was happening far to the north in a place called . . . Timmins.

On any normal day you can board one of the red and white Air Canada D C-9s at Toronto International Airport, fly north for exactly forty minutes and touch down briefly at North Bay on Lake Nipissing, Ontario.

A ten-minute stop to take on and disembark passengers and then on again, still north, for a further forty-minute flight over a vast and never-ending sea of fir trees and frozen lakes. Too numerous to count, these lakes stretch to every horizon like pieces of quicksilver dropped carelessly from a giant's hand. Up here, around latitude 48, there is little evidence of man – the occasional ruler-straight fire-break cleft from the forests, the seldom-seen ribbon of Highway II off to the right as it curves up from Georgian Bay to swing round past Kirkland Lake, Kapuskasing and Geraldton to Thunder Bay on the western shores of Lake Superior.

Even under the first warmth of spring the country strikes fear into the pampered heart of the city-dweller with its casual, terrifying emptiness, its utter disregard for the puny restraints imposed upon its face by Man, the exploiter. The few towns that have carved names for themselves amid the vastness of silver birch, amid the lakes that abound in trout, bass, pickerel and pike, seem on a normal day to be small indeed, no more than the inconsequential punctuation marks upon the rolling chapter of northern Ontario.

This far north the inexperienced traveller finds his mind turning uneasily to thoughts of engine failure, of survival down there among the firs and the grizzlies, of the flimsy creature comforts abandoned so readily far to the south. Thus it is that when at last the smudge of low buildings finally begins to roll over the horizon, it is hailed with an inner relief that looks fondly, blindly, upon a town with a population of 44,000 but which has little architectural merit. The air brakes go down and the smooth, practised descent into Timmins begins.

On a normal day.

Which only means that none of that was happening at Timmins. Not today.

Now there were no anxious passengers counting lakes, no smooth let-downs into Timmins, no aircraft in the circuit.

The airport was blind.

For the last two and a half hours Timmins airport had been without radio, radar or telecommunications of any kind. Flights in and out of the town's only tarmac airfield had been cancelled or diverted back to Toronto in the face of massive electronic interference on the 9.00–22.00 MHz waveband.

The signal that caused such confusion in sensitive landing-assistance aids and such bitter, ill-directed blasphemy among the fleet of part-time taxi drivers and the Duty Flight Controllers was clear and unmistakable.

Cutting across all forty channels within that frequency band, it sounded exactly as though someone very near at hand was knocking two pieces of mahogany together with great force and at great speed. At times the interference was deafening, painful to the ears. At others, it dropped away to a muted, sibilant whisper. Interference, listed in the Duty Logs as QRN – man-made interference – had been persistent now for two hours thirty-five minutes and even at its lowest volume it defied all attempts at over-ride. Its presence, its source of origin, was a mystery. In Timmins, quite simply, they'd never known anything like it.

The airport was the place, perhaps, where its effect was most obvious: 428 miles from Toronto, more than 300 from

Sault Ste Marie to the south and west, the small town relies heavily upon its air link with the outside world. But there were other locations within Timmins where the interference was to have results that could be measured in blood, in suffering and in the thin, narrow line between life and death.

Timmins is a busy, thriving, highly mechanized mining town with lumber as its stable secondary industry. Nine mines operate in Porcupine: The Aunor, Dome, Hallnor, Sidex and Pamour mines bring out the gold; the mines of Texasgulf, Texmost and Langmuir chase out a combination of nickel, silver and copper.

Only, right then, one of those mines had a problem: there had been an accident 600 feet underground at the stope – the working face – on level six at Sidex Exploration.

Safety is of particular concern to all within the Canadian mining industry and Sidex Exploration prided itself upon a safety record that was better than most. Until that evening their 'Days Without Accident' board at the head of the mine had read one hundred and seven. Campbell had just spoilt all that.

Campbell had been a twenty-three-year-old apprentice three-boom jumbo drill operator at the stope understudying drilling technique until the moment he stepped down from the massive rig to adjust the square red battery pack clipped to the broad leather belt worn by all miners underground.

Somehow – no one would ever know just how – Campbell had slipped beneath the wheel of the vehicle at the moment Operator Martin engaged reverse. Martin had spun the wheels away and killed the engine but by then Campbell was pinned by his right thigh beneath four and a half tons of machinery and his screams were echoing down the vaulted cavern like shouted messages from hell itself.

Martin kept his head and activated the procedure they had all practised a hundred times before. He punched in the Rescue Call-Pak that was carried on the vest of each shift leader and crawled unhesitatingly beneath the vehicle with tourniquet and morphine syrette, comforted somewhere amid his own horror and Campbell's screams of pain to know that even now the rescue team would be racing towards him, each man alerted by the call patched through to the small metallic bleeper carried upon pain of dismissal by surface personnel wherever they went.

What Martin had no way of knowing as he crouched down among the grease, the heat and the broken ore trying to stem Campbell's pumping femoral lifeblood, was that the closed circuit of the alarm system carried his message no further than the site control office at the head of the shaft. From there, each bleeper was activated by electronic pulse – a signal which, that evening, was jammed because it fell between 9.00 and 22.00 MHz. The rescue team was scattered over the site's six hundred acres, and the doctors, nurses and heavy-duty mechanics had to be contacted and assembled by phone, truck and word of mouth. To Martin's tear-streaked disgust it took the sweating rescue team twenty-four minutes to reach the stope and get Campbell away to the surface.

There were other problems elsewhere: all four radio stations, together with the three TV stations, went off the air; police communications were disrupted, traffic lights froze on red, and garage doors refused to obey the signals beamed at them from frustrated owners sitting behind the wheels of their cars. However, for Campbell it had by that time all become rather academic.

In Washington's Pentagon, Captain Paul Fisher handed over temporary command of the Air Force Intelligence Desk (Analysis) and hurried along the busy corridor towards General Freeman's office, his interpretation of Timmins's QRN clutched in his hand. Unlike many of his colleagues, Fisher took the General's beam weapon theories seriously, and, moreover, he was coming to believe in them himself. Several months ago Freeman had issued a memorandum outlining the possibility of this sort of electronic development as an indicator – a signpost – whose discovery would suggest the scale of the weapons system it would serve: such a weapon, Freeman reasoned, would require advanced radar warning of missile launch far in advance of any traditional early warning system.

His own professional analysis of what he called the

'Russian Woodpecker', with its characteristic 'toka-toka-toka-toka', suggested there might be as many as four different stations radiating the same signal from different locations. To his specialized mind, the pattern screamed over-the-horizon radar. The pinpointing of Gomel as one of the sources of origin merely confirmed what he had suspected: the signals must come from some kind of west-ward-looking backscatter OTH radar with a skip distance far in excess of anything he had encountered before.

Ten minutes later General Freeman tossed the report aside and tilted back in his chair. He tapped a pencil against his teeth and gazed up at the ceiling. Captain Fisher waited patiently. 'Gomel – you're certain?'

'Yes, sir. And it checks out. Four hundred miles south-west of Moscow and –'

'Eight hundred in line-of-flight from the satellite launch site at Kapustin Yar,' finished Freeman.

Fisher nodded. 'Yes, sir.'

'OK, Captain. Leave it with me.'

Fisher saluted, turned smartly on his heel and returned to Operations Intelligence.

When he had gone General Freeman reached out for the intercom and buzzed through to his secretary. 'Laura – I want the files on the following: Gomel – the industrial town in Byelorussia; anything and everything we've logged in Analysis on QRN over the last six, nine months; and the latest update on that Russian kid Prolev, Misha Prolev, now aged about ten. Where he is, what he's doing, the works. You got that, Laura?'

'Gomel, QRN, Misha Prolev – got it, General.'

It was after 9 p.m. that evening before General Freeman pushed the last of the papers aside and reached for the phone. He punched out a number and stood there drumming his fingers with impatience as the soft burring tone rang on in his ear. Come on, get on the job . . .

'Yes . . .?' A male voice, rumpled and creased from the pillows of sleep or fornication. Knowing a little about Tom Greener and a lot about the current credibility of the

Central Intelligence Agency, Freeman reckoned it was probably both.

'Hello? That you, Tom?'

'Who is this?'

'Clarke Freeman. General Clarke Freeman.'

'Oh.' The welcome ran out of the voice like water out of a tub. Freeman heard a woman's whisper in the background, accompanied by the rustle of sheets. 'Forgive me, General, but do you know what time this is?'

'I know what time it is –'

'Well? Can't it wait? My office opens –'

'No, it can't wait. I want you to get the Nuclear Intelligence Board together for an extraordinary meeting. Soon as you can.'

'You *what*? You want the NIB –?'

'That's right, the NIB. You people hold the statutory powers of assembly, don't you?'

'Well, yes, but –'

'Then I'm invoking my right to convene that meeting as Head of Air Force Intelligence. You want me to go higher, I'll go higher, Tom. I'm through fooling with you people.'

OK, OK, take it easy. Give me a call in the morning. We'll work something out then.'

The line clicked in Freeman's hand.

Tom Greener rolled over among the blankets and reached for his spectacles. Suited, stern and commanding among the trappings of power at the CIA Headquarters in Langley, Virginia – the contrast now was almost total.

'What's the matter, hon? What is it?' asked the young woman curled naked beside the middle-aged Assistant Director's unappetizing body. Tom Greener was sitting upright in the wide bed, a ludicrous, indignant and almost hairless figure in the near-darkness.

'Damn that man,' he muttered at the far wall. Freeman and he had clashed often in the past, particularly so in recent weeks since Freeman had gone public on what he saw as the Agency's increasing inefficiency, a cry that had struck chords with both the Senate Investigations Committee and the publication of Stockwell's *In Search of Enemies*.

Now Greener sat there, frowning at a parade of dismal thoughts: NIB, indeed. Why was that sonofabitch invoking his right to a hearing now? Why now – with the MX debate all but cut and dried and the Senate Foreign Aid hearings scheduled for next month? It was bound to mean trouble. Trouble for the CIA, for his department, maybe for himself. Tom Greener reached out absently for the whore's large breasts and began stroking softly. 'Damn the man,' he repeated, though this time the words carried rather less anger.

The woman's expensive fingers may have had something to do with that.

Two hours later, as Tom Greener's latest purchase reached for her shoes and cast a pitying glance at the snoring hump under the blankets, Frank Yates linked his hands behind his head and stared open-eyed up at the ceiling.

He had introduced Lydia Prolev to his daughter and for the next hour he had held his breath awaiting the detonation of tearful anger that never came.

Frank had given Lydia the spare room, shown her where the bathroom was and then slipped outside to buy supper for the three of them. When he returned the apartment was in total silence and he had burst through into the lounge expecting to find justification of his wildest fears. Instead, he discovered Lydia Prolev on her knees in the middle of the carpet calmly dressing a doll while Louise looked on with the rapt attention only a six-year-old girl can donate to such a task.

Lydia had risen smoothly to her feet with a little smile of embarrassment, taken charge of the food he had purchased and vanished into the kitchen to produce an appetizing supper all three had eaten seated around the deal table in the kitchen. After Lydia had marvelled at the choice, the quality of the food and at the dresses Louise had amassed for her dolls, it had been Louise who had done most of the talking. Frank had listened silently, subdued, awkward among the rekindled memories of another domesticity. Yet once, perhaps twice, he caught himself following Lydia's figure to the stove, found himself noting the soft curve of hair at the nape of her neck.

Now there was a soft knocking on his bedroom door.

'It's open.' The handle turned slowly and Lydia Prolev stood in the doorway, framed in the light from the hall. She was still dressed, a newspaper held down by her side.

'I could not sleep,' she said simply. 'I thought that perhaps you would like to talk. About this business . . . about Viktor, perhaps.'

Frank swung his legs down to the floor and reached for his robe. 'Sure. Why not?' He moved forward out of the bedroom and closed the door firmly. 'Drink?' he asked quietly over his shoulder.

She nodded. 'That would be good.'

'Scotch?'

She nodded again and Frank gestured to one of the armchairs. 'Go ahead – I'll fix the drinks.'

He went over to the sideboard and poured two generous shots of whisky into square, thick glasses that gleamed in the pale lamplight. Outside, beyond the drawn curtains, he could hear the steady murmur of traffic. It was peaceful and silent inside the apartment. He glanced now over his shoulders. 'Nervous?'

He handed her a glass.

She smiled tautly, fingers laced around one slim knee. Then, to Frank's alarm, she tossed back the scotch and swallowed two dollars' worth of expensive import at a gulp. Without pausing to splutter or cough, she placed the glass firmly on the glass table in front of her and leant forward. 'Captain –'

'Whoa there – hold on a minute! You're supposed to sip that stuff slowly – not knock it back like you're about to rescue a swimmer in difficulties!' He smiled.

'I am sorry?' She looked up, embarrassed.

'It isn't vodka, you know. You're supposed to take it down slowly.' He refilled her glass.

This time Lydia sipped with exaggerated caution. 'Is better?'

Frank nodded. 'Much better.'

She sipped again, then 'Captain . . . Yates? I would like you to know –'

'Frank. Make it Frank, OK?'

Again she smiled that taut smile. 'Frank. I want to tell you that . . . today, with Viktor? I said things to you that were unnecessary, cruel, you remember? I am sorry. It is only because I am scared . . . frightened. Just a little bit. You know?'

Frank studied the bottom of his glass. 'Sure. Forget it.'

There was a sudden awkward silence. Lydia Prolev swept her eyes around the room searching for a conversation piece. They alighted upon a smiling photograph of Louise. It was an unfortunate choice. 'You have a lovely daughter, Frank. She is very much like you – to look at, I mean. Her mother, is she –?'

'Did you get to meet the General?' demanded Frank abruptly, wrenching the conversation around on to safer ground. The snub flashed into Lydia's eyes and she picked up her glass, long, elegant fingers cradling the amber fluid.

'Yes, I meet with your General,' she said quietly. 'He is the one who first questions me after Vienna, you know? Frank, I am sorry. I did not mean to –'

'That's OK. Forget it. Her mother was killed thirteen months ago in a boating accident. I was the captain.' His voice sounded very bitter. 'I don't want to talk about it, OK? So – what did you make of him? General Freeman?'

Again that expressive shrug. 'It was not the time to make a favourable impression, I think. He wanted certain information that I was . . . not permitted to give to him. He was very angry.'

'Information?' asked Frank, deadpan.

Lydia Prolev glanced up. Despite herself she was smiling as she wagged a slim finger in his direction. 'Information, Mr Intelligence Officer! Yes, information! What do you think?' She leant forward to rummage inside her plastic handbag. Presently she produced a creased black and white photograph which she handed to Frank as though it was something very, very precious. 'You see?' she said softly.

'I too have a child. A son.'

The snapshot showed a smiling boy sitting on a playground swing, muffled in a thick coat against the snow. 'That is Misha.

Lydia Prolev spoke so quietly Frank had to lean forward to catch the words. 'He is just ten. Ten and a half.' She paused. 'If I say nothing to your General it is because I am here, and Misha, he is still in Russia. It was not . . . it was not planned in such a manner. I came to the West by an easy route because of my work, you understand? The others . . . they do not manage to come over. I do not know why.' She made an effort to rouse herself. 'So – when Misha is here with me, safe, then I will talk with your General Freeman. Until then, I say nothing.'

'You expect General Freeman to get Misha out of Russia for you? Mount a rescue operation, send in the troops?' demanded Frank incredulously.

'Would it be so impossible?' she wiped her cheek dry with the back of her hand. 'He is very important, very powerful, this General of yours, no? He tells me so himself.' She raised her glass wryly. 'To your General Freeman.'

Frank raised his glass. 'To General bloody Freeman,' he echoed, stunned.

*

Frank Yates and Lydia Prolev talked on into the night, the rush of traffic and the muted whisper of aircraft overhead muffled by the thick curtains that added to their feeling of safety, of insulation from the outside world. Both might have sat less easily in their chairs had they known that one of those jets high above carried Ferris safely into Washington's National Airport.

*

On the seventh floor of the drab grey apartment block two kilometres to the south of the Semipalatinsk space faculty, a ten-year-old boy watched fearfully through the crack in the door as the blue-raincoated security man shook his head sternly and pointed back towards the head of the concrete staircase. The boy opened the door a crack wider to catch the words as the old woman tried to argue, pointing beyond the folded arms towards the apartment door. The man shook his head emphatically and raised his voice. The woman's shoulders sagged in defeat and she turned away, beaten.

As she disappeared down the stairs once more Misha Prolev closed the door quickly and hurried back into the communal bathroom shared by the four families on the same floor. What had happened to Auntie Irena? Why wouldn't they let her visit him like she usually did?

He slipped the bolt on the ill-fitting door and sat down on the toilet seat in this, the only room in the block that offered temporary privacy. Choking down the fear that was familiar now to a boy without mother or father who was living with uncaring foster-parents selected by the State, Misha turned to the mirror above the enamel basin and carefully removed his metal spectacles. He closed his right eye and stared bravely back at his own solemn reflection. Then, slowly, he opened his right eye again, prised down the lower lid with a finger and leaned forward. The thick scab of damaged tissue seemed to be healing slowly. He dabbed the eye with cold water, replaced his spectacles and slipped back the bolt on the door just as Alexei began hammering on the partitioning. 'All right, all right. I'm coming,' he grumbled.

A ten-year-old's self-consultancy is rarely accurate. The spray of jagged glass fragments that had been part of the crash that ended the abortive escape attempt to the West had caused serious, progressive damage to the cornea of his right eye.

Misha Prolev was going slowly blind.

*

Professor Eduard Ryabov laid his newspaper aside and listened intently.

'Irena? Is that you?'

The door of their home on the recently built estate of

attractive, low-timbered dashas on the outskirts of the new township that had sprung up around the Professor's work at Semipalatinsk had just opened and then been gently closed. Uncharacteristically, there had been no cheerful call of greeting.

'Irena?' The Professor laid his spectacles aside and made to rise.

'Yes, Eduard. It is me. Who else would it be?' She sounded tired, defeated.

He rose to his feet and moved forward to greet her. 'Irena? What is it? What is the matter?'

His wife came through wearily from the hallway, her thick coat buttoned still against the chill wind outside. As she stepped nearer he saw that she had been crying.

'Irena! What is it?' He placed his thin arms around her and rocked her gently towards him.

'Oh, Eduard – why? Why do they do it?'

The tears started again and the Professor felt the beginnings of real alarm. She was usually so cheerful, so comfortable, so ... so solid. Tears were a rare thing indeed. He drew her gently away from his shoulder and studied her face intently. 'You will tell me. You will tell me now, Irena! If it is those Cronin boys again, then I personally –'

A tired smile broke through the tears, perhaps at the picture of her man of such brilliant ideas surging forth in braces and shirtsleeves to do battle on her behalf. With the children gone now, Irena Ryabov wondered suddenly if he realized just how much she still loved him. She shook her head. 'No, Eduard – it is not the Cronin twins. I almost wish that it was.'

'What, then? People on the tram? In the street?'

Again she shook her head. Since their niece had left, it had been her kindness to call each week to see Lydia's boy, Mishinka. Each week Irena took with her something tasty from her oven – an apple-cake, perhaps, or maybe a delicacy from the Commissary inside the complex. Now she wiped the back of her hand over her worn, lined face and made an effort to pull herself together. Used to shielding her academic husband from the harsher realities of their simple life together, she felt dimly ashamed of giving way.

Professor Ryabov guided her gently into an armchair over by the log fire and poured out a full measure of the thick apricot wine he kept on the shelf for special occasions. Eyes fixed upon his wife, shoulders stooped to the weight of the concern he felt for her, he handed her the glass and stood over her menacingly, a matron giving out medicine.

'Drink, Irena – every last drop,' he ordered sternly. She did so and gave a little shudder.

'More?'

She shook her head and grimaced as the fire burnt deeper. Eduard Ryabov placed her glass aside. 'So, so tell me. Who is it that makes the finest woman in all the Republic return home in tears?'

'It is the same as usual: I take the tram and I get to Mishinka's people the same time as I always do, a little before seven.'

'Go on.'

'I . . . I went upstairs –' she fiddled nervously with her fingers – 'And, as I approach the door, as I get there, there is a man. A man from State Security.' She paused and her husband leant forward, his bony hands gripping the arms of his chair. 'He . . . he asks me if I am the wife of Professor Eduard Ryabov – not . . . if I am *Irena* Ryabov, but if I am your . . . your wife. Then he asks for my papers. I showed them to him. Then I am ordered to wait. Only I must wait below. Downstairs.' She held up a shaking finger. 'For one hour, Eduard – for one hour exactly they made me wait.'

The Professor flinched visibly, fingers curling tight against the crude, calculated indignity. Irena Ryabov was sixty-three.

The apartment was on the seventh floor. There were no lifts.

'At last I am permitted to return,' she continued. 'I approach the seventh floor. Only this time there is another man, a different man.' She shook her head, and with a stab of alarm her husband saw that the tears were about to start again. 'Do you know what he tells me, this . . . this man?' Eduard Ryabov shook his head. 'He tells me there has been a change. That I am no longer permitted to see Mishinka. You and I, Eduard – do you know what we have become? We have become – what did he call it? – a "sphere of bad influence".' She reached out and clasped his hand tightly. 'What does it all mean? Why are they doing this to us? When I tell him about Mishinka's eye condition, he just shrugs – and I can *see* the boy, peeping at me through a crack in the door like some . . . some animal. Why, Eduard?'

Her husband patted her arm absently, his mind darting ahead swiftly. Deeply alarmed by the tenor of the Moscow meeting and by the talk, however 'hypothetical' of offensive beam weapon development, Ryabov had penned a résumé of his fears to Marshal Gladky himself. Up until this moment he had received not the slightest acknowledgement that his letter had been received, and his fears had only grown in the darkness of a private imagination.

Many years ago, long before Fuchs helped him to the position of prominence he now enjoyed both within the limited physical boundaries of Semipalatinsk and within the boundless intellectual frontiers of the Soviet Academy of Sciences, Professor Ryabov had stilled the early growlings of conscience amid the unaccustomed opulence of his surroundings by the sure and certain knowledge that he was working for peace and national security in a manner that would push the possibility of a drift towards the horrors of international nuclear conflict into the dim reaches of improbability. Yet in recent years that comforting certainty had wavered as the growlings of doubt, of conscience, became more pronounced.

He had not told Irena about his fears, about his recent meeting in Moscow or about his certainty that men known to them both, colleagues and friends they had entertained amid warmth and laughter here in their own home, had been systematically eliminated by the agents of the Government he served.

'I do not know why,' he lied gently.

Ferris had been met at Washington National Airport by the
man he knew as Nicholson, who worked for the Rezidentura
from behind the façade of a fashionable florist on Duport
Circle. Now Ferris followed Nicholson through the heavy,
perfumed jungle of the darkened shop, their rubber-soled
shoes making no sound as they crossed the thick cork tiling
between the laden shelves of indoor ferns and chic office
decorations, the display stands of potted plants, climbers
and blossoms, to a narrow staircase at the back of the shop
that led directly to Nicholson's rented apartment above.
They climbed this swiftly and Nicholson led the way into
the apartment, drew the curtains and switched on soft side
lighting.

Ferris stood by the door listening quietly, his single piece
of luggage still in his hand. Nicholson tossed his jacket on
to the settee and reached for a bottle and a couple of glasses.
'Drink?'

The drive to the airport, the hanging around outside
among the uniformed police officers and the airline staff,
had made him more nervous than he had realized. You
didn't have to be careless for your luck to change – you just
needed to discover you were in the wrong place at the wrong
time. Airports, stations, places of transit – all were among
Nicholson's list of Wrong Places.

But this guy seemed to have no nerves at all. No tongue,
either – they had exchanged less than a dozen sentences on
the way over.

Now Ferris shook his head at the bottle and walked briefly
round the small apartment sniffing out the geography, the
danger areas, the blind spots. 'Got a coffee?'

'Sure.'

Nicholson went through into the kitchen. Ferris followed him. As the water drummed noisily into the kettle 'This place been cleaned recently?'

He didn't mean with a vacuum and a handful of dusters.

'Guys came through three days ago. Part of your welcome procedure.' Nicholson handed Ferris the coffee and led the way back into the lounge. The apartment had an air of raffish, artistic neglect: colourful soft cushions, warm pastel colours, modern paintings in steel frames, subdued lighting and plants in untidy profusion. It looked like the home of some artisan dedicated to the pursuit of the gentler goals in life. Nicholson, who was not queer, had meant it to look that way. A great deal of hard, intelligent thought was rewarded by Ferris's look of disdain as he glanced about him. It was all a long way from Kutuzovsky Prospekt.

Nicholson gestured around them at the soft, effete furnishings and patted his own velvet-trousered leg. 'Don't let it fool you,' he said with an edge to his voice that Doris Freeman would certainly never have recognized. 'Don't let any of it fool you for a moment. I've used this as cover for the last three years. It works.'

Ferris inclined his head. 'Congratulations – I was beginning to wonder.' He paused, watching Nicholson steadily, shrewdly over the rim of his coffee cup, weighing the trust he felt for the man. He put his coffee aside and leant forward.

'We'll start at the top,' he decided. 'How much have they told you?'

Nicholson shrugged. 'The usual: very little. Only that I was to pick you up, provide you with whatever "good services" you required and act as cutout between yourself and any dealings you may have with either the Embassy here, the Rezidentura or the UN delegation.'

'And that was all?'

'One thing more. Several weeks ago I was told to look out for references to an American Air Force General – a General Clarke Freeman. Head of Air Force Intelligence and one of the more outspoken hawks on the establishment.

He's been making a lot of smoke recently about US preparedness and the inadequacies of the ICBM programme over here. Before that, he was sounding off about nuclear shelters and the civil defence programme in the homeland. Anyway, I've checked him out. I think maybe I've found a back door into that situation. I was in his home earlier today.'

'Explain,' demanded Ferris shortly.

Nicholson told him about Freeman's wife and her activities for penal reform, and about his own natural insertion into those circles via the supply of floral displays for her many functions. Ferris was impressed. Nicholson went on: 'This General Freeman seems to be a man without many friends in the Pentagon. The papers call him a "hotshot" General. Last month he was in open conflict with the Assistant Director of the CIA and his own superior, General Holt –'

'Why was that?' demanded Ferris, sensing a lever of opportunity.

'The MX debate. The General has been leaking angry letters to the Washington papers. They're anonymous, of course, but there's not much doubt where they're coming from. I have them here should you wish to see them.'

'Later. Tell me: the name Prolev, Lydia Prolev – does that name mean anything to you?'

'Lydia Prolev.' Nicholson turned it over in his mind. 'No, I have never heard it before,' he said finally.

'Soviet scientist,' supplied Ferris. 'She defected to the West a short while ago. We are told she is in this vicinity also. The discovery of her location is my – and now your – primary task. It takes priority over all others.'

'What about our agents-in-place? Informers within the service, the government? The Pentagon? CIA itself?'

Ferris shook his head emphatically. 'Prolev is not in the care of the CIA – nor is her location known to US Naval Intelligence or the Federal Bureau of Investigation – that much we know already: there has not even been the usual internal circulation of tape transcripts following her defection to the West. As far as those US Departments are concerned, it is as though she does not exist on this side of the Atlantic.'

'Pictures? Photographs?'

'They should be coming through in the next day or so.'

'And this man General Freeman? Where does he fit into all this?'

'It is believed his position – the stance he has taken regarding certain matters – would be greatly strengthened in the military were he to produce Prolev as a witness who could endorse some of his more . . . far-fetched suggestions. With General Freeman identified as the man most likely to benefit from whatever evidence she has brought with her, it follows he may well be the one who is hiding her, or at least knows where she is hidden.'

Nicholson considered this. Then 'If they are right, if he is the man who is shielding her, hiding her, why has she remained silent for so long?'

'There are still family ties back in the home country that have ensured her silence in the past – the fear now is that, as time passes, these may prove insufficient. We are now looking for a more permanent solution.'

'And that has been sanctioned?'

'At the highest level.'

Early the next morning, in Hagerstown, Viktor Pligin, the former airline steward who had hidden Lydia Prolev, stood at the top of the bare wooden stairs leading down to the front door and searched his soul for the courage that would take him downstairs. Just now there had been the bang of a letter box.

Pligin was scared, frightened half out of his mind. For now, added to the controlled, natural fear of detection that had lain with him like some sluggish, chained beast ever since he had walked out of that stopover hotel and sought asylum in the United States, lay a feeling of isolated vulnerability, a feeling that had grown within him ever since he had watched from behind drawn curtains as that

American in the battered station-wagon had driven Lydia away without so much as a backward glance.

In the weeks that he had shielded her, Pligin had found warmth in her company, in the linguistic small-print of home he would never erase from his memory. Now she was gone, swept out of his life as suddenly as she had arrived because 'they' decided his apartment was unsafe. She was gone and he was left, forgotten. There had been no phone call, no letter of thanks and reassurance, nothing from the security men once pledged to ensure *his* safety.

It was as though he had been written off.

Perhaps this letter, the one in the white envelope he could see at the bottom of the stairs, perhaps this one held the news he was waiting for.

Pligin picked up the heavy poker and began treading downstairs, the steps creaking beneath his weight as he descended slowly, one step at a time.

He got to the bottom, peered fearfully to either side of the front door, scooped up the envelope and scuttled upstairs to safety.

He paused at the top of the landing, heart pumping furiously beneath his thin shirt. He listened anxiously. A car drove by, and he could hear the distant shouts of children playing on the worn grass outside. Nothing out of the ordinary. He pushed the letter into a pocket, wiped a shaking hand across his forehead and hurried through into the lounge, turning the envelope over in his hands.

It was addressed to 'The Occupant' and contained details of an amazing new carpet shampoo on special offer in the next fortnight.

Pligin mashed the circular into a ball and hurled it across the room in his anger, his fear. He would *not* be discarded so easily – had he now no rights, no further claim to protection?

Suddenly he remembered the note the American had brought from the General when he came to collect Lydia. It was still here, somewhere. Pligin laid the poker carefully aside and began to rummage around in the litter and discarded beer cans that had quickly replaced the woman's tidiness. He'd call the General himself, shake things up a bit! Yes – and he would call him Collect into the bargain! Show a bit of style, a bit of cheek! They were not about to discard Viktor Pligin so easily!

Fear coupled with anger: these two powerful emotions were about to stifle the law of caution and anonymity that had governed Pligin's new and secret life with such nondescript success these last few years. Pligin crossed to the phone, smoothed out the sheet of notepaper and peered short-sightedly at the number. He went through to the operator and presently the call rang through into the General's private home in Beachside Landing. Pligin listened to the tone anxiously, anger subsiding into nervousness as he planned how he would disguise his plea.

'Yes?' A woman's voice, puzzled at the Collect Call. The maid? His wife? 'Who is this calling?'

'I . . . I wish to speak with the General,' said Pligin nervously.

'Well, I'm sorry. He isn't in right now,' said Doris Freeman. 'May I take a message? Who is this?'

'No . . . no, I will call again.' Pligin replaced the receiver hurriedly, but he was already too late.

The call had been booked, logged and calibrated somewhere within the vast machinery of the telephone system. If anyone was looking, there was now a physical record of a link between the General's plush home on Beachside Landing and a run-down apartment in Hagerstown. Ordinarily, that would be of little consequence.

Except that, right now, somebody was looking. The die had been cast.

*

Ferris crossed M Street NW beside the bank with its gleaming gold dome and pushed into the welcome of Nathan's Bar, Georgetown. It was another of the day's little ironies that he was no more than five hundred yards from the woman he was looking for.

Nicholson was already seated on a high stool by the bar.

Ferris ordered coffee and then waited until the aproned barman had moved to the other end of the counter. 'Anything?'

Nicholson shook his head. 'Not a thing. Nothing with our people in Aliens, Civic Allocations, Located Personnel or the State Department. Not a word. I've a trace going through Cuttings right now. Otherwise – nothing. You?'

'The same.'

The two men had fallen swiftly into a carefully planned sequence of investigations. Working independently, they held brief, daily liaisons like this in one of a dozen different pre-selected bars and eating houses, each rendezvous ninety-five minutes earlier than the one of the day before. Working in isolation because ignorance of each other's contacts was the best protection of all, each was incapable of compromising the other: Nicholson had no idea where Ferris was staying; Ferris did not know the cover name of a single contact supplied to the more exposed and expendable Nicholson by New York Field Office. Secure, discreet, isolated, the two men worked efficiently through the pack of possibilities.

'State Department came up with one interesting thing,' continued Nicholson quietly. 'That General Freeman's been active again – going through the CIA to tie things up with the Nuclear Intelligence Board. They're to meet the day after tomorrow. Special summons.'

*

General Clarke Freeman was on the phone again. This time he was speaking from the Pentagon to Tom Greener's office at CIA Headquarters in the Virginia countryside outside Washington. Freeman was pleased. Three hours earlier he had received some good news: with much grumbling and grousing, Greener had arranged for the six-man NIB Committee to gather at 14.00 the following afternoon in Room 2300 of the New Senate Building. With Greener's gruff 'It just damn' well better be worth all this running around' still sounding in his ears, Freeman had just terminated the arrangements and asked a messenger to come to his office.

*

Frank Yates and Lydia Prolev were building castles out of toy bricks on the kitchen floor with a happy, carefree absorption that had taken years off their lives. Thanks to their cold-blooded efforts the girl seemed blissfully unaware of the state of siege that had subtly transformed their home into a jangling box of tension that seemed to shake every time the phone rang.

The game, in any event, was pathetically transparent to anything but the eyes of a child. Usually, as she herself pointed out, Louise would play in the lounge. It was warmer in there, there were carpets on the floor and all her toys were close by. Frank was hard put to argue. You cannot explain to a six-year-old that the windows overlooked the street and thus offered an easy target to anyone with a bomb or a rifle, a grenade or even a can of petrol mixed with soap-flakes.

But they were not entirely defenceless: there was a loaded .22 hunting rifle on top of the bookcase at the end of the hall and a .45 automatic pistol on the top shelf in the ice-box.

There was a short ring on the doorbell.

Lydia Prolev started violently, and the careful pile of bricks toppled over.

'Oh, I'd nearly finished it,' began Louise.

Lydia managed a smile. 'Sssh – we'll build another castle in a moment,' she whispered, anxious eyes following Frank as he crossed to the ice-box and, with his back to Louise, stuffed the automatic into his waistband. He turned to Lydia.

'Stick close to me. Watch me – watch me all the time.' They rose, closed the kitchen door and crossed the lounge silently. Frank handed down the .22, placed it into Lydia's hands and gripped her shoulders gently. 'OK?' he whispered. She swallowed and nodded.

Frank took up his position further down the corridor, pressed his back against the wall and called softly 'Who is it?'

'Captain Yates?' The voice sounded muffled, anxious. 'Message from General Freeman, sir. Contact Delta.'

Contact Delta was Air Force parlance for person-to-person communication via a single messenger. But Frank wasn't buying it yet.

'Show me your ID. Drop it through the letterbox.'

'Yes, sir.' The letterbox opened and the familiar oblong of blue and white plastic fluttered on to the doormat.

'You alone, Marshall?'

'Alone? Yessir.' Frank slipped the chain on the door and a startled, fresh-faced Air Force Lieutenant stepped nervously into the narrow hallway. Frank flicked at the gleaming buttons, the neatly tailored uniform. 'This your smart idea, Lieutenant?'

Marshall fumbled inside his tunic and pulled out a letter and signature pad. He glanced up, noticed Lydia with the .22 for the first time and swallowed. 'The ... er ... the uniform, sir? Routine. Strictly ... strictly routine. Here's ... here's the message, sir. I ... I guess I'll need your signature too.'

Frank signed for the letter and tore open the envelope. The message was brief: General Freeman required Frank at his office immediately. Lieutenant Marshall would stay in his location until his return.

Frank was shown into the General's office without delay. Freeman was dictating captions from the back of the latest batch of satellite reconnaissance photographs into a tape-recorder. He glanced up as Frank entered. 'The device appears to be powered by a series of magneto-explosive generators mounted on firing tables – they could be concrete – behind shielded walls that separate power units from the accelerator. Energy content is estimated in the region of 5 megajoules/Kg. Period.'

He tossed the photographs aside, snapped off the machine

and shook his head disgustedly. 'What'll it take to convince those bastards – blood? Take a seat, Frank.'

Frank sat as Freeman leaned forward abruptly. 'Tell me this – what do you know about the NIB, the Nuclear Intelligence Board?'

Frank blew out his cheeks and thought briefly. 'Very little, General. I know they're heavy. They carry a lot of weight up on the Hill. They're responsible for R & D priority allocation, if I remember rightly. Politicians, scientists, a couple of congressmen – that kind of mixture. They meet – what? Once, maybe twice a year. Their findings are classified, naturally.' He paused. 'That's about it, I guess.'

Freeman nodded. 'Not bad – you've got the weight of it anyway. They meet officially twice a year – unless someone calls an extraordinary meeting.' He smiled grimly. 'Under my statutory authority, Frank, I've done just that.' Briefly he explained how the QRN interception at Timmins had tipped his hand. 'However,' he continued, 'as at this moment we are still a little short on good, old-fashioned evidence.' He rose and began pacing his office. Then he turned and pointed a finger directly at Frank. 'Evidence, Frank, that I believe *you* can bring me.'

'Me, General?'

Freeman smiled briefly, enjoying Frank's look of genuine amazement. 'You, General. I believe these photographs –' he tapped the pile of glossy twelve-by-sixteens – 'coupled to this report on those OTH signals, carry us two thirds of the way there. Two thirds. Any ideas, Frank, what might bring in the missing one third?'

There was silence while Frank got there all by himself:

'Personal evidence,' he said slowly. 'Testimony from someone who was there, someone who knows what they're talking about.' He felt the first stirrings of suspicion, of exploitation. With them came the first awakenings of anger. 'Is that why you moved her in with me, General? To try for the personal touch? Expose her to the widowed Air Force pilot and see what happens?' His voice rose. 'Get her to open her heart while the trusty USAF tape-recorder picks up every creak of the bedsprings? Jesus, General!' Frank was on his feet now, pacing angrily.

'Take it easy. Sit down,' said Freeman wearily. He had expected a more balanced response from the younger man. Frank appeared not to have heard. 'I said: sit down, Captain!' The words, the reminder of role, slashed across the office, and there was an electric silence as Frank stared back in angry defiance. 'Go on, Frank – take a seat. Relax,' commanded the General more quietly.

Frank dropped back into his seat, anger suddenly spent. He ran a hand through his hair. 'I'll tell you now – she's not about to change her mind. Not for you, not for me, not for a million bucks. Not with her son over there. Not in a hundred years.'

'I still need you to try, Frank – to gain her confidence. Her evidence could really help before the Board.'

'What do you need to know? Specifically?'

'Anything. Anything and everything. As much as she'll give you. Anything at all about her work in Semipalatinsk. Just the barest confirmation that Hammer is moving forward.'

'And the boy? What if she asks about him? That's the way through, General.'

Freeman shook his head. 'There's nothing yet. I can't offer her a damn' thing.'

As soon as Frank had left, General Freeman dialled another number. 'This Leningrad trip planned for the Russian boy Prolev: I want detailed plans showing the exact location of the Eye Hospital, its proximity to tourist routes and recommended entry and exit points for clandestine lifting.' He paused. 'One more thing – tell Sabre Four he is authorized to make contact with that Jewish Soviet action group. But nothing obvious, nothing specific. He can test the water, that's all.'

Nicholson stood silently beneath the bare trees that flanked the asphalt walk-way leading to John F. Kennedy's graveside, his hands thrust deeply into coat pockets as he waited for Ferris to arrive.

The Kennedy Memorial lies deep in the heart of the Arlington National Cemetery, its importance almost hidden among the smooth, rolling hills that have been pushed into regimented columns of sad headstones by the violent appetite of history. Yet, even as he waited, another coach pulled to a halt nearby, laden with those driven by curiosity or a sense of private pilgrimage to see for themselves the resting place of two murdered brothers, the eternal flame of a nation's conscience and the proud, dated legacy of a young President's finest words etched deeply into weathered marble.

Anoraked schoolchildren raced on ahead as the new arrivals washed past Nicholson to mingle with the tide of visitors returning to their coaches, their pilgrimage complete. Ferris was somewhere there, among the sea of bobbing heads. Presently the two men walked off together away from the main party. It was their second meeting of the day and, as such, justified immediate explanation.

'Cuttings gave us nothing,' reported Nicholson briefly as their heels crunched in unison along the gravel path and up a slight rise. 'But one of our telephone engineers may have come up with something. He works out of the Trident Automatic Exchange.'

Ferris nodded, his eyes on his shoes. 'And?'

'T A E covers Annandale, Fairfax and Springfield. Beachside Harbor Landing subscribers come under Springfield zoning.'

'So?'

'We traced the General's private usage rate.' Nicholson shrugged. 'Nothing much going out: the usual number of calls, both local and long-distance.' He grimaced. 'Doris Freeman and her little friends, I shouldn't –'

'Get to the point,' said Ferris curtly.

'I'm coming to it.' Nicholson stopped and held up two fingers. 'Two calls, right? Both today, both for the General personally, both from the same number – and both Collect.

It's a private subscriber in Hagerstown, Virginia, about forty miles from here.'

'That's it?'

Nicholson shook his head impatiently and the two men walked on. 'Our man put a trace through, you know? he taps out a bogus technical clearance sequence, the number's flashed back logged through the maintenance sheets, and then the rest is easy: all you have to do is trace the subscriber's name through records, right? Only it didn't work like that this time – he'd no sooner begun the trace through records than the Circuit Supervisor comes through demanding security clearance before actioning further disclosure. Our man backed off, claiming he'd knocked in the wrong number, and that was that –'

'What are you telling me?' demanded Ferris impatiently.

Nicholson sighed. 'I'm telling you that number was protected – privileged within military circuits. Collect calls from a private subscriber in Hagerstown that's given Military security status to prevent a trace? What does that sound like to you?'

For the first time Ferris smiled. He clapped Nicholson on the shoulder, and the two turned and began to walk back to the coaches.

'I think we just found our pigeon.'

7

Nicholson's hired dark-green Lincoln rolled to a stop out-side Pligin's apartment in Hagerstown, and the two men sat there quietly in the evening darkness going over their plans, the engine plinking in front of them as it cooled. Ferris stared up at the single lighted window and caught the reflected neon glimmer of a television as a shadow moved across the upstairs window. He pulled back. 'OK.'

Nicholson nodded, half waiting for the word of praise that never came. He had tracked down the apartment in three hours flat: a drive to the telephone depot, a fifty-dollar bill had changed hands, and he had been left alone for five brief minutes with only the Installation Log for company. It had been all the time he had needed, and the rest had been simple, straightforward elimination.

Ferris tapped Nicholson on the shoulder and they rolled forward, turned a corner and halted. Ferris got out, the car moved on, and Ferris stepped silently into the shadows. Five minutes and half a dozen cars rolled by, then Ferris walked round to the flimsy door, hammered briefly on the partitioning and stepped back against the outside wall. He looked around at the nearby houses. All eyes were turned inward.

Pligin was upstairs watching television, the doors that led to the kitchen and bedroom closed firmly around him in illusory protection, the remains of a meagre supper laid out on a tray beside him. He was watching a western, and at first he thought the sound came from the TV. Then it came again and the last of his meal turned to cardboard in his mouth.

The hammering came again: sudden, violent, impossible to ignore.

Pligin darted through into his bedroom and swept up the cheap alarm clock with trembling hands: seven fifteen. Who could be calling at such an hour? Back into the lounge, heart pounding. He turned down the sound on the TV and stood there in his baggy trousers watching the empty, empty pictures, waiting for the hammering to come again.

The hammering came again.

Pligin pulled a hand through his hair distractedly, his eyes rolling around the room like frightened black marbles.

He crossed to the back window, pulled back the blind and stared out into the darkness, but the light from within prevented him from seeing anything beyond his own frightened reflection, and he cursed weakly. He went over to the far wall, turned off the light and blundered over to the front window.

Ferris outguessed him effortlessly.

Pligin tugged back the yellow blind and stared down. Nothing. No one parked outside, no one waiting below.

And again that fearful hammering.

Pligin opened the door to the stairs and stood there, mumbling his fear to himself as the door shook once more. Then he went down his stairs, the poker clutched in his hand.

Perhaps it was just the kids, he reasoned; there'd been a lot of trouble recently. Or maybe a parcel – or someone from the General, he grasped greedily: perhaps his message had got through at last. Laying the poker aside he eased open the door as far as the security chain would permit. 'Hello? Who's . . . who's there?' he called fearfully into the darkness.

There was no reply.

Against every precept of caution and common sense, Viktor Pligin began to slip the catch on the chain. He would take one quick look outside. Kids – it was probably kids . . . He opened the door a crack and stepped hesitantly forward. Things became horribly, violently confused.

Ferris smashed the door back with his foot, cannoned into Pligin's slight body and sent him hurtling back to crash cruelly against the bare boards of the stairs. Before Pligin could move or cry out for help from an indifferent world outside, Ferris had whipped the door shut. Pligin was inside, Ferris was inside, the door was closed, and as far as the rest of the world was concerned, all was quiet, domestic normality.

Except that Viktor Pligin's nightmare was about to begin.

Ferris turned, stood back silently and looked down at the pathetic bundle with scant interest. So this was the man who had been calling the General, Collect. He had expected rather more. He slipped the chain carefully on the lock, merely lifted the butt of his automatic from his pocket so that the man saw it and prodded him with his foot.

'Come on, you – up,' he ordered shortly. Pligin watched him with terror, a hand clutched to his mouth as he searched the stranger's face for weakness, comfort, re-assurance. He searched in vain. The pistol appeared. 'I said: up!' Ferris kicked and Pligin scrambled to his feet. Ferris gestured up the stairs with the gun. Pligin began to move upwards in a curious crab-like shuffle, his eyes flicking between the mouth of the automatic and the eyes of the stranger.

Pligin fetched on to the top landing and stood there panting as Ferris rose easily beside him. He pushed him through into the lounge and Pligin collapsed into a chair to stare with sightless eyes at the mute pictures on the television.

Ferris checked each room briefly in turn and returned to the lounge. Pligin sat there beside the congealed remains of his supper, his eyes glued fearfully on the TV as Ferris walked quietly around him, gazing down at his victim, con-sidering.

He leant down and turned off the set, stuck the pistol away in a coat pocket and dropped into a chair opposite Pligin. Pligin pulled his legs up on to the chair and gnawed on a knuckle, his fear a palpable, ugly thing in the silent apartment. Ferris regarded him silently, impassively.

'Well . . .' he said finally. 'Don't you want to know who I

am? Why I have come here? Or perhaps you know already —'

With a superhuman effort, Pligin wrenched his eyes round to face his attacker and forced himself to press on with the charade. 'What . . . what do you want of me?' he managed, the dread large in his eyes. 'If . . . if it is money you are looking for —' but Ferris shook his head tiredly.

'No, it is not money.'

'I . . . I do not understand what it is you want with me. I am just . . . I am just . . .' The gabble of words choked off into silence as they ran up against that hard, implacable stare.

'Tell me your name,' ordered Ferris softly.

Pligin swallowed. 'My name? You want my name? Sure — it is Arnold. Saul Arnold.'

Ferris nodded, as though satisfied, and Pligin felt a brief flaring of hope.

'Tell me, Mr Arnold: are you an American? A citizen of the United States? Your accent would appear —'

Pligin nodded hurriedly, the Adam's apple jerking on the scrawny, stubbled neck. 'Yes. Yes, I am. I was naturalized fifteen, twenty years ago. You see, my father —'

'And before that?' Ferris watched closely, and when the fear lanced deeply into the man's eyes it did not escape him.

'Before that? Let me see . . . originally, I came from Saporoshe — that is a region of the Ukraine, of Russia, you know? I came here first a long time ago, after the . . . after the Second World War,' he lied.

'The Great Patriotic War,' corrected Ferris quietly. 'I too am from the Soviet Union. From Kutaisi. In Georgia. Perhaps you know it?' he asked politely.

'Oh, Jesus, no. I . . .' blurted Pligin as true realization dawned. 'Before God, I . . .'

'Tell me,' said Ferris conversationally, 'why did you call the General?'

The question popped into the silence and took Pligin by surprise. He looked up and was lost. 'The . . . the General?' he managed, in a pathetic caricature of surprise. It was so transparent that Ferris laughed aloud. That too was not a pretty sound.

'Come now, Mr Arnold – or whatever your name is: you can do better than that. How about: "The General? What General? I have no idea what you are talking about!" But just "The General . . .?" Really, that is too bad!'

Pligin stared at his broken fingernails and prayed for death to take him.

Ferris rose and began to pace the apartment. Pligin followed him with his eyes and felt a fresh stab of fear turn his bowels to water; suddenly it became desperately important for Pligin to distract him, keep him talking, because there, on top of the television set, was the note written to him by General Freeman. And the name on the envelope was not that of Mr Arnold but of Pligin, Viktor Pligin . . .

'Oh, yes. General Freeman – General Freeman, you mean?' rushed Pligin as Ferris stopped in mid-stride and turned to face him with the pleasure of a teacher who gets the right answer from the bottom of the class.

'General Freeman – very good, Mr Arnold. At last we are beginning to make progress. Why did you call him? Why did you call him twice – Collect on both occasions?' Ferris resumed his pacing. He was coming back from the bedroom, back now towards the television and away from the landing and the stairs that led to the front door –

Pligin uncurled his legs and leaned forward. 'General Freeman? Oh – I knew him a long time ago when –' He leaped to his feet, scuttled round the sofa and lunged for the stairs. Ferris moved swiftly to his left, raised the pistol and smashed it sideways against Pligin's temple as he darted past. The legs buckled and the man went down on the threadbare carpet like a sack of dirty washing. Ferris hauled the crumpled body to his feet, inspected the ugly gash where the foresight had caught him above the eye and dumped the unconscious figure unceremoniously on the sofa.

When Pligin regained consciousness ten minutes later Ferris was standing over him waving General Freeman's note gently between finger and thumb.

'The time for games, for deception, is over, comrade –' Pligin looked up fearfully. 'I am not interested in you, particularly, but in the woman who lived here with you: tell me what I need to know and it is just possible that you will live. Your words, then, for your life.' Pligin moaned and pressed a dirty handkerchief to the ugly bruising on his temple. 'Now – this man . . . this United States Air Force officer who comes here to take the woman away on the General's orders – what was his name?'

Pligin shook his head. 'I do not know – he did not say, I swear to you! God above, if I knew, do you . . . do you think I would not tell you? Do I look to you like a brave man, a hero?' He shuffled away from Ferris to the far corner of the sofa. Ferris watched impassively.

'How did he come here?'

'By car . . . by car. Private car.'

'You are sure?'

'Yes . . . yes, I am sure. Certain. You have my word.'

Ferris smiled dryly. 'Thank you for that. How are you sure?'

'I watched them. Here, from the window. I watched them leave.' He tried to get to his feet and then sank back as nausea washed over him. 'I . . . I think I am going to be sick.'

Ferris hauled him to his feet, pushed him through into the small bathroom and stood over him impassively while he heaved his supper into the toilet pan. Then Ferris pushed the stumbling figure back into the lounge.

'OK – so he came by private car. Describe it.'

With shaking hands Pligin wiped his mouth with his handkerchief, sat down and buried his head in his hands.

'It was a station-wagon. Yes, yes – a station-wagon. A VW – but an old model, yes? Four, five years . . . something like that.'

'Colour?'

'Brown. No, no – dark green. Yes – dark green. I am sure of it.'

'On your life?'

Pligin's head jerked forward. 'Yes, yes – I am sure.'

Ferris tossed a coat over the man's bent shoulders.

'Come on, old man – I think it is time you and I went for a little walk.'

Pligin looked up with haunted eyes, a Dachau inmate told that at last the showers were working again. 'Relax,' soothed Ferris. 'We are just going to make a phone call. From somewhere a little less – obvious, yes?' Pligin nodded with relief and began struggling into his overcoat.

Ferris led him to the top of the staircase and gestured for him to lead on. At the bottom, just as Pligin reached eagerly for the door catch, Ferris stopped him with a hand on the shoulder. He turned him round and pressed him up against the wall. Then, very slowly, Ferris drew the automatic from his coat pocket and placed the barrel against Pligin's mouth. Then he reached out, grabbed a handful of lank hair and jerked viciously. Pligin's head went back, he opened his mouth to cry out and the barrel popped inside. It was quite a neat fit. Pligin's eyes bulged from his head as Ferris thumbed back the hammer with an audible click that turned each half-second into yawning canyons of lost time. Ferris pressed even closer.

'Before we go out there, Mr Pligin, just remember: I am always with you. This gun is always with you. If you call out, I will kill you. If you run away, I will kill you. Believe it. If you do none of these things, then your life may be permitted to continue.'

Pligin nodded grotesquely, his mouth full of pistol, as Ferris withdrew the barrel slowly, obscenely, its metal gleaming with spittle.

'After you, Mr Pligin,' offered Ferris graciously, uncocking the pistol and placing the weapon carefully in his coat pocket. Pligin fumbled open the front door and the two stepped out into the darkness.

They walked in silence for twenty-five minutes, their collars turned up against the evening, before stopping finally at an empty phone booth near a road junction. Ferris went inside while Viktor Pligin stood beside the door. Ferris dialled a local number, and presently Nicholson answered from a motel across town.

'Call me back at this number,' ordered Ferris briefly. Two minutes later Nicholson did so and Ferris passed on the details of Frank's car. Then 'One more thing before you go,' remembered Ferris with a glance at the man standing beside him, the prisoner chained to his side by a lack of courage, hands thrust deep into coat pockets, thin hair blowing around his face in the chill wind. 'Find out what we know about a Pligin. Viktor Pligin. Aged about forty-five, fifty. Born in Saporoshe, Ukraine. Call me back on this number in half an hour.' He replaced the receiver and stepped out of the phone booth. 'Now, we will walk some more, Mr Pligin. Exercise is good for you.' He tucked Pligin's arm firmly in his and the two set off along the deserted sidewalk.

Promptly on the half hour, the phone rang out again in the sidewalk phone booth. Nicholson, once again, had been very efficient. The only serving Air Force officer who owned a 73 VW station-wagon was a Captain F. T. Yates, a former fighter pilot with 388th Tactical Fighter Wing now attached to USAF Intelligence and living in Georgetown, Washington; the only Viktor Pligin the Soviet Rezidentura in New York had been able to come up with had been a Soviet airline steward who defected to the West almost ten years ago.

Corner Tower lies a little to the south of Moscow's Marx Prospekt and directly behind the Square to the 50th Anniversary of the October Revolution. Built in the nineteenth century, it stands at the apex of the Kremlin triangle that runs south to the Moskva River and whose flanks are the Alexander Gardens to the west and Red Square itself to the east.

This triangle, known the world over as simply 'the Kremlin', is completely enclosed by a high, crenellated wall that is studded, in turn, by a series of elaborate gated towers, four of which – the towers of St Nicholas, Trinity, Saviour's and Borovitsky – are topped with stars which glow at night: red stars.

In the northern segment of this triangle stands the three-sided building where meets the Council of Ministers formed by the Supreme Soviet of the USSR and which is second in national importance – on paper, at least – to the Praesidium itself.

But the seat of real power lies just through a thin belt of trees nearby. The former Arsenal holds that distinction, not because of quaint shot and shell stored in its ancient magazines, but because it is within a part of this thin, rectangular building that the Politburo meets to formulate policy and guide the historic march of destiny through socialism towards communism, that perfect state that is the true focus of a nation's remorseless strivings.

The Politburo is the 'Cabinet' of the Communist Party of the Soviet Union. There is no higher ideological body than this, and because it is the Party and not the State – despite its cumbersome, wasteful, layer-cake bureaucracy – that truly rules the Soviet Union in its every waking and sleeping moment, it follows that it is the fifteen members of the Politburo who control in their tight grip the destiny of a nation of more than 250 million.

With a single-mindedness that should be the envy of less aggressive, more liberal regimes, everything within the Soviet Union – every school, every textbook, every place of work, every nut and bolt, every factory, metre of cloth, rifle, soldier and peasant working on his *sovhozy*,* meshes tightly into the iron embrace of the Politburo's Gosplan, its five-yearly overall national masterplan, first introduced in 1920 and which has been taken as the metre-rule of progress ever since.

The Head of the Politburo, Chairman of the Praesidium, President of the USSR, Marshal of the Soviet Union and, most important of all, General Secretary of the CPSU this morning was still the ageing and infirm Vasili Travin. Only recently returned from another of his periodic absences from the public eye that had renewed the incessant rumours of ill-health, sudden death, resignation and Politburo re-

Sovhozy: State farm.

shuffle, he now moved uncomfortably in his chair, the pain of his infection deep within him.

Ranged around the table beside him were the powerful, watchful Party members who had shouldered their way with him on to this slender dais of supreme power. Igor Bayev, the newly appointed Head of the KGB's First Chief Directorate, waited patiently until Marshal Gladky had finished outlining the glittering strategic opportunities he saw presented by the recent successes in the Skyshroud programme. Then, when he had finished, 'Security in this matter remains unimpaired,' he reported. 'Executive action sanctioned within this chamber several months ago – you will recall the names: Viklov, Osipov, Lyudin – is now almost concluded. There is one name remaining, and that is being dealt with at present.' He laid a slim folder on the polished table but made no move to reveal its contents. He paused and glanced around the table. 'However, comrades, the Americans are not stupid. Such disposals may well, in themselves, have triggered an awakening response within their intelligence groups. This risk is one we have always recognized, one we chose to accept in view of what was at stake.'

Bayev looked around calmly at the nodding heads, searching for the look of dissent. He did not find it. 'In the last few hours we have learnt that the American Nuclear Intelligence Board has been summoned to an extraordinary meeting. Such a decision, taken at this time, is curious, comrades.

'The Board has been summoned at the insistence of this man –' Bayev flipped open the folder and passed out copies of a large black and white photograph. It showed General Freeman talking earnestly to another uniformed colleague at some official function. Freeman's head and shoulders had been ringed in red and on the back of the photograph were pasted brief details of his career. 'General Clarke Freeman, Head of USAF Intelligence. A bright, perceptive general – a hawk, as the Americans would say. *He* is the man behind this summons, comrades, although just why he has done so, at the precise moment when most of his colleagues appear to be rubbing their hands together at the prospect of increasing national reliance upon the next generation of intercontinental ballistic missiles, remains unclear. We are investigating.'

There was silence save for the squeak of a chair as President Travin swung away to gaze down at the inner courtyard beyond the narrow windows, his thick brows furrowed in thought. Then he swung back with a grimace of pain as his massive body pressed forward against the table. 'You are suggesting we could still find ourselves in a technological race for supremacy in the field of beam weapon technology, even at this late stage?'

'Much would depend upon the specific reason for the summons – but, certainly, we cannot rule out such a possibility,' said Voskoboy from across the table. There was another silence, heavier this time, as Politburo members considered the implications of the recurring nightmare in which careful, ponderous Soviet development was suddenly, almost carelessly, overhauled by rapid, flexible American counter-measures supported by the twin pillars of lavish resources and massive financial aid.

'What would satellite reconnaissance have given them?' demanded Travin finally.

Gladky shrugged. 'Food for thought, certainly, Comrade Chairman. But nothing definite, nothing specific, I am certain.'

'Do you wish to add anything before we debate the matter? Comrade Gladky?' A shake of the head. 'Comrade Voskoboy?'

Voskoboy leant forward. 'Comrade Chairman, comrades – I gave earlier my reasons for supporting Comrade Gladky in pushing for a change in role for Skyshroud. Let me now emphasize – there can be no room for half-measures. My requirements – which you are, of course, at liberty to reject out of hand – are quite specific. Firstly, rapid acceleration of the development programme – not from four years to two, not to months, but to weeks! That is my first requirement. Secondly, it will be necessary to expand our perception of target strike capability quite dramatically before we can parade this development with absolute confidence, understand that.'

'Target strike capability? What do you mean?' asked the minister responsible for social programming.

Voskoboy looked up, the soldier's dislike of the civilian writ large on his face. 'It is quite simple: I mean, comrades, that we must be damned sure the thing works –' he shook his head – 'not just against deserted bunkers stuffed full of sheep and a few miles of waste land, but against a target with realistic characteristics.'

The room was very still.

'Such as?' asked Social Programming quietly.

'A village, a town somewhere,' expanded Voskoboy carelessly. 'Somewhere where there are people, buildings –' The room stirred suddenly around him and there was a low murmur of disapproval.

'You're mad!' stammered the minister, aghast. 'You'd test this . . . this *thing* of yours on people? On *our* people?'

Voskoby shrugged. 'Nowhere important, nowhere particularly large. There must be somewhere suitable – a penal colony, perhaps. A small –'

'You'd never get away with it!' flustered Social Programming. 'The people would tear you –'

'The people? What have they got to do with it?' demanded Voskoboy softly.

'Comrades, comrades!' Chairman Travin began to interrupt and then broke into a bout of prolonged coughing, aware as he did so that not every eye regarded him with comradely concern: soon, he knew, the jackals would begin to tear at the carcass of succession. 'The choice . . . the choice that faces us is basically a simple one.'

Again there was that long, laboured silence as he gathered his breath. 'One – that we proceed as planned, course unchanged. We ignore what Comrade Marshal Gladky described as the enormous offensive potential of such a weapon based in space and continue to accord Skyshroud the same financial priority as before, regarding it simply as an anti-missile system to be deployed in existing silos around this city, with possible expansion at some future date. Two – that we massively increase that commitment and that, after tests, we go over to the offensive, space-based deployment of Skyshroud for use against land-based targets in Western Europe, Britain and the United States.'

'You would actually advocate a pre-emptive strike against American missile silos and British nuclear bases, using this system?'

President Travin shrugged. 'That is what we must shortly determine, comrade.'

Behind the modest, low-beamed exterior of the Chalet de la Paix restaurant on Arlington's Lee Highway outside Washington, Sam Tolland, one of the members of the Nuclear Intelligence Board, began forking the first of a dozen fresh oysters into the folds of his mouth. Juice spurted from the corners of his lips and he dabbed freely with a snowy white napkin as Jacques, the head waiter, arrived at his side with the telephone trolley. He made the connection in the wall of Tolland's secluded, oak-panelled booth. 'A call for you, M'sieur Tolland.'

Tolland nodded, dabbed again with the napkin, and reached out a plump hand for the call. 'Sam Tolland.'

'This is Michael, Sam. Good afternoon. Are you well?' asked the quiet voice politely.

'I was expecting your call. Have there been any developments?'

'No, none. None at all. Your instructions remain unchanged. You are simply to apply constant, steady pressure. Get the man to reveal early on the scope and dimensions of his submission to the Board. We need to know what he has as early as possible. You will please report back to me at the usual number at your earliest convenience. But that is all – nothing too obvious, nothing too pointed, do you understand?'

'Sure. That would be in character, anyway,' he chuckled fatly.

'Goodbye, Sam.'

In Washington, Sam Tolland was marked down as a powerful opportunist, a wealthy businessman whose reputation did rather less than hold him forward as a shining example of others before self. Ambitious, ruthless in the pursuit of his diverse and often clouded commercial ambitions, major stockholder in no fewer than three of the capital's five major industrial corporations, Tolland's appointment to the prestigious Nuclear Intelligence Board had appeared, to some, almost inevitable.

It served, however, a darker purpose.

The phone call to the Chalet de la Paix was merely the latest link in a long chain of deliberate, almost casual national betrayal, for the man on the other end of the line was Major Dmitri Muratov, Field Officer at the Soviet Rezidentura in New York.

Successfully blackmailed by the KGB over his undeclared sexual preferences, as revealed in a series of photographs taken at a beach chalet in Wildwood in the days when sexual deviation of any kind spelt professional oblivion if it became known to a wider public, Sam Tolland had been kept sweet by a succession of generous bribes. These were married to infrequent requests for information that he discovered he was able to provide with almost child-like ease and at absolutely no risk to himself. With time, initial fear and anger gave way to acceptance, even to a twisted enjoyment of his new role as Tolland found himself prospering under the feather-light control of his new masters.

He might have proceeded a trifle more cautiously had he known that the information he was required to provide had been selected precisely because its acquisition presented negligible risk to the informer. From the late 1950s onwards the KGB had chosen to cultivate, in addition to its vast network of spies, agents and informers overseas, a stable of agents-in-place. These agents-in-place were listed by the massive KGB computer in Moscow as 'Mutzchpan' – offerings – and that clipped, terse title exactly describes their real value to the Soviet Union.

Agents-in-place are expendable. They are pawns of limited value whose timely 'detection' has gone a long way in the past to ease a greater deception down the suspicious gullet of the intelligence services of the western world. It was a measure of the importance of the business in hand that, despite his placing within the Nuclear Intelligence Board, Sam Tolland was still classified as 'Mutzchpan'.

As Sam Tolland returned to his oysters, Major Muratov finished his sandwiches and then bent over his cluttered desk to compose a suitable signal for inward transmission to 'The Centre' in Moscow.

Presently, across the Atlantic, far away in The Centre outside Moscow, there was a rap on the inner door of the office belonging to the Chairman of the KGB, Yuri Chekhov. He glanced up with impatience and took the message flimsy handed across his desk by his efficient male secretary. He scanned the message briefly and then handed it wordlessly to Igor Bayev, with whom he had been in conference ever since they had left the Politburo meeting.

The two men had emerged from that meeting called to decide the future deployment of Skyshroud with their ears ringing to the blows of argument and revelation. Having set the scene, Chairman Travin had sat back thankfully and listened with half-closed eyes as the debate unfolded.

Predictably, it had been Minister of Defence Marshal Voskoboy who had begun. Swiftly outlining the historic, ideological conflict between East and West, a conflict that relegated the Great Patriotic War to little more than a brief interruption of a wider conflict of interests, Voskoboy launched into his own bleak scenario of the future, in which the trembling fingers of a sick western world fumbled off the covers of their nuclear arsenals as the fabric of their corrupt, decadent societies crumbled like sandcastles beneath the churning, remorseless progress of socialism – a last, despairing heads-we-win, tails-you-lose gesture of global dismissal that left Europe a smoking, contaminated ruin.

Then Voskoboy was off again, banging a different drum this time as he pointed towards the ominous signs of a halt in the West's slide towards military oblivion: Britain's Iron Lady was goading the henchmen of imperialism towards a new appraisal of their military needs, and there were signs that the peanut farmer from Georgia was already beginning to lose the dewy-eyed idealism that had swept him to office and permitted such easy Soviet erosion of the 'back-yard deal' that had restricted Soviet expansionism so successfully under stronger presidents. The West was now in a position of unparalleled military inferiority, but it would be foolish to believe such a condition would endure for ever. The Soviet Union's destiny was linked indissolubly to the historic march of socialism, but over-riding all else came still the need to ensure complete security of the Homeland against attack. The way to do that, the way to exploit what even the western world, with a rare and prophetic insight, had come to recognize as the Soviet 'window of opportunity' was simple.

Strike first.

Voskoboy sat back for a moment in the silent room, a hand raised to signify he had not yet finished. He waited a small moment for those seated beside him to turn the suggestion over in their minds, to get the feel of a concept that was full of sharp corners and terrifying, angular new surfaces. Then he leaned forward once more and continued: 'That phrase I used then, "window of opportunity" – it would suggest that time is on our side? That the sands of time are running in our favour to the ultimate confusion of our enemies?'

He shook his head sadly. 'Windows can be closed. Time runs also, comrades, against ourselves.' He paused again as the heads came up. 'We have not, you will all be aware, been able to rise to our present position of military superiority without great cost to the economy elsewhere: in terms of gross national product alone, defence spending has risen from nine per cent fifteen years ago to the present *published* ceiling somewhere in excess of sixteen per cent.' He grimaced. 'I need hardly remind you what could have been achieved if something in excess of ninety-seven billion roubles had been diverted away from defence spending.

'We have discussed such matters before and will return

to them again, because the question refuses to go away: how long can we continue to spend such sums at the expense of a society becoming increasingly restless in the face of denial?' He began to tick items off on his fingers, a shopping list parading the shortfalls of socialism: 'The growing unrest within the Republics which clamour for a truly autonomous identity; a decrease in the size of the truly Russian population; the near-certainty of a series of poor grain harvests in the immediate future; the fact that we will soon be forced to become a net *importer* of oil; the growth of a religious revival within the Islamic communities coupled to renewed stirrings in Iran; Afghanistan; the emergence of the People's Republic of China as a power capable of adding nuclear weapons to her armoury of teeming millions – that above all.' Voskoboy looked up calmly to regard the sober, watchful faces of the other Politburo members. 'Comrades, my point is made. Action in the manner I propose, though extreme, though in many ways regrettable, would be one way of stopping that clock at a time of maximum advantage to ourselves and to our allies.'

He sat back and there was silence. Then Travin's chair creaked protestingly as he leant forward to point a finger across the table at Pelske, the minister responsible, in part, for economic planning.

'Comrade Voskoboy himself talks about the effects of such defence spending in the past,' began Pelske slowly, quietly. 'Does he have any idea what would be the financial implications of this proposal to change the role of this weapon almost overnight? It would mean stagnation, total stagnation! The implications almost defy imagination! There would be massive, almost terminal crippling of every other arm of the Soviet economy, be it industrial, monetary, agricultural, hydro-electric! . . . You talk, comrade, as though putting such a system into space, keeping it there, assembling it, was as . . . as simple as dropping apples in a barrel! Even I understand there is more to this business than simply bolting the bits together and firing the lot into space! If we vote in favour of offensive deployment, that will be just the beginning. It will be months, perhaps years, before we are able to exploit such an advantage! And, by then, who knows what the Americans may have achieved?'

In the short silence that followed, Commander-in-Chief of the National Air Defence Forces, Marshal Gladky, caught the attention of Travin at the head of the table, paused for his nod of assent and then leant forward.

'I should begin by stating that we have perhaps been a little unfair to our Politburo comrades. Comrade Voskoboy? If I might be permitted to speak for one moment on your behalf?' Voskoboy inclined his head with the beginnings of a smile that suggested he knew what was coming. 'We know something that has not been shared with our Politburo comrades before now, for reasons of national security.

'As some of you may be aware, the Soviet Union produces and assembles two Salyut-T space stations each year, roughly speaking. These are usually allocated to scientific research, to our space-life sciences, our Military Applications Division and so forth. They are adequate for our needs and augment the existing launch programme satisfactorily.

'In the last three years, however, that earth-to-space ferry system has been upgraded, with the result that today our palleting, transportation, orbital launch and dry-dock characteristics are vastly improved. Guiding our efforts in this field, comrades, has been the knowledge that we might, one day, be required to lift a palleted payload of considerable dimensions into space for assembly and operational, offensive deployment. We call such a system Proton-Soyuz. I reveal this to you now, Comrades, because a debate such as this would be less than balanced if only myself, Comrade Voskoboy and Comrade Chairman Travin were aware of the fact that we could place Professor Ryabov's project in space – and keep it there – within a short space of time.'

'How short?' snapped Pelshe, miffed at the exclusion of himself and others on the Politburo from so crucial a development.

'A few days,' admitted Gladky, as the chamber erupted around him.

Two hours later Vasili Travin concluded the business of

the day with a compromise that satisfied no one, merely postponing final commitment for a few days longer. A prototype Skyshroud weapons' package would be prepared for offensive space deployment immediately. Once launched and positioned, it would be assembled and fired against a suitable land target within the Soviet Union. The selection of that target – with one important proviso – would be left to Marshal Gladky.

Much would ride, quite obviously, on that first crucial test against the target chosen by Marshal Gladky. The proviso? The site must, regrettably, be populated.

So it was that KGB Chekhov and Bayev, Head of the First Chief Directorate, the two KGB men co-opted on to the Politburo for the Skyshroud talks, met now to amend the role of their organization in view of this sudden somersault in strategic thinking. Bayev was angry. He banged his hand on the desk. 'Not a word, not a bloody word! At least Gladky could have –' Chekhov raised a hand and Bayev fell silent.

Chekhov lit his pipe and began puffing gently. When it was drawing to his satisfaction he waved the smoke away and pointed with the stem of his pipe at the signal he had just received from Muratov in New York. 'When you have read that, I think we should have a talk with the Head of Department A – what's the man's name again?'

'Boychenko, Comrade Chairman.'

'Ah, yes – Boychenko.'

Department A is responsible almost solely for *dezinform-atsiya* — disinformation.

*

In General Freeman's Beachside Landing home outside Washington, one of Doris Freeman's afternoons was in full swing: '. . . but there won't *be* any change until we stop locking away the young offender and ignoring the grass roots of the problem: basic housing, basic education, the rights of –'

'You're so right, so right,' agreed Doris Freeman with animation, her eyes blinking earnestly behind the enormous horn-rimmed spectacles she wore to what she privately thought of as her 'intellectual gatherings'. And Martin, as usual, *was* so right – he brought such perception, such animation to the group. Thank goodness there were still enough of the younger people who cared, who took a real interest in turning away from the harsh, outmoded politics of suppression to push forward new ideals –

Martin Nicholson talked on to the little group of women that surrounded him in Doris Freeman's elegant lounge overlooking the lawn that led down to the river. There had been a break a little over an hour ago for the drinks and the trays of tasteful canapés Doris always provided on these occasions, and, as usual, her committee of gorgeously dressed, elaborately coiffured and middle-aged ladies had simply cooed their pleasure. It was all so, so *satisfactory*, somehow, so worthwhile . . .

Doris bobbed away from Martin's little group in a haze of self-satisfied enjoyment, swept up a tray of canapés with practised grace and, trailing chiffon from each arm, circled round to descend upon another little cluster of Social Awareness over by the French windows:

'Say, Doris, do tell me –' one of the grande dames fastened a horny hand around Doris's wrist and dragged her down to a glittering, hungry smile – 'who is that *divine* young man talking to Mary Ellen over there by the piano? I do declare he's quite the most *gorgeous* creature I've ever seen at one of your afternoons.'

Doris turned and followed the pointing, red-tipped talon. It was, inevitably, Martin: the velvet suit, the fine head of rich black hair, the slim, almost athletic thrust of his thighs . . . Doris looked away distractedly and brought her hand hurriedly away from her ample bosom, to which it had unconsciously strayed.

'Now, Margaret, just you mind your manners, you hear?' She smiled dangerously. 'But, since you ask – that's Martin Nicholson. He runs – owns, I should say – a florist's near Dupont Circle, so I believe.'

'Wherever did you discover such a man, Doris? I congratulate you. Quite a catch.'

'Well –' Doris bent down conspiratorially – 'he found us, actually. Read about the work of the committee, isn't that gratifying? Came up from the Mid-West somewhere where he first got involved in The Movement . . .' Doris Freeman chatted on, ever the charming hostess. She distributed canapés, mint tea and coffee to her little gathering and moved carefully from group to group, eyes flashing behind enormous spectacles. Presently it was her pleasurable duty to move round to Martin's group again. It seemed only natural that soon the two were in private conversation.

'Er . . . Doris,' murmured Martin, lowering his voice to a suitable pitch. She leant forward eagerly. 'I'm sorry to bother you with such a . . . a delicate matter: is . . . is there a men's room nearby?'

He smiled pleasantly and her heart warmed to him. 'Why, of course!' she exclaimed with a motherly smile. 'You go through those glass doors to the hall . . .' Martin followed her directions. He smiled his excuses, slipped out through the glass doors and pulled them carefully closed behind him.

He had, he estimated, no more than four minutes.

He slipped past the toilet, looked carefully to right and left and listened intently for a moment longer to the hum of empty chatter from the lounge. Satisfied, he tiptoed softly to the head of the stairs and began descending swiftly.

The stairs led directly to the door of General Clarke Freeman's study, and, Nicholson discovered, that door was not locked.

*

Professor Eduard Ryabov stood on the narrow wooden porch of his attractive, low timbered dasha and watched, in a mood of deep depression, while the twin red brake lights of the official Chaika glared briefly at the corner and then disappeared as the limousine gathered speed and roared away importantly into the darkness.

Ryabov turned round slowly, returned indoors and closed the door firmly behind him as though thus he might shut out fear and unwelcome knowledge with the cold winds of the evening. He crossed to his favourite armchair and sank down among the brightly coloured cushions, aware suddenly of the weight of every last one of his sixty-five years. Irena was away for the evening, out with friends nearby, and for that, at least, Ryabov was thankful. For that, and for not much else, he pondered bleakly.

Twice before in the years he had spent here outside the space faculty at Semipalatinsk, the arrival of important news relating to the Skyshroud project had been heralded by the brief instruction, received at the laboratory the day before, to remain indoors the following evening and await the arrival of the chauffeur-borne emissary from Moscow.

They had wasted little time on pleasantries when the visitor arrived, and dislike had been mutual, instantaneous. The meeting had not lasted long and the stranger had departed into the night leaving the Professor a sealed envelope with instructions that it was not to be opened until after the visitor's departure. The man from Moscow left him also with verbal confirmation of the worst suspicions he had harboured since the day he had been summoned to appear before PKO in Moscow.

Professor Ryabov sat quietly in his chair for a long time, the sealed letter forgotten, gazing with sightless eyes across the room at his wife's empty chair, seeing nothing beyond the folly of a trust misplaced and the crystal-clear consequences that stemmed from a life of brilliant technological isolation. He lifted his arms to run brittle fingers through his thinning hair and noticed, with only mild surprise, that his hands were shaking.

Skyshroud was going to be tested for offensive deployment. If those tests were successful, then his brain-child would be used, not as a defensive, life-saving system, but as an offensive weapons system fired and deployed from some sort of space vehicle out there somewhere in space.

His visitor had begun by apologizing. For the harassment of his wife, Irena. It had all been a mistake. She had been mistaken for somebody else. Would they both accept their apologies and would he – one hour after this meeting was over – would he please care to open the enclosed letter, which, he assured him, contained nothing but good news. The very best news. Gold teeth glittered at the corners of the smile.

Oh – and something else: the boy – the boy Misha Prolev. He was shortly to go to Leningrad for specialist treatment for his eye. The very best treatment the State could provide. It was the least they could do to make amends.

Ryabov had welcomed the news and winced inside at the crude tactics of intimidation: a glimpse of the stick and then a bagful of sweets.

Ryabov had taken the letter and thrust it into an inside pocket while the visitor outlined the decisions that had been taken – and Professor Eduard Ryabov, the man who wanted peace, felt the fist of a cold and alien fear close around his heart. When the man began to talk glibly about deployment against a land-based target –

'What target?' demanded Ryabov sharply, the memory of that bunker complex and the stench of roast mutton suddenly yesterday-fresh in his mind.

The man had shrugged in an offhand fashion and become silkily evasive. He really had no idea, and, in any event, it was a matter of little concern to the Professor. He was concerned only with the functional efficiency of the system's components. Target acquisition was being arranged by Launch Control. It was a different operation altogether.

Oh, quite, murmured Ryabov.

And so the man from Moscow had clambered back into the high, dated body-work of that most prestigious of Soviet status-symbols, the chauffeur-driven limousine, and retreated behind the sanctuary of the little grey curtains that shielded the occupant from the gaze of the curious and the fearful.

Ryabov sat on in his armchair, his thoughts chasing one another through the labyrinth of his own conscience.

Test firing was tentatively scheduled for Monday, 3 May. Against a target or targets unknown.

Half an hour passed before Ryabov rose suddenly to his feet, struggled into his overcoat and climbed behind the wheel of his own private car to drive swiftly back along the narrow, frozen roads to the space complex at Semipalatinsk.

He showed his pass to the uniformed guards on the barrier, who recognized him instantly and waved him through, their breath pluming above fur caps in the cold, harsh glare of the arc lights as they stamped their booted feet against the bitter cold that is reserved by a malicious providence for the bored sentries of every nation.

Professor Ryabov drove a further three miles inside the guarded perimeter fences, turned left past the long, low, funnel-shaped building that ended in a massive, man-made sand-trap and which housed the core of all his experimentation, and pulled in to the reserved parking space opposite the office complex. He slipped his security pass into the special holder on the windscreen and crossed to the building with a nod to the security guard in his insulated glass cubicle by the entrance porch.

He knew the man would log his arrival at this late hour, but that was of little consequence; he had long been used to working as mood and enthusiasm took him and the security teams at the base had, in turn, become accustomed to the professional whims of their brilliant scientist.

Now Ryabov was relying upon two simple facts. First, that Control would have received notification of both the intention to launch and the target co-ordinates for the ground test – without such information, Ryabov reasoned carefully, preparations would be meaningless. Secondly, that no one would challenge his right to that information. He swallowed. Unless he betrayed himself by sounding nervous, uncertain. Confidence – confidence and the deliberate exploitation of his own prestige – there lay the key to success.

He let himself into his office and sat at his desk, his face in shadow beyond the single pool of light thrown by his desk lamp. Listening to the stillness around him, fearful in the waiting silence, he was aware of his own heart thudding painfully beneath his ribs. He licked dry lips. There was little point in waiting. Better get it over with ... He lifted the receiver and dialled through.

The call was answered instantly: 'Control.'

'This is Professor Ryabov over in Amst Nine,' announced Ryabov with what he hoped was the right abruptness.

'Yes, Professor? How may we help you?'

'A simple matter: would you just confirm you are preparing the Skyshroud prototype launch for Monday, 3 May?'

There was a pause and Ryabov heard the rustle of papers. 'That is correct, Professor: 0600 Monday, 3 May.'

Ryabov drew a deep breath. 'And the co-ordinates for Land Target Acquisition?'

This time there was a longer pause and for a terrible moment Professor Ryabov thought he had gone too far.

'Er, Professor. You should really –'

'Quick, man! I haven't got all night,' snapped Ryabov with a bite to his voice that took them both by surprise.

'Yes, yes. Er ... of course. Target co-ordinates are as follows: sixty-one degrees, twenty minutes north, one hundred and twenty-two degrees, forty minutes east. But, Professor –'

'*Forty* minutes east? You're quite sure about that?' said the Professor sharply as he scribbled down the information. 'I was sure I had it as twenty minutes east.'

'No, no – forty, I am certain. I am reading it now, just as it came to us off the Mission Authorization form.'

'Good. You have been most helpful. That will be all. Good night.'

'Good night, Professor.'

The line went dead and Ryabov replaced the receiver slowly. He sat back, relieved. It had been as easy as that. The hardest part satisfactorily concluded, the rest should be easy.

It was. Another brief phone call, a reminder of his status within the faculty's scientific community, and he was striding briskly across the hardened snow to the Centre of Cartography. The pass he would require would be waiting with Security when he arrived.

Before the German offensive against the Soviet Union in June 1941, detailed and accurate maps of the Soviet Union – including the sensitive border areas – were readily available. In all, some 100,000 of these, set to a scale of 1/50,000, had been printed and openly distributed for purchase on the open market both at home and abroad. With the war's end four years later, no less than 80,000 of these maps were discovered in the possession of Hitler's Third Reich. Belatedly, the Soviet Union attributed much of the massive damage suffered by their industrial institutions to Luftwaffe bombing that had taken its devastating accuracy from the 'white' intelligence gleaned from the efforts of Russia's own cartographers. It was a lesson learnt.

With the exception of exploded views and panoramic cartoons showing the relative relation of one town to another, it is today impossible to obtain truly accurate Russian-made maps of the Soviet Union. Most certainly, a general map is roughly accurate, but it would be useless for any offensive, military purpose: today's maps omit whole towns; between one edition and another, the location of entire communities is significantly altered, and place names change overnight. It was not until American astronauts and technicians visited the Tyuratam launch site in Kazakhstan for the Apollo-Soyuz Space Project in 1975 and actually compared their Soviet-stated position with the evidence of their own BigBird photographs that they realized they had been deliberately misled for years as to the centre's true location.*

Accurate maps were kept, however, at Semipalatinsk. They were locked away in a secure, low-ceilinged bunker

* The Soviet Union gave the position as 43° 30′ N, 65° 50′ E. The correct position – then and now – was 45° 60′ N, 63° 40′ E.

complex a little apart from the other low concrete buildings that served Control. Ryabov went there now, collected his security pass and was soon poring over huge rolls of maps, the co-ordinates of each obligingly printed in the top right-hand corner.

His late-night visit to the map centre attracted a first, curious glance from the bored loggist behind his desk at the far end of the brightly lit chamber, but the Professor was left alone to study without interruption the rolls of maps that were brought, at his request, from their fire-proof depository below ground.

He bent over the numbered sheets for long minutes, working slowly with pencil, ruler and paper as he plotted the information he had extracted from a careless Duty Officer in Launch Control. 61′ 20° N, 122′ 40° E – that placed the target area somewhere to the south-west of the Lena Plateau and rather north of Olekminsk.

Pencil and ruler came together. Ryabov made a tiny mark on the map and straightened up slowly, easing the pain in his back as he studied the map spread out in front of him.

He frowned and reached for the phone.

'Those figures you gave me just now: sixty-one twenty north, one hundred and twenty-two forty east – is that correct?' There was a doubt to his voice, an edge of un-certainty, that an actor would have found impossible to imitate.

Now there was a pause as the same Duty Officer con-sulted again the Mission Authorization papers. 'Sixty-one twenty north, one hundred and twenty-two forty east, Professor. That is what I said, yes. That is correct.'

'You are certain?'

'Absolutely.'

'I see. I . . . I . . . thank you,' he murmured dazedly.

He would not remember later how it was that he returned the maps to the loggist, climbed behind the wheel of his car and drove slowly home along those dark, frozen roads, but he managed it somehow – managed it, with his mind full of a hideous, burgeoning horror.

He had good reason to trust the accuracy of those particular maps; he had used them often before for reference points, for the location of complex, practical experiments. He was unable, therefore, to comfort himself with the thought that there had perhaps been a mistake of some kind. Instead, he had to face the certainty that the co-ordinates were accurate; that when the map indicated that a small town called Kafiyevka stood at that exact same point on the map, it was almost certainly telling the truth.

It was only later, when he was undressing slowly to climb beside the sleeping form of his wife, that Professor Ryabov remembered the letter from Moscow he had thrust into an inside pocket. Now he crossed over to the window, tilted the sealed letter against the moon's soft rays and slit open the envelope with his finger. A single sheet of folded notepaper crackled stiffly in the silence as he peered closer.

Long years of dedication were to be rewarded. His selfless work in the defence of the Soviet Union was to be formally recognized by the award of the Order of the Red Banner for 'outstanding services over a period of years'. He would receive the award from the hand of Comrade President Vasili Travin himself at a ceremony in Moscow on Tuesday, 4 May.

A dull, sullen anger grew within him as he pictured his wife climbing fearfully up and down a series of cold, concrete stairways – a victim of intimidation by the organ of State Security.

First the stick, then the carrot. And so now *they* would choose to honour *him*?

Professor Ryabov tore the letter into tiny pieces and watched without interest as they fluttered to the floor.

: : 9 : : : : : : : : : : : : : : :

In Frank Yates' Georgetown apartment, Lydia put down her glass.

'Frank? Something is troubling you, yes?'

Frank shook his head silently and resumed his study of the bottom of the glass, hoping, almost unconsciously, that the action would of itself prompt more inquiry. They had eaten supper early, Louise had gone to bed and they were sitting together in the lounge, a half-empty bottle of scotch beside the coffee cups on the table between them.

'Tell me what it is. I would like to be of help,' concluded Lydia practically.

Frank glanced across the room with a wry smile. If only it really was as simple as that: ask and ye shall receive ... She was sitting opposite on the sofa, her hair pulled back and gleaming in the lamplight. Twice before this same evening he had steeled himself to break the fragile mood of relaxation – of intimacy, almost, that had grown between them with each evening spent together in this anxious isolation. Twice he had steeled himself – and twice he had steered the conversation away to safer ground as courage failed in the face of a selfish enjoyment of the woman's presence. He shook his head at his own weakness. These were hardly the attributes of a good lieutenant – or even a good captain, he mused idly, as the scotch began to wash away the sandbags of caution.

'That messenger this morning – the young Lieutenant Marshall? I had to go and see your favourite American General.' Frank paused to toss off the last of his drink. 'For orders.' He glanced up. Lydia had stiffened perceptibly.

That's how it's done, thought Frank bitterly: a few careless words for the Good of the Service and you can stand

: 128

back and watch friendship and intimacy disappear like magic, courtesy of the United States Air Force. Lydia Prolev sat a little straighter among the cushions.

'What orders did the good General give you? Or am I not permitted to ask?' Her voice was level. Nice and neutral. Without a trace of tension. Almost.

'They were about you, Lydia,' continued Frank slowly, taking masochistic satisfaction from the simple, inevitable way in which the fragile bricks of trust and friendship were turning to dust before his very eyes. 'He's up before the Nuclear Intelligence Board tomorrow. Very important people.'

'I do not understand,' said Lydia Prolev shortly. There was ice in her voice and the once warm face looked cold, flat and hard. You see, he chided himself mirthlessly – it's easy. Out loud:

'He's going to tell them all about Hammer – or as much as he knows, anyway.'

'Hammer?'

Frank nodded. 'Project Hammer. That's his name for what your people are doing at Semipalatinsk. He's got a thing in his head about it. Fixation, almost.'

Lydia gave a sigh of anger, of exasperation. 'Again! Every week, every month – Semipalatinsk! Semipalatinsk! Sometimes I believe that is all your General has to worry about –'

'He thinks you're holding back – that you have crucial evidence that –' but Lydia was on her feet, stalking across to the bedroom. She went inside and slammed the door angrily behind her. Frank Yates was left on the sofa to stare stupidly at his stupid scotch. Top marks, Yates, he thought bitterly – top fucking marks. There was silence from the bedroom. He rose, crossed to the door and knocked softly. 'Lydia?'

He tried the handle and the door opened under his hand. She was standing over by the bed, her anger, her fear, a palpable thing there in the darkness.

'That won't solve a damn' thing,' he said quietly. He

reached out, took her arm and led her gently back into the lounge. Lydia sat down again, and there was silence as Frank poured drinks for them both.

'This General Freeman of yours –'

'He's not *my* General. You make him sound like some –'

'No,' she agreed sadly. 'He is not your General. But you are his Captain, no? There is a difference. General Freeman – he expects me to go before these nuclear people and – and do what?'

Frank glanced up. 'Give evidence. Tell them what you know. Back up the General, I guess.'

She nodded. 'Back up the General, I see. And Misha? What about my boy, my son?' She paused, choosing the spot for the killer punch. 'What if it was Louise? What if it was *your* daughter? What then?'

There was silence. Lydia leaned forward. 'Frank, answer me! I ask you a question: what about Misha?'

Frank spread his hands helplessly. 'I'm not in a position to say. Ask General –'

Lydia set her glass down on the table with a dull smack. 'I will *not* ask him. I will ask you! I am asking you, now. What would you do?' She paused, breathing deeply. 'My silence is all that I have. It is what keeps Misha safe and alive. And you think I should put that at risk just so that –'

'Look, Lydia: all I'm saying is –'

'Do you not understand that I come to the West because I am tired of all this? Tired of the politics, the military, the pressure on the scientists to think, to work, along certain lines only, to suppress?

'Forget what General Freeman says to you, Frank – forget it! I do not come here with my head full of secrets to give to the West – I come because I am tired, yes? Tired, tired, tired: tired of the drabness, tired of the little things: I am tired of seeing my son and husband living four families to an apartment with the only toilet at the end of the corridor; I am tired of queueing, queueing, queueing for the things you spoilt Americans take for granted: for meat, for milk, for eggs; for flour that is always gone when it is your turn – for the things of quality that you discover are only for *pokazukha* . . . how do you say it? . . . for show? Yes, for show.

'What do we have? Oh, we have other things. Very important things.' She went on with heavy sarcasm: 'We have vodka. And salt. And, last year – pen-knives. Every shop has many, many pen-knives. It is curious, is it not? Pen-knives and vodka. But milk? No. No milk. And do you know what else we have, Frank?' She leant forward to tap the side of her nose conspiratorially. 'We have the . . . we call him the *upravdom*.'

'The *upravdom* ?'

'The *upravdom*. The Director of the House. He must report everything to the authorities, the KGB' (she pronounced the letters 'kay jay bah'), 'Oh – and, of course, we have passports, passports, papers, for everything: for moving districts and to get a new apartment – do you know, Frank, that people get *married* to people they do not love or even know particularly well, just so that they can live in one of the big cities? It is a major industry – that and the search always for something that is *firmenny*, a thing that is imported from outside the Soviet Union, something that will make you feel a little good inside, yes?'

'Fine, Lydia, but –'

'Wait! One moment – everywhere there are spies, there are informers. I will tell you: some friends of mine, they were not very good members of the Party, do you understand? They have a little girl, a nice little girl of five, maybe six years. And, one night, in the apartment block, they have a party and they get a little drunk.' She smiled without humour. 'On vodka, of course. And they begin to shout. They begin to sing. They sing things that are not very . . . very *politik*, yes? The *upravdom*, he listens to this, but he does not stop it. He listens. And he makes his report. Two days more and the little girl, she is taken away. Because her parents are not teaching her to live in accord with the Moral Code of a Builder of Communism.'

Lydia paused again, her eyes staring off into a foreign distance. 'They do not see that little girl again.' She looked up. 'You, you Americans with your three cars, your swimming pools and your easy freedoms – can you comprehend that?'

'You're kidding,' said Frank and regretted it instantly. It was a stupid thing to say.

'No, I am not "kidding", as you call it, Frank. Do you think Misha would be safe if I talk to those people for your General? Do you still believe I should tell the General what he wants to hear?'

In Hagerstown, Ferris leant forward and prodded Viktor Pligin with the toe of his shoe. Pligin started violently from his position on the sofa and glanced across at his captor with haunted eyes. He had slept uneasily, curled on the sofa, while Ferris sat awake opposite like some sinister baby-sitter, his contempt for the man he dominated by fear alone shown earlier as he had replaced the pistol in his coat pocket and laid a heavy carving-knife on the arm of his chair. That chill reminder of the penalty for disobedience had crushed even the flicker of rebellion, and Pligin had passed a wretched night huddled amid his cold, grim thoughts while 'The man' sat reading opposite, glancing up occasionally to study his prisoner with detached, professional interest. Like a hangman gauging weight.

'On your feet,' ordered Ferris now. 'Time we found another phone booth.'

With Louise away at school next day, Frank Yates and Lydia Prolev were alone once more in the apartment. Frank, defying his own edict about movement in the lounge, was lying full-length on the sofa, hands clasped behind his head. He was deep in thought: the simple passage of time had brought his own conflict of loyalties into sharp focus – in just five hours' time the General would step before the Nuclear Intelligence Board and start presenting his evidence – evidence that, he knew, would almost certainly contain the promise of testimony from a new and secret source. Some time before that moment he, Frank, had to decide where his loyalty lay. Now, as the phone began to ring, he swung his feet to the floor and crossed to the desk slowly, his thoughts still focused inwards.

'Captain Yates?' A male, friendly voice.

'Speaking.'

'It's Mr Needham here, Captain Yates – Needham of High Hills Junior school? We haven't met yet, I'm sorry to say. I'm Junior Principal. Took over from Mr Spilburg at the end of the fall –'

'What can I do for you, Mr Needham? I –' High Hills was Louise's school. 'Louise – is she all right?'

'We don't believe it's anything serious,' assured the friendly voice easily. 'You know what these kids are, Captain Yates. One minute you've got your eye on them and then next –'

'What's happened?'

'Well, now – she's taken a slight fall. Nothing serious, you understand. It seems she was playing on the swings just a short time ago, and, well . . . one of her little classmates –' Frank clenched his teeth at the picture. He hadn't even kissed her goodbye that morning, he remembered bleakly.

'Is she badly hurt?'

The tone of his voice brought Lydia Prolev through from the bedroom, anxiety fresh in her eyes.

'There's been a little concussion – otherwise it's mostly cuts and grazing. Shock too, I guess. I've tried calling your Mrs Headley but there's no reply. I thought you'd appreciate it if I called you direct.' The voice paused for the clincher: 'She's been asking for you.'

There was a silence while Frank juggled priorities. No contest.

'I'll be with you in half an hour,' he decided impulsively.

It took Frank fifty-five impatient, horn-blaring minutes to cut his way across town to his daughter's school. Now he indicated he was about to turn right, slid through a narrow gap in the thundering river of oncoming traffic and braked to a halt on the gravel track that ran alongside the high wire fence bordering the school playground.

A playground without any swings.

Frank got out of the car and jogged across the asphalt, his coat flapping as he ran. He pushed through the double doors and stepped into a bright Gulliver world of low-ceilinged changing rooms with their coats and schoolbags hanging motionless like firemen's uniforms on rows of neat, low pegs. The musty smell of books, of ink and sneakers, damp socks and youthful sweat rekindled memories of his own as Frank lunged out of the changing room into a passageway with a sense of awful, nagging urgency. The doors banged shut, and the echo rolled on around him.

A playground without any swings.

Now Frank forced himself to stand motionless for a moment. To think. He was half-way down a long, gleaming corridor, its walls lined with bright young paintings of stick-legged mothers with gap-toothed smiles. A door opened suddenly a little further down the corridor, and a young teacher emerged from another classroom carrying a pile of books. Frank started after her.

'Excuse me.'

The woman turned and waited, puzzled, wary of a strange adult in a children's world as he ran lightly towards her. 'Can I help you?'

'Yes – yes, you can. Tell me – where are the swings? Your playground swings? Do you have any swings here?'

The woman looked alarmed. He might have asked for the machine-guns. 'I'm not sure I understand what you –'

'Please. It's very important – are there any swings here? I saw when I came in just now that –'

'We've no swings here. None at all,' replied the teacher emphatically. 'There used to be some a long while back, I guess. Then they got, you know, vandalized and – are you sure you're OK?'

'Yes, yes – I'm fine. Really. My name's Yates – Frank Yates. You've got my daughter here? Louise Yates? Third-year kid. Long fair hair and –'

The teacher was nodding. 'Sure. I teach her math.'

'Tell me – how is she?'

'How is she?' The cautious look was back in her eyes as she recalled all the world's crazy stories of demented fathers, mad axemen and child molesters who ever held a school to ransom: it was a favourite nightmare of hers. She swallowed uneasily – but not High Hills Junior – pray God, not High Hills Junior . . .

With something of an effort, Frank forced himself to pause, take breath and then start again more calmly. 'Let me explain – I had a phone call just now – well, about an hour ago – from your Junior Principal. He said Louise had had an accident, here at the school. She'd fallen off the swings – don't ask me which swings – and she had con-cussion; a few cuts and bruises. That's why I asked about the swings, do you see? Only I couldn't see any when I came in?'

The woman nodded, relieved. Perhaps he wasn't a mad-man after all. 'I guess that makes sense, Mr Yates. Only that –'

She paused again, puzzled, and began leafing through a pile of exercise books.

'Only what?'

The teacher held up an orange notebook. 'I thought so – I just gave her eight out of ten for her sums, Mr Yates – and whatever else your daughter may be suffering I guess I'd put concussion at the bottom of the list. There must be some mistake. Look –' she craned past Frank to peer on tiptoe through the glass window set in the top of the door – 'I'm sure she's there now.'

The teacher swept the formation of bent heads expertly, a classroom fighter pilot scanning silhouettes of the enemy. 'Yes – there she is,' exclaimed the teacher. 'Second row, third from the left.'

Frank looked. A small, familiar blond head bent over a textbook. As he watched, the head came up and an arm shot out to answer a question from the teacher. No grazes. No bruises. No concussion. No question.

The math teacher was regarding Frank rather oddly. 'Who did you say called you?'

'Your Junior Principal,' explained Frank patiently, for all the good he realized it would do. He was too late. Much too late. 'A Mr Needham.'

The teacher looked almost relieved. 'I'm afraid someone's been making a bad joke at your expense, Mr Yates.' She ticked off the points patiently on her clever little fingers: 'In the first place, we don't have any such title here at High Hills Junior – "Junior Principal" is a term we simply don't use –'

'And in the second?' asked Frank bleakly, as stomach-rolling certainty took hold.

'We've no one on the staff called Needham,' finished the teacher simply.

'Jesus.' Frank groaned, turned on his heel and thus missed the frown of disapproval from the woman who also took Morning Prayers. Over his shoulder 'Where's the nearest phone?'

'At the end of the hall on your –' but he was off, pelting down the polished corridor, his heels rapping out the noise of his stupidity as the woman's final words floated after him – 'but it doesn't work.'

Five minutes later Frank pulled in off the highway, ducked under the perspex shield of the phone kiosk and punched in his own home number. The phone began to ring. He pressed the receiver against his ear and willed the machine to pluck the woman out of the trouble he had made for her and dump her back in the kitchen where she could cross to the wall, reach out for the phone – she's reaching for the phone – she's reaching for the phone now – now – now.

The phone rang on unanswered.

He smashed the receiver back on its hook. Gone. He had thought too little, too slowly. Now Lydia – his charge – was either dead in his own apartment, a cold, grisly trophy to his inadequacies, or else she was taken.

He closed his eyes and leant his head against the clear perspex of the kiosk. And someone, sometime, would have to tell the General.

*

Dead she was.

Dead, physically, she wasn't. She was unharmed and, in that sense alone, she was in perfect physical health. Her death was in the mind – in that small area of consciousness where live all hope and optimism, where flickers the smallest flame of determination to fight on, to defy the cruel cards of a malicious providence.

Twenty-five minutes after Frank Yates had left the apartment, there had been another phone call. With a glance at her watch, Lydia had calculated it was probably Frank calling back from the school with news of his daughter. Her guard was down, therefore, as she took to her belly the stream of cold, deadly words that stretched out from her homeland to nail her heart against darkness.

They knew where she was. Whenever they wished they could pick up her son. She was to return now, of her own free will, to an address they would give her shortly.

If she agreed to this instantly, then the boy, conceivably, might live. If she disobeyed this one, final instruction, then they would send her, over the next few weeks, detailed coloured photographs of her son's castration and eventual, merciful, execution.

And then they would come for her.

She was to take a taxi . . .

Dry-eyed, leaden-shouldered, she took a taxi.

Frank Yates fumbled for his keys, opened the front door of his apartment and pushed it wide. It banged back emptily and there was silence as he stepped slowly over the threshold.

'Lydia?'

There was silence. The silence, almost, of derision. Of course there was silence. What did he expect, a twelve-piece band?

He closed the door softly behind him, slipped on the lock and chain, and walked silently down the hallway towards the horrors that must surely await him.

A step at a time. And still no sound.

'Lydia?'

He took down the hunting rifle from the top of the book-case and eased back the bolt with careful, practised fingers. He slid the bolt back a fraction and slipped his index finger into the breech, his eyes still on the turn ahead that led into the lounge. The weapon was still loaded, the round still chambered. Bolt closed, finger curled around the trigger, Frank stepped slowly forward, the butt cushioned into the base of his right shoulder.

A quick, sweeping glance into the lounge, head and eyes scanning from left to right. Nothing. The lounge was clear. The bedrooms? That too. Spare rooms and bathroom also. And the kitchen.

The .45 Colt 1911A1 automatic was still inside its plastic bag in the ice-box, and Frank unwrapped it and cocked the action, preferring to carry that weapon now as he completed a swift, thorough inspection of the apartment that yielded nothing: no bodies in the freezer, no corpse in the wardrobe or behind the sofa, no signs of a struggle, no blood, no broken ornaments. Just nothing.

Frank pushed the phone book aside, hoisted himself on to the kitchen counter and forced himself to sit there and think clearly, logically. He had found nothing. That, in itself, must tell him something. He'd been lured away from the apartment for a purpose: to give them a clear run at the woman.

Options? There were two options, he reasoned carefully. One: that she had been taken by force, against her will. He glanced around him once more. Force? That didn't seem likely. If she had gone out that way there would be some sign, somewhere. Yet the apartment was immaculate, nothing was out of place. Therefore, he reasoned, she had not been dragged away by force.

Yet she had gone.

Option two: that she had left of her own free will, had a change of heart. Under pressure, perhaps, but she had placed one foot in front of another all the way to the front door because she chose to do so. Why? All right, then, picture the scene: she's standing here in the kitchen – or in the lounge, maybe – and they make contact. How? One of two ways – they either bang on the door – hardly likely: for all they know, half Washington's National Guard is waiting round the corner for just such a move, their arms full of Mace and shotgun shells. Too risky, too conspicuous. So they didn't ring the doorbell.

Maybe they got to her the same way they'd lured him away to the school.

By telephone.

For the first time Frank's gaze fell on the open phone book. It had been pressed open at a page marked 'Taxi service'. He ran a thumb quickly down the list of numbers. There were dozens of them – probably hundreds. If she was travelling, using a taxi, she might have picked any one of a dozen different companies. He twisted round suddenly and scanned the scratch board pinned to the wall beside the phone. There was a list of groceries, a reminder about dry cleaning, a scrawled note to Mrs Headley – and half a dozen phone numbers. Frank recognized and discarded most of the numbers. He ripped out the page from the phone directory and held it up against the wall as he scanned both sets of numbers for similarity, for the match.

He found it.

232-9171. Phoenix Cabs. He hopped down off the counter and punched out the number. The call rang out and was answered.

'Yeah?'

'Phoenix Cabs?'

'What's your problem?'

'I'm calling from Dumbarton Street, Georgetown. Can you tell me – have any of your people been out here just recently? To pick up a fare? It's very important. A matter of life and death.' He grimaced. Pure cornball.

'Yeah? No kidding?' responded the controller, with as much excitement as a beaver rolling off a wet log. Just now there'd been that crazy dame shouting off about what the neighbours were doing next door. Who did they think he was all of a sudden, Kojak? And now this guy –

'Can you tell me: have you picked up a fare out on Dumbarton Street? Any time in the last hour, hour and a half?'

'Hold your water, mac. I'll have to check it out.' The phone went down with a crash, and Frank heard someone rooting around among a mass of papers like a hog in close country. 'Dumbarton Street NW – No. 315 – would that be the one? Two Zero Six tabbed a fare over there half an hour back.'

'Did he say where the fare was to?'

'Well, now, sure he did.' The voice was suddenly sugar. 'Gave me the fare's age, address, next-of-kin, all that stuff. What d'you think, mac?'

'OK, OK – but did he say where the fare was –' Another phone began to ring in the controller's office, and Frank heard the sudden hiss and bark of static from an incoming radio transmission.

'Listen, I've gotta go, OK?'

'Tell me! Where was he going? Was it far? Long-distance?' He was almost shouting.

'Hagerstown somewhere, I guess. Only just where he –'

'Thanks. Thanks a million.' Frank dropped the phone back on its cradle with a crash, jammed the automatic in his waistband and took off at a run.

Hagerstown!

The driver of cab Two Zero Six regarded the woman doubtfully. 'You want me to wait, lady? You look kinda shook up to my way of thinking, if you'll pardon me.'

Lydia Prolev shook her head. 'Thank you, no. It will be all right. You must leave me here. Thank you.'

She crushed dollar bills into the man's open hand and turned away. The driver shrugged again. 'Whatever you say.'

The window went up and the car pulled away. Lydia Prolev watched it disappear and then turned to face the house that had been her home for four and a half months. She closed her handbag and stepped off the sidewalk on to the worn grass. As she approached the door with the familiar peeling paintwork it opened suddenly and a young man with a head of glossy hair stood framed in the doorway. He was smiling the pleasant, assured smile of victory. 'Lydia Prolev?'

Her head went up and she looked ahead defiantly, determined to keep to herself the quaking fear.

'That is I,' she acknowledged calmly.

'Come along in. We've been expecting you.' The man stood aside politely as she stepped over the threshold.

'You surprise me,' she managed with a brief, taut smile. The door closed behind her and the chain went on with the rattle of finality.

'Upstairs,' he ordered briefly. Lydia Prolev did as she was told, her slow steps heavy and hollow on the bare, worn tread. As she reached the top of the staircase another door opened and a tall man, balding and unsmiling, beckoned her forward. She moved into the lounge and started as she saw Viktor Pligin hunched into the corner of the sofa, his arms clasped about his shoulders in a caricature of self-protection. He regarded her awkwardly and moved dry, cracked lips.

'I am sorry,' he whispered huskily. 'There was . . . there was nothing I could do, Lydia. Nothing! They said they would . . . they would kill me if I did not . . . if I did not help them.'

Lydia reached out a hand and patted the thin, frail shoulder. 'It does not matter,' she said softly. 'Sooner or later, it was going to happen anyway. If not from you, Viktor, then from someone else. It is of no consequence.'

She listened dully to her own words and felt the weight of defeat settle around her shoulders like a cloak. She had been wrong to believe it would be possible to start again, wrong to clutch at the – the tall, balding man, the older and infinitely more sinister of the two, had closed the door softly, crossed to where she was sitting and bent down slowly, his eyes upon her face, to pluck her handbag from unprotesting fingers. He rummaged inside briefly and then, apparently satisfied, tossed the handbag back into her lap and walked over to an armchair. He sat down and regarded the two captured defectors silently, both hands stretched out along the arms of the armchair.

Lydia Prolev watched him steadily, and it was the man who, finally, dipped his head in acknowledgement, perhaps in salute. 'You are a brave woman, Lydia Prolev. It is a welcome change –' He nodded contemptuously towards Viktor Pligin. Pligin flinched at the barbed words, and his fearful eyes darted away. His captor paused, considering. Then 'Where was Yates? When you left?'

'He had gone. To the school. He received a phone call. It was about his little girl. She had –'

'We know about Louise.'

She nodded. She had worked that much out already.

'What will . . . what will happen to my son?' she asked calmly as the door opened and the younger of the two men came in quietly behind her.

Ferris shrugged. 'As far as we are concerned, we have no further interest in the boy. He will be perfectly safe. He is simply a tool, a device that has enabled us to make contact with you. He will not be harmed – provided you do what you are told.'

'I have made my decision. I give you my word I will return to the Soviet Union, I will say what you want me to say. That will be enough, no? There is no need to involve Misha further. He is just a child.'

'I am sure that is so. But we are just messengers, you understand, we –'

'Messengers! You are butchers, murderers!' Viktor Pligin waved a wild finger at Lydia Prolev, his voice balanced on the very edge of hysteria. 'Do you know what he did, Lydia? He came –'

'Be quiet, you! Quiet – or you will be silenced.' The cold, chill words of warning froze the gush of accusation, and Pligin subsided into silence as Ferris turned to face the woman once more. 'We'll leave this apartment shortly, move somewhere a little more ... comfortable, a little less obvious. First, however, I want a little private conversation with your colleague here, Comrade Pligin. You will excuse us?'

Ferris rose to his feet, regarded the former airline steward dispassionately and beckoned him to his feet with a crooked finger. 'Come on, you – up. We have things to discuss: the terms of your silence, for example.'

Pligin cowered deeper into his corner and remained there until Ferris hauled him to his feet by a handful of soiled shirt front. He nodded again at the woman. 'We will talk again soon, Mrs Prolev. You will excuse me for a little while.'

He shoved Pligin against one of the thin plywood doors, and the two disappeared into the spare bedroom.

The door closed softly behind them.

:: THE HEARING : DAY ONE

The tall windows that lined the entire west wall of Room 2600 of the New Senate Building had been opened to take advantage of the fine spring weather, and the blue-clad figure standing erect at a raised wooden dais had to raise his voice slightly against the murmur of Washington traffic below as he began to unfold his deposition before the six members of the Nuclear Intelligence Board.

Standing before a venerated board of national experts, General Freeman and his aides were alone in a room that could have seated two hundred with ease. Yet the public was absent, the press tables were empty and the microphones inert. To ensure that such privacy continued, armed guards stood in the corridor outside, their backs to the high locked doors.

Already General Freeman could sense the hostility seeping towards him across the gleaming oak and polished maple like nerve gas. He reminded himself it was no less than he expected – he was, after all, the bringer of bad news. More than that, he was presuming to tell the Board that their thinking was outdated, that they were wrong.

'. . . and you are aware, I suppose, General Freeman, that it is less than one month since the members of this Board gave their unequivocal support to Pentagon proposals to reinvest heavily in the next generation of silo-based and submarine-launched ICBMs? Something in the region of five thousand billion dollars by fiscal' 82? A recommendation endorsed, incidentally, by your own service?'

'I am, sir, yes.'

There was silence. Sam Tolland leant across and murmured something to Tom Greener. Both men smiled briefly at some inner amusement and then sat back to resume their languid inspection of General Freeman. The enemy.

'And?' demanded Tolland.

'I will not deny that my stance – my appearance before you gentlemen today – is a cause of some embarrassment within the Air Force. However, I believe I have a duty to the country I serve that transcends a narrower loyalty to my own particular service. I truly wish that my views chimed with those of my superiors. However, they do not. I am obliged, therefore, to follow the dictates of my own conscience regardless of any personal, professional considerations.'

'How commendable,' commented Greener dryly. He paused. 'So tell us, General – why you have chosen this particular time to exercise your statutory right to summons the Board? Your initial call –' Greener coloured for a second as he remembered the exact moment of interruption – 'suggested there was reason for haste.'

General Freeman hesitated. It was on the tip of his tongue to reveal the contents of Captain Fisher's report on the OTH characteristics recorded at Timmins, but he bit back the words. 'If I may, gentlemen, I will come to that a little later. The shape of my submission to the Board falls into three parts: my preamble, which you will hear in a moment; the outline of technical submission which will support that preamble; and the personal sworn testimony of a leading Soviet scientist who will be able, through personal knowledge of a most detailed, intimate nature, to confirm the existence of what I have come to believe constitutes the single, most awesome Soviet development since 1945.'

There was a stirring of interest as the heads turned one to another.

'Go ahead, General,' ordered Sam Tolland.

General Freeman stepped down from the raised platform and moved crisply to the projector set on the table beside his aides. They watched him impassively as he clicked a switch and the motor whirred warmly. Freeman turned round, tugged down the tail of his uniform jacket and began speaking once more, his voice clear and firm. 'I'd like to take you back, gentlemen – back to 1 March 1950. To London, England. And to this man.' Click. A slide snapped on to the blank screen. A thin, balding man in round pebble spectacles wearing an ill-fitting shirt and tie, and hand-cuffed to two police officers. 'This man is Fuchs. Klaus Emil Julius Fuchs, the nuclear scientist. The former member of the German Communist Party. Fuchs the traitor.'

There was a stirring of impatience from the members of the Nuclear Intelligence Board. Both Fuchs and the story of his treachery were known to them all. It had been the discovery of the extent of Fuchs' systematic betrayal of the West's most secret nuclear discoveries that had wrecked Anglo-American trust and co-operation for eight long years. They all knew that. None of this was new –

'General Freeman,' began Professor John Rogers, senior Consultant to the Atomic Energy Authority, 'I really think we –'

'Bear with me, Professor,' commanded General Freeman. The Professor shifted in his chair and fell silent. Freeman went on: 'On that date, gentlemen, Fuchs appeared before Lord Justice Goddard in Number One Court at the Old Bailey, where he was charged with two offences under Britain's quaint but nevertheless effective Official Secrets Act. One: that on a day in 1947, for a purpose prejudicial to the safety or the interests of the State, he communicated to a person or persons unknown information relating to atomic research which might be useful to an enemy.' Freeman paused to glance down at his notes. 'Two: that during 1945 he committed a similar offence here in the United States. At that time Fuchs had been employed by the Atomic Research Department at Los Alamos, New Mexico. Prior to that date he had been engaged on the gaseous diffusion process at Oak Ridge, Tennessee, where he was closely involved in the then top-secret process involving the separation of fissionable uranium 235.'

Now General Freeman killed the projector and stepped away from the machine. 'In July 1949 Great Britain and the United States of America were deeply alarmed to discover there had been an atomic explosion – a test – within the Soviet Union. It had taken five years for the people at Los Alamos, working in great secrecy, to complete their re-research, to build that first atomic weapon. Now the Soviet Union – that nation of poor, dumb peasants – had done it in two.'

Click. Another slide, this one showing Fuchs sunk in the back of a police car between two large plain-clothes detectives, the glint of steel at his wrists just visible beneath the folds of a blanket. Freeman paused while they studied the photograph, silent now as they waited on his words. 'There was your reason, your leak. Having confessed to his old friend Wing Commander Arnold, Harwell's security officer, who was already hot on his tail, Fuchs was sentenced to fourteen years in prison.'

Click. Another photograph. Fuchs mounting the stairs to a Polish airliner. 'He served nine, gentlemen – just nine. Notice the smile? Professing a genuine regret that he had harboured communist sympathies, made all those dinky little trips to the Soviet Embassy, Fuchs flew out to Schonefeld, East Germany, in June 1959. After a summer spent with his ailing father in a chalet somewhere to the north of Berlin, Fuchs disappeared from sight. Within a few short weeks, the western world lost interest in him. Out of sight, out of mind. There were other spies, other scandals.'

The room was silent as Freeman stepped back behind the projector once more. 'The end of the story? Not quite. Prior to his "confession" to Arnold at Harwell – a confession that, in any event, only pre-empted his arrest for treason by a few short weeks – Fuchs had been working with the British team investigating the beam weapon concept as Head of Theoretical Physics. Shortly after his arrest, you may remember, the project was abandoned: there was no way they could generate enough electrical power with the available technology. It was –' he searched his mind for a suitable analogy – 'it was like trying to channel every single power source, every single electric light and power station in the British Isles into one single light bulb for one hundredth of a second.' He shrugged. 'Naturally enough, in those days, it simply couldn't be done. The work was shelved, filed, forgotten. The project abandoned – no great sweat, they thought: if we can't do it – hell, there's no way anyone else can, either! Least of all those poor, dumb, stupid peasants inside the Soviet Union!

'And so Fuchs went back to Germany. To the People's Republic.'

He had them now. He had them and they were silent.

Click.

A smiling, older, fatter Klaus Fuchs at some lavish formal banquet. Men were standing around him, clapping, while a familiar figure placed a ribboned medal around his neck. 'Some change of heart,' continued Freeman quietly. All eyes were on the screen. '13 December 1971: Communist Party Chairman Herr Ulbricht presents our little fella with the East German Order of Merit of the Fatherland in gold.' Click: a close-up of the award itself dangling around Fuchs' thin neck. 'In *gold*, gentlemen! Last man before Fuchs to receive that award was Nikolai Alexayev, Soviet Deputy Minister of Defence for Armaments and principal delegate to SALT in '69.

'We've done some checking: it's fairly certain Fuchs spent several years after Schonefeld at the Yefremov Institute in Leningrad. He spent some time working with Andrei Sakharov, father of the Soviet H-bomb, who, in his later work, proposed a way of creating super-magnets with sufficient charge to power the particle beam weapon concept. Together with Lyudayev, Smivov, Plyushchev, Pavlovsky, Zysin and others, he published his findings, "Magnetic Culmination", in DAN SSSR in 1965. Now, it is our belief that both Fuchs and Sakharov worked with this man –' click: the same function and a close-up of another dinner-suited guest – 'Professor Eduard Ryabov, one of the Soviet Union's leading high-energy physicists. Professor Ryabov is currently head of development at Semipalatinsk.'

General Freeman switched off the projector and moved round to the table with the written evidence he would shortly lay before the Board. He picked up the nearest file, riffled through a batch of satellite photographs and held them briefly aloft. 'BigBird photo-reconnaissance. With the current state of the art, we can tell if the can of beer you're holding in your back yard is open or closed. In the next three or four days I will reveal what I believe to be the true depth of Fuchs' betrayal. I intend to show you also just why I believe the intellectual arrogance of our learned scientific community constitutes the single major post-war disservice to the North Atlantic Alliance. The dimensions of that blind, arrogant, self-serving underestimation of Soviet ability and determination are tantamount, I believe, to nothing less than an act of gross national betrayal . . .'

Frank Yates drove into Hagerstown and parked in a quiet side street a hundred yards from his objective.

Picking his route carefully, working always with the blind side of the building in his favour, he jogged swiftly over the grass and across the sidewalk. Jacket buttoned, automatic still tucked into his waistband, he made the last few yards under cover of the neighbour's parked camper and flattened himself against the weatherboard walls of Pligin's apartment.

No sound came from within the building as he stood there planning his next move. There were no cars parked nearby, no clues. Tucked away out of sight from both the main road and the neighbours nearby, Frank felt he was in no immediate danger of detection. He eased his tight grip on the butt of his weapon and swallowed. Pligin might be in there alone. Or he might be out; the place could be deserted, empty. Probably was. Christ, what a mess!

He settled, finally, upon a compromise: he would remain where he was for a further half hour. If nothing had happened by then, he would hammer on the front door, take his chances. He reviewed the alternatives glumly. Short of calling up the US Marines and taking the place by storm, there weren't any. Call in the local police, the FBI, Military Intelligence? He grimaced. They'd all be able to read about it in the papers. The General would love it, love it to pieces.

Twenty minutes rolled by, and Frank began cursing under his breath. Then, quite suddenly, he heard the sound he had been waiting for, hoping for: the thump of a man's tread as he came down that bare interior staircase. He pressed back against the wall, drew the pistol and gripped the butt firmly, the weapon still hidden beneath his jacket.

There was the rattle of the chain on the door and the dry creak of hinges as someone stepped out on to the porch and pulled the door closed behind him. As it shut, Frank heard the low murmur of voices from somewhere upstairs. He waited a few moments longer, pressed flat against the blind side of the old building and then risked a single, snatched glance around the wall at the back of the retreating figure. Male, slim, early thirties – with a mane of thick, glossy hair.

The man disappeared. Four minutes passed and then there was the surge of a car's motor drawing closer. The vehicle idled slowly along the pathway and braked to a halt around the corner from Frank's position, so close he could have reached out and patted the bonnet.

The engine stopped, a car door opened and there was the whine of the audible seat-belt warning indicator. The car door closed and there was the faint jangle of keys. The apartment door opened and closed to the creak of dry hinges and the thump of steps as the man climbed the wooden stairs to Pligin's apartment.

Frank let out his breath in a soundless sigh and risked another glance around the corner, a plan pushing him towards a decision. He glanced down at the heavy pistol, checked the magazine and slipped off the safety catch.

Upstairs, Ferris heard Nicholson return and, leaving Pligin in the spare bedroom, slipped back to the landing. 'OK?'

Nicholson nodded. 'Ready to go. It's just outside.'

Ferris nodded and turned to Lydia Prolev. 'Time to go, lady.'

'And Viktor? What about Viktor?'

'I'll see about him.' He opened the bedroom door and slipped his head inside. 'You're to stay in there, understand? One full hour – and you can forget about the phone. I'll see to that right now.' He banged the door closed, crossed to the telephone and ripped the line out of its socket with one savage jerk.

'OK, we're moving: you first –' he jabbed a finger at Nicholson – 'Then the woman, then me. Let's go.'

Frank heard the steps on the stair. One – two – three different people, he judged, all coming downstairs, accompanied by the low murmur of voices. The chain came off the door and the voices were suddenly right in his ear:

'. . . chose to come with you.' That was Lydia.

'. . . discuss that later.' One of the men.

Frank began counting under his breath: one monkey – two monkey – three monkey – four monkey and –

He spun round the corner, left hand gripping the edge of the wall, right hand holding the levelled pistol across the support of his own left forearm. He thumbed back the hammer.

'Stand perfectly still,' he commanded. 'Move and I fire.'

'Frank!' Lydia spun round and took half a step towards him.

'Freeze! You too, Lydia!'

They froze.

His ears had not deceived him. There were three of them. One man was frozen in the act of reaching down to the handle on the car door, the keys in his hand; a pace or two behind him stood Lydia Prolev, clutching her handbag, half-turned towards Frank; and a tall, balding man bringing up the rear, frozen now with his back to Lydia as he bent to lock the apartment door behind him.

'What do you –' began the man by the car.

'Don't talk. Don't move. Don't anything,' snapped Frank, the dark gleaming mouth of the automatic covering them all with impartiality. A basic animal sense warned him that the man by the apartment door represented the greatest threat, and the muzzle of the gun moved a quarter of an inch. 'You – the man by the door – spread your hands against the door above your head. That's right, that's good. Now I want to see you press against that door. Go on, press! Good – keep it like that. You – the man with the car keys – drop them on the ground. Do it now, slowly, slowly – or I'll blow your head off. Good.'

The keys dropped to the ground with a tiny tinkle. Frank's hand came off the edge of the wall and he moved position, both hands now clasping the gun, legs bent and flexed slightly as he moved around the little group. He could see the man by the door watching him under his raised arms.

'OK. We're going inside again. Lydia goes first, then you, then Mr Tall. Lydia – you're to go up the stairs and stop on the landing. Clear?'

'But I –'

'Is that clear?' he snapped.

'Yes, I understand.'

'Then do it. The man by the door: three paces back, arms still raised. Do that now.'

They went upstairs. On the landing 'Lydia: into the lounge. Both of you: you're to lie down on your stomachs on the landing. LIE DOWN!' They lay down and Frank stepped slowly over their legs, the muzzle of his pistol pressed tight against the base of each neck as he moved past them and towards Lydia. Finally, he called the two men through into the lounge. Presently all three were seated facing him across the small room.

'Now what?' asked the taller of the two with faint amusement. He might have been about to suggest a new indoor game on a wet afternoon. Frank glanced from one to another. What indeed? He looked across at the telephone. Reinforcements? Most definitely.

He picked up the receiver and placed it carefully on the table. He bent down to dial – and heard the single, broken signal.

'And there was nobody there,' chided the tall man with a gentle smile. 'What a pity, Captain Yates. You're all alone.'

'If you want to keep the use of your hands, be quiet,' ordered Frank softly. 'Lydia – are they armed? Do they have any guns?'

'I don't think so. I . . . I don't know.'

'OK, I'll have to search them. Come over here –'

'Frank –'

'Come over here, point this gun at them –'

'Frank! Listen to me! It's over, finished! I have to return to the Soviet Union. They have my son. They have Misha!'

'Say all that again, slowly,' commanded Frank, his mind reeling.

'Soon after you left for the school, the telephone, it goes again, yes? I think it is you but it is these . . . these men. They say that Misha will be . . . harmed if I do not return. He will be killed if I do not go back immediately. They tell me that if I do this, if I go back, he will not be harmed.'

'And you believe them?' demanded Frank roughly.

'I *must* believe them. What else can I do? They have told me also that –' the words broke off and Lydia's eyes flew suddenly wide with horror – 'Frank,' she whispered in a small voice. Frank almost fell for it, almost spun round to follow that slim, shaking finger –

'What is it?'

'Under . . . under the door. There is . . . something. I think . . . I think . . . oh, God – Viktor . . . I think it is . . . it is blood.' She half rose to her feet as thoughts snapped together in Frank's mind. He sprang away, gun still levelled.

'Sit down! Pligin. Viktor Pligin. Where is he?' Again Lydia raised that slim finger, her eyes clamped wide to a spot at the base of the bedroom door.

'Don't pay any att—' began the tall man. The gun snapped round and he fell silent.

'That man – the tall one,' whispered Lydia huskily. 'He says he must talk to Viktor. In private. In there.' She frowned. 'But . . . just before we go we hear them! We could hear them talking, talking! In there.'

'Hear them?'

Lydia paused as realization flooded in. 'No,' she said slowly. 'No, we heard only one. We heard only that man.' The finger moved to point accusation at Ferris. A flicked glance over his shoulder told Frank that Lydia Prolev was not lying.

Blood was seeping under the bedroom door.

He backed towards the bedroom, jerked open the door and glanced inside. He banged it closed a second later and stood rocking gently on his feet, fighting in full view of his prisoners to keep the waves of nausea and vomit behind clenched teeth.

Ferris and Nicholson watched him closely through narrowed eyes, watched as the pistol came up and the finger tightened bone-white on the trigger guard. Frank's index finger slipped on to the trigger itself and lay there. Quietly. New death, fresh death, was suddenly very close.

The room was still.

'You did *that*?' asked Frank quietly, the gun pointing rock-steady at Ferris's temple. 'You did that and then *pretended that thing in there was still alive*?'

Ferris remained impassive. Nicholson glanced at him briefly but said nothing.

Frank glanced at Lydia. 'And you say you're going back to the Soviet Union? With people like *these*?' He took a deep breath. 'I want you to go in there, Lydia. Go on, take a look.'

'No, no. I –'

'TAKE A LOOK, DAMNIT!' shouted Frank. Lydia stood up slowly and walked hesitantly towards the last room Viktor Pligin had entered in his life. Frank backed with her towards the door. He opened it and pushed Lydia forward. 'Go on, take a look,' he ordered more gently.

Lydia stepped into the bedroom.

Lydia Prolev glanced inside the room, let out a single gasp of horror and then backed away blindly, a hand to her mouth.

'Seen enough?' demanded Frank roughly, his eyes on Nicholson and Ferris as they sat forward silently, gauging their moment, the chances. 'You still want to trust these two bastards? You still want to go back to sweet mother Russia with these shits?'

'I have no choice, Frank! They will kill him, don't you understand? They said they would *castrate* him; they would send me pictures . . . photographs, if I did not do what they say. But . . . but *that*?' Her head turned towards the half-open door, her eyes looking through the partitioning to the bleeding corpse her mind saw still.

'You go back with these two and you're dead anyway, Lydia, you understand? You're dead, Misha's dead – you've both had it, wiped out. It's the only currency they know –'

'I must go with them, Frank! I have no other choice –'

'You have a choice! Right now – I'm giving you one! Stay here – stay here with me. We'll get him out. Christ knows how, but we'll get him out, I promise you! We'll –'

'Frank! You mean that? Truly – !' She turned and jarred Frank's pistol arm in her eagerness.

It was all the opening Ferris needed, all he had been waiting for.

As the gun went up Ferris flung himself to his feet, lashed out at the coffee table in front of him and rolled over the back of his chair towards the door. Nicholson leapt to follow as the table crashed into Frank's legs with agonizing force. Frank cursed, pushed Lydia sprawling into a corner, hopped awkwardly over the coffee table and lunged after them towards the door. Ferris was already halfway down the stairs, Nicholson four paces behind. Frank closed the distance with Nicholson, raised the pistol and chopped once, hard, at the back of that gleaming head of hair. Nicholson went down without a sound. By the time he had stepped over the sprawled body the front door was banging back on its hinges and the tall man had gone.

Frank ran downstairs, looked outside, locked the door and returned upstairs. Then he bent over the crumpled shape of Nicholson, inspected the thin trickle of blood that seeped from beneath the glossy hair, and straightened up. He'd got one, anyway. That at least was something, some small kernel of satisfaction to be gleaned from the débâcle. Meanwhile, Viktor Pligin was still lying sprawled on the bare mattress behind that door, his throat neatly cut from ear to ear, a heavy carving knife lying behind the body. Frank glanced at Lydia. She sat quivering in an armchair, her eyes still sick with the horror of what she had been forced to see.

Frank crossed to the main bedroom, ripped a blanket off the bed, twisted open the door to the spare room and stepped inside, his mind and stomach steeled against the thick, sickly-sweet stench of death.

Pligin lay sprawled back, almost spread-eagled against the dirty mattress like some shabby offering, his eyes staring wide at the ceiling as though witnessing their own extinction. As Frank paused at the threshold, a fat fly crawled greedily across the staring face towards the rich feast below the ugly, gaping mouth. Frank stepped carefully over the pools of congealing blood towards the stiffening corpse. What did they say, eight pints? Seven? With Viktor Pligin, it looked as though someone had been generous. Frank tossed the blanket over the butchered remains of the former airline steward. Even as he turned away, the first dark stains began to seep through the thick blanket like dark ink through blotting paper. Frank stepped outside, closed the door firmly and kicked the rug over the stains beneath the door.

Lydia Prolev was watching him intently, a slim trembling

hand unconsciously clutched to her own throat. 'What have you done?' she asked now in a low frightened voice. 'What have you done to him? To . . . to Viktor?'

'One thing I didn't do was give him mouth to mouth.' She flinched at that as though struck and Yates regretted the words instantly. 'I'm sorry, Lydia, I didn't mean that. I've covered him over. It'll have to do. It's time we were moving.'

The woman made no attempt to get to her feet but just sat there listlessly, her mind still grappling with the realities of death and the fresh after-taste of terrors unimagined. At last 'You meant what you said?' She roused herself. 'About the boy? About Misha?'

Frank's attention was elsewhere as he bent low over Nicholson, searching through his pockets urgently, counting the seconds they delayed their flight. He found nothing. He laid a finger lightly against the man's bare throat and Lydia started violently as though he was about to pay the man back in kind. He smiled grimly. Did she really think he was capable of that?

'It's OK,' he reassured her. 'I'm just checking his pulse.' There it was, steady and strong.

'Frank – about Misha: you meant what you said? You promise?'

'Yeah, sure – I promise.' They'd have to move fast. But not back to the apartment in Georgetown – anywhere but there. To a motel somewhere. Anywhere. He grabbed her wrist and tugged her none too gently to her feet. 'Come on – time to be moving. We've got to go. Unless you want to be roped in with that?' He jerked a thumb roughly at the closed door behind them, and the stark reminder jolted her out of that state of leaden, stunned resignation. Lydia began to move slowly towards the stairs. Frank scooped up her handbag, crammed it into her hands and propelled her sharply towards the stairs with a last backward glance at the apartment. They descended the bare staircase with Frank moving impatiently behind the woman. At the bottom he held her back, opened the door and peered cautiously outside.

Nothing. A few kids over in the distance, the whine of an early lawnmower somewhere across the block. The man? He considered him briefly. He'd be long gone. 'Come on, Lydia – with me, now. Quick as you can – and keep your eyes open.' Lydia stepped reluctantly out of the apartment, Frank banged the door, locked it behind them and then led the way swiftly across the grass towards his car, a hand on the butt of his gun beneath his jacket.

They reached his car without incident. Other vehicles passed by quietly; pedestrians waited to cross by the lights further up the street, and a delivery van was pulled in to the kerb half a block away – but that was all. Of the tall killer there was no sign. Lydia reached for the door catch and slipped into the front passenger seat as Frank glanced about him and then dropped to his knees to look beneath the chassis. No tell-tale wires. He rose and brushed the dust from his trousers. He looked around hurriedly; still there was no sign of danger. 'There's a catch under the dash,' he told her urgently. 'A lever. Pull it towards you.'

She glanced, fumbled, pulled – and the hood popped up. Frank lifted the engine cover and inspected the motor with a swift eye. Nothing there, either. He banged down the hood and climbed behind the wheel. He turned on the ignition and the engine sprang to life. Lydia Prolev leant across and grasped his arm. 'Frank, I want to –'

'Later, OK? Let's get clear first,' he interrupted, assuming carelessly that grateful, perhaps even tearful, thanks were on the way. He was wrong. Lydia Prolev leant over and almost wrenched the keys out of the ignition.

'Frank, look at me!' she commanded. Startled, he glanced across at the tense, pale face, at the brown eyes now wide with shock and the beginnings of something else – anger.

'OK, Lydia: so tell me. I'm looking.'

'We have a bargain now – a deal, you will remember?' she said gravely. 'I have your word: you and the General – you must find a way of getting my son away from those people so that –'

'Just how the hell am I supposed to persuade the –?'

'I have your word, Frank! Do not try and change things

now! Back in there with those . . . those animals, you made
to me that promise –'

Frank banged the steering wheel in exasperation.
'Lydia, I rescued you from those bastards. Don't you
think –?'

'I did not ask you to come, to . . . to interfere! And if you
had not given me your word regarding the boy, then I
would not be with you now! I would be with them! Do you
understand? It is my son that is important to me – not your
America, your General, not poor Viktor – not even you,
Frank. Misha. Misha is what matters to me! All that matters
to me,' she ended.

Frank looked at her silently and felt a sudden sadness. A
long moment passed and then she reached out and squeezed
his arm impulsively. 'I am sorry, Frank, that I must be so
cruel, but it is true. And yes, thank you,' she added simply.
'Thank you for coming to the rescue like . . . like your
Seventh Cavalry, no? You . . . you were very brave.'

'Bullshit,' snapped Frank. 'Bullshit and crap, Lydia.
Pure crap.' He twisted the key in the ignition, banged in
the handbrake, and the car shot out into the quiet street in
a spurt of angry gravel.

:: THE HEARING: DAY ONE (CONTINUED)

'. . . what I am saying, what you will find amply supported
in great detail in those papers before you, is that the Soviet
Union is now close to perfecting a charged-particle beam,
an anti-ballistic missile system that will shortly be capable
of vaporizing our ICBMs as they re-enter the earth's
atmosphere and head down towards their target –'

'It's a silo-based system, I take it?' interrupted Sam
Tolland with heavy, crude sarcasm. 'Or maybe it's fired
from space?'

'My information is that it is a land-based system,'
replied Freeman evenly. 'Space deployment would be too
costly, too advanced – at this stage. It's a defensive system,
gentlemen. We can be grateful for that, at least.'

'You maintain the Soviets have damn' nigh perfected a

way, not just of *containing a nuclear explosion* in a man-made sphere, but of actually switching it to some kind of holding point and then squirting the resulting stream of atomic particles – electrons, protons, neutrons, the whole works – out into space to zap our missiles as they re-enter the earth's atmosphere – am I getting it about right?'

Freeman nodded. 'That's about it.'

'By implication, General Freeman, you're suggesting the credibility of deterrence, of mutual assured destruction – the balance of terror, as the newspapers like to call it – all that is falling apart?' said another voice quietly.

Freeman turned and nodded sombrely at Professor James R. Disman, a colleague from his early Pentagon days and the nearest thing he had to an ally in the room. 'That would follow, Professor, certainly.'

'And the MX project?' added Disman softly.

Freeman shrugged. 'I don't care how you hide them, gentlemen – you're not gaining a whole heap of beans if they're punched out of the sky the moment they try to achieve penetrability. You might as well save yourself the fare.'

He paused, then 'I want to go back to concepts: one of the hardest elements to grasp in this whole business, this whole particle–beam scenario, is the enormity of the proposal itself. It's wide open to ridicule, just for a start – hell, we tried it, didn't we? Back in the fifties? We tried it and got nowhere. So what we're up against here, apart from a bad case of scientific indigestion –' Disman alone smiled – 'is the original Not Invented Here attitude, the exact same trap we in the Air Force fell into over the Army's Jupiter missile programme back in the fifties.' General Freeman waved a hand at the thick manila folders he had lain before the Board. 'Those reports you have there outline the six main road-blocks, the main technical road-blocks, facing the Soviet Union or anyone else who attempts to develop a beam weapon.

'It is my belief – one, I assure you, I have arrived at only after the most careful study I have ever devoted to any single subject in my entire career – that the Soviet Union has overcome them all.'

He paused to hold up a hand and tick items off on his fingers: 'Explosive generation, flux compression, power transportation, energy storage, the switching mechanism itself and, finally, electron injection.

'My belief that these problems have been solved is confirmed not simply by the content of my report which you will shortly read, but by at least one academic footnote the significance of which will not be lost on any of you.'

Freeman paused to pick up a copy of a Soviet weekly newspaper. He folded the paper open and glanced up. 'In recent weeks no less than four top Soviet physicists have been elevated to the Soviet Academy of Sciences: G. A. Mesyats, for his work on switching mechanisms; A. I. Pavlovsky, for work with pulsed power systems; V. M. Titov, for his work on energy generation; and S. L. Mandlestam, for contributions to accelerator development.' He laid the newspaper carefully aside. 'That information is not assembled at random by United States Air Force Intelligence – I read it to you just as it appeared in *Izvestia*, 1st February.' He paused. 'If I am allowed one projection to add to what I see as the significant pattern in that development, it would be this: for the last five years at least, each of those men has been working at a place called Semi-palatinsk. Under a Professor Ryabov. Professor Eduard Ryabov.'

General Clarke Freeman stepped back behind the projector and paused, finger on the switch. 'Semipalatinsk: what do we know about it?' A slide snapped into view showing its exact location south of Novosibirsk and north-east of Lake Balkhash. Click again, as General Freeman switched to slides showing a series of sequential 'Early-Bird' satellite reconnaissance photographs. 'It's the underground test centre for ABM warheads – that much the Soviets have as good as admitted already. They do nothing without good reason, and that, in my opinion, suggests it's a blind. Certainly, it's one of the most secure Soviet nuclear faculties within the Union – more remote, more protected, even, than Tyuratam away there to the south-west.'

He glanced at his audience. All eyes were on the screen. 'Yet we believe all that is almost – he searched for the right word – 'almost *unimportant*, compared with the real function and purpose of Semipalatinsk. Take a look at these photographs.'

The projector blinked away, and for the next six minutes General Freeman took the members of America's Nuclear Intelligence Board past the wire, the fences and the sentries, the dogs and the surveillance devices, on a flat, one-dimensional bird's-eye tour of the nuclear site that was so safe from physical infiltration, yet so vulnerable to the high-definition cameras working away in eerie silence 50,500 feet above the earth.

Presently General Freeman's fingers fiddled impatiently with the focus ring. Snapping into sharp detail came a close-up of a long, low building. An anonymous technician was caught, frozen, as he walked towards a stationary truck parked beside a building nearby. The intrusion of frail, fallible humanity into so sterile, so specific, so sophisticated an environment looked almost – untidy.

General Freeman pointed briefly at the larger building. 'We believe this building pictured at the west of the complex, within this inner security fence, houses the first Soviet collective accelerator,' he announced simply. 'The building itself is two hundred feet wide, over seven hundred feet long, and has walls of reinforced concrete that are, by our estimation, more than ten feet thick. What you see there –' he pointed – 'is a sand butt at the end of the building.'

Another picture slid into view. 'We've been watching this place for quite some time – what we've learned has more than rewarded our patience, our series of informed hunches. At a conservative estimate, the Soviet Union has ploughed something in excess of five hundred million dollars into this one complex alone. Look here.' Again the picture changed. 'Four deep holes, each dug through solid granite formations to a depth of three hundred feet; mine-heads built over each opening, the tons of rock removed to leave a large underground chamber at least fifty-five feet in diameter. IR photography shows they've shifted something in excess of twelve thousand cubic feet of material. Why? Well, one answer may be here.' Click.

The slide showed heavy transporters moving huge metal dishes along a concrete causeway. 'What are these spheres for? We think they're the thick outer shell the Soviets will use to contain that underground nuclear explosion. The one that can't possibly exist. Only we've checked against the dimensions of that hollow underground chamber. The measurements fit. Exactly.'

The slide changed again. 'This satellite photograph is the most recent taken of the Soviet experimental installation at Sary Shagan near the Sino-Soviet border. It's a Pavlovski generator – an explosive-drive magnetic flux device used to convert chemical energy into explosive energy. As the chemical has a very light weight-to-power ratio it is possible to construct very compact power sources with a high energy output. Fantastic as it might sound, these power packs are so light they could one day be put into an earth-orbiting satellite and used as a weapons concept that we may have to consider seriously in the not too distant future. However, that day isn't here yet.'

He paused, glanced up at the silent, listening faces.

'Two final items for you today, gentlemen. One: a town in Ontario, Canada – a place called Timmins – suffered massive electronic interference on a scale never experienced anywhere else before: airport shuts down, radios are jammed, the whole town just folds up. They thought at first it was freak atmospherics – northern lights.' He shook his head emphatically. 'It wasn't. Not by a long shot. Source of origin? The Soviet Union. We believe it was the first-ever deployment of over-the-horizon radar. OTH would be essential, gentlemen, if you're about to test just such a beam weapon. That beam weapon would only be as good as the "eyes" that gave it early warning of imminent target acquisition.'

The chamber was absolutely silent.

'Your second item?'

'Two: just under a year ago, we ran a series of routine photo-recon missions over a whole series of Soviet nuclear test sites. Strictly routine. On more than one occasion in the past we've caught them out in the open with a process in hand they've been protecting so secretly we *could* only stumble upon it by accident, by chance. Eleven months ago we took pictures, satellite pictures, of this test site –' click – 'the bunkers there to the right of the picture are old. They were used years ago to house SS-7 test personnel. See them? They're quite distinct. Now, take a look at this – same site, same location, exactly the same co-ordinates, taken about a month ago. Notice anything different?'

Freeman glanced at the members of the Board and saw the eyes widen in realization. 'Right! Where are the trees? Where's the bunker complex? There's nothing, nothing but a heap of rubble. And the course of the river – see? It's been changed. Oh – and one more thing, gentlemen: it's radioactive. IR trace-back samples indicate it's radioactive. Four square miles of it.'

An hour later General Freeman was killing time, talking desultorily to his two aides in the large empty chamber as they waited for the six-man Nuclear Intelligence Board to complete their analysis of his first technical report.

Suddenly General Freeman was aware of a man standing at his elbow. He turned to acknowledge the rigid salute of one of the uniformed guards. 'Yes?'

'General Freeman? Urgent message for you, sir. Would you come this way? There's a phone right along the corridor.'

Freeman followed the man's respectful pointing finger and picked up the receiver. 'This is General Freeman.'

'Captain Yates, General. I'm calling on an open line –'

'Frank? What's the word?'

Briefly, Frank explained. Then 'She'd been picked up by the other firm. She wanted to go back with them. She wanted to go home. They were most persuasive.'

'She *what*?'

'They told her there was some trouble at home. With the family. There was pressure on her to go back to the old country.'

'Do you have any idea how important –'

'I think it's OK, General. I persuaded her to stay.'

'Good, Frank. Good –'

'At a price, General.'

'Price? What price?'

'I said we'd look after the boy ourselves.'

'Be more specific,' snapped General Freeman.

Frank drew a deep breath. 'I made a promise, General. I said we'd help her son. Over here. I said we would arrange it ourselves. It was the only way: no son, no evidence.'

'Jesus Christ,' muttered Freeman. There was a short, glacial silence, then 'Where are you now?'

'On my way in. With the lady.'

'Don't let her out of your sight, Frank –'

'There's more, General – and none of it's good. Our steward friend won't be making contact again. The other firm had a word with him. He's closed down operations.'

General Freeman glanced down the corridor. The green light above the tall polished doors was winking steadily, indicating that the Board was about to resume.

'We need to talk, Frank – you, me and the woman. Call me back in a couple of hours from somewhere secure. I'll come out to you there. In the meantime – don't lose her. Right now that woman's more precious than diamonds.'

Freeman replaced the receiver and strode back towards the hearings chamber.

*

The KGB's selection of Ferris had taken many years. It had been a long, laborious, painstaking process as, around him, others less suited to the subtle rigours of foreign operations were weeded ruthlessly from the ranks of potential recruits to the First Chief Directorate's Department V. Among much else that went with the planting of an Illegal, Ferris had been trained to recognize and instantly crush the false pride, the doggedness, the stupid, blind, press-on-regardless determination which was so beloved by the West and was wilfully, criminally encouraged by authority as a ready substitute for clear, rational thinking. Ferris was trained, therefore, to cut and run, to recognize developments and to extricate himself instantly from an operational situation deteriorated beyond his total control. To step on to dangerous ground through miscalculation, blind chance – through error, even – was one thing; to remain there was crass stupidity, whose just reward was detection, humiliation, even death.

Thus a western operative would have disguised the extent of his error, delayed reporting in and then misled Control as to the likely consequences of his mistake. Ferris simply reported that the Prolev woman had been retaken by the American, sketched out his plans for retrieval and awaited confirmation from New York Control on the other end of the phone.

Seated behind his desk in the Soviet Rezidentura in New York, Major Dmitri Muratov was not unhappy. He was pleased, not simply because Ferris had reacted according to training but because even this latest development played perfectly into the wider picture sketched by Moscow earlier that same week. Briefly, and in a few short words, Muratov brought Ferris up to date.

*

The Nuclear Intelligence Board had taken little more than an hour to digest and absorb the broad import of General Freeman's highly technical submission, and whatever naive, subconscious hopes the General might have harboured about a sudden, almost biblical conversion to his own beliefs had been still-born the moment that heavy door had opened and he glanced at his watch. Seventy, seventy-five minutes. That was all the time it had taken. It was a bitter realization, which brought with it a bleak, despairing anger as the six men walked out on to the raised platform, their brows furrowed in . . . in . . . what had it been? Disapproval? Impatience? Something like that. Only one man, Professor Disman, had shot him an apologetic glance as they settled down in their high backed chairs.

Seventy-five minutes. He had expected they would spend a couple more hours at least just exploring the full technical linkage of the submission he had taken so many grim hours, so many months, to distil into cold, hard print. Yet here they were, loaded for bear and hunting trouble.

Once again, it was to be Sam Tolland who was the first to take careful aim. 'They tell me two swallows never make a summer, General. I guess you could say that applies here too.' He leaned forward fatly, comfortably, and Freeman realized with disgust that the man was actually *enjoying* himself. 'No one here, not one of my colleagues on the Board, disagrees that *something* a mite unusual is going on at this place, Semipalatinsk, but it's the "what" that sticks in our throats, General. That's where we part company.'

He waved Freeman's report carelessly, as though it was a paper of little consequence. 'Your report here spends most of its time suggesting that the Soviet Union is engaged in developing the components for high-energy technology – right, General? But there's nothing *new* in that. We don't need –' he flicked through the bound pages – 'we don't need fifty-nine pages just to tell us something we know already. As a matter of fact, the Soviets themselves make little attempt to deny such work is in progress, isn't that the case, Professor Rogers?'

'That is so,' nodded the Professor.

'As for the rest,' continued Tolland, 'your theory's just too far-fetched for serious consideration. How the hell can you ask us to accept that the Soviet Union, the people who run a traditional second-best to the US when it comes to sophisticated technology, have found a way of actually welding two steel halves together that's strong enough to contain a major nuclear explosion?'

There was more like that. A whole solid hour and a half of scorn, disbelief and scepticism, first from Tolland and then from Tom Greener. Shortly after 4 p.m. the Board adjourned. General Freeman would have a chance to continue his presentation at 10 a.m. the following morning. As General Freeman gathered up his notes and the few papers with a low security classification that would not remain under armed guard in the chamber overnight, he had been approached almost diffidently by the one ally he had on the Board, the only man he believed might yet throw in a word or two in his support once the Board retired behind locked doors, Professor James Disman.

The two shook hands. 'Hello, Jim. How am I doing?' asked Freeman softly, grimly. Both men knew the question was unnecessary. Disman shrugged narrow shoulders and gave a theatrical swallow as though forcing down something unpleasant.

'That early stuff, Clarke – all that business about Fuchs and his Soviet award? Your Int. about that place Timmins and the bunkers out there in the middle of the desert?' Freeman nodded. 'That was good, Clarke – sharp, too. It made an impression. You really had them going with you for a while. Not far enough, you understand, but, nevertheless, it was impressive.'

'And the rest of it? The report itself? That was the guts of it, Jim. You know that.'

Disman shook his head sorrowfully. 'You know that. I know that. But those people?' He jerked a thumb over his shoulder. 'Rogers, Tom Greener, Sam Tolland? You're cutting no ice with them, Clarke, believe me.'

He gripped Freeman's uniformed sleeve suddenly. 'You haven't got *enough*, damn it! You're falling short, Clarke, you're falling short every time! You'll need more than that to convince people like Tolland. They're –'

'A .45 would convince Tolland, Jim. That and about damn' all else. Why, the man's –'

But Disman was shaking his head sadly. 'Listen to me, Clarke: this thing you've got about particle beams: you're out on a limb – way out. As we've left things tonight you're not going to be on your feet this time tomorrow *unless* you've something pretty damn' conclusive up your sleeve. Greener's going to throw it out – and he'd be right, too.'

Disman gathered up his coat and turned to leave. 'I tell you this, Clarke, for the old days, you know? Because back then you had a lot going for you. We both did. But now? This thing could sink you, Clarke – sink you without trace. And shall I tell you something? Half my fellow Board members would cheer as the ship went down. You want to think about that.'

It was after 6 p.m. that same evening before General Freeman had showered, changed into civilian clothes and slipped
behind the wheel of his wife's white sports car for the hour-
long drive north to the nondescript motel beside the pike
road leading to Dulles International Airport where Frank
Yates and Lydia Prolev were hiding.

The drive through Fairfax and Vienna was swift, the
traffic surprisingly light despite the hour – yet Freeman
felt himself to be in the grip of post-combat exhaustion,
weighed down beneath a heavy, dark brooding as he
remembered Disman's parting, prophetic words of caution
to an old friend: 'something pretty damn' conclusive' –
wasn't that what the man had said was required? Well, he
hadn't got that.

Not by a long shot.

The motel was up ahead somewhere, away on the right.
Freeman lifted his foot, and the sports coupé began to slow
down. Well, he'd know soon: he had to return to Washington this night with nothing less than the promise of whole-
hearted co-operation from a Soviet scientist who had just
been dragged away from the KGB who held her only child
hostage against her silence. Freeman grinned without
humour as he swung the little car off the highway and
crunched across gravel. That shouldn't be difficult, then:
the woman had a straight choice, hadn't she? The life of her
only son against the reputation of an old American war-
horse with a kink in his brain about beam weapons, an old
American war-horse who, by rights, should have died in his
P-38 over the Pacific thirty-five years ago. He swung the
car into a parking bay, switched off the engine and got out.
No problem, then. She'd side with the war-horse, with him.
With freedom, with democracy.

Of course she would.

With a careful glance behind him, General Freeman walked slowly towards the dim low line of chalets, his hand on the unaccustomed weight of the service automatic jammed into a coat pocket, his stern face lit by the flashing glare of the motel sign. He mounted the wooden sidewalk and began counting cabins, his heels echoing hollowly as he walked slowly towards cabin 59. There was the sound of television from within and the glare of the small screen flickered against the drawn curtains. Freeman paused and then knocked softly. He knocked again, louder this time, and the voices fell suddenly silent. He knocked once more.

'What is it?'

A male voice. He recognized it as Yates'. There was an audible click. He recognized that, also.

'Freeman. I'm alone,' he said quietly, his mouth close to the door. As he spoke, a cabin door opened a few paces away and a man staggered drunkenly towards him, a bottle in a brown paper bag clutched in tight fingers. The man stumbled past Freeman on a wave of bourbon fumes and disappeared towards the parked cars as a woman's querulous voice wailed after him like a police siren:

'Harvey! Har-veee – come back here, hon.'

Harvey had the sense to keep going. Now Frank was fumbling the chain off the door. It opened and Freeman slipped quietly inside. The door closed swiftly behind him. Frank uncocked his automatic and laid it carefully on the chipped dresser beside the door.

The room reeked of plastic, disposable austerity. The black and white television was bolted to the floor, and the room, like the liaisons it was most frequently used for, held little of value to either party. It was a place of transit, an anonymous rendezvous for illicit couplings, and as such it suited General Freeman's purpose perfectly.

'Evening, General,' said Frank quietly, his back to Freeman as he slipped the chain on the door.

'Frank – Mrs Prolev.' Freeman nodded briefly at the woman sitting tensely on the edge of the bed, her knees drawn tightly together as though she feared invasion, assault. The woman nodded warily and Freeman unbuttoned his coat. He laid it on the bed close at hand, the pistol making an obvious bulge in the pocket. The woman noticed the weapon, and Freeman watched as the fear sprang into her eyes. He moved casually to block her line of sight and then reached for the bottle of scotch that stood already opened beside a cone of plastic cups and the remains of some pre-cooked meal lying amid the ruins of two paper plates. The scotch was already a quarter empty, and Freeman didn't blame them: the depression inherent in the squalid, silent little room seeped into his soul like some slow poison. As the silence built around him Freeman poured himself a drink. He knocked back the scotch, crumpled the plastic cup into the waste bin and sat down on the edge of the bed.

'OK,' he said finally. 'So tell me: what went wrong. Frank?'

Frank told him.

'Pligin's apartment? How the hell did they cotton on to that?' demanded Freeman angrily.

'Christ knows – and Pligin's not about to tell you, either. He's not about to tell anyone anything. They took him out with a nine-inch steak knife. So much for your security, General.'

Lydia shuddered and reached across for the scotch.

'They? How many of them?'

'Two. Two at least. Maybe more. Two that I saw, anyway.'

'What happened to them?'

'One I left in the apartment. He'll have a headache when he comes to, but that's about all. With any luck the police will be standing over him when he wakes up. I gave them the word as we left, tipped them off about Pligin.'

'And the other one?'

'The other one? Christ knows. He got away. I had him, but he got away.'

'He got *away*? Jesus, Frank –'

'Look – General: he got away, right?' Frank shook his head angrily. 'You've one helluva nerve, General! Sir. Just a few days – that's what you told me: just a few days. And when I asked if Louise would be safe you as good as laughed in my face! Safe? She'd be better off playing with hand grenades!'

'OK, Frank, OK – take it easy. Have a drink –'

'I don't want a drink, damn it! I just want to get this bastard over with, OK?'

'OK, fine.' General Freeman studied his hands, aware that the time for protocol, for insisting on a return to the proper formality, was a long way off. There was an awkward silence. Then, 'You winning before that Board of yours, General?' asked Frank.

General Freeman pulled a face and glanced across at Lydia. 'Could have gone better. Could have gone a whole lot better, matter of fact. That's why I'm here – among other things.'

'And you expect me to – how do you say? – to pull your fat out of the fire? Isn't that the phrase?' asked Lydia quietly, speaking for the first time.

Freeman glanced up sharply. 'Well, certainly, I'd hope that –'

'Frank I trust,' murmured Lydia quietly. 'But you, General?' She glanced up quizzically. 'You, I am not so sure. There is too much anger, too much pressure, aggression. Do I have your word also? The word of the Head of United States Air Force Intelligence?'

Freeman looked at Frank as though he could not believe his ears. Frank smothered a smile: it was probably the first time in his entire service career that General Freeman had been given anything less than a top security clearance.

'I'm not in the habit of breaking my word, Mrs Prolev,' said Freeman frostily. 'But then I'm not aware I've given it – yet. Captain Yates has no authorization to promise United States intervention on foreign soil, far less the snatching of a Soviet national. However, that's by the by: if, after you've given evidence to the Board that is found to be helpful, I can persuade –' but already Lydia Prolev was shaking her head angrily, emphatically.

'When my son Misha is here with me, safe, and un-harmed, then I *might* be prepared to talk to these people of yours. Not before, General. Do you think I am a complete amateur in such matters?'

Freeman glowered at her angrily. 'You don't understand the picture, Mrs Prolev: I can't just wave some kind of fairy wand and pluck whomsoever I want out of the middle of Russia! That sort of –'

'Why? Why cannot you do that? You have done so before –?'

'It has happened, yes,' admitted Freeman grudgingly. 'But that kind of operation takes time: time to make plans, get clearance, sanction funds. It takes a helluva lot of time. It's out of the question.'

'Then so too is the matter of my appearance before this Board of yours, General Freeman. When my boy is here, *then* I might be prepared to co-operate.'

'Look ... er ... Lydia,' tried Freeman clumsily as he leant forward persuasively. 'For the last eleven hours I've been trying to convince a lot of sceptical nuclear scientists that it's time we, the US, paid special attention to the work you and your scientists have been doing at Semipalatinsk. This country's yours now – it's where you're going to have to make your home, with or without that son of yours. If you were prepared to testify that, as a nuclear scientist –'

'Me? A scientist?' Lydia spread her hands expressively. 'How many times must I tell you, General: I am *not* a scientist – I am a psychiatrist. You know? To do with the brain, with the mind. I know nothing about these nuclear matters at ... what was the place? Semi ... Semi ...?'

'Jesus, lady! Who're you trying to kid?' exploded General Freeman angrily. 'You think we're a bunch of goddam amateurs ourselves? You think we don't know about you? You think we haven't been following your career? Christ – we know every move you've made from the day you left Kurchatov! We know who you were working with at Plesetsk, we know why you were transferred to Moscow District, we know when you moved to Semipalatinsk; so don't come the wide-eyed innocent with me, lady – we're just not that dumb!'

Now it was Lydia who spoke. She spoke slowly, quietly and very distinctly. 'You are a stupid man, General Freeman – stupid. You want to know why? I shall tell you: it is for all this, for all these angry words that you use – for your attitude, for your lack of warmth, for your professional desperation that comes with you into this ugly little room like the sickness. But most of all I think, General, because you do not truly care about the little things; about the people, about the families. To you, I and my problems are of no consequence. I am merely a cipher. You are a man of stone. It is good, therefore, that you are with the military. You are made for it. For the life and death, of uniforms, of killing. And you think I am going to talk for you? To save you?'

She smiled like a small child who realizes suddenly that by hurting himself deliberately he will hurt the hateful adults also. 'For you then, General, I will always remain this one thing: a psychiatrist. So go to hell, General: go right to hell.'

*

Most of Moscow was still abed as the teleprinter clattered once briefly and then rattled off the coded prefix that alerted the duty watch: a secret communication was about to be flashed into the Dzerhinsky Square building for the attention of the Head of Directorate T.

The message that followed, handled forward, as always, by the KGB's headquarters on the city's outskirts, was heartening; it was waiting for Mikhail Kostikov a little later in the morning when he arrived at his desk and it was on the top of the folder he took with him for his daily meeting with Igor Bayev, the Head of the First Chief Directorate.

The message came from Rezident Muratov in New York and contained, amid a great deal else, a detailed résumé of the information Ferris had passed on by phone from Hagerstown. Now Igor Bayev studied the signal unhurriedly and then glanced across at his junior.

'It is almost,' he mused quietly, 'almost as if . . . as if they were playing into our hands.' He paused. 'Is that possible?' he asked shrewdly. 'Could *we* be the ones that are being tricked? Duped?'

Mikhail Kostikov shook his head decisively. 'I think not, comrade.'

'May I be permitted a question of a more . . . a more personal nature, comrade?' asked Kostikov as he gathered up his papers to leave.

Bayev looked up guardedly. 'Please.'

'Do you think this General Freeman will bite? Do *you* think he will put aside the coincidence, go for the bait?'

There was a short silence as Bayev pushed a row of sharpened pencils into a neat line.

'Who knows?' He shrugged. 'Most certainly, he will be suspicious. He will check. But – yes, I think he will. He will bite – what choice does he have? What real choice, eh, comrade?'

*

It was cramped, crouched in the back of General Freeman's white sports coupé, cramped and uncomfortable. Lydia had her knees drawn up painfully beneath her chin, her eyes just inches away from the short, stiff hairs on the nape of the General's neck as he drove swiftly down the broad ribbon of highway towards the centre of Washington.

Frank Yates was in the front passenger seat beside the General, yet they drove in silence, with only the car radio to bridge the hostility that had accompanied Freeman's sudden, unexplained decision to take them both back with him into the centre of the city. Lydia had no idea where they were going. She knew only that her legs had gone to sleep and that the General was driving with a fast, fierce anger that was directed back at her. A lorry swept past, sweeping them with its dazzling headlights, and Lydia looked away painfully.

The car pulled to a halt and the three got out on to the rain-slicked sidewalk. Freeman led the way swiftly up a steep flight of marble steps towards the front of an imposing building.

'Frank?' Lydia stumbled and caught his arm. 'What is this place? Why do we come here?'

'It's all right, Lydia: I think I'm getting the picture. This is the New Senate Building. Scene of the General's latest battle, and all that? This is where he's giving evidence to the NIB.'

'But now? It is almost tomorrow. He must be mad,' whispered Lydia.

Frank nodded. 'I'd say that was a distinct possibility.' He put his hand under Lydia's elbow and the two set off again up the steep marble steps. General Freeman was waiting impatiently before a pair of wide glass doors. There was a light beyond in the wide hallway and, beyond that again, darkness save for a further pool of light illuminating a single uniformed security guard seated behind a desk, reading.

General Freeman banged on the glass doors and the man looked up suspiciously. He moved from behind the desk and came forward slowly, a hand resting on the butt of his holstered sidearm, the badges, buttons and appointments of his uniform glittering in the overhead light.

Freeman fished inside his coat and produced his own security pass, which he pressed flat against the locked glass doors, the information it contained proffered inwards. The guard peered forward, nodded in swift recognition and began unlocking the doors top and bottom.

'Evening, sir. May I help you?'

'Good evening, Corporal. General Freeman. Guess you'd say I'm one of the stars in there.' Freeman treated him to a gruff smile and then paused to glance directly into the man's face: 'You're working kinda long swings, aren't you, son?' It was the man who had shown him to the phone earlier in the day. The guard smiled, mollified by recognition. 'I've left some papers inside. OK with you if I go on in and pick them up? Oh – and don't worry about these people, Corporal: they're with me.'

'Well . . . er . . . General, sir. The thing is –' began the guard awkwardly as Freeman began to move past him – 'I really need to –'

'Fifteen minutes, son. That's all. Just fifteen minutes.'

'Well . . . very good, General, sir,' muttered the young guard with a frown of unease as Freeman, Frank and Lydia Prolev manoeuvred quietly past him. They walked down a long, dark corridor, their steps echoing against silent black walls of stone, until, turning a corner, General Freeman passed the phone he had used earlier and saw before him the polished oak doors of the now deserted hearings chamber. Before it, beneath a pool of yellow light, was the figure of another uniformed sentry, busy tugging down the hem of his tunic and adjusting the gleaming black pistol belt at his waist.

With some inner portent of what was to come, the sentry snapped ramrod straight as the party approached, a wisp of smoke spiralling incongruously from the hand held behind his back. General Freeman stopped before him. He sniffed. Then he treated the unfortunate to the swift, glacial glare of inspection he usually reserved for recruits, a glare that missed nothing between the crest of the No. 1 dress hat to the toes of the gleaming patent barrack shoes.

Freeman reached out and gently fastened a blouse pocket before slipping his identification under the man's startled nose. The sentry glanced down. A general, no less. He swallowed hastily and resumed his intense study of the far wall.

'Drop it,' advised Freeman gently. 'Drop it now and stomp it out.'

'Sir?'

'You heard me the first time,' said Freeman, his words echoing into the quiet darkness. 'You're either smoking on post or you're about to burst into flames. Drop it.'

'Er . . . yessir.' The butt fell to the ground, the man managed a small, military step backwards and crushed it out. 'Sorry, sir. It won't happen again.'

'If it does –' Freeman glanced at the name above the right breast pocket – 'Collins, I'll have your hide, you understand me?'

'Yessir.'

'Good. This door locked?'

'Yessir.'

'Open it. I'm going inside for a few minutes. These people too.'

'Right away, sir.' There was a hurried jangling of keys, the creak of heavy oak – and the place was theirs.

*

Despite the forceful arguments, the aggression, he had exhibited before his fellow members of the Nuclear Intelligence Board that morning and afternoon, Sam Tolland leaned, in truth, towards the gentler pursuits of life.

His fellow members would have been surprised, for example, to learn that the overweight Washington businessman with a fabled tolerance for expensive food was the legitimate owner of one of the finest collections of French eighteenth- and nineteenth-century fans in America. They would have been more surprised – and alarmed, and offended – had they learned that such an expensive collection had been assembled with a lavish care funded, not by the fruits of the man's intellectual prowess or business acumen, but by the tawdry currency of treachery and national betrayal converted into negotiable American dollars by an anonymous KGB fund-master.

Now bathed, changed, lightly powdered and wrapped in a pure silk dressing gown one of his former young friends had brought home with him from Saigon, Tolland allowed his eyes to feast greedily upon the contents of a glass-fronted display cabinet as his fingers toyed gently with the slender stem of a chilled wine glass.

Tolland was pleased with himself. Pleased too that very soon the distasteful business of the General would be concluded; pleased also that the call he was expecting at any moment would finally sever the chains of servitude shackled to his fat wrists all those years ago.

He sighed and reached for a large cigar from the inlaid humidor at his side. He lit the cigar carefully, rolled it around his small mouth and puffed wetly. Well, it was all drawing to a close at last. Well, wasn't it? Hadn't it been that man Michael in New York himself who had set the deadline, promised total withdrawal and a return of all compromising papers, documents and photographs after this one last service? Tolland raised his glass and swallowed back the beginnings of excitement.

The phone on the nineteenth-century French side table with the ornate ormolu mounting began its soft, discreet burring. Tolland drained his glass swiftly, patted his lips, laid his cigar carefully aside and reached out a pale, fat hand. 'Yes?' he said carefully.

'Good evening. This is Michael.'

'Good evening, Michael,' replied Tolland cautiously.

'Good evening. You have something for me, I believe?'

'An indication, I'm afraid, Michael. No more than an indication.'

'Do not worry. I am sure that will be sufficient. My people would be most grateful for anything of that nature.'

'Really? Well, then –' Tolland paused, choosing neutral words that would be innocent, meaningless, to a third party. 'I can tell you that it is not going well for the . . . for the party you asked me to look out for, yes? I myself have done all that I can to ensure the questioning is . . . what shall we say . . . reserved? Sceptical? At times, even . . . hostile.'

'Tell me: there are – what? Five of you? Listening?'

'Six. Six including myself.'

'Six. And tell me – how do they divide – as things stand tonight? For or against further action, investigation? Referral upwards?'

'Including myself? Four, possibly five would be against. One definitely in favour of referral upwards, as you put it – but he is a man of little real consequence; a spent force.'

'Good, good,' soothed Michael from New York. 'Do you foresee any difficulties ahead?'

Tolland paused and considered. He recalled Freeman's

promise of his star witness, the scientist from Semi-palatinsk, his ace in the hole. He told Michael this and was mildly surprised when he simply brushed the reference aside and began, instead, to heap effusive thanks on his informer. Tolland therefore judged it prudent to jog the man's memory. 'You haven't . . . er . . . forgotten what was said when last we spoke?'

'About our deal? No, I have not forgotten. The deal stands, Sam. It still stands! Nothing has changed. Your papers will be returned and our . . . arrangement terminated, you have my word.'

'When?' prompted Tolland cautiously.

'I am coming down tonight. I will bring everything with me, personally. I will be arriving shortly after 1 a.m. at the airport. Could you perhaps meet me there? Then I can ensure you are satisfied, that we have forgotten nothing, and then I can return. Would that be satisfactory?' asked Michael unnecessarily.

In his expensive two-storey house outside Washington, Sam Tolland began to tremble. 'Yes . . . yes, that would be . . . satisfactory. Most satisfactory. I . . . I shall meet you. Without fail.'

'Until then – goodbye.'

'Good . . . goodbye.' Sam Tolland replaced the receiver and walked slowly back towards the bottle of white wine cooling quietly in a silver ice-bucket. He tumbled wine into his glass, climbed the fine staircase and entered the master bedroom. He sat for a moment on the heavy pink quilting and regarded himself with suppressed excitement in the mirror on the wall opposite.

There were mirrors on all the walls and there was a mirror, also, on the ceiling. Sam Tolland liked mirrors.

He stood up and raised a glass to his several reflections. 'Out of the woods, Sam boy,' he beamed, he chortled. 'Out of the goddam woods!'

As Sam Tolland toasted his foolish reflections, Nicholson too was waiting for a phone call. Unbeknown to both men,

Nicholson's had been attendant upon the successful conclusion of the conversation between Muratov and Tolland.

Recovering swiftly after Yates' departure and before the police arrived, Nicholson had stumbled away from Pligin's apartment to make his way south to Washington. En route, he too had received new orders. The first of these was to collect a certain package from the mainline station. This he had done. The package stood opened before him on his coffee table. The second instruction was to do nothing, but wait for this phone call.

Now Nicholson was sitting in near darkness, and the welcome gloom of his surroundings had done much to soften the trip-hammer blows that pounded the base of his skull. Presently the phone began to ring. Nicholson winced and lifted the receiver hurriedly.

'The store is closed now,' he opened.

'You have the package?'

'Yes.'

'And the letter?'

'That too.'

'Any problems?'

'No.'

'Good. He will move, I suspect, between twelve and twelve thirty. You will have ample time.'

'On my way.'

'Goodbye,' said Major Dmitri Muratov. He meant it too. In New York, Muratov replaced the receiver and resumed the detailed briefing of his replacement. He had, he assumed, no more than twelve hours.

Behind the gleaming, high oak doors of the New Senate Building's hearings chamber, there was silence.

Most of the sixty-five seats, spread out in a generous half-circle before the speaker's raised platform, were in deep shadow, the only light coming from the single shaded desk lamp at the front of the chamber and the white beam of the slide projector shining ahead on to a blank screen. The atmosphere was tense, theatrical, and the chamber itself had become a place of shadows, of whispered, echoing confidences. Sitting alone two rows back in the shadows, Frank realized it was most certainly calculated. He glanced sideways at General Freeman, who was standing motionless beside the projector. Lydia Prolev sat a few paces in front of him at the illuminated desk, her dark head bowed over a sheaf of papers.

She was reading the General's report, his submission to the Nuclear Intelligence Board.

More time oozed by. Fifteen minutes, twenty, with the only sounds the faint hum of the projector and the regular rustle of pages being turned. Finally Lydia laid the report aside and twisted round.

'Well?' demanded Freeman, the harsh edge to his voice betraying an inner tension. 'Am I right?'

Frank Yates watched the woman shrewdly in the taut silence.

Then Lydia smiled, quizzically. 'Very interesting. Very interesting indeed, General, although –' she paused deliberately, shrugged, and tapped the thick report in an offhand fashion – 'as a mere psychiatrist it is, of course, beyond my –'

'Don't give me that crap!' roared Freeman, smashing his

hand down on the table beside him. Lydia jumped. 'You come on with that kinda talk just one more time and –'

The heavy oak doors opened. 'General? Is everything all right, sir?' asked the guard as he stood framed in the doorway, a hand on his pistol belt.

General Freeman whirled round. 'Get outa here. Everything's fine. Just dandy – go on, beat it.'

'Er . . . yessir. Sorry, sir. On my way.' The man withdrew hurriedly, and the doors closed swiftly behind him.

'You seem to be a little . . . frayed, general?' mocked Lydia.

Frank closed his eyes and sank a little lower in his seat.

'Frayed? Frayed, you say?' demanded Freeman, his voice lashing across the darkened chamber with iced menace. 'Let me show you something. Let me show you something that should put a stop to that "psychiatrist" crap of yours once and for all – your introduction, Mrs Prolev! Your introduction to the members of the Nuclear Intelligence Board! You should find it interesting.'

Lydia said nothing as Freeman turned, swept up a magazine of slides and loaded it deftly into the machine. He paused, gathering his thoughts, buttoning down his anger. When he resumed talking, his voice was quite normal.

The first slide snapped into view: it showed a large, grey building with a line of black limousines drawn up before a flight of imposing stone steps. Flags fluttered at the bonnets, and people were clustered on the steps, talking.

'We could play Guess the City, but I guess you'd start with an advantage, Mrs Prolev. Vienna, Austria: 11 August 1977. The building? The Austbeilung Institute of Nuclear Physics – but then you know that too, don't you, Mrs Prolev? You were there, after all. At the Ninth International Scientific Seminar, you remember?' Using a pointer he picked out a woman in a smart black suit standing on the steps talking to a cluster of white-haired gentlemen. 'There you are, large as life. Guest speaker, if I remember correctly, was Professor Sheyndlin, also from the Soviet Union. Only he went back and you didn't. You came over to us. Turned up at the American Consulate, cool as ice. They must have missed you: the only "psychiatrist" to attend such a select, scientific gathering.' The sarcasm was very pronounced. Lydia said nothing.

The slide changed to a grim, grey frontier post somewhere along the East–West German border. 'Hof, West Germany – just,' supplied General Freeman.

There was a road leading past a line of concrete cones to a lowered red and white barrier beside a low building surrounded by high barbed wire fences. An open-backed lorry was slewed across the road twenty yards behind the barrier, its windshield shattered by gunfire. Long-coated border guards were frozen in mid-stride as they ran towards the lorry, their rifles raised.

Immediately there was an involuntary gasp from Lydia. She was leaning forward intently, her hands gripping the arm-rests of her chair. The picture changed to a telephoto close-up of the lorry's licence plate. 'Recognize the number, Mrs Prolev? You should do. The truck belonged to your husband.'

Before she could reply Freeman snapped on another slide.

A man was outside the lorry now, his hands raised high in the air. A Vopos' ambulance had backed towards the incident and two soldiers were moving towards the open doors carrying a laden, blanket-draped stretcher. 'No!' gasped Lydia, jerking to her feet.

'You had the easy part, Mrs Prolev,' said Freeman sadly. 'Crashing through the border is for amateurs, Mrs Prolev, strictly for amateurs. They never had a prayer. All you had to do was walk up and bang on the front door.'

'No! That's not true! I–'

'Your husband was arrested. After a secret trial he was sentenced. He died soon afterwards in one of the camps on the Archipelago.'

Lydia nodded silently, the tears glistening on her cheeks in the gloom.

'So – what happened to Misha? Whatever happened to your son?'

'I –'

'I'm not really asking the question, Mrs Prolev. We know

that too. We know exactly what happened to Misha.' Freeman raised a pointer so that its shadow fell on to the screen.

'That's him there, on the stretcher,' he said quietly.

'Misha!' The word was ripped from her heart with searing pain.

Freeman waited a cold moment and then held up a hand.

'It's O K. He was sitting up front in the cab with your husband. By some miracle he came through that first fusillade of shots unscathed –'

'I do not understand –' began Lydia. Frank hunched forward, feeling the words with her.

'There was a lot of glass flying about,' continued Freeman remorselessly. 'Cuts to the face and arms, mostly. Damage to one eye. Your son's due to attend the Leningrad Eye Hospital for examination any day now. Trouble is . . .' he paused, stopped there deliberately.

In that moment Frank hated him. He leapt to his feet in the shadows. 'General – there's no need to –'

'Stay out of this, Frank.'

'What the hell are you doing to the woman? Can't you see – ?'

'SIT DOWN, CAPTAIN, GODDAMNIT!' General Freeman whirled and stalked furiously to where Frank was standing. He grabbed him by the arm and pushed him away to a corner out of the woman's hearing. 'What the hell're you trying to pull, Frank? You screwing with her or something? You think –'

'Say that again,' invited Frank with cold, velvet anger.

Freeman shook his head impatiently at his own stupidity.

'I apologize. I didn't mean that, Frank. Listen –' he hissed – 'you think I'm *enjoying* any of this? You think this is how I get my jollies?'

Frank nodded. 'It's possible.'

'Well, screw you, Captain. You're wrong!' Freeman pointed a strong finger towards Lydia, watching them anxiously from within her pool of light as his voice sank to an urgent whisper: 'I'm gonna spell it out one more time, then Christ help you if you foul up on me again.'

He paused, breathing deeply, and then leant closer, a

finger stabbing the air for emphasis. 'We – America – have just ploughed all our trust, our national heritage, every goddam thing we value, into a new generation of missiles that will be as out of date as the bow and arrow long before that daughter of yours is at high school – you reading me, Captain? *That woman there –*' he pointed at Lydia – 'has the details of the Soviet defensive system that's blowing a hole in the very core of deterrence even as we're standing here; she knows all about the Soviet beam weapon that puts all that rinky-dink hardware of ours out on the junk heap – are you getting this, Frank? She holds the key – and with her testimony I can maybe stop this nation of ours becoming as defenceless, as open to Soviet aggression, as a new-born baby. Do you understand? I F I can get her to testify.' Freeman paused. 'Now, I don't give a fuck if I've got to burn a few tails in the process: I'll burn hers, I'll burn yours, I'll even burn my own if it'll help, kapich?'

'I get the picture, General.'

'You bet your goddam life!' Freeman turned abruptly on his heel and returned to the front of the chamber.

'I was telling you about Misha's eye,' continued Freeman smoothly, as though there had been no interruption. 'We understand the condition itself isn't serious, but delay between examination and treatment that could take months –'

'General? What are you trying to tell me?' asked Lydia coldly.

'Your son is suffering from what your medical people call PCD – progressive corneal decay. It means, Mrs Prolev, that your son is going slowly blind. I'm sorry. An immediate corneal graft and the implantation of a plastic lens would arrest the deterioration, but –' Freeman shrugged – 'I don't suppose the sons of defectors come very high on the Soviet priority list.' There was a long silence. Then –

'Such treatment is available here? In America?' Freeman nodded. 'And if . . . if Misha was here and I . . . I gave you what you wanted – it would be available?'

'It's possible –'

'Tell me, please: where is he living? Who is looking after him, caring for him, for his condition?'

'Foster-parents appointed by the State. Now – last picture.'

General Freeman strode briskly to the front of the chamber and glanced up at the screen.

It showed Klaus Fuchs receiving his Order of Merit of the Fatherland in gold at the special dinner in his honour on 13 December 1971. General Freeman pointed now to one of the nearby dining tables. Smiling, dinner-suited men, elegant ladies in long evening gowns, all with their hands frozen in the act of approbation behind the flower arrangements, the glittering glass and polished cutlery.

Freeman tapped the screen itself with his finger. 'His uncle and aunt are allowed access, Mrs Prolev – Professor Eduard and Mrs Irena Ryabov.'

The finger moved slightly in the silence and then settled on a younger, smiling woman in a low-cut evening dress seated directly to Professor Ryabov's left. 'This woman worked very closely with the Professor, Mrs Prolev. She was his aide, his assistant, his technical confidant. If anyone knows the inside of that man's brain, Mrs Prolev, it's her. This woman, Mrs Prolev, is you.'

Outside somewhere a clock chimed the hour.

General Freeman walked slowly back towards the projector. He paused, then – 'Mrs Prolev, let me ask you again. That report – am I right? Nearly right? Or have I got it all wrong?'

'You haven't got it all wrong. Not at all. The defensive system is almost complete,' said Lydia in a small voice.

Frank flicked a glance at the General. Freeman remained impassive, the contest so nearly his. 'And if Misha was here? Alive, unharmed and about to undergo the medical treatment that would save his sight?'

There was silence, then 'I would tell you. I would tell you everything. You have my word.'

General Freeman breathed again.

'OK,' he said finally. 'We'll do it. We'll go for the boy. So help me, we'll get the boy out.'

General Freeman stood on the steps and watched pensively as the cab carrying Frank and the Russian woman to another anonymous motel turned the corner and vanished from sight. He dug his car keys out of his coat pocket, tossed them briefly in the air and caught them firmly. The boy's extraction would take a little time – more, certainly, than he had at his disposal. He needed, therefore, a further adjournment.

And the only man who could give him that was Tolland. Sam Tolland.

Freeman strode to his car and climbed behind the wheel. As he swung on to the gleaming, empty streets the electric clock on the dashboard said 12.15. Tolland's home, Freeman estimated, was no more than twenty minutes away . . .

As General Freeman closed the distance between the centre of Washington and Sam Tolland's expensive, tree-shrouded, lawn-surrounded home to the east of the city, Sam Tolland glanced at the heavy gold watch on his plump wrist and decided it was time he made a move towards the airport. He leaned awkwardly across the arm of his chair and crushed the stub of his cigar against the side of a heavy glass ashtray. Then he rose to his feet, slung a heavy sheepskin coat over his broad shoulders and walked through to the expensive automobile standing idle in the illuminated car port beside his home. Moments later the engine snarled into life and Tolland rolled down the ramp of his driveway towards the airport and his rendezvous with Michael.

From the shadows, Nicholson watched him go.

Nicholson sank a little lower in his seat as the car swept silently past, headlights blazing their expensive brilliance, driver pressed fatly behind the wheel. Nicholson watched from the side road as the red brake lights glared angrily at the corner and then disappeared. The sound of the engine receded swiftly and there was silence. Nicholson rolled down his window and listened intently. Nothing. In this part of the world the wealthy paid much for that nothing, that silence. He gathered up the things on the seat beside him, listened a moment longer, glanced up and down the empty road and stepped out.

They didn't just pay for silence out here; they paid, also, for seclusion. Still no one in sight. Firs shielded the house from the outside world. They shielded Nicholson as he slipped silently across Tolland's lawn, lifted the flower pot laid carelessly against the base of the outside wall behind a small shrub and reached unerringly into the small hole it had hidden. His fingers encountered a switch, which he pressed upwards. Intruder alarm immobilized, Nicholson crossed confidently to the front door, fitted a key into the lock and turned the handle. The door opened.

He would have been most surprised if it hadn't.

He stepped inside and reached for the light switch. The lights snapped on, and Nicholson glanced about him. He had never been within a mile of Tolland's home before, yet the photographs and the briefing Michael had sent him made a prior visit unnecessary: it was not for him to ponder whose 'good services', whose eyes, had made him instantly familiar with a stranger's domestic surroundings: the photographs, the briefings, the documents, the key in his hand, the cigar of the right brand – all were simply the tools of his trade. Builders dealt in bricks. Nicholson dealt with both black and white Intelligence.

Slipping on a pair of plastic gloves, he walked through to the lounge. He checked the curtains were securely drawn and then switched on the lights. A moment here, glancing first at the contents of Tolland's antique desk and – with particular care – at the remains of Tolland's cigar in the ashtray beside the chair in which his unwitting host had so recently been sitting, and then Nicholson flitted silently upstairs. Again there was no pause, no hesitation. A glance at the bedroom, a few moments confirming the arrangement of the bedroom – and Nicholson set to work.

He opened the file he carried and slipped a selection of distasteful magazines into the drawer of the table beside Tolland's wide bed. He crossed to the built-in wardrobe and placed two reels of his own films among the row of cans beside the 16 mm projector Tolland kept nearby for his own curious enjoyment. Returning swiftly downstairs, Nicholson slipped three pages of documents into the right-hand pigeon-hole of Sam Tolland's beautiful antique desk. The fourth and last document he slid beneath the pale green jotter until it was almost – but not quite – hidden from view. Lastly he tossed two black and white pornographic photographs on to the settee.

Now Nicholson stood back and reviewed his actions slowly, critically, searching for the flaws. He found none.

Still wearing his gloves, Nicholson picked up Tolland's evening paper, turned to the arts page and sat down in Tolland's chair. Instead of reading the paper he simply allowed the pages to slip limply from his fingers and slide unheeded on to the carpet around his feet. Then he picked up Tolland's heavy glass ashtray and carefully tipped the contents into a little plastic bag he took from his pocket. Lighting the cigar he had brought with him with Tolland's own lighter, Nicholson rolled the cigar wetly around his mouth and puffed gently until the cigar was drawing well. He sat back, puffing contentedly at the cigar. Minutes passed. Then Nicholson balanced the cigar on the edge of the ashtray, paused – and flicked the cigar on to the open pages of the newspaper at his feet.

The paper smouldered, turned brown and then flicked into flame with a dull whoomph. The flames ate through the newspaper hungrily and attacked first the expensive wool carpet beneath and then the slender, expensive legs of the occasional table itself.

Nicholson got to his feet carefully, crossed to another chair and sat down unhurriedly.

Five minutes later, coughing amid the clouds of billowing smoke, the crackling flames and the heat, Nicholson backed carefully towards a side door. It wouldn't burn the house down, he reasoned – but it would bring out the neighbours, the fire department, the police – maybe, even, the press. And that was all they wanted.

General Freeman estimated that, if his last set of directions had been correct, Sam Tolland's house should be just around the next bend in the gravel road. First he should see a blue and white mail box, then a clump of bushes standing alone. Tolland's home should then be at the end of the first driveway on the right. Hands turning the wheel, Freeman picked up the mail box and drove on slowly. And there were the bushes. He pulled in to the kerb and killed the engine. He glanced about him. Nice, quiet, secluded. Despite his dislike for the man, he was impressed. He could almost have picked it himself. Somehow he had not associated the portly businessman with such expensive good taste. He got out. It was cold now, cold and quiet. He reached inside the car for his coat and tugged it on, his breath pluming away into the darkness.

He sniffed the air.

What was that? Burning? Yes – burning of some kind. But not from a wood fire. Something else. He crossed the lawn in the darkness and began picking his way through the fir trees towards the dim shape of the house, whose white front door he could see gleaming in the darkness. As he drew closer the smell of burning grew stronger. Freeman frowned. It seemed to be coming from the house, from Tolland's house. Suspicions aroused, he rang the doorbell and waited. Nothing happened. But there was a noise of some sort in there, a faint crackling. And the smell of burning was much stronger.

Freeman crouched down and prised open the letter box. Smoke immediately seeped towards him out of the rectangular opening. Beyond he could see the glow of flames, hear the crackle of fierce burning. He hammered hard on the door. 'Tolland!' he yelled. 'Sam Tolland – you in there?' He placed his shoulder against the door and rammed, hard. The door didn't move. He hammered again, his eyes hunting furiously to left and right for another way into the burning building.

As he glanced to his right he sensed rather than saw a door open and close. In the instant the door opened a figure was framed against the glow from within. The figure darted away silently into the darkness. Freeman whirled round. 'Hi! You – stop!' He turned, ducked beneath a branch and set off after the fast-moving figure. It was a man. He could see that now – a man running fast and hard, head low as he twisted and turned through Tolland's fir trees towards the road. Freeman remembered suddenly that they gave out soon and that the runner – whoever he was – would have to cross open lawn to gain the road.

Moving swiftly now despite his bulk, his age, Freeman cut across to intercept, hand reaching for the weapon in his pocket. He drew the gun and cocked it almost from reflex as he waited for the man to emerge from the woods. He was breathing hard, tense with an old, forgotten excitement – there! Off to the right –

'You! Stop!' ordered Freeman curtly. The man raced on without a glance, a dark, shadowy figure, head tucked down between the shoulders, arms pumping hard as he ran. 'Halt!' repeated Freeman. He raised the pistol at arm's length and fired once into the air. The man's stride hardly faltered. He ran on unheeding as the shot crashed out into the stillness.

So that's the way you want it, muttered Freeman, as training stepped in to take the place of compassion. The pistol came down, Freeman dropped into the marksman's crouch and cradled the heavy sidearm in both big hands. He settled the notched vee of the foresight on to the man's swaying, pumping shoulders. As he took up primary pressure on the trigger the man half turned to glance back over his shoulders. Perhaps he thought he was safe. Out of danger. Out of the woods.

He was wrong.

Freeman fired twice. Double-tap.

Arms flung wide, the figure smacked aside, crashed on to

the ground with a dull thump and slid down the last few feet of manicured lawn to sprawl head first on to the gravel of the road beyond. It lay still, staining the well-kept darkness with the careless, rag-doll abandon of death. Freeman lowered his pistol.

As he moved towards the body, lights sprang on in a house half hidden among more trees on the opposite side of the road. A front door opened and banged closed somewhere else nearby. Voices shouted questions in the darkness. Freeman moved down to the road as a car suddenly appeared from nowhere and jammed to a dry halt, slewing across the road in alarm as its headlights cast cruel, heartless illumination on the sordid moment of Nicholson's death.

'Jesus Christ –' began the man behind the wheel, his eyes wide with fear as he glanced first at the crumpled figure and then at Freeman walking slowly down the lawn towards him, pistol lowered in his hand. He swallowed. 'Now, Mister –' he began.

Freeman cut him short. 'You live around here?'

'Back . . . back there. But look now, I –'

Freeman gestured him to silence impatiently. 'Get on the phone. Call the police – and the fire service too. There's a fire going on in there,' he pointed back towards the building. 'The place is on fire, you got that? Number Six.'

'Six? Jesus – that's Sam's place! What in hell's happening around here? Who's this –?'

'Christ knows. I caught him running away from the house. I told him to stop but he just kept right on going. I warned him.'

'So you shot him?' demanded the man incredulously. 'You just shot him? For that?'

Freeman looked up angrily. 'You want that house to burn down while you're standing here sounding off? Go on – make that call. I'll still be here when you get back.' The man reversed his car and roared back up the road. Freeman bent down beside the body. It was too dark to see clearly. He crossed to his car for a torch.

His shots had gone high. His first round had entered just

below the right eye and exited behind the left ear. Pale pink brain tissue and slivers of bone mingled with the dark blood that trickled slowly down the slope of the damp lawn to gather in a little puddle on the dusty roadway beside the grazed, still cheek. Freeman's second shot had taken the man in the top of the right shoulder as the first bullet had wrenched him round. Freeman shone the torch on the handsome face and sighed. He sighed for the waste and he sighed with the knowledge that this body, this killing, was about to add hideous complication to an already complex, tortuous tale. He studied the wide staring eyes, the rich, gleaming hair now clotted with blood and dust from the roadway. The man had really been very good-looking. Once. Freeman leant forward and began searching the man's pockets.

*

Sam Tolland was puzzled. Puzzled and alarmed. He had met the flight from New York, scanned the face of each disembarking passenger most carefully – but there had been no sign of Michael. He was sure there had been no mistake. He was definitely meeting the right plane.

He checked with the flight desk: yes, that *was* the last flight from New York; the next flight would arrive shortly after 7 a.m. the following morning. Tolland tried to call Michael direct, but the line, for some reason, was unobtainable. Then he checked with reservations; but without a surname to go on he was able to confirm only that there had been no last-minute cancellations between the time Michael had called him at his home and the time the flight closed a few minutes before take-off.

Somewhere beneath his overcoat there were the first stirrings of alarm, of fear.

Tolland climbed behind the wheel of his expensive car and began to drive slowly homewards, the radio providing soothing music for his troubled mind. He was still asking himself the same unanswered questions as he turned up the slip road that led to his house. What could it mean? Something must have gone wrong in New York, he decided.

There could be no other possible explanation. Gradually, he became aware of the glow of lights up ahead. Someone must be having a party, he thought. Yes – New York would have the answer. He would call again just as soon as he got in. He would – he stopped the car, thunderstruck.

Fire engines were blocking the road, their hoses snaking across *his* lawn, through his trees towards . . . good God . . . towards *his* house! For a moment Tolland watched wide-eyed from the warm cocoon of his car. What was happening? What in God's name was *happening*? There was a police car – an ambulance too! No, *two* police cars, their lights flashing urgently across the sky, and – Tolland snapped off his car radio and wound down the window to listen with mounting dismay as the car filled with the pant of powerful engines, the crackle of radios and the shout of orders as police and firemen strode purposefully across his beautiful lawn towards his house; and – Christ above – there was *smoke* coming from the house! Tolland wriggled feverishly from behind the wheel.

'Sam, Sam – thank God you're back,' panted Elmer Stans, his neighbour, pushing through a crowd of dressing-gowned spectators to paw ineffectually at his sleeve, a dark blue dressing gown at incongruous odds with the big vehicles, the lights and the gleaming male machinery that is attendant upon civil misfortune and the loss of private property.

'Elmer! What is all this? What the hell's going on?' demanded Sam Tolland fearfully as he began to stride up the grass slope towards his home.

Elmer had to run at his side to keep up. 'We don't know, Sam. No one has an idea! There was just this fire and this shooting an' all –'

'Shooting? Jesus – what shooting, Elmer?' Tolland grasped his arm, swinging him round.

Elmer ran a hand distractedly through his thinning hair. 'Like I said, Sam: I don't know – none of us do! We were all inside – asleep mostly, in bed, you know?' Tolland nodded impatiently. 'We heard what sounded like a pistol shot. Then, straight off, there's another one, Sam, same as before. Next thing we know old Jim Hacker, he's roarin' down the road, blaring away with that horn of his, shouting about how there's a guy up here with a gun an' all, your place is on fire and there's this other feller lyin' back there in the road –' he gestured vaguely behind them both, and Tolland turned to see a white-roofed ambulance backed towards a huddled, blanket-covered shape on the edge of the grass, around which stood a cluster of police officers. A taller figure – strangely familiar, yet indistinct in the false lighting – stood talking to another police officer, who was taking notes, slightly apart from the others. Tolland frowned, then pushed the puzzle aside. It would keep until later. He turned back towards the house and shouldered his way impatiently through the knots of firemen and spectators cluttering his lawn, standing carelessly on his carefully groomed flower beds.

A press photographer, perhaps sensing ownership, dodged suddenly forward, camera raised. Tolland pushed him aside too as the flashgun crackled in his face. He stumbled over a length of hosing and stepped on to the path leading to his front door. Several hoses snaked past him through the splintered remains of his doorway and disappeared into the expensive interior of a home now ugly with the smell of chemical foam and the thick stench of burning. A charred side-table lay beside the broken French windows, and one of Tolland's display cabinets filled with eighteenth-century French fans stood propped against an outside wall, one leg broken, its glass smeared with smoke, its priceless contents spilling unheeded into the garden. Tolland hurried forward –

'Don't touch those, sir, if you please. They're still the property of the owner,' ordered a well-meaning fireman in a white helmet.

Tolland turned on him. 'Owner? I'm the goddam owner,' he snarled. 'These are mine. All this is mine!' He made a grand sweeping gesture that embraced half the State of Maryland.

The fireman made allowances. 'You're Mister –' he consulted a notebook – 'Mr Samuel Jonathan Tolland, right?'

Tolland nodded angrily, his anger directed at the fireman because there was no one else.

'Sorry about this, Mr Tolland. We came as fast as we could. You're kinda difficult to get to out here,' he added, striking an unconscious blow for his fellow have-nots when confronted with one of the haves. He clumped forwards in his boots and stood beside Tolland. Together they surveyed the sorry scene. 'It looks a lot worse than it is, Mr Tolland, believe me. It's really not that bad inside.' He shrugged. 'I mean: it's bad, sure – and you've taken some damage to property. But your house isn't in danger, know what I mean? It could be a lot worse, understand what I'm saying?' He took Tolland's arm and guided him gently around the corner. 'Now, sir: if I could just ask you for a few details about the property . . .'

Sixty paces away General Clarke Freeman was answering the same cold questions, fielding the same cold stares of disbelief from the detective at whose feet lay Nicholson's blanket-shrouded body. Chewing steadily, the man flicked over a page of notes and twisted round towards one of his colleagues standing over by the neighbours taking statements. 'Hey – Carillo: you've searched the guy, right? What ID d'you make?'

The man excused himself and came over. 'Not a thing, Lieutenant,' he said quietly. 'The guy's as clean as a whistle.'

The Lieutenant's eyes opened with surprise. 'Sure?'

'Sure I'm sure, Lieutenant. The guy was clean.'

Freeman would agree with that, at least. He had gone through his pockets first. The Lieutenant dismissed Carillo and returned to flick idly through his notebook. He shook his head sadly. 'I still don't get it, General Freeman. Why did you fire? The guy was running away, right? Did he shoot at you? Here you say no. Did he turn to point a gun at you? No. Did he have a weapon of any kind? No. So what I'd like to know, General, is this: why did you drop him?'

'I told you. I keep telling you,' snapped Freeman, 'I saw him running away from the house *after* I discovered it was on fire. I told him to stop. He didn't. I told him again: I shouted at him. He kept right on going. I fired once into the air. I ordered him to stop once more. He ran on. So I fired – I wanted to bring him down. I did not intend to kill him. The shots went high.'

'Yeah, I've got all that, General. That's what you keep telling me. Let me ask you a couple more questions, put my mind at ease: one – what were you doing here in the first place? You're a long way from home, right?

'And two - why were you carrying this piece anyway?' He hefted the General's automatic pistol, sealed now along with three empty brass cases in a plastic exhibits bag. Freeman sighed, loath to confide in so junior a police officer.

'I had business with Mr Tolland. I wanted to see him about some urgent matter that couldn't wait until morning – will that satisfy you?'

The Lieutenant wrote it all down slowly. He looked up. 'What sort of business?'

'Jesus, Lieutenant –'

'What sort of business, General? I need to know. You're going to tell me. This isn't some Air Force base out in the boonies – you're on my ground now. So tell me: what was this urgent business that brought you out here with a loaded sidearm shortly after midnight?'

There was a pause.

'It's tied in with National Security.'

'Yeah?' The man didn't even stop chewing. 'National Security, eh?'

'Look, Lieutenant – I'd advise you –'

'Why don't you tell me about it, General? I've got all the time in the world – and that means, right now, that you have too.'

Inside Tolland's home the firemen were cleaning up. The worst was over, the flames had been put out and the young firemen had pushed aside their constricting breathing masks and were beginning to enjoy this legitimate browsing amid the possessions of the wealthy. One of the men dusted off the cushions on the sofa, stooped, and held up one of the curling black and white photographs he had discovered. 'Coo-eee, Charlie-boy. Take a look at this!'

Another of the yellow-coated young firemen sauntered over to peer over the other man's shoulder. White teeth flashed behind the smoke-smudged face. 'Must have been some kinda party. What with all the boys being so friendly, and all.'

They grinned. The photograph was tossed aside and they resumed the official search for fire damage, the serious, professional business of the night disguised now by a healthy interest in another man's pornography.

The firemen's browsings led them in due time to Sam Tolland's antique desk standing a little away from the seat of the fire. Apart from some scorched paintwork that was probably repairable, the desk itself was undamaged. Gloved fingers wiped away the smoke grime and began flicking idly through the contents of the pigeon-holes, searching, officially at least, for sparks. Presently the gloved fingers paused and the desk jotter was lifted carefully aside. The fireman nipped the end of his glove between strong white teeth and drew off the thick gauntlet.

'Hey, Pete – take a look at this,' he said quietly, picking up the embossed paper that had caught his attention. Sensing the discovery of more salacious photographs, Pete stepped over quickly with a grin of anticipation. The grin faded as, together, they read the document Nicholson had planted beneath the jotter for their very eyes, less than an hour earlier.

'That's heavy, man,' whispered Pete in something like awe. The other nodded slowly.

A minute more and the document was being inspected carefully by the site's Incident Officer. A detailed search revealed similar papers nearby. A little later a white-faced Lieutenant of Detectives had cleared the room and was busy dialling an unlisted number at the Central Intelligence Agency's Headquarters at Langley. As he did so he cast his mind back feverishly over a less than respectful conversation with the man he belatedly recognized as the Head of United States Air Force Intelligence.

And by then he had stopped chewing.

Another hour and the scene outside Sam Tolland's home had changed drastically. The hoses had been rolled away, the fire engines had gone; the ambulance had wailed away too, taking with it Nicholson's stiffening corpse. The dressing-gowned spectators, the knots of anxious neighbours, had been persuaded back behind their locked doors, and there was now only a token presence of uniformed police officers guarding the stable door. But the change that had been wrought had to do more with atmosphere than mere numbers on the ground: the calibre of those remaining had altered also, the civic concerns of Homicide and Fire Department replaced now by the quietly-spoken, softly moving, graven-faced Agency men who were combing the woodland, sifting painstakingly through the charred remains of Tolland's lounge. Those same men had searched the house thoroughly. Dismissing the man's personal sexual preferences with hardly a glance, they had taken away two rolls of film and a selection of secret documents, payment slips and Soviet Intelligence memoranda for interpretation and analysis.

The two firemen whose sharp eyes and base curiosity had made the initial discovery had been taken aside and spoken to quietly before their machines were allowed to pull away. Now, despite a natural and frank enjoyment of their role at the very centre of such mystery, despite the merciless joshing they received at the hands of their intrigued colleagues, neither was saying a word.

Sam Tolland, expensive French fans forgotten, was sitting between two men in the back of a dark limousine at the bottom of his own driveway. In addition to a stunned, fearful expression, he was wearing a pair of steel handcuffs that bit cruelly into his wrists.

General Clarke Freeman walked slowly across the lawn and up towards the house, his head bowed in thought as he tried to analyse the importance of the night's events, to separate the merely spectacular from the quietly important as he gauged the professional repercussions of the killing he had done and the firemen's later discoveries that had led to Tolland's arrest.

He moved across the lawn and stepped on to the paving. The fall of his step made another raincoated figure swing round. It was Tom Greener, the Agency's Assistant Director and Tolland's friend and confidant on the Nuclear Intelligence Board.

'Evening, Tom,' tried Freeman quietly, waiting, hands thrust deep into coat pockets. Greener regarded him quietly, eyes glittering with anger.

'You sonofabitch,' he managed finally. 'You stinking sonofabitch. You really think you're going to get away with it? Pulling a stunt like this? I'll see you're finished, Freeman. Wiped out. I'll see to that personally.'

He turned on his heel and strode down towards his waiting car.

Because of the CIA's involvement in the fire and Tom
Greener's ingrained suspicion and dislike of US Air Force
Intelligence in general and Clarke Freeman in particular, it
was long after 3 a.m. before the General was finished with the
statements and the questions and permitted to return home.

Now he locked his wife's coupé into the garage, slung his
coat over his shoulders and let himself quietly in at the side
door that led through into the kitchen. He stepped softly
on to the polished floor and closed the door. He listened
intently, anxious to avoid waking Doris – anxious, most
particularly, to avoid the stream of empty, endless questions,
the bitter whine of disharmony that would better keep until
breakfast. He winced grimly. By then it would probably be
all over the newspapers and TV anyway. Let it keep until
then. Meanwhile, there was time to let his brain grapple
quietly with the facts, the theories and the outlandish
possibilities thrown up in his path by the night's developments – time and the silence he needed. Freeman laid his
coat on the hall chair and walked downstairs to his study.
His place of thinking.

Switching on the single lamp on his wide desk, he slipped
into his swivel chair and hunched forward to sit motionless
for long moments, head cushioned on open hands, his eyes
closed. Then he reached into his jacket pocket and took out
the plastic envelope he had taken from the man he had
killed.

Freeman held the little bag up against the light and peered
forward to study its contents minutely: the crushed butt of
an expensive cigar and an inch or two of ash. That and –
he dipped again into his pocket – that and this single yale
door key was all that the man had carried.

As Freeman had left to make his formal statement one of the officers nearby had belatedly noticed a deserted car parked in the shadows against the verge a few hundred yards from the house. They would, presumably, trace the owner, the driver – maybe the thief – through the car licence plate, the car hire documentation, the fingerprints. Then they would have a name, an address, an identity.

But that would be all, predicted Freeman. Because he was the one who held the evidence, the proof of sinister, deliberate intention.

And he was sharing it with no one.

He held another advantage also. Unlike the Agency men, the police and the fire service – unlike even a few of his own colleagues – he alone knew what he had seen. *They* might doubt his story, believe his presence outside Tolland's home at that particular time on that particular night was due to more than just charitable coincidence, but he *knew*. He alone knew that his arrival was the result of a sudden, random decision, impossible to predict, which he had shared with no one. Whatever he had stumbled upon as he waited for Sam Tolland to open his own front door, therefore, had been unrehearsed. That at least had been an accident.

This knowledge gave him one single, tremendous advantage, because the ash he studied in its little plastic envelope, shining now beneath his desk lamp, confirmed that the man he had killed had been prepared to go to extraordinary lengths to establish *beyond forensic dispute* the authenticity of the 'accident' that had started the fire at the home of the General's greatest critic on the Nuclear Intelligence Board – a critic that now, *because of that fire*, was revealed to have been a Soviet agent.

And that worried Freeman. It worried him greatly.

So who? And why? One of his rivals within the service? Someone from DIA, NSA – Tom Greener himself, perhaps? Someone from within the Federal Bureau's Division Five? Any one of these – or none at all.

Freeman rose, pushed open the French windows and

stepped out on to the dark, cool lawn to walk down slowly towards the river at the bottom of his garden, breathing in the silence that rolled softly towards him as the house receded over his shoulder. His shoes made no sound as he walked across the damp grass, reviewing for his own peace of mind the blur of action between the moment he had stepped out of his car and caught that first faint smell of burning and the half-second before his finger closed irrevocably on the trigger.

He reviewed each action dispassionately, pressing his inquiring mind into the fuzzy corners of his memory to unearth conscience, guilt or the buried bones of wrong-doing. He found nothing with which to reproach himself, and yet the line of his mouth tightened: no doubt others would have no such difficulty. Soon, in addition to his private battle of conviction with the members of the Nuclear Intelligence Board, he would be battling to retain the confidence and support of superiors who had long ago marked him down as a dangerous, volatile and outspoken ingredient in the chemistry of their own promotion.

Freeman turned and began to walk back towards the house, the cold striking now through shirt and jacket: he had challenged the man to stop. He had refused. An innocent man with nothing to hide would have stopped – if not on the command, then most certainly on that first warning shot into the air. The man had not stopped. Ergo, he was not innocent. Freeman stepped inside his study, closed the French windows, slipped home the bolts and pulled back the curtains. No, he was not innocent, decided Freeman finally, formally. And the proof of his guilt was there, on his desk. In a little plastic bag.

General Freeman crossed the study and took one of his own cigars from a box on the side table. He snipped off the end and lit the cigar carefully. When it was drawing well he laid it in an ashtray and stood over it, watching. Within minutes Freeman was nodding with grim satisfaction. The cigar had gone out.

General Freeman pulled his rocker over to the window

and sat down to wait for two things. The first was for the dawn to come up. The second – the arrival, by special Pentagon messenger, of certain documents. And while he waited, General Freeman's mind turned over a new and terrifying suspicion. What would be the implications if – just suppose – someone within the Soviet Union actually wanted his arguments to prevail before the Nuclear Intelligence Board? What would *that* mean?

*

Frank Yates was also awake.

Sharing another anonymous motel bedroom with Lydia Prolev, he was curled uncomfortably on the couch while the woman slept in the bed. She had turned in with hardly a word shortly after he had phoned in their new location and had slept almost immediately, a slim arm crooked behind her head, her body hummocked among the shadows that fell from between the open curtains.

Perhaps an hour went by – and then the telephone on the bedside table began to burr softly. Frank crossed the room in two swift strides. 'Yates.'

Lydia rolled over, instantly awake, her eyes wide with expectancy.

'Captain Yates? General Freeman wants to see you at his home, sir.'

'When?'

'Now, sir. Right away.'

'Now?' Frank frowned into the phone.

'Now, sir. Car's on its way to your location.'

General Freeman was waiting on the lawn, hands thrust behind his back, a coat thrown over his shoulders. He nodded a brief greeting, turned on his heel and led the way up to the house, some new, undefined tension etched in the dark outline of those broad, hunched shoulders.

Frank fell into step and studied the man critically as they moved silently across the grass. Something had changed, he could sense it. Alerted first by the General's distracted greeting, Frank was confirmed in his feeling now by the lines of strain he saw in the General's face.

Freeman opened the front door and led them through into the hallway.

'What's the word, General?' asked Frank quietly.

With his hand on the banister rail leading down to the study, Freeman turned. Talking in a low half-whisper, he then brought them swiftly up to date: he told them about his sudden decision to plead with Tolland for more time, about the shooting and about the blackmail evidence discovered by the firemen in Tolland's desk, which showed that his attacks upon Freeman's testimony had been orchestrated by someone codenamed 'Michael' in the Soviet Residency in New York.

Freeman did not tell them about his growing suspicions, or about the plastic envelope of cigar debris he had found in Nicholson's pocket. That he kept to himself.

Then he picked up the heavy buff envelope delivered to his home by Pentagon messenger not half an hour earlier. 'Movement details, Frank. Because of this shooting business I'm bringing things forward. Contacts, timings, routes in, routes out – it's all there. Learn and destroy. You're on your way later this morning.' He handed Frank the package and led the way slowly down the stairs to the study.

As Freeman closed the door behind them and waved them to seats, Lydia looked at the General in disbelief. 'You can do this? So soon? But only last night, a few hours ago –'

'We've had contingency plans set by for some time,' said Freeman vaguely. 'Now – Frank: where are you staying?'

'Motel about fifteen minutes from here. 215 Salvador Drive.'

Freeman nodded. 'OK – but we've got this slight problem: between the time Frank leaves and the time I can get over after the hearing, you'll have to be alone in that motel, Mrs Prolev. Think you can handle that? Stay low, keep out of sight – you should be safe enough. I don't want to bring anyone else in at this stage, you understand?'

Lydia shrugged. It was obvious the prospect held little attraction. 'Do I have any choice?' she asked rhetorically.

Exactly on schedule, the taxi pulled in to the kerb outside the motel and waited silently, the roads almost empty in the thin light of early morning. Frank and Lydia exchanged glances. Frank zipped shut his holdall and turned towards the door. 'OK, Lydia. That's it, I guess. Time I was moving.'

Lydia nodded silently from the armchair as Frank turned away, his hand reaching for the catch. Then, impulsively, she came out of the chair, crossed the shabby room and laid a gentle hand on his shoulder. Frank swung round. She watched his eyes gravely. 'Please, Frank – be careful, yes? Do not do anything foolish – not only for the sake of Misha, but for you, also. You are a good man, I think.'

She leant forward and kissed him gently on the lips. Frank stiffened and then relaxed. Then he broke away and turned abruptly towards the door. 'See you,' he managed gruffly.

Lydia locked the door carefully after he had left and then watched from the window as he slung his bags into the back of the taxi and climbed in beside the driver.

'Andrews AFB, right?' asked the driver, chewing steadily as the car pulled away from the kerb.

Frank shook his head. 'Wrong. I want to make a slight detour first. Dumbarton Street, Georgetown, OK?'

'You got it, chief.'

Mrs Headley came to the door, her hair tousled from sleep, her eyes peering painfully into the light. 'Frank? What are you doing here? Where's Lydia?'

'It's OK, Mrs Headley – everything's fine. I've . . . I've just got to go away for a few days, that's all. Thought I'd stop by and tell you.'

'What? Again? Where is it this time?'

'Not too far,' evaded Frank. 'Er . . . Louise – she all right with you for a few more days?'

Mrs Headley nodded, smiling. 'Sure, Frank – same as always. You know that.'

'Thanks, I appreciate it. She asleep? Right now?'

Mrs Headley grinned, wrinkled her nose and beckoned Frank over the threshold. 'Sure she is – you want to take a peek?'

Frank grinned sheepishly. Mrs Headley led him through her comfortable, cluttered living room and up the stairs. She stopped outside a small bedroom. 'She's in there, Frank. Go ahead. I'll be downstairs if you need me.' Frank nodded gratefully and cracked open the door.

Louise was lying fast asleep on her back, her arms flung wide across the pillows, her hair falling forward over closed eyes. Frank brushed the hair away gently and planted a kiss, feather-soft, on the child's smooth forehead as the old, familiar pain of loss built within him. Louise stirred sleepily, a small smile starting on her lips. She was so like Carole . . . 'Cuggles,' whispered Frank quietly: it was a baby-word with special meaning from her childhood. 'Cuggles, little one. I love you,' he whispered softly. Then he turned, crept towards the door and closed it firmly behind him.

'. . . Fire Chief Harold S. Birley told this reporter the fire is believed to have been started by a lighted cigar falling on to the carpet. Final confirmation of that theory must, however, await the forensic report expected around noon. This is Cathy Winslow for Station WXKC returning you now to the studio.'

'Thank you, Cathy. We'll be returning to that location later in this programme.' The anchorman spun round in his chair, glanced at his notes and looked directly into the camera with practised confidence. 'Facts concerning this story are still confused. What has emerged, however, is that the man who fired the fatal shots that resulted in the death, seven hours ago, of the young man – still to be identified by the police – outside the exclusive Sunrise Hills home of industrialist Sam Tolland is none other than General Clarke Freeman, the controversial Head of US Air Force

Intelligence. It's to his home on Beachside Landing that we take you now –'

'Thank you, John. Good morning – this is Peter Coles reporting. I'm standing outside the General's home right now. There's been little activity so far this morning – and the General isn't talking to reporters. With the exception of a brief appearance at that door a little over an hour ago when he issued a terse "No comment" to the reporters you can see behind me here, the General has remained indoors.'

Coles glanced briefly at a clipboard. 'General Clarke Freeman is a career Air Force officer with a distinguished record as a fighter, both on the front line and back here in Washington. He first jumped into the nation's headlines a little less than a year ago with a scathing public condemnation of US nuclear preparedness that caused a powerful political detonation both within Pentagon circles and up on the Hill among those who believed a serving officer had no business speaking out against government policy while wearing the uniform of the US armed services. Twice decorated for valour during World War Two, informed sources tell me General Freeman needed all that courage and more when he decided to speak out against the combined weight of traditional military thinking. Here's what he said then –'

'Jesus, not again,' groaned Freeman. He rose to his feet, placed his coffee cup aside and twisted down the TV sound with a quick, deft movement. He moved cautiously across to the window, lifted an edge of the curtain and peered outside. ENG cameras to the shoulder, there were at least two TV crews that he could see, together with a handful of photographers and half a dozen newspaper reporters with notebooks. Freeman felt his anger come to the boil: they were walking all over his lawn, peering into his home with undisguised, naked curiosity. As he watched, one reporter flung a half-smoked cigarette into a carefully tended flower-bed and sauntered over to another colleague with the insensitive arrogance of his breed. As Freeman held his curtain back still further and craned forward, he was spotted. A finger went up, an arm shot out, heads turned and one of the ENG cameramen swivelled in his direction. Freeman let the curtain drop hurriedly and turned back into his study as the camera's picture was carried instantly on to his own television set. Freeman watched on TV as his own curtain settled back into position. It was unnerving, and the General felt trapped, pinned into his lair by the baying hounds of a public's breakfast-time curiosity.

Now the picture changed to a recent photograph of himself in uniform. Almost against his will Freeman felt compelled to turn up the sound as the reporter reloaded with a fresh belt of information: '. . . the day before yesterday. By tradition, NIB hearings are held in secret, so we can only speculate as to the reasons for the General's unprecedented emergency summons of the –'

'Clarke?'

General Freeman spun round to see Doris, his wife, framed in the doorway of his study. Swathed in a mauve housecoat, feet encased in puff-ball slippers of shocking pink, her face a frozen, unpainted mask of alarm and consternation, she stood motionless in the threshold, a hand gripping the edge of the doorjamb for support. 'What's happening, Clarke? Why are all those reporter people outside? And the phone –'

Her husband crossed the room swiftly and turned down the television set. Doris made a vague, distracted gesture with her hands. 'Don't turn it off, Clarke. I want to see. What is it? Tell me: what's going on?'

She came forward hesitantly, a coffee cup balanced carefully in her hand. 'I tried to use the phone –' she wavered, glancing across at Freeman's desk. The receiver there was off the machine and lying on its side. She crossed the carpet and replaced it. She had hardly turned away when the phone began to ring once more. Without a word General Freeman crossed to his desk, lifted the receiver, broke the connection and replaced it on its side.

Doris stared at him as though he had suddenly begun

throwing the best china through the French windows. Her chins began to wobble. 'Tell me, Clarke – what's *happening*, for goodness sakes? Why are all those people outside? Why won't the doorbell –?'

'OK, Doris, OK. Take it easy. Come on now, sit down,' he soothed. Despite his irritation at the priorities she accorded to her life, at the circle of friends she enjoyed and at the issues she took to her well-meaning bosom, he felt an unexpected stirring of sympathy: this was still the woman he had married, still the woman he lived with after all these years. In an unconscious rebirth of an intimacy that had been lost between them for almost fifteen years, Clarke Freeman stretched out his hand, grasped her wrist gently and tugged her down beside him on the couch. His problems touched her also. She was entitled to a little of the truth, an explanation to take to those friends of hers in that world he could never share or understand.

'Doris, listen to me,' he began softly, choosing his words with care. 'At about midnight last night, while you were in bed –'

But he got no further. Doris Freeman's coffee cup slipped from her fingers and fell to the floor with a shattering crash as she raised a hand to point at the television screen. General Freeman turned. A reconstructed photograph of the man he had killed filled the screen. Printed across the staring face in block lettering was the word SLAIN.

'That's Martin – Martin Nicholson,' whispered Doris Freeman. 'I'm sure it is. I'd recognize that face anywhere.'

'You *knew* him?' demanded her husband urgently. 'You're sure? Certain?'

She swallowed and nodded several times. 'As I'm sitting here – that's Martin. He owns a florist's out on Dupont Circle somewhere. He used to come to our coffee mornings and . . . oh my, how . . . how awful. I must tell Mary –'

She made to get up but her husband restrained her. 'Sit here a moment, Doris,' he said gently. 'We have to talk. Tell me about him – about Martin Nicholson.'

Half an hour later General Freeman was alone in the house,

his wife gone to spend the day with friends, her cosy, ordered world up-ended by the ugly realities of her husband's revelations. She had listened wide-eyed as he told her what he believed she should know. When he had finished he wondered if it had been worth it. He had expected anger, accusation. Instead, his words had been met by a blank silence which suggested that full understanding had yet to sink in. Luckily, friends lived nearby and while Doris changed upstairs General Freeman had used the phone. Soon a car had drawn up, Doris had struggled tight-lipped through the barrage of press inquiries that had greeted her appearance and then vanished down the drive in a swirl of dust and a hurled handful of unheeded questions.

For a moment then the reporters had converged on the front door and tried shouting their questions from there. General Freeman retreated upstairs to change, and presently the press withdrew to the edge of the lawn and settled down to wait. They were used to such sieges.

Sitting once more in his study with one eye on the clock and the moment when he must go outside and get in his car if he was to arrive at the New Senate Building in time, General Freeman stirred now to a renewed chorus of questions outside followed shortly by a brief staccato hammering on the front door. Patience exhausted, he took the stairs two at a time, tugged back the bolts and fairly flung open the front door.

'General Freeman – a word, please!'

'Got a statement yet, General?'

'Is it true the man you killed had his hands in the air, General?'

'Let's move in out of this shall we, Clarke?' suggested the tall uniformed officer mildly as he turned away from the harsh lights and the flash units that glared down on to the porch. It was Brigadier-General Irwin Holt, Freeman's direct superior within the Air Force, the pack of newsmen yapping their questions at his polished heels.

'Certainly, sir. Come this way.' Freeman stepped back, Holt came forward, and Freeman closed the door smartly behind them. The noise died suddenly and Holt regarded his subordinate in silence for a moment. 'Goddam vultures,' he grunted. 'They'd film their mother's funeral.'

Freeman nodded, waiting, as the hawk-nosed, thin-cheeked officer glanced unhurriedly at his surroundings. 'Thought I'd come by myself Clarke. I'd like to get it from you direct. Seems you've kicked over a whole heap of apples.' He frowned. 'And not for the first time either, as I recall.'

'No, sir. Would you follow me – we'd best talk in here.' General Freeman slid open the glass doors and led the way through into the lounge. He gestured Holt to a chair over-looking the wide sweep of lawn leading down to the river. Brigadier-General Holt seemed in no hurry. He sat back among the cushions, his hands resting on the arms of his chair as he studied Freeman's garden with evident pleasure. 'Do your own gardening, Clarke?' he asked mildly, as though that was the real reason for the visit, the killing, the fire, Tolland's arrest and the intelligence discoveries just the excuse.

'When time permits, which isn't often. There's a boy comes in maybe twice a week. My wife likes to arrange the –'

'They're saying you set the fire, Clarke.' Holt's eyes snapped round. They were blue, hard – and they missed nothing. 'They're saying you set the whole thing up to get Tolland off your back: that you started the fire, planted the evidence – maybe even nailed the guy who helped you do it to add local colour.'

'They?' demanded Freeman.

Holt paused and then allowed himself the smallest crack of a smile. 'Let's just say there are those within our circles who watch your progress with ... particular attention. Especially when you take a stumble.'

'And you?' asked Freeman. 'You believe those rumours?' For months now he had placed Holt as a neutral. Maybe he had been wrong. Yet the man was here now, giving him the word. There was a long silence.

'Frankly, Clarke, I don't know. My guess is this first

flush of accusation will die down in a day or two. When the smoke clears we'll see what's left. For the moment I'm keeping an open mind. I want to hear it from you. But I'll tell you this –' he levelled a slim finger across the room – 'if you're going down another of those private rivers of yours, Clarke, tell me now: get it out in the open. Pressure's building already to get you suspended right away pending a full investigation –'

'Suspend me!' exploded Freeman. 'They must be out of their goddam minds! Don't those sons of bitches know I'm half-way through –'

Holt raised a hand in interruption. 'OK, Clarke, OK: take it easy. Go ahead – convince me. That's why I'm here.'

Freeman began to try.

*

Across town Ferris punched money into the payphone and dialled long-distance. Presently he had the information he needed. Lydia Prolev was hiding out in a motel: on 215 Salvador Drive.

As General Freeman began to attempt to justify his actions
to Brigadier-General Irwin Holt, the television set in his
study continued to fill the empty room with its soundless
pictures. Both Freeman and Holt would have instantly
recognized not just the street but the building itself that
had now captured the attention of the cameras. It was the
Soviet Residency in New York.

A reporter was standing in front of the Residency's
imposing metal gates. A large black limousine rolled into
view, paused at the gateway and then turned right into the
main road, where it picked up speed and disappeared from
view. The TV cameras managed a quick glimpse of the car's
interior: three men – a uniformed driver, a front-seat
escort and a single lone passenger hunched grim-faced in
the back of the car. The reporter's words, had they been
heard, would have made sense of the pictures they were
supposed to accompany: Major Dmitri Muratov, Military
Attaché at the Soviet Residency and the one Soviet contact
compromised by the inclusion of his codename in the documents discovered on Sam Tolland's desk, was being expelled from the United States. Muratov's codename had
been known to the CIA for some time; now there had been
a frosty exchange of notes, diplomatic status had been summarily withdrawn and Major Muratov was required to
board the first available flight back across the Atlantic en
route to the Soviet Union and whatever fate might be
reserved for a disgraced KGB officer.

Later, as General Clarke Freeman trotted brisk and stern-
faced up the steep stone steps leading to the entrance of the
New Senate Building, as the press and TV crews closed in
hungrily, sensing public appetite for a story they had almost

totally ignored the day before, a dark blue open-backed Air Force truck turned in a wide half-circle across the sprawling concrete vastness of Andrews Air Force Base on the southern outskirts of Washington DC.

Frank Yates sat alone beside the young black driver. He was dressed in nondescript airforce coveralls, his civilian clothes and documentation in the grey zippered holdall on the metal floor between his feet. Now the driver lifted a gloved hand and pointed with studied nonchalance beyond the rows of parked aircraft belonging to Military Airlift Command. 'There she be, Captain – the bird on the left there.'

Frank looked beyond the gloved hand, impressed as ever by the sheer majestic size of the Lockheed Galaxy C-5a that was now growing rapidly before the windshield and which would soon be carrying him on its regular transatlantic hop to the US Air Force Headquarters at Ramstein AFB in West Germany.

The young driver glanced across at his passenger and grunted. 'Some piece of aircraft, huh, Captain? Nearly a hundred yards long. Guys say she's the biggest thing in the air anywheres. Had some trouble a while back, so I hear, what with fatigue an' structure weight and all, but I guess they've hacked all that by now.' He shot Frank Yates a wide white grin. 'Sure hope so, Cap'n, anyways!'

He spun the wheel expertly and the tiny, toy-like vehicle slid beneath the mid-morning shadow cast by one of the vast back-swept wings. Frank reached down for his gear, tossed it out on to the concrete and climbed down. The pick-up pulled away and he paused to glance about him, the memories stirred instantly, fanned into flame by the smell of sun-warmed metal, the high-octane shimmer on smooth aerodynamic surfaces, the tyre-stained expanse of a dozen different airfields instantly recalled in the here and now of Andrews AFB. Frank bent, unzipped a side pocket and smoothed out his travel authorization documents and Air Force ID as a member of the aircraft's flight crew stepped through the gloom towards him, his

eyes lost and expressionless behind the mandatory sun-
glasses.

Some things didn't change, Frank thought as he held
out his papers.

At the exact moment that Captain Frank Yates made his
introductions to the pilot, a commercial wide-bodied 747
lifted ponderously into the air from Kennedy International
Airport.

Take-off checks completed, the aircraft swung away to
the north and eased its rate of climb. Presently the Fasten
Seat Belts/No Smoking signs were extinguished. Tensions
were eased, seat belts clicked open up and down the aircraft
and soon the team of smiling hostesses began distributing
aperitifs and the elaborate menus that were themselves a
stimulating appetizer to the lunch that would be served in a
little less than an hour as the jet whispered gently higher
towards the northernmost traffic corridor that would carry
it safely across the cluttered Atlantic airspace.

Major Dmitri Muratov sat in an economy window seat.
The seat was paid for by the Soviet government and permitted by an angry and offended US State Department.
Muratov studied the menu carefully and then raised his
head to smile pleasantly across the cabin at the attractive
young woman passenger sitting across the aisle beyond
three vacant seats. The woman returned his smile politely
and then resumed her own study of the menu before
reaching an elegant hand to the call button above her head.
When the steward arrived she ordered a martini. Major
Muratov watched her pleasing, gracious movements: he
would miss all this when he got home, he decided – miss
the pampered elegance, the unconscious luxury of choice,
of colour, of fashion he had been able to observe and enjoy
en passant during his attachment to the Soviet Rezidentura
in New York.

He glanced about at the luxury of economy travel: all
this would soon be gone. The steward was moving slowly
down the aisle towards him and, on impulse, Muratov
held up a hand. The man stooped attentively. 'Sir?'

'A bottle of champagne, if you please?' he decided politely, pointing at the listed beverages on the menu.

'Champagne? Certainly, sir. A full bottle, sir? Or merely a half?'

The Russian glanced across the empty seats towards the attractive young woman he had smiled at a few moments earlier. 'Oh, a full bottle, I think.'

Two hours later, their pleasant lunch concluded, the young woman excused herself from Muratov's side, slipped back to her own seat and settled down for an afternoon nap, her soft hair cushioned against one of the crisp white pillows provided by a thoughtful, competitive airline. Muratov watched her with a slight smile, his critical faculties mellowed considerably by an excellent lunch washed down by the chilled champagne. The meal had been perfect, he decided, capped by idle, flirtatious and amusing conversation with a beautiful, intelligent woman. Soon he too allowed his head to tilt back against the pillows. He slept.

The sleep of the expelled Soviet diplomat was genuine. That of the woman was not. It was an old and sometimes successful ploy, this planting of a CIA observer on the very last stages of the route home to listen for the unguarded word as the mental defences began to slip down in the geographical no-man's-land high above the Atlantic. Now, behind gently closed eyes, the woman strove to interpret the strange behaviour of a man who considered champagne a suitable intoxicant to mix with the drugs of removal, disgrace and dishonour.

Professor Eduard Ryabov, his wife Irena and the boy Misha stuck close behind the polished heels of the tall, uniformed MVD* security officer as he carved a rough passage through the tight knots of burdened passengers towards the antique grandeur of the passenger express that would shortly carry Irena Ryabov and the boy on the first stage of their long journey to Leningrad.

The civilians moved aside without protest, few sparing

* MVD: Ministry of Internal Security.

more than a shrug and a glance at the blue and white of the officer's shoulderboards, resigned as ever to delay and confusion – resigned also to the knowledge that the *vlasti*★ had, as always, this State-condoned right to brush them aside as they struggled with their cheap suitcases, their lumpy paper packages tied with string, their little packets of food and watery beer that threatened to burst all over the platform in sticky, sweet confusion.

The escorting officer now grasped the hand-rails of the metal staircase leading to their compartment and paused, his boot on the bottom rung of the ladder, to bawl angrily at the old woman in black coat and ancient scarf who was blocking the top of the stairs. Clutching a bulging parcel of brown loaves, she struggled aside as the party climbed up and moved past her down the narrow corridor to the sanctuary of their reserved compartment. As Professor Ryabov dumped their suitcases on the floor, Misha darted to the window and strained sideways to glance down the length of the train, excited at the prospect of so adult a journey.

The Professor straightened painfully and then paused to catch his breath. 'I wish to . . . to talk privately to my wife and to the boy here for one moment. You will please wait outside. It will only take a moment.'

The escorting officer merely nodded, slid back the door and stepped out into the corridor. The door rolled shut behind him as a whistle blew from somewhere near the front of the train. Professor Ryabov felt the rising bile of urgency, of panic. He had only moments left now. He leant forward and embraced his wife clumsily over the suitcases and patted her shoulder awkwardly through the combined bulk of their thick overcoats. 'Do you have everything?' he asked anxiously.

'Yes, yes, Eduard. Don't fuss so –'

'And you . . . you understand –' he glanced over his shoulder at the officer's broad back – 'about what may happen? About what you are to do?'

★ *Vlasti:* powers-that-be.

Again she nodded impatiently, anxiety mingled with exasperation at her husband's flapping attention to the details they had gone over again and again the night before.

'Eduard, if it happens as they say, it will be all right – truly. Now – quickly: you must go. Enough of this waiting,' she decided briskly, taking charge.

'Yes, yes – you are right,' agreed her husband, turning to the boy. 'Mishinka, come here,' he commanded, a thickness in his voice betraying the onset of an emotion he had resolved to hide. The boy turned from the window, the right eye closing slightly against the angry infection within.

'Uncle Eduard, the train is –'

'Forget the train for a moment.' He stooped and held out his arms. The boy came forward hesitantly, embarrassed by this sudden display of emotion. His uncle hugged him fiercely, his eyes tightly closed as he felt the boy's narrow shoulders beneath his hands. Then he held the boy away at arm's length studying his nephew with a sad, lingering finality. 'You are to take care of yourself, Misha Prolev,' he said quietly, dropping the diminutive for the first time. 'Do you hear what your old uncle is saying? You are to do everything your Aunt Irena tells you – everything, is that understood?' he insisted. 'I do not want to hear any bad reports about you.'

'Yes, uncle.' He looked resigned, puzzled. He would only be gone two or three days, four at the outside. What had got into the old man all of a sudden?

'And the camera I gave you? Where is that?' demanded the Professor with a hand on the boy's arm.

Misha twisted free and pointed to the school satchel he had laid on the wooden seat. 'In there. With my books, uncle.'

Professor Ryabov nodded and ruffled the boy's thick black hair. There was nothing more to say, and further delay was suddenly unbearable. He straightened and turned abruptly out of the compartment. The officer watched silently as he brushed past and climbed down from the train as another whistle blew. From the platform below he stood for a moment looking up at the faces of his wife and nephew as the train began to move. He stood there for a long, lonely moment, waving until the train had dwindled into insignificance. Then he turned and walked slowly back to his car.

As the distance widened between boy and uncle, Misha bounced down on to the hard wooden seat and turned to his aunt. 'Auntie Irena,' he asked quietly, 'I think Uncle Eduard was crying. Why was that? Why should he cry?'

The few sentimental tears had been brushed impatiently aside by the time Professor Ryabov slipped behind the wheel of his car for the short drive back to the space faculty. By then his formidable intellect was wholly concentrated once more upon what he had come to describe to himself as an act of international madness, perhaps of self-immolation: the offensive deployment of Skyshroud.

If his wife had been able to ignore the presence of the security officer sitting with them now in their private compartment, she might have answered Misha's simple question by saying that partings at railway stations were always painful. Yet such a response would have touched only lightly upon the true depths of a moral sadness that had climbed down to the very pit of her husband's soul as the true purpose of his work had leapt suddenly into clear and terrible focus beside which further intellectual blindness was impossible.

That final process of revelation had begun two days ago.

He had been working in Number Three Laboratory in the eastern end of the Semipalatinsk faculty when he was summoned suddenly to the office of the faculty's Director. That in itself was nothing new. Professor Ryabov had merely shrugged away the irritation of another distraction and hurried away along the gleaming corridors, intent only upon making the disruption to an already tight schedule as brief as possible.

Looking back now, he realized with a start of alarm that even *then* it was the work he had been putting first, the work in isolation from its wider application in the world of people and other living things beyond the stainless-steel walls of his laboratories. Yet even as he walked up the sloping ramp towards the Director's offices he had reminded himself of that dark intention to test Skyshroud shortly against a very real Soviet village. Perhaps there had been a change of policy, of target, he thought. Perhaps even at this late hour humanitarian considerations had triumphed over military strategy; perhaps they had decided to spare the village, to change the target's co-ordinates – perhaps, please God, they had abandoned all thoughts of offensive deployment altogether. His steps quickened.

They hadn't.

He sensed that the moment his pass had been returned by the guard outside and he had been ushered through into the Director's office. The Director was absent, his office occupied by three men in civilian clothes. Two were seated in the chairs reserved for visiting dignitaries, while the third was standing behind the Director's desk, his hands clasped behind his back.

All three looked up and smiled pleasantly as the door opened, relaxed and at home amid unfamiliar surroundings. Glancing through the window into the private car park beyond, Professor Ryabov had a moment to glimpse the large black Volga with the discreet MOC licence plate of the Party as the men came forward to shake hands. All were strangers, yet he sensed all knew much about him.

'I was told Comrade Director Ivassov wished to see me,' said Ryabov to the three strangers equally.

The shortest of the three – portly, grey, mid-fifties – shook his head briefly. 'I am afraid not. The Director has been called away. We judged it easier to reach you without attracting unnecessary attention if we said the summons came from this office. Our apologies.' The head bowed without apology. The summons. The word brought a chill into the room.

'And you are . . . who?' prompted Ryabov, ignoring the hand that gestured him to an empty chair.

'From State Security,' announced their spokesman simply. The others watched silently.

223 :

'I see,' pretended Professor Ryabov. 'And how may I help the Party, comrades? Forgive me, but certain . . . decisions taken recently mean that I am extremely busy.' The edge of bitter sarcasm crept in unintentionally.

'We understand, Professor.'

There was a pause as the three exchanged glances. Secret signals flashed between them: they had expected anxious, malleable co-operation. Trained to detect the nuances of fear, guilt, and anger, they were puzzled by the man's air of suspicious hostility towards them and – far more important – towards the requirements of the State. Wasn't this the chosen recipient of the Order of the Red Banner, the award of which would ensure a standard of living for his lifetime that would almost equal that of the most decadent western nation?

One of the men sat back, unbuttoned his jacket and folded his arms. 'We come to you, Professor, on a matter of the utmost delicacy. The utmost secrecy.'

He paused. Professor Ryabov waited silently, forcing them to come to him. How ridiculous they looked, how earnest, in their tight dark suits and their Party expressions! The man shifted awkwardly and began again. 'It concerns your nephew, Professor. The son of the Prolev woman. Lydia Prolev.'

There was a stirring of embarrassment from the man's companions as he spoke the name, a mental intake of breath, as though verbal association with a defector of such prominence was enough to rot the entire barrel of Soviet solidarity.

'Misha?' Professor Ryabov leant forward frowning, his veil of detached, faintly hostile curiosity pierced by this sudden unexpected reminder of family loyalty. 'What about him?' he demanded sharply.

Again there was that faint stirring. The man behind the desk glanced at his silent companions as though seeking Party support for whatever he might now feel compelled to disclose. 'We want you to understand, Professor, that our visit here has been authorized by the highest authority. It further follows that nothing of what you will shortly learn here is to be divulged to any third party: is that understood?'

Ryabov nodded impatiently, adding dryly: 'I am not unused to keeping secrets.'

'Good. Now – the boy: this trip of his to Leningrad. The business of the eye. With whom will he be travelling? Yourself, or your wife?'

'My wife. I do not have the time – not even for the boy.'

The man nodded. 'Of course, Professor. That is as I expected. It is as well that he travels with someone with whom he is totally familiar, somebody he loves.'

He paused, flicked open a slim dossier and bent his head over a copy of Muratov's recent signal to Moscow, a signal that contained Ferris's warning that an attempt might soon be made to lift the boy from within the Soviet Union. 'It is only fair to warn you, Professor, that we have it on good authority that an attempt may be made to kidnap the boy and take him over to the West, to his mother.'

Professor Ryabov's eyebrows rose in disbelief. 'What? You can't be serious –'

'We are perfectly serious, Professor. The proximity of Leningrad to neutralist countries, its use for such operations in the past, all these facts suggest that such an operation may well be attempted. The party will travel, therefore, with an escort. There are certain ways, however, in which *you* can be of assistance . . .'

:: WASHINGTON

Alone now in the anonymous motel on Salvador Drive, Lydia Prolev felt caged, restless. She got up and paced the cramped, mean little room as she tried to squeeze the exciting thoughts of reunion from her mind, imagining, even as she failed, the converging paths of Frank Yates and the son she had not seen for almost two years. And who was going blind . . .

How would he have changed? He would be taller, of course – and perhaps his shoulders would have broadened also. Would he be fatter? Or slimmer? And his studies – how would he have been coping without his mother to prod him in front of his homework every evening? Her mouth softened into a smile. Particularly with mathematics. He hated mathematics. That had been a favourite joke between them, and, at times, a cause of bitter argument: the scientist mother and the young boy who still had trouble adding up the price of a handful of groceries. And her uncle and aunt – how were they coping now without her? How was he coping with the professional stigma of her departure, the shame of her defection? Too important to be punished, too vital to be removed, he was not too important a member of the State to be immune to the glacial eye of official displeasure, perhaps even of suspicion.

Lydia forced herself to put away this warm glance at the past; the pain it brought was still too great, made more poignant now by the sudden possibility that within a few short days she might be permitted to see her son once more. If all went well. Please, please, let it go well; let it be so.

And if it did? Then she would make a home for them both in this new and exciting land of boundless, numbing plenty glimpsed so briefly from the isolation of the series of 'safe' houses she had been shuttled between since the very moment of her defection. Perhaps, she thought, perhaps it would not be so difficult: once she had told the American General all she could remember she would be of no further use. Then, surely, she would be allowed to disappear into the vast American hinterland, and then soon – with a little help – she would be able to find a job: as a teacher, perhaps. Her English would become fluent, the accent would begin to disappear and they would finally lose the stigma of fugitive. Misha would work hard, perhaps work his way through college, as was apparently the custom. And then? She shrugged. There was an awful lot of 'maybe' and 'perhaps', and the future stretched away uncertainly into the distance as her mind frolicked over the freedoms that had been revealed to her so fleetingly, so carelessly, in this generous, profligate land.

In the cabin next door someone turned up the television, and the sound hammered through the thin dividing walls. On impulse Lydia turned and lifted her coat from the hook behind the door. She began to slip into the sleeves and then stopped, her eyes caught by her own reflection in the mirror on the cheap dressing-table: General Freeman had ordered her not to move, not to answer the phone, not to open the door. She was to remain alone until the evening, when he would come out and collect her himself.

Only now she was restless.

The television set was turned off abruptly next door and now she heard a man and a woman laugh together intimately. There was a squeal of feigned surprise from the woman, and presently Lydia heard the bed-springs begin to creak up and down, up and down. She felt shame, shock, embarrassment – a voyeur caught with her eye to the keyhole. Fastening her belt hurriedly, she fluffed her hair outside her collar and turned towards the door, a decision suddenly taken.

She'd only be gone an hour, she told herself. An hour at the most.

She stepped out of the motel and paused on the sidewalk, alone and unescorted for almost the first time since her arrival in the United States. Cars and lorries blared past noisily.

Lydia looked about her suddenly, her senses battered by the onslaught of new sounds and colours, like a hospital patient confronting the outside world after months of isolation. Lydia opened her handbag. She had a few dollars Frank had given her a few days ago against what he had vaguely described as 'emergencies'.

Summoning her courage, Lydia decided she would now face her problems head-on: she would walk for a while and then find somewhere she could sit, drink a cup or two of coffee, and watch go by the world she hoped soon to join. She walked to the corner and waited there amid a cluster of pedestrians opposite a red light that warned DONT WALK. She stood there looking about her, desperately anxious to conform, to learn.

On a stool near the window of the lunch bar opposite, a man tossed his newspaper aside, laid two dollar bills beside his plate and walked unhurriedly to the door, his eyes on the woman standing on the opposite corner. There was a break in the traffic, and he sauntered across the street and fell into step twenty paces behind Lydia Prolev. Despite the front-page picture of Nicholson in his paper, despite the news of the fire, Tolland's arrest and the expulsion of Muratov from New York, Ferris was in no particular hurry. He already had his instructions.

:: THE HEARING: DAY TWO

'Thank you, General Freeman. We'll take a break there.'

Freeman nodded, stepped back from the raised platform in the well of the hearings chamber of the New Senate Building and made his way back to his seat.

Where before, earlier that same morning, there had been angry hostility and open suspicion as a direct result of Freeman's prominence in the morning newspapers and on breakfast television, there was now a keen, almost polite interest in the General's continuing submissions regarding the Soviet defensive beam weapon system.

Once past the reporters gathered on the steps outside the New Senate Building, the General had encountered a volley of questions within, as first one and then another of his critics fell over themselves to condemn Freeman's actions in the roundest possible terms.

That assault had lasted exactly twenty-five minutes.

While it persisted, the move to suspend both Freeman and the hearings he had instigated rose to a fever pitch against which the cogent reasonings of the General's one ally, Professor James Disman, had been swept aside. Then, at exactly 11.45, the mood passed its crisis and fizzled away to be replaced by this new, sheepish attentiveness.

It had fallen, with neat justice, upon Tom Greener, the Assistant Director of the CIA, to deliver Freeman with whatever dignity he could muster from beneath that cloud of suspicion.

Greener had arrived late at the hearings. As he told his fellow committee members in the hushed silence that greeted his arrival, the papers discovered at Sam Tolland's home had been verified as genuine beyond any doubt. Traced back swiftly into the administration's bureaucracy, and binding Tolland to his treachery by the text they contained, the evidence of the depth of his guilt was suddenly all too clear. Doubts that had beset the Agency for months were suddenly doubts no longer; other intelligence agencies were called in too as the rich documentary pickings found in Sam Tolland's home led back into the Soviet Residency in New York, and the true purpose of Tolland's verbal attacks, his attempts to undermine the importance of Freeman's allegations, became known.

The silence had deepened as Greener sketched in the details, and more than one committee member glanced across at Freeman with a new and startled respect. As to the shooting itself – Freeman's own arguments carried the day, given forcefully as they were after Greener had finished speaking: while accusing him of the murder of a stranger outside Tolland's home might satisfy some immediate, basic hunger for a scapegoat, however improbable, it was accepted now that such a theory was hardly worthy of serious or prolonged consideration. Freeman was off the hook.

He sat down beside his assistants, aware of a fresh and not unwelcome respect in their glances. The next development was not long in coming: a side door opened and Tom Greener began walking across towards Freeman. He stopped in front of his table and stuck out his hand awkwardly.

Freeman rose, knowing what the gesture cost him.

'General Freeman – my apologies. About what I said last night out there. I was wrong.' They shook hands, Freeman nodding gruffly.

'Oh, say –' added Greener. 'By way of a peace offering. Picked this up on the way over. What d'you make of it?'

He handed Freeman a flimsy message form. It was an agent's field report transmitted from the flight deck of a 747 high above the Atlantic and it brought together two strange bedfellows: disgrace and champagne.

*

'Will you come this way?' The young waiter led Lydia Prolev through the crowded restaurant towards a small table tucked away against the wall near the kitchens. The table was laid for two although the chair opposite was empty. The waiter brought a menu to the table, placed a glass of iced water beside her napkin and sauntered away.

Lydia studied the menu intently for some moments, covering her confusion behind lowered eyes. It was lunch-time and the place was crowded with cheerful, chattering young people. Lydia covertly studied the bright shirts and blouses, the jackets and the jeans, the expensive jewellery so casually worn, so flamboyantly displayed. The different hair styles, the profusion of cigarettes, drinks and money, made her awkward, uncomfortable, acutely aware both of the few dollars in her purse and of her own muted, conservative appearance. How poised, how confident these Americans appeared!

'You about ready to order now?' The waiter stood beside her, pencil poised.

'I would like . . . I would like a coffee, please.'

The waiter frowned. 'Just coffee? That's all? It's lunchtime, you know, and –'

'Of course, of course –' She consulted the menu hurriedly and chose something at random, anxious to avoid attracting attention. 'I shall have a fresh salad also.'

'Fine. Cheese? Ham? Egg? Anchovy? House Special – what'll it be?'

'Er . . . cheese.'

'One cheese salad, one coffee coming up.' The waiter scribbled on his pad and disappeared into the kitchens. Lydia shook her head at her own confusion. Be patient, she counselled herself. Have patience. It takes time, that is all.

In a very short while – 'This seat taken?'

She glanced up.

Ferris.

The menu slipped from her fingers as she stared aghast across the intimate little table into the clear, steady eyes of the man sitting comfortably opposite.

'You're being a little careless now, aren't you, Mrs Prolev? I mean –' Ferris glanced easily about him – 'I don't see any knights in shining armour ready to ride to the rescue. Not this time. Your Captain Yates know you're out playing hookey?'

'What are you doing here?' she whispered. 'What do you want?' Behind the pleasant lunchtime chatter that surrounded them, Lydia suddenly saw Viktor Pligin lying spread-eagled across a dirty mattress, his throat neatly cut from ear to ear. Ashen-faced, eyes wide with the fear that rose to engulf her – 'Why do you do this? For what purpose? What is it you *want*?'

'What do I want? Let me see now –' he pretended to consider the matter deeply – 'Yes: I think I shall start with the salad too. They say the –'

'Here you go: one cheese salad. Coffee'll be up in a –' Lydia pushed the table away, rose violently to her feet and hurried past the waiter towards the exit. Ignoring the startled faces, the hands half-raised in protest, she hurried blindly towards the street and away from the terrors that stalked behind her. Pushing now through a knot of dawdling customers she burst out on to the sidewalk. She paused, panting hard, to look wildly about her: there was a corner fifty feet away. She glanced behind her, expecting at any moment to see the doors thrown back as the man closed in, yet they remained shut; there was no sign of pursuit. She turned and ran down towards the crossroads, her heels tapping terror on the sidewalk.

Ten yards to the corner. Five. Three – and still no signs of pursuit. Now she was round the corner. Lydia forced herself to slow down, to walk, to blend in with the other pedestrians, who were her only protection. She searched desperately for a bus, a taxi. There! An empty cab out in the middle lane cruising slowly up from the corner as it waited for the lights to change. As she watched they showed green and the lines of traffic began to surge forward, gathering speed. Ignoring the horns, Lydia ran out into the traffic, darted round the bonnet to a squeal of angry brakes and hammered on the window.

'Jesus, lady! You tired of livin' or somethin'?' demanded the startled driver.

She climbed in, the door banged shut behind her and the cab shot forward.

'OK, OK – so you made it. So where's the fire?'

'Just go – go,' she panted.

General Freeman glanced again at his watch. The committee had been studying that latest batch of satellite reconnaissance photographs for the best part of forty minutes. He smiled grimly. Things were looking up at last. A day or so ago they'd have tossed them back in his lap within a matter of minutes – nothing like a dash of awakened guilt to prompt attentive study. When they returned he'd reveal what –

'General Freeman, sir?'

The General turned to see one of the uniformed guards standing at his elbow. 'You're wanted out in the lobby, General. Someone there to see you. A woman. Says it's urgent, sir.'

Frowning, Freeman rose, laid his papers aside and walked briskly down the long, echoing corridor.

Lydia Prolev was standing nervously in the lobby, her hands clasped tightly together in front of her. Freeman strode towards her angrily: now what the hell?

'Mrs Prolev? What are you doing here? I thought I told you –' he hissed as she grasped his arm.

'That . . . that man? The man who killed Viktor, Viktor Pligin? He came after me! He found me!'

'In the motel? How the hell did he –?' but she was shaking her head:

'No, no – not to the motel. To a . . . a restaurant.' Briefly she told him what had happened. Brushing aside unproductive anger, Freeman listened attentively and then, taking her arm, led her gently to a leather-backed sofa set into an alcove. They sat down together in an echoing silence, Lydia glancing about her nervously, her eyes fluttering wide at every strange sound.

'Try to relax, Mrs Prolev. I want to ask you a few questions, OK?' She swallowed and nodded. 'When did you first see him?'

'As I . . . as I looked up. He was there. Sitting there.'

'At your table?'

'Yes.'

'And before that? On your walk from the motel to the restaurant?'

She shook her head.

'And he came straight to your table?'

'Yes, that is so.'

'Was that the only empty seat in the restaurant, can you remember?'

She considered this carefully:

'No, no – there were others. I am sure of it.'

'And he said – what? Can you remember? The exact words?'

'He . . . he said that I had been careless. And that he could not see Frank. Frank Yates.' There was a pause.

'Anything else?' asked the General.

She frowned, trying to remember something, then 'You have a word – hooking?' she asked earnestly.

Despite himself Freeman smiled. 'Sure,' he admitted. 'We have such a word. It means selling your body for gain: prostitution.'

Lydia shook her head impatiently. 'No, no – not like that.' She paused. 'Hookey,' she decided finally. 'Is that

233 :

also a word? The man asks if Frank knows that I am "play-ing hookey" – would that be correct?'

'That would make sense, yes,' admitted Freeman slowly, his mind already ahead of his words. He rose suddenly and Lydia watched him apprehensively. 'I want you to stay here one moment – don't worry, you're quite secure, I'm going to get one of my officers stay with you 'til I'm through. Then you're to come back with me, to my home. We'll take it on from there, OK?'

She nodded as Freeman began to walk away. Then he stopped and turned, a finger pointing at the woman. 'And one more thing, Mrs Prolev: no more walks, no more little trips, understand?'

Deafened and numbed by the austerity of his military flight across the Atlantic aboard the giant Lockheed Galaxy, Frank Yates had spent most of that interminable trip playing cards, losing badly to a grinning black Load-Master, and drinking hot coffee out of plastic cartons.

On arrival at Ramstein he was handed a new passport and identity by a nervous Embassy official and then bundled across country to Mannheim for the afternoon flight to Helsinki, Finland.

He slept then, wearied by noise, packet food and plastic coffee, battered also by that special exhaustion reserved for those faced by two Time Zone changes with a third on the way. Travelling now under the name of John Albert Coning, Citizen of the United States, Frank was looking forward to a long, uninterrupted sleep in his Helsinki hotel just as soon as this glide down over the scattering of offshore islands was completed. The DC-9 wobbled a little on final approach, yawed as it crossed the perimeter of the municipal cycle track beneath their port wing and then touched down lightly enough with the double thud-screech of rubber on concrete that spelt safety. Airport clearance formalities took another forty minutes and then he was free to pick his way through the concourse to the line of taxis waiting outside. He glanced up at the large clock on the terminal wall, dropped his bags on to the glass-polished pine of the airport floor and adjusted his watch. Here it was shortly after 8 p.m. Frank felt exhausted. He hefted his bags and hailed a taxi.

The Hotel Posion could have been any large hotel in any prosperous town in any one of a score of different countries. Only the signs and the language were different. There was a pleasing abundance of polished pine and subdued lighting, fresh flowers and gleaming glass, and Frank felt some of the tensions of travel ooze from his body as the girl at reception smiled and booked him in with swift, practised efficiency.

In a matter of moments he was following the young uniformed porter to the bank of lifts and rising silently into the core of the modern building. They rode to the sixth floor, Frank's replies to the boy's tip-conscious politeness restricted to a grunt and a nod. Down the quiet, carpeted corridor they went before the boy showed him into a double bedroom, spent the obligatory half-minute fiddling with the curtains while he waited for Frank to remember where he kept his change and then retreated, closing the door softly behind him.

Frank groaned, stretched, kicked off his shoes and walked through to the bathroom. Then he returned to his holdall, hauled out his toilet kit and began ripping off travel-stained shirt and trousers. He thrust them in an untidy ball into the bottom of his bag and stepped through to the shower. Ten minutes later he called room service and ordered a cold chicken supper and a couple of bottles of chilled beer. Later, empty tray outside his bedroom door, he slipped naked beneath the light, fluffy duvet.

His last waking thought as he gazed up at the pale pine ceiling was that it was now up to them: he had booked in, followed instructions to the letter. 'Them'? he wondered drowsily: who were 'they'? He rolled over and stretched tired toes down into the starched coldness of fresh sheets. He had no idea. No idea at all . . .

*

It was three hours later and there was a faint, muffled knocking. Frank murmured something indistinct and rolled over into the warmth of the duvet. The banging came again, more distinct now, as he began to surface from the pond of sleep. He groaned, rolled on to an elbow and jabbed about for the light switch, eyes blinking in the strange twilight that streamed in from around the edges of the drawn curtains. He found the switch and sat up abruptly, leaden-headed from too much travel and too little sleep.

The knocking came again, insistent now. Frank swung his feet to the floor, tugged the duvet around his naked waist and padded across to the door. He opened it a cautious half-inch. Nothing. He threw off the chain and opened the door wide. Still nothing. Frank craned out and glanced up and down the corridor. No one but a couple walking slowly towards another room, their hips grinding together with each step.

'Excuse me: was that you just now? Knocking on my door?'

The man turned round with the lazy smile of the slightly drunk and nearly laid. '*Bitte?* I am sorry?' queried the German politely. The blonde rested her head against the man's shoulder and regarded Frank fondly.

'It's O K – forget it. My mistake,' corrected Frank hastily, noticing for the first time the elevators a little further down the corridor and the red light that blinked steadily down the level indicator column. He stepped back into his room and closed the door. As he did so he glanced down and saw the white envelope that had been thrust beneath his door. He slipped the chain back on the door, took the envelope over to the bedside table and sat down. He examined the envelope carefully: John Albert Coning. Frank slit open the envelope and tugged out a single sheet of paper:

Presently the phone in your room will ring twice. Exactly four minutes after that you are to leave your room, take the elevator to reception and order a taxi to take you to Temppeliaukio Church. There you will be contacted.

He read the note once more, jotted down the name of the church, burnt the note and began to dress. He had almost finished when the telephone beside his bed rang twice. He glanced at his watch, paid off four minutes and stepped out into the deserted corridor. He depressed the call button and the lift doors sighed open. He stepped forward into the narrow little cage with its wall mirrors and advertisements for gift shops and local restaurants. A man with pale, lank hair was standing facing him, his hands clasped lightly in front of him. They nodded one to another and then averted their eyes as strangers do when thrust together into the intimacy of such surroundings.

The lift doors hissed closed and the elevator dropped silently through the levels towards the reception area.

Level three, level two, level one – reception. The lift kept on going. Frank banged futilely on the stop button as the lift came to an abrupt halt in the car park basement.

'I was supposed –' he began with a wry smile and then stopped. The lift's only other occupant had gripped him tightly by the arm.

'You are to come with me, please, Mr Coning,' he announced quietly, pushing him firmly out of the lift towards a silver-grey Mercedes that now rolled towards them, the note of its powerful engine beating deeply against the enclosed concrete walls.

'What do –?'

'Please. Everything is in order. We know about Temppeliaukio Church. I am your contact. Will you please stand still for one little moment, Mr Coning? Purely a formality.'

With that he ran a hand expertly over Frank's shoulders and back, under his armpits, around his waist and then up and down the inside and outside of legs. Finally he squeezed his crotch lightly. 'My apologies.' He smiled briefly. 'It is necessary to be sure.' Frank nodded, impressed by the man's competence.

'Now,' the man continued, opening the rear door of the Mercedes, 'please get in.' Frank did so. 'There – on the seat beside you – you will find a simple mask. You are to put it on now and to keep your head on your knees. It will not be for very long, I assure you.' Once again he did as he was ordered; the man got in by the opposite door and the car rolled up a steep ramp on to the street above and pulled away. Within minutes he had lost all sense of direction and his muffled questions were greeted by total silence.

Finally the limousine made an abrupt turn to the left, another to the right and then stopped. There was a rolling sound above, and Frank had the impression he had entered some enclosed space, for the smell of oil and petrol was suddenly pronounced. He felt a light tap on his shoulder.

'Good. You may remove the mask now, Mr Coning. Sit up. We have arrived.'

Frank peeled back the mask and looked about him. They were inside someone's large double garage. Glancing behind him, Frank saw that the sound of thunder had come from the heavy metal door that had rolled down behind them. There was a heavy trestle bench running across the end of the garage. On the bench stood several empty bottles and glasses, with, beside these, a tray bearing the remains of a selection of open sandwiches. Beside the tray and the trestle bench stood three men, all listening now to Frank's escort as he made his report. They nodded once or twice and glanced occasionally towards the car – three calm, tough men all in their mid- to late thirties and all with that same unmistakable air of cautious, wary professionalism.

The driver sitting in front of him turned his head briefly at a signal from the tallest of the men. 'You may get out.'

Frank stepped down and, following the silent, pointing finger of the man who was obviously in charge, sat down facing the four on a backless wooden stool. He tried to look unconcerned as he caught the low murmur of foreign voices. Now one of the men turned, picked up the tray of sandwiches and advanced towards him. 'Sandwich?'

He shook his head. 'Thank you – no.'

The other three men had turned to lean back against the trestle, their arms crossed as they watched him closely beneath the harsh, functional neon lighting. There was silence for a moment broken suddenly by the whir of an extractor fan.

'So – you are Mr John Coning.'

Frank nodded warily.

'I am Paul,' said the man holding the tray.

'And?' demanded Frank.

'And the music is getting louder every day.'

'I long for the good old days,' completed Frank. 'Thank Christ for that!'

'Tell me, Mr Coning, what were you told?' demanded Paul, replacing the tray and moving round to rejoin his companions. 'What have your people told you?'

'Only that the boy Misha Prolev is rumoured to be travelling to Leningrad some time between 4 May and 9 May.'

Paul nodded. 'It is more than just a rumour, Mr Coning – it is confirmed. The boy will arrive there early tomorrow morning. He is travelling with a woman, a relative.'

'And the trip's genuine? Legitimate?'

'It would appear so. The boy has a serious eye condition. The hospital that specializes in such treatment is in Leningrad and Leningrad only – that we know. Our sources there show that the boy's appointment for treatment was made more than four months ago. Our people there have been very thorough. They have checked the records – it is genuine.'

'And you understand that I am responsible merely for the boy's safe passage, the return? The snatch itself – that has nothing to do with me?'

'That is the way we would want it, Mr Coning. Forgive me – but you are on our territory now. We are the experts here; we know what we are doing.

'One thing more, Mr Coning, before we move on to other matters.' He paused. 'What is her place in all this –

the woman? The woman who is with the boy? We understand she is some kind of relative.'

Frank shrugged. 'She has no role as far as we're concerned; no tactical value. She must be ignored or dealt with as your people feel fit. We know nothing about any woman.'

'Good,' said Paul as the others nodded their relief. 'It would have added a new dimension of difficulty. We have never attempted this with more than one person before.'

'O K. So what have you got to tell me?' asked Frank.

Now another man came off the edge of the bench and unfolded his arms. 'First – you must do some shopping, here in Helsinki: simple, everyday things. Most important, you must buy a camera, a polaroid. You must buy that, together with a bottle of hair dye. Black hair dye. Before you leave we will give you the name and make of a suitable substance –' he saw Frank's eyebrows rise sceptically – 'don't worry, Mr Coning. It is not for you. Oh – and a powerful light bulb also, something in the region of one hundred and fifty watts.'

He turned and now it was Paul who came forward to pace slowly up and down the garage. He paused, hands resting flat against the bonnet of the Mercedes. 'It is, of course, almost impossible now to get either you or the boy – or indeed both of you travelling together, since I understand the child is too young to travel unescorted – through any sort of Soviet border control: car stowaways, false papers, disguises at the frontier, bribery – even cars that have been specially armoured in order to simply crash through the checkpoints themselves – all have been tried; all are passé – what do you Americans call it? Blown?'

'Blown,' agreed Frank readily, a reservation removed with some relief from his mind. At least they didn't intend knocking on the front door.

'There is, however, one method of gaining temporary, restricted access to the Soviet Union without a visa and with only the most perfunctory of passport inspections – a crossing point, a place of access, where all that matters is numbers: numbers in and numbers out – do you follow what I am saying? Such a visit is only possible between two places on this earth –' he paused to point dramatically at the concrete floor – 'Helsinki, and –'

'Leningrad?' offered Frank.

Paul nodded. 'Leningrad. Exactly. It is possible for tourists to join a four-day excursion cruise from the port here – a cruise that goes east along Finska Viken – the Gulf of Finland – to the city of Leningrad itself. The sea passage is of some fourteen hours' duration, I believe. Once there, the tour concerns itself with the usual things: the Hermitage, St Isaac's Cathedral, the Peterhof, matters of that nature.'

Frank was nodding silently, sensing the way in.

'Naturally, the tour is closely escorted. Once you arrive at the Soviet Union there are certain . . . restrictions, but these are not insurmountable, as we have discovered to our advantage in the past. The important thing is that entry by this method is not restricted to visa-holders only. There is less control: you are required to surrender your passport upon arrival when you disembark with the rest of the tour and simply reclaim that same passport when the tour is over.' He paused now and folded his arms. 'There is something else I shall tell you also that is connected with this business of numbers, of counting heads. Almost a thousand kilometres due north of where we are standing, vast herds of our Finnish reindeer are about to be moved to spring pasture. They move for days over the frozen lakes and the open tundra – perhaps you know this? Anyway, they move for days and days – vast herds of these animals – thousands upon thousands, escorted by their Lapp herdsmen and their families as they move slowly eastwards.' He smiled. 'Naturally, it is no easy matter to ensure that animals and herdsman stay behind the Finnish border – a border which, in any case, is little more than a line upon a map in those northern latitudes.' He shrugged. 'In fact, it has been known for those Finns to cross quite a long way into the Soviet Union, Mr Coning. Quite a long way . . .'

It was after 3 a.m. Helsinki time before Frank Yates was

ushered politely back into the Mercedes, blindfolded and driven back to the Posion Hotel.

Eight hours later he stood at the corner of Norra Esplanaden on the city's southern outskirts, watching the tourist-laden pleasure steamers butt out into the sheltered bay towards Suomenlinna. It was a dry, warm day, a time of balmy winds and strong shadows cast on to the sidewalk by pleasant, purposeful people. Even the thick belt of pine trees that rose on the western slopes beyond the moored ferries seemed to add a note of nordic clarity to the bustling, colourful seaport. He glanced up and began scanning faces, enjoying, beyond the immediacy of his task, the pleasure and stimulus of a foreign country.

He glanced again at his watch. Two minutes to go. He flicked open his tourist's guide and consulted its pages. In the plastic bag at his side lay the camera, hair dye and light bulb he had been instructed to purchase. All he needed now, he told himself a trifle self-consciously, was someone to play with.

'Mr Coning? Paul sent me – I believe you are expecting me?'

Frank swung round. A short, seamed little man was smiling pleasantly up into his face, his eyes crinkled against the sunlight. In his late forties, he had a face browned and beaten by the weather. 'It would be as well if we both consulted your map, perhaps?'

Frank smoothed out the coloured pages, and the man laid a thick finger against it. 'My name is Halle,' he said quietly. 'Seppo Halle. If you raise your head now and look directly across the square towards the sea – that is good – you will see a young boy sitting alone on a public seat beside a red automobile that is just beginning to move . . . so? You have seen him? See? He is moving now towards the fishing boats.'

'I've got him.'

'Good. That is Jakko, my son, Mr Coning.' He paused, watching Frank shrewdly. 'The age is good? It is acceptable?'

'Looks about right from here. I'll need to take a closer look before I can be certain. The hair will –'

'The hair is not important. That we will change – but certainly: you must take a closer look. You must be satisfied, yes?' He smiled up into Frank's face. 'Where are you staying, Mr Coning?'

Frank told him his hotel and room number. Seppo Halle nodded approvingly. 'It is the right place. Large and efficient – yet impersonal also, yes? We must meet there – shall we say in one hour? One hour from now?' He held out his hand politely and Frank took it. It was dry and firm.

The man turned on his heel and strolled away. Frank watched the boy dart across the street, and presently father and son were swallowed up in the hurrying, sunlit crowds.

One hour later there was a gentle tapping on the bedroom door. Frank opened it cautiously and Seppo and Jakko slipped quietly into the room. This time Seppo was carrying a small holdall. He dropped the bag and came forward to shake hands warmly, his weathered face creased in smiles. 'We are here as promised, Mr Coning. One hour exactly.'

He stepped behind his son and ruffled his hair fondly. 'This is Jakko, Mr Coning. He is twelve years. The middle of my sons.'

The boy was pale and thin. Long skinny wrists poked out from the sleeves of his jacket. He pushed the hair out of his eyes and gave Frank an uncertain, lopsided smile.

'Would you stand over by that light for one second, Jakko?'

Seppo bustled his son over to the standard light while Frank took out a dog-eared photograph loaned to him with great reluctance by Lydia Prolev. He studied the photograph briefly, pressed the boy down into an armchair and stepped back, the picture of Misha held at arm's length while he compared likenesses. Not bad, he conceded critically: not bad at all. The same strong features, roughly the same age – the hair was all wrong, of course, but that could be changed.

'Good?' asked Seppo anxiously, moving around his son,

inspecting him critically as though he were some prize exhibit under the judge's scrutiny.

Frank took his time, refusing to be railroaded. Now was not the moment for errors, for hasty judgements; the success or failure of what followed would depend upon this judgement. Finally he straightened up and slipped the photograph back into his wallet.

'OK,' he said quietly. 'I think we might be in business.'

Seppo's brown little face lit up like a warning to shipping. Frank held up a hand. 'First, I want a word with you alone, Seppo. Ask the boy to wait in there.' He indicated the bathroom. Seppo spoke rapidly to his son in Finnish and the boy disappeared obediently into the bathroom. When the door had closed 'How much does he know about all this? How much have you told him?'

Seppo made a throwaway gesture.

'He knows only that he is to travel with you to Leningrad, where he will be reunited with his mother. He has been told to follow your instructions exactly. This he understands.'

'And the risk? Does he understand the risk too?'

'There is little risk,' Seppo shrugged. 'We know about these matters here, Mr Coning. It is quite straightforward: one year it is for the Americans, a few months later, another year maybe, it is for the Danes, or perhaps maybe the Belgians. And always there is no problem.'

'You make a living out of this?' demanded Frank incredulously.

Seppo spread out his hands and sighed. 'You Americans are so naive: what do you think, Mr Coning? That we do it for love? For – what do you call it? – Democracy? Most certainly we do it for money: for US dollars, French francs, Israeli pounds –'

'Russian roubles?'

The smile slipped a little. 'You think perhaps that I betray you? That I am a double-agent? No, Mr Coning: not Russian roubles. I am a businessman. I believe in free enterprise,' he said with simple dignity.

'And the boy – what about him?'

Seppo shrugged. 'I have five sons, Mr Coning. Five sons and one daughter. Today it is for Jakko to come with me, that is all. He is the most suitable.'

Frank sighed, conscience appeased. 'OK, Seppo – he's your son. You can bring him back now.'

Jakko rejoined them as Frank returned to his case and dug out the visa-free tour application.

'Please, Mr Coning, before we start: a small favour?' Frank looked up. 'Is it possible to order something to eat before we start this business?' Jakko smiled uncertainly at the American, his long wrists dangling at his sides.

'Sure, why not? Help yourself. Room service is –'

'Nine. I know. I have been here before.' Seppo crossed to the phone and dialled the number, rattled off what sounded like a menu for a state banquet, replaced the receiver and shrugged apologetically. 'Don't worry, Mr Coning – don't worry. It is all expenses, no?'

The food arrived on gleaming metal trolleys. Frank signed for the lot and then watched, with the righteous anger of the cruelly exploited, as two bottles of Teachers whisky were swept off the trolley to disappear into the depths of Seppo's capacious holdall. 'For the emergencies,' offered Seppo with a sly grin.

After a decent interval, in which trays of expensive food were emptied with the lightning speed of a conjuror's sleight of hand, Frank dragged them back to the purpose of the meeting. 'Right – to work,' he said sternly, an earlier tolerance replaced by a grim determination to justify the alarming hotel bill. 'Jakko – over there.' He pointed to a chair.

Jakko nodded, crammed the remains of a delicate soufflé into his mouth and ambled obediently to the chair. Seppo burrowed into the depths of his holdall and emerged – after a shoft clinking of bottles – brandishing a pair of metal-rimmed spectacles. 'I was requested to bring these –' he burrowed again – 'or these?' A lighter pair this time, plastic with pinkish arms. Frank regarded them doubtfully as Seppo darted across to his son and slipped the metal spectacles on to his nose. Still bending, he turned towards Frank. 'With the wearing of these, Mr Coning, it is not the shape or the style that is important, you comprehend, merely the fact that they are either there or not there, do you understand?' He shook his head impatiently. 'It does not matter if this boy of yours has a different style – almost certainly that will be so. All that the Soviet official will remember – and if he is bored or it is raining, he will remember nothing at all – is that the boy was or was not wearing spectacles as he left the ship.'

'OK, we'll try it,' agreed Frank, bowing to experience, to logic. He loaded the polaroid, wound on the film, laid the camera aside and studied the boy critically. 'The clothes,' he decided slowly. 'The clothes are all wrong. We'll try a few photos first to get the lighting right. Then I want you to go out and buy a coat, jacket, trousers – OK?'

Seppo nodded readily, his eyes glittering at opportunity. 'That will cost some money,' he agreed with relish. 'American clothes are expensive in Helsinki. Very expensive.'

Frank sighed. 'I'll take care of that.' He picked up the powerful light bulb and fitted it into the lamp behind Jakko. He turned it on, and the boy instantly averted his eyes beneath the painful glare. 'Good,' approved Frank. 'That's how I want it.' He spent the next few minutes constantly adjusting either the boy, the chair or the position of the lamp until he was satisfied. Then he lifted the camera and set to work.

Irena Ryabov was tired and strained from the train journey
that had carried her and the boy first to Moscow and then
on to Leningrad itself. Now she started violently at the
sound of knocking on the wooden door of their bedroom
on the sixth floor of Leningrad's Pushkin Hotel.

A hand clutching the throat of her ankle-length flannel
night-dress, hair-net already in place, she paused as the
hammering came again. 'Mishinka, quickly now – into the
bathroom,' she commanded, pushing the boy past her. He
was also dressed ready for bed as, grumbling, he did as he
was bid. Irena Ryabov closed the door firmly behind him
and stood for a moment, heart thumping, unsure what to
do. Then she walked slowly towards the door. 'Yes? Who
is it? What do you want?' she wavered.

'Open the door, Mrs Ryabov.'

Recognizing the voice of the uniformed security officer
who had accompanied them for the entire duration of their
journey from Semipalatinsk to this strange, huge city,
Irena Ryabov sighed and fumbled the chain off the door.

'You frightened me, banging on the door in that manner.
I am not used to visits late at night,' she complained,
clenching closed the neck of her night-dress between frail
fingers.

Unlike the Professor's wife, Kapitan Simonov, their
escort, was still fully clothed: the top button of his closely-
fitting tunic was still fastened, the boots still gleaming.
Irena Ryabov wondered if he had polished them just now,
specially for this night-time visit. It would be in character,
certainly. Kapitan Simonov of the MVD had been every
inch the stiff, formally correct, watchful official for every
mile of their endless rail journey.

Now he stepped abruptly into the room and swept the twin-bedded apartment with eyes that missed nothing – not the drab green walls, the scuffed ancient wooden furniture, the sealed window that looked out beyond dirt and cobwebs to a grey stone courtyard below   nothing. He spun round sharply. 'And the boy? Where is the boy?'

'Mishinka – come out of the bathroom. It is all right. It is only the Kapitan. Again.'

The door opened and Misha emerged in his pyjamas brushing his teeth. He regarded the officer with the fearless dislike of a ten-year-old. If it was possible to brush teeth rebelliously, Misha Prolev now strove to do just that.

'So,' said Kapitan Simonov softly, 'you are settled? All is in order? It has been a long, tiring journey for you both.' He brought his heels together sharply. 'Mrs Prolev – I shall see you both in the morning. Breakfast is at 08.00 downstairs.' He nodded.

'Good night, Kapitan,' said Irena Ryabov wearily. 'And please – do not come banging on that door again. It frightens me. We shall still be here in the morning.'

'It is my duty to see that you are. That you come to no harm.' He smiled thinly and bowed once more. The door banged closed behind him. Irena Ryabov stood motionless watching the door blankly while she thought the thoughts she was unable to share with a ten-year-old. How she wished Eduard was here to help her, to take the strain. She glanced round. Misha was scowling at the door, toothbrush clenched tightly in his fist.

'Why is he like that, Auntie Irena? Why are they all like that?' he demanded, his mouth full of toothpaste.

'Like what?'

'Like this –' He puffed out his chest and, attempting to look down his nose, began to strut around the cluttered bedroom. After a few steps the effort failed and he dissolved into a bout of frothy coughing.

His aunt smiled. 'It is the training,' she said absently. 'It is nothing, Mishinka – just the training. Now –' she turned to the boy and clapped her hands together sharply – 'now you – comrade Mishinka: bed – bed – bed – quickly, or I shall call the good Kapitan.'

Kapitan Simonov stepped quietly away from where he had been listening by the door and walked slowly down the thinly carpeted corridor. He paused at the closed door of the *dezhurnaya*,* pushed it wide and strode in. The woman was sitting in front of a small black and white television watching the City Lottery intently through a haze of cigarette smoke. Glancing first at the uniform, then at the shoulderboards, then at the face, she stubbed out her cigarette and turned off the television hastily. 'Comrade Kapitan? May I be of some assistance?'

'I have to make an important telephone call. You will take me to the hotel switchboard,' he ordered. The old woman rose to her feet without protest and led the way to the ancient elevators. Once downstairs she took him past the kitchens and along a stone-flagged corridor to a small office without any windows. She paused outside a door of frosted glass. Simonov nodded and the woman scuffed away in her slippers. Inside there was another old woman sitting at the switchboard. He told her the number he required and then told her to wait outside, to go to the kitchens for a cup of coffee. Rising without complaint, the woman did as she was ordered. Soon the call went through, and Kapitan Simonov hunched forward.

In his office above Dzehinsky Square in Moscow, Mikhail Kostikov of Directorate T, KGB, replaced the receiver, spun back in his chair and buzzed through on the private intercom to the office of Igor Bayev, Head of the First Chief Directorate responsible for all KGB Foreign Operations. Despite the hour, Kostikov knew that his superior would be waiting for this call. 'Comrade Direktor,' he began, the note of satisfaction travelling down the line with his words. 'The project we were discussing earlier? First phase is now complete: woman and boy have arrived in Leningrad. They are staying in an hotel not six hundred

* *Dezhurnaya:* house warden.

metres away from the eye hospital itself – just a short walk away. And they are under constant surveillance.'

'Discreet surveillance, I assume?'

'But of course, comrade.' Mikhail Kostikov contrived to sound injured, and his superior laughed down the phone.

'Good, good. Then we can only wait, eh, Mikhail? The next move is up to the Americans.'

'And if there is no "next move", comrade – what then?'

'With the boy in Leningrad? There will be, comrade, there will be!' He laughed once more. 'I have it on very good authority! Good night, comrade.'

'Goodnight, Comrade Bayev.'

General Freeman and Lydia Prolev were sitting in the car together on the way back from the conclusion of the second day's hearings before the NIB. Now Freeman swung the wheel and the car crunched up the driveway outside his home.

It was early evening, twelve hours after the press had laid siege to Freeman's home. Since then there had been other stories, more pressing deadlines, so that now the driveway was deserted and Freeman was able to enjoy once more the early shadows that dappled the privacy of his surroundings.

Doris Freeman was still away with friends and the General had been able to offer Lydia the spare bedroom without fuss or explanation. In those few hours since she had arrived in a state of high nervous tension at the New Senate Building where Freeman was presenting his technical evidence to a Board that seemed to respond to his allegations in a new mood of silent, sombre attentiveness, there had been a subtle transformation in their stormy relationship that both had secretly welcomed, a new mood of relaxed tolerance and mutual dependence to replace anger, hostility and suspicion.

'So?' Lydia glanced quizzically at the General as he turned off the security alarms and ushered her through into the kitchen. 'How do you think you are doing?'

'On Day Two?' Freeman shrugged, opened the ice-box and took down a jug of chilled orange juice. He poured a glass for them both. 'Hard to say – we're rocking 'em –'

'Excuse, please. This is real? Real orange juice?'

'Sure. Florida orange juice.'

'And you buy this? Whenever you want it?'

Freeman grinned. 'That's the idea.'

Lydia sipped cautiously. 'It is marvellous. Truly marvellous. I am sorry, General: you were saying – about the hearing?'

'It's hard to say – we're rocking 'em, I can feel it. Especially after the business with Sam Tolland. They're not the same bunch of disbelievers they were a couple of days ago, that's for sure.' He pointed a thick finger at Lydia. 'But I'm still going to need that testimony of yours, Mrs Prolev – that's going to be the clincher.'

Lydia sipped and nodded. Then, almost unconsciously, she glanced at her watch, her thoughts once more of her son inside the Soviet Union. 'Perhaps now?'

Freeman glanced at his own watch, made a swift mental calculation and shook his head briefly. 'Not a chance. A few more hours to go yet. I'm not expecting to hear a damn' thing – good or bad – until some time late tomorrow. You'll have to possess your soul in patience.' He smiled sympathetically.

'I am sorry, it is just that, you know, it has been so long –'

'Sure. Try not to think about it. Time'll go a lot faster that way.'

They lapsed into silence, then 'That colleague of yours, Professor Disman,' Lydia mused. 'He was the most interesting. At first I believed he was going to speak against you, to support the others, but then –'

'Jim? Jim Disman? Hell, no – he's an old friend from way back. More of an ally in the enemy camp.'

'And what does he think? Does he believe you are – how do you say? – winning the day?'

General Freeman shrugged. 'He's not saying – not out

front, that is. Between you and me? Yeah – he reckons I'm in with a chance. Now, if you'll excuse me, there's a whole heap of papers I've been avoiding down in the study. If you want anything, just holler.'

An hour later he was finding it hard to concentrate on a batch of classified documents detailing the fiscal arguments likely to be deployed supporting the MX project. His mind still toying with his performance before the Board that afternoon, he suddenly pushed the papers away violently. They slid across his polished desk and knocked the silver model of the P-38 on to the floor. Muttering an oath under his breath, Freeman rose from his chair, went to the front of his desk and dropped to his knees. The model had rolled against one of the legs of his desk, and he had to adopt a very un-General-like position to recover it. As he straightened up, he banged his head against the corner of his desk – then froze, bruise forgotten.

Just in front of his eyes, pressed in tight among the shadows on the underside of his desk, was a flat metallic disc the size of a dime. General Freeman fetched a torch. The shaft of light confirmed his suspicions: he was looking at an automatic listening device.

The private study of the Head of US Air Force Intelligence had been bugged.

General Freeman switched off the torch and laid it softly aside, his mind racing. He walked back to his desk, flicked open his diary and turned back several pages, suddenly conscious of every sound he made in the listening room. There! Twelve, thirteen days ago – that was the last time his Electronic Countermeasures team had swept the house for electronic intrusion. Thirteen days. Thirteen days of what, Freeman? Think! Of idle conversation and domestic chit-chat and – a chill settled on his heart: they had been standing in the study when Frank Yates had told him the address of their motel in Salvador Drive! *That* was how the man had traced Lydia Prolev so easily – through the listening device! Freeman ran down the logic remorselessly: the man had been working for Soviet intelligence; ergo,

Soviet intelligence – the KGB – had planted the bug. Take it on further: suppose the bug had been planted by Nicholson, who had gained access to his study via Doris Freeman's social afternoons – the soft underbelly? Then Nicholson had *also* worked for Soviet intelligence.

Yet the papers that Freeman now believed Nicholson had planted at the fire had led to two things: firstly, the detection of Sam Tolland as a Soviet agent-in-place; secondly, *a massive boost to the credibility of both General Freeman and his defensive beam weapon concept before the previously sceptical five members of the Nuclear Intelligence Board.* And that meant . . .

Jesus. Oh, Jesus . . .

Easy, Freeman, easy. Take it easy. One step at a time. Slow it right down and think things through. That's what they're paying you for; that's what comes with the brass, the salutes and the pension.

General Freeman closed his mind to the need to hurry, shut himself off from the electronic ear and the revolving spool of tape waiting somewhere to record his every heartbeat. He sat on at his desk, his mind twisting into the tactics of domestic infiltration, his eyes gazing sightlessly at the silver model of his P-38 as a few more pieces of the puzzle slipped quietly into place. He was sitting there still when there came a soft tapping on his study door. He looked up, a decision taken.

'General Freeman? May I come in?' asked Lydia Prolev.

Freeman nodded and half rose from behind his desk. 'Sure you can. What's on your mind?'

She came in hesitantly, her fingers locking and twisting together. 'I have been thinking,' she began, walking slowly forward in time with her words, 'about what you have done for me. I have been thinking too about what I have said – about you and about your work. I would like you to know that I am sorry. You have been under much pressure. I apologize –' she managed an awkward little smile – 'it is something I find I am often doing in this situation. It is new for me.'

General Freeman smiled and said gruffly 'Your apology's not necessary – but it's accepted nonetheless. Thank you.'

There was an awkward silence. Lydia covered it by glancing once more at her watch. 'Do you think perhaps that now –?'

General Freeman shook his head, considered the bugging device beneath his desk, and weighed his words carefully. 'It'll be a while yet. By my guess the ship'll still be well inside Finnish territorial waters – and it's a fourteen-hour trip from Helsinki to Leningrad even under optimum conditions. Frank's got a while to go yet before that RV with Misha.'

Lydia nodded as, unbeknown to her, the bug picked up every word.

General Freeman's estimate was slightly inaccurate.

As his words were automatically transmitted to the listening ears of the Soviet SigInt* team sitting in a stuffy, smoke-filled room behind the façade of Washington's Soviet Trade Mission, Frank Yates was standing alone on the promenade deck of the MS *Finnstar*, leaning against the teak-capped rail and watching astern as the twinkle of Helsinki's lights sank slowly below the horizon. They had sailed shortly after 6 p.m. It was now 8.30, and they would dock at Leningrad after breakfast early the following morning.

The ship rolled and plunged, and Frank swayed easily with the motion. Already the five-thousand-ton cruise ship's bows were cutting briskly through the choppy seas out in the gulf, and the stiff offshore breeze had driven even the romantics below decks to the warmth and comfort of their spotless cabins.

He turned his face into the wind and gazed back into the gloaming, his eyes following the lazy rise and swoop of the gulls as they wheeled astern to bicker over a bucket of scraps thrown overboard by a white-coated steward: so far so good. Frank licked the salt from his lips and smiled down a little grimly at the racing wave crests. Twelve,

* SigInt: Signals Intelligence.

:254

twenty-four hours from now and it might very well be different, yet, so far – he rapped a knuckle against the teak rail-capping – the mission had progressed without a hitch: his trip out to the Linnanmäki Amusement Park, where the US Embassy contact had returned their doctored passports with a nervous haste that had bordered on the farcically indecent; his subsequent visit to the Vinkler Travel Bureau and then on to the shipping office armed with their franked visa-free tour applications – all had passed without incident, and he had been forced to acknowledge the competence of Seppo Halle, the strange little Finn who, having nursed him through the formalities in the hotel bedroom, had then cast him loose with his own son to complete the embarkation formalities alone.

Frank peeled back his cuff and glanced at his watch. He had left the boy Jakko in their shared cabin on B deck. Seppo was travelling independently with a cabin of his own somewhere below them on C deck. Should they meet in a corridor or in the restaurant, each would ignore the other completely; they had planned a clandestine meeting in a few minutes' time in the men's toilet directly behind the restaurant.

He turned away from the rail and ducked below. He swayed down the carpeted corridor past pale-faced passengers who lurched by clinging grimly to polished pine handrails. He stopped outside their cabin door and knocked softly.

'Yes – kom,' called out a cheerful voice. Frank kommed.

Jakko, resplendent in light blue slacks, white tennis shoes and yellow windcheater, dark dyed hair awry, was lounging across the lower berth, the fruit bowl resting comfortably in the crook of his arm. As Frank entered he glanced up, swallowed, spat a stream of grape pips across the room into the handbasin with unerring accuracy and raised a bunch of grapes in nonchalant salute. 'Ah, Mr American. Everything is OK? Everything is – how do you say? – hunky-doodle?'

'Yankee-doodle. Hunky-dory,' corrected Frank. He

255 :

noticed that the fruit bowl was already half-empty. The biscuits had gone too. And the bottles of mineral water. Despite himself, he grinned. The soap would probably go next. Then the light fittings. 'I'm off to see your old man. Your father, OK? Back in five –' he held up the spread fingers of his hand – 'five minutes, understand?'

The boy nodded enthusiastically. As Frank turned towards the door Jakko began peeling an orange.

Frank found Seppo washing his hands at a basin in the men's toilet. As the door banged closed behind him Seppo glanced up into the mirror and then resumed washing without a flicker of recognition as another passenger pushed out of one of the toilet stalls and joined Seppo beneath the mirrors. Frank crossed to the urinals and undid his fly.

When the man had left and they were alone 'Everything is all right?' asked Seppo quietly.

Frank nodded. 'Everything's fine. Jakko's in the cabin eating. I think he's about to start in on the bunk fittings.'

'I am sorry?'

Frank shook his head impatiently. 'Joke. Forget it. Any change in the schedule? What did you find out?'

Seppo moved closer. 'The tour stands as arranged. Everything is to schedule; everything is routine.' He pursed his lips. 'It is possible, of course, that there may be some last-minute security consideration when we dock, but that is not likely. Now – remember: as soon as we are alongside, the port security police will come on board. Passengers wishing to go ashore must present their passports to him. You will hear the instruction to go to the purser's office on the . . .' He gestured impatiently at the loudspeaker grilles.

'PA system?'

'Ja – the PA system. Then you must wait. That is very important. Do not go immediately: wait until there is a long line of people, yes? Until the man he is very busy, under much pressure. Now – on no account is Jakko to go with you when you hand over your passport, do you understand? If he asks, then the boy is packing, or playing somewhere, he is unwell – something of that nature.'

Frank nodded.

'Good. So – you and the boy will accompany the morning visit to the Hermitage and St Isaac's Cathedral.' Seppo prodded a bony finger into Frank's chest. 'Remember, remember, remember – you are to stay back, to keep the boy as far away from the other passengers as you can, so that your companions remember nothing later about the boy – that too is very important.'

Seppo shrugged. 'It should not be difficult: they will be looking at the sights, at their precious cameras, not at you. In any case, I shall be near. If I think that you have brought too much attention upon yourself, then I shall take the decision to abort. Do I make myself clear?' Again Frank nodded. 'After your tour is concluded you will eat a meal with the others at the Aurora Café on Nevsky Prospekt: that too is all part of the tour. In the afternoon –' Seppo broke off as another passenger stepped over the combing into the toilet. When he had gone and Seppo had turned from drying his hands for the third time, 'After lunch you will be permitted to do some shopping before strolling north towards the River Neva and the Summer Garden of Peter the Great. By then it will be between three thirty and four in the afternoon. Now, listen carefully: there, in the Summer Garden, there is a Summer House, a – yes? Something is the matter?'

Frank was frowning. 'We sail at eighteen hundred, correct?'

'Yes.'

'And the boy comes through between three thirty and four? Why not leave it until later? Till the last possible –'

Seppo silenced him with a withering look. 'And let every Russian in uniform put the timings together for himself?' He shook his head decisively. 'There is no other way. And besides there are the diversions; there is the hospital itself to consider.'

He paused and then added soberly 'I hope you have good nerves, Mr Coning. Maybe you will need them before this business is through.'

Presently they separated. Half an hour later Frank and Jakko went into a sadly depleted restaurant for dinner as the MC *Finnstar*, ablaze with lights, butted heavily eastwards along the darkened Gulf of Finland towards the Soviet Union.

In Leningrad's Pushkin Hotel, on the sixth floor, Irena Ryabov bent over the sleeping form of the boy and gently brushed a strand of dark hair away from the closed, damaged eye. God knows he has reason to be tired, she thought wearily: they had spent the entire day shunted from one medical department to another in the Potseluyev Eye Hospital. Tests, examinations and then more pointless, endless waiting as first one and then another specialist bustled in to confer over the results of the latest batch of tests.

And so back to the hotel, with Kapitan Simonov riding silently at their shoulder.

Irena Ryabov straightened up from the bed and walked slowly over to the couch beneath the window. She eased off the tight shoes and breathed a sigh of relief: all that waiting around; all that sitting and standing – and even when they returned to the hotel it had not ended, she recalled: even inside their own room there had been that rapping on the thin door. And again – Kapitan Simonov: was everything in order? Oh – and there was, he regretted, a fresh set of restrictions: they were not to go outside, they were not even to take the elevator downstairs, without first consulting with him. If there was anything they wanted, anything they required, they were to call him first.

And then, dear God, if he hadn't already done enough, he had strolled over to the chair, picked up Misha's gleaming new camera, the present he had been given by Eduard, glanced at its simple mechanism and sauntered over to the window, his polished heels leaving little pressed crescents in the worn carpet. Irena Ryabov ran a shaking finger over her forehead at the memory: thank goodness the view from their room looked out on to dustbins, courtyards and cobwebs: had there been trees and parks – a glimpse, perhaps, of the river, Kapitan Simonov might have been tempted to take a picture, even to wind on the film.

And that would have spelt disaster.

:: LENINGRAD – 3.04 P.M. THE FOLLOWING DAY

The bored Soviet sentry at the southern entrance to Leningrad's Potseluyev Eye Hospital held up his hand and the grey laundry van squeaked to a halt, its dusty bonnet almost touching the striped barrier. Officially, the hospital was a civilian institution but, like everything else within the Soviet Union, the military had first call on its facilities. Now the guard checked the van's arrival against the printed schedule on his clipboard and glanced up at the young, dark-haired driver. The van he recognized but the driver, the man's face, was new. He shrugged: so what? They were always changing. Still 'Where's the old man?' he demanded, reaching up for the proffered papers.

'Alexandrov? Taken a few days off. Family bereavement. His mother-in-law just snuffed it – lucky sod.' The driver smiled disarmingly and the sentry relaxed. A smile: that made a bloody change. Anyway, two weeks six days from now and his two years' initial service would be up; then he'd be off, away home. He slung his weapon over his shoulder, stepped round to the back, glanced through the rear windows and rubbed a finger against the glass, seeing beyond the accumulated dust of several months a pile of wicker laundry baskets stacked almost to the roof. The guard walked slowly round to the front of the vehicle, jotted down the time of arrival and waved the van on. The barrier rose into the sky and the van rumbled forward with a smile and a nod of thanks from the driver.

The laundry van turned left across the forecourt and drove slowly round to the side of the vast concrete building, past the entrance to the communal nuclear shelter and down a steep service ramp, where it braked sharply before backing up to the rubber swing doors that gave on to the basement corridors, service lifts and maintenance area. The guard at the gate lost interest and sauntered back inside his little cubicle. When he had gone, 'OK, it's clear,' murmured the young driver over his shoulder as he killed the engine.

There was a moment's silence. Then, in the dark interior of the stuffy van, two young men and a girl with short cropped hair eased their cramped muscles and rose to a crouch behind the heavy laundry baskets, their nervous breathing loud in one another's ears, the smell of their fear, their tension, mingling with the starch and the sour bite of soiled bed linen.

Now the girl, their leader, pushed aside one of the heavy baskets, twisted open the rear doors and jumped down to the ground, her movements stiff and awkward after the long confinement. The two men quickly followed, bending to rub their limbs vigorously before straightening to look to the girl for their instructions. Young, dark-haired and in their mid-twenties, all three – all four including their driver – were Jewish. The girl glanced about her slowly, missing nothing, while the driver sat impatiently behind the wheel of the van, his hands drumming nervously against the string-bound steering wheel. 'Come on, come on,' he muttered under his breath.

Finally, satisfied, the girl nodded. 'We go.'

The two men tugged one of the laundry hampers towards them across the metal floor of the vehicle. Its metal skids screeched protestingly, setting teeth on edge. The girl spun round. 'Quietly!' she ordered, eyes flashing her anger in the gloom.

The men stopped the hamper on the lip of the van's floor and flicked off the leather fastenings. Wrinkling his nose in disgust, one of the men threw back the lid and tossed a bundle of soiled bed linen towards the front of the van. He then reached deeper into the hamper and handed a green surgical gown and mask to each of his comrades. A brown workman's overall he laid aside for himself. Wordlessly, working to a well-rehearsed drill, the three began dressing, the man with the beard and the girl turning their backs one to another as fingers flew on the tape ties. Surgical masks looped loosely around their necks, they paused when they had finished, as though to postpone, or at least to mark, this moment of armed commitment to the cause they had for so long defended over their coffee cups. The girl glanced about her, sensing their hesitation. 'Now! There is no going back. Now we do it!' she hissed.

Again those hands went deep into the hamper to emerge clasping a thick, bulky parcel about four feet long wrapped in a dirty sheet. The sheet was unfurled impatiently, like some dusty ensign awaiting battle. A moment's pause and the man began handing out the weapons: 7.62 mm SKS carbine to his friend; AK47 to their leader, the girl; 7.62 mm Tula Tokarev automatic pistol for himself. The carbine and the Kalashnikov were unsuitable, too bulky, too long in the barrel for concealed work indoors but all they had been able to capture: resistance fighters couldn't afford to be choosy. Not yet. He shrugged. They'd do.

He cocked the pistol and thrust it into the waistband of his trousers beneath the brown workman's overalls. He would stay with the driver, secure the escape route. Now he slammed back the hamper lid, thrust the basket back into the gloom of the van's interior and nodded at the girl. 'Good luck. We will be waiting. We will not fail you.'

The pipes above their heads rumbled suddenly and there was a muffled bang inside the hospital as a door slammed shut somewhere. Off to the right there was the rattle of a trolley and then the bark of sudden laughter. It was not a good place for waiting. Perhaps sensing the courage it would take to remain inactive, the girl suddenly smiled, reached forward and kissed the man swiftly on the cheek. 'Nor we you,' she promised before turning to her team-mate. 'Ready?' she demanded.

The man with the beard swallowed nervously but his answer was steady enough. 'Ready. We go along this corridor to the third floor. Through that to the inside staircase. One floor up and we –'

'Come on.' She turned on her heel and led the way swiftly down the corridor.

: : 19 : : : : : : : : : : : : : :

Misha Prolev was lying on a doctor's couch, his head tilted back beneath the strong glare of the specialist's lamp. Irena Ryabov sat opposite on a hard wooden bench, her hands toying nervously with the boy's camera as the doctor peered intently into the boy's right eye before moving across to his colleague by the window. Heads bent, they began murmuring together, referring often to the boy's case-notes.

Misha twisted his head to watch and his aunt smiled. He was enjoying all the attention, the novelty of this treatment for which he had waited so long.

Standing by the far wall, Kapitan Simonov watched the doctors quietly, his arms folded across his chest. Now there was a clearing of throats, and one of the doctors turned towards Mrs Ryabov. He was waving the boy's case-notes gently between finger and thumb. 'In view of the boy's youth, it might perhaps be as well if we arranged for –' He got no further. The door to his right suddenly burst open and the girl receptionist who had been in the outer office stumbled forward with a small cry, propelled by an unseen hand. 'What on earth –?' began the doctor. The door crashed back. A woman and a man in doctors' masks and gowns stood immobile in the threshold, eyes hunting rapidly over the faces before them. Both were armed with automatic weapons.

There was silence. Then 'Nobody move. Everybody is to remain quite still,' ordered the girl quietly, her words muffled by the mask over her nose. As she spoke she stepped to one side and the man moved swiftly through her line of fire. Misha had struggled upright from the couch, eyes goggling as he looked from the guns to the eyes and back to the guns. Irena Ryabov watched the two sinister

: 262

figures through a haze of fear that carried somewhere within it a rising bubble of excitement. Eduard had been right! He had said that some time during – she had shifted impatiently on her hard chair and now froze into immobility as the man swung abruptly towards her, rifle levelled at her chest, finger curled around the trigger. And as he turned, Kapitan Simonov moved.

Simonov lunged forward, fingers scrabbling at his fastened holster. He was too slow. The man turned, raised the wooden butt of his rifle until it was almost parallel with his own jaw-line and then swivelled sharply on heel and toe, rifle held rigidly at high port. The wooden butt scythed round and smashed into Simonov's face. The Russian collapsed to the floor without a sound. As he fell, his arm brushed against a tray of glass phials, which crashed and tinkled on to the floor beside him. The man with the rifle stepped aside and inspected the results of his handiwork with satisfaction. Rifle trained on the two doctors, he dropped to one knee, tugged open Simonov's holster, removed his automatic and spare magazine and stuffed both beneath his gown. He rose to his feet as one of the doctors stepped forward to help the downed man, then thought better of it as the girl's AK47 swung across to cover him. 'You – the boy. You will go next door. Move, please.'

Misha scrambled down, fumbled for his glasses and started hesitantly towards the door. Irena Ryabov moved to join him, but the girl raised her weapon threateningly. 'Just the boy. Only the boy – the boy Misha.'

Heads jerked up at the girl's use of the boy's name.

'But he . . . he is only a child,' protested Irena Ryabov.

The girl flicked the muzzle of her weapon towards the door impatiently. 'Misha. In there,' she ordered. She turned to the boy's aunt. 'Don't worry – he will come to no harm.' The girl went through into the outer office, verified that the door into the corridor beyond was still locked and then gestured Misha towards her. As he moved, bewildered past his aunt, Irena Ryabov leant suddenly forward and thrust the camera into his arms.

'A new present,' she explained. The girl frowned but let the action pass without comment as she pointed Misha to the chair behind the receptionist's desk.

'What are you after? What do you want?' demanded one of the doctors in a voice intended to sound stern and indignant but which emerged strangled and high-pitched, choked on his own fear. 'I ... that is, we ... we demand to know –'

'You? You will demand nothing,' countered the rifleman flatly, jabbing the barrel of his weapon towards the doctor. 'If you have so much air to spare, you and your friend: pick up that pig.' He gestured at Simonov's crumpled body. 'Get him on that couch.'

The two doctors stepped forward, eyes locked on the gunman. Simonov's head lolled drunkenly as bright spots of blood dripped on to the shining floor. The doctors grunted with the effort of moving their bleeding burden, but presently he was there, slumped face downwards on the plastic sheeting, his gleaming boots jutting incongruously over the end of the couch.

'Please, I want –' began Irena Ryabov.

'Do not talk,' ordered the man with the rifle as he began to back towards the inner office door. He opened it and said quietly over his shoulder 'OK, you can make a move. No problems here. Go now. Quickly.'

Irena Ryabov swung round, startled. 'But the boy! What about the boy? Don't you see that –'

The gunman closed the door firmly and faced his captives. 'Be silent, old woman.'

He eased himself on to the corner of the desk and placed the rifle across his knees. With his hand on the trigger he groped with his left under his gown for the automatic pistol. He pulled it clear, checked that it was loaded and hefted it comfortably in his hand.

'What is it that you want from us?' asked the other doctor quietly, reasonably, glancing up from the bloodied mess of Simonov's mouth, which he was busy swabbing with cotton wool. 'There is nothing here you could possibly want. One small boy –'

'Of you? I want nothing of you and your kind – for years you have given us nothing, ignored our very existence,' he said venomously. 'Why should we be any different from you?' Realizing he had been stung into self-betrayal the man fell suddenly silent. He moved the pistol in a gentle circle that encompassed them all. 'You may smoke if you wish,' he said conversationally, with a trace of his earlier composure. 'We will be here, together, for a little time.'

In the other office, behind the closed door, the girl was trying to break through into the boy's understanding, to push past that look of fear and distrust – and there was so little time. Now she tried a different tack: she crouched down beside him until her eyes were on a level with his. Then she tugged down her mask and smiled. 'Do not be afraid, Misha,' she said quietly. 'Do not be afraid of the guns –' she shook her automatic as though it was a tool of little purpose – 'or the masks. See? I am just like you – and we have come to help you, Misha; to make you happy. You want to be happy, yes?' Slowly the quiet, gentle words began to work. The boy nodded warily. 'We are taking you to your mother, do you understand? To your mother – you would like to see her now, wouldn't you? Wouldn't you?' She waited until she caught the boy's silent nod.

'Is she near here?'

'Not so very far,' evaded the girl. 'But if you want to see her you will have to do exactly what I tell you to do, is that clear? If you do not, then I and my friends will be caught and you will never see her again.'

The boy paused. 'And Auntie Irena?'

'She will be coming too,' lied the girl. 'So – we have a deal? You do what we tell you and we will take you to your mother.'

'You mean it? Truly?' asked the boy with the beginnings of a fragile belief in the impossible.

'Come – I will show you.' The girl rose to her feet, folded down the butt of the Kalashnikov and slipped the weapon beneath her gown. Then she began walking towards the door. After a moment's hesitation, Misha followed.

Ten minutes passed, then fifteen. Simonov, still unconscious, was lying slumped on the couch, his breath sawing harshly across broken teeth. The two doctors were sitting side by side at the desk, their hands flat in front of them, with the terrified receptionist frozen at their side. Irena Ryabov, having twice been silenced as she attempted to talk to the gunman, sat nervously on the hard wooden bench watching as the man kept glancing at his watch, his hands opening and closing on the butt of the automatic. Now his eyes flicked once more towards the phone: why didn't the damned thing ring? What had gone wrong? Surely it must ring soon; surely . . . there! The phone began to ring! One of the doctors made to answer it and then stopped, hand over the instrument, as the pistol was raised threateningly.

'No! Let it ring!' commanded the gunman.

Once, twice, three times the tone rang out. Then it stopped, and the gunman hopped down from the desk grinning his relief. They were out of the hospital – they had got clear!

Working deftly, the man unloaded the rifle, pocketed the shells and began stripping down the weapon: with only the pistol to conceal he would be able to move faster, attract less attention, diminish the risk to himself and thus to the others. They should be safe now, out there somewhere in the city. He glanced about the office and then locked the separate pieces of the rifle into a steel filing cabinet. He slipped the key into his pocket and moved towards the door, Simonov's pistol held across his body.

Once again the old woman made to stand up, her hands twisting in agitation. 'I . . . I must talk with you,' she begged. 'It is important. Very important – important to –' she glanced nervously at the silent doctors – 'to you. To your people.'

Something in the urgency of her demand arrested the man's impatience. He jerked his head towards the now empty outer office. 'Very well, in there. But I warn you –'

Ignoring the glances from the other captives Irena Ryabov hurried through to the outer office. The man followed and stood up against the half-open door watching both rooms. 'Well?' he said impatiently.

Irena Ryabov, hidden from the others by the thin door, licked dry lips. 'That . . . that camera,' she whispered. 'The one the boy carries?'

The man frowned. 'What about it?'

'Ssssh – not so loud! It is very, very important. Look inside – look in the back, in the back of the camera. You will find there some microfilm, information from the boy's uncle that –'

'The boy's *uncle*? What is this madness?'

'Sssh, you fool: not so loud! The boy's uncle is Professor Ryabov. Professor *Eduard* Ryabov? You have heard of him, perhaps?'

The man shook his head and Irena rolled her eyes upwards. But the gunman was grappling with a darker realization. 'You *knew* this would happen? The guns – us – here? You *knew*?' he demanded urgently, the other prisoners forgotten, his fingers biting cruelly into the old woman's arm.

She winced and then nodded. 'We were told only that such an act was possible. Eduard . . . my husband believes that –' She shook her head at the impossibility of rapid explanation. 'Look inside the camera, that is all. That is what you must do. You must look. Promise me!'

The man nodded, and Irena Ryabov sighed with relief. It was done. Somehow word would get through. Now she raised her voice for the others. 'But if you harm so much as a single hair of that boy's head –'

The man pushed her roughly back with the others. 'Enough of your empty threats, *babushka*! You don't get special treatment. None of you do.'

With that he slammed the inner door and turned the key. He spun round, jammed the automatic into his waistband beneath his sweater, tore off gown and mask, threw them into a corner and picked up a file of papers. Then he stepped boldly into the corridor, locked the outer door, lit a cigarette and began walking briskly towards the exit.

The way was clear.

The long gleaming corridor was almost empty: a nurse in a white coat was walking away from him, her arm around an old woman leaning heavily on a stick; a hospital porter was pushing a laden trolley slowly towards him – and that was all. He began to hurry, his footsteps echoing off the high plastered walls. A few more minutes and he would be out too. A clear run. He glanced ahead: there were a couple of turnings off to his right before the corridor curved away to the stairs and the side exit. He walked on, eating the distance, winning with each crisp step the race towards the safety of those anonymous crowds that waited for him beyond the hospital grounds.

Suddenly he heard voices and the bark of male laughter from around the corner just ahead. Aware of the pistol digging into his ribs beneath his sweater, he hugged his papers closer, drew on his cigarette and quickened his steps as a crowd of armed soldiers swung easily round the corner. They were laughing and joking as they turned towards him, their attention focused on a sheepish-looking young soldier in their midst whose left eye was heavily bandaged. As the men approached down the corridor they fell silent and he felt their veiled hostility as they took in the dark curly hair and the wide, hooked nose. He walked on looking straight ahead. Ten paces, he told himself: ten paces more and he would be past them. Nine . . . he couldn't make it. He turned suddenly, blindly, down the first of the two corridors to his right. He took it on impulse, not knowing where it might lead, knowing only that he had to get away from those hard, flat, staring faces. He breathed again thankfully as the banter resumed behind him. He heard a sudden chorus of shouted ribald farewells and the sound of heavy boots on concrete as one of the soldiers turned down the corridor behind him.

Fighting the urge to run, the man walked on, realizing belatedly and with cold dread that the corridor led nowhere; it ended a few paces on at the entrance to the lifts that served the lower floors. It was too late to turn, to late to do anything but wait, brazen it out. The soldier stopped beside him, glanced at him curiously and then reached past to stab a thick finger on the call button. There was a whirring from somewhere below and the two men waited silently together. The gunman glanced out of the corner of his eye: the soldier was swarthy, thick-set, in his late twenties. He looked fit and hard. His short blond hair gleamed in the strong overhead light and the man could smell the soldier's body, distinguish the individual blend of rough cloth and gun oil, garlic and barracks' bread. The lift arrived, the metal gates banged back and the two men stepped into the lift. They had to stand close together as the doors clattered closed behind them. The lift began to drop slowly towards the basement.

The soldier adjusted the sling of his AKM more comfortably over his shoulder, reached into his tunic pocket, took out a packet of cigarettes and held one forward unlit.

'Light?'

He was watching the civilian with interest, noting the thick curls, the beads of sweat starting now at the temples.

'Light? Yes – yes, of course.' He held out his cigarette. The soldier shook his head. 'The box, Jew. The box.'

The man groped hurriedly in his trouser pockets, aware that the automatic pistol in his waistband was just inches away from the soldier's belt-buckle. He pulled out the matches and offered the box to the soldier.

'Go on then, Jew: light it for me, light it for me.' The man clasped the file of papers between his knees and began fumbling with the matchbox, aware all the while of the soldier's pale eyes as they ran over his face, his body. The match spluttered and flared. He held it forward and glanced up into the soldier's face in time to see a sudden look of fear and surprise coupled to realization. The soldier puffed on the cigarette, blew out the match with a plume of smoke and turned abruptly away as the lift sagged to a stop.

The doors banged back and the soldier gestured with his cigarette 'After you.' The gunman nodded thanks and stepped forward, thankful to be clear of the claustrophobic metal box. Thank God, it was over: he'd seen nothing, suspected nothing that – he fell sprawling, knocked almost unconscious, as the soldier's rifle smashed across the top of his shoulders, driving him to the ground in a blinding haze of pain. As he lay there, dazed and half-conscious, the soldier's rough hands hauled him over on to his back, tore away the sweater and ripped the pistol from his waistband. Another blow – this time from a boot to the side – and the soldier stepped back breathing deeply, his rifle levelled. He glanced quickly down at the pistol.

'So – the little Jew-boy likes to play with guns, does he? On your feet, scum – go on, move!' The soldier kicked cruelly once more and the man rose groggily to his feet, stunned by the blows and by the savage speed of his downfall. 'We'll see what the people upstairs have to say about you.'

The gunman stumbled forward: if they got him inside, under custody, they'd make him talk. One day, perhaps two – maybe a lot less – and he'd be finished. They'd always said that, always known that, as they soberly plotted the worst over their coffee cups. Better to end it now, they'd agreed, to make a run for it; to give the others a chance. He owed them that. Through the mists of pain he peered painfully down the deserted corridor. Ahead there was another turning, a little further down to the left. Perhaps if he could just ... he stumbled, turned and lashed out at the soldier, shoving him sideways and off balance, the rifle swinging wide.

He ran.

He ran blindly, weaving to right and left as the corner swam slowly nearer: if he could only make the corridor turning he'd have a –

'Halt! Stop!'

He looked wildly over his shoulder. The soldier was struggling with the sling of his rifle, struggling to bring the weapon up into the aim. He jinked to the left again as the first shot crashed out to echo deafeningly down the corridor. Two more steps ... The soldier fired again.

Arms flung wide in supplication, the man sprawled forward to smash into the wall and then tumble, loose-limbed, across the corridor towards a wall of velvet, painless darkness. As he fell one of the cheap black shoes he was wearing came loose and rolled along the floor.

When the shoe came to rest the man was still also.

Irena Ryabov's message died within him.

Now there were shouts and screams in the ringing, post-shot silence as the first wide-eyed spectators began to edge cautiously round the corner. The soldier shouted, waving them away. He dropped into a crouch and advanced carefully, slowly, towards the sprawled body. Rifle levelled rock-steady on the corpse, he stopped a few feet short and glanced down. His second shot had entered between the man's buttocks. There was much blood and the dead man had fouled himself involuntarily on the moment of death. The soldier regarded his work dispassionately and uncocked his weapon as the crowd gathered around the silent, in-elegant tableau, their mouths babbling questions.

Two kilometres away, near a tree-lined square on the corner of Zhukovskova and Ligovsky, the driver of the dusty grey laundry van glanced once more at the girl sitting on the battered seat beside him and shook his head. They were waiting for the phone to ring in the public call-box a few paces from where they sat. Iosef was late; he should have called in by now.

'What shall we do?'

The girl glanced at her watch. She was puzzled: there had been no alarm, no sirens wailing across the city like their last abortive attempt at something of this sort – and they did have the boy. He was sitting quietly in the back among the laundry baskets with Stefan. Besides, they needed not just the money but the status, the trust of others in the world outside, if they were to expect backing for what they planned would follow later in the summer.

The girl made her decision. 'We go. We go on as planned. He may still turn up. We go on to the Summer House.'

The driver nodded. 'We're moving,' he warned the others over his shoulder. He started the engine and the van lumbered forward into the traffic.

'. . . and we will now move on towards one of the city's finest buildings: the Marble Palace on the Neva Embankment. If you will follow me . . .' The middle-aged Soviet guide with the mannish haircut turned slowly, waved her guide book over her head and led her group of tourists along the gravel path, their heels crunching, their cameras clicking happily. 'In 1937, you may recall, the Palace was converted into a branch of the Central Lenin Museum in front of which you will presently see, set on a granite base, the historic armoured car from the turret of which Comrade Lenin spoke upon his final return from exile in April 1917. It is perhaps interesting to note that . . .'

The high-pitched voice droned on as the group shuffled forward obediently. Frank held out a restraining arm and Jakko paused as the tourists moved past them. Together with several other parties of tourists, they had been picking their way through the ornamental gardens, pausing dutifully to admire the symmetry of well-shaped hedges and the goldfish whose pools had been stocked by the dying Russian Empire, when Frank had suddenly caught sight through the trees of a low green wooden building. He glanced at his watch: 3.34 p.m. They walked on. As they turned a corner there was Seppo reading his guide, waiting by a stone bench.

As they sauntered forward – Jakko chewing busily on a chocolate bar – Seppo began in a low voice: 'There is the Summer House before you. There – through the trees. In a moment the guide will lead the party through the ground floor and out of that white door over there to your left.'

Frank picked out the door without difficulty. 'Seen,' he murmured as they walked slowly past Seppo without stopping.

His nose buried in his guide book, the little Finn fell into step a few paces behind. 'You will wait for my signal,' he ordered quietly. 'We are close now – very close. Be ready.'

Gravel crunched underfoot and there was a pause lasting several paces as Seppo glanced up and looked about him casually. Frank felt the tension dry his mouth and tauten the muscles of his stomach. He glanced across at Jakko. The boy grinned, then 'They are here!' whispered Seppo excitedly. 'See? The grey van: there, beneath the trees.'

As Frank looked, a dusty grey van began rolling slowly forward. 'Now – go on,' urged Seppo suddenly. 'Catch up with the rest of the party.'

Frank and Jakko joined the last of the knot of tourists waiting to walk through into the Summer House as the van disappeared from view. Now they passed out of the sunshine into the cool gloom of a tiled hallway full of musty grandeur and the elegance of an age swept away by revolution. Their group was one of several clustered around their guide in some confusion, oohing and aahing near the roped-off entrance to the grand dining room.

Seppo waited a moment longer and then jogged Frank's arm. 'Follow me.' He turned abruptly down a gloomy, wooden-floored corridor, lifted the roped barrier aside and gestured Frank through impatiently. 'Quickly, quickly – we have minutes only.' As they hurried down the passage-way the guide's voice receded behind them.

There was a plain unpainted wooden door directly to their right. Seppo rapped softly and the door was opened instantly from the inside. They passed through and the door closed behind them.

They were standing in what had once been the scullery. Furniture had been pushed here into temporary storage and it cluttered the floor beneath drab dust sheets. The room smelt of age and caustic soda; the double doors at the far end of the room had been thrown open, and Frank could see the rear of the laundry van beyond, with the driver sitting at the wheel.

Three people were waiting for them in the room: a dark-haired girl of about twenty-five, a man a little younger, who carried a drawn pistol – and a boy standing a little apart from the woman regarding them gravely through huge dark eyes.

'Hello, Misha,' said Frank softly, recognizing the boy instantly from his mother's picture.

The boy said nothing. Seppo Halle clicked his fingers impatiently. 'The letter, the letter. Give the boy the letter.'

Frank opened his jacket and tore with quick fingers at the bottom of the lining. He reached inside and pulled out a crumpled envelope. He handed it to the boy. 'It's from your mother, Misha. It explains what is to happen – why we are here. You can trust us. Read it –'

He shook his head in exasperation as the boy regarded him blankly. The girl stepped forward and translated swiftly. Misha took the letter slowly and Frank nodded his thanks to the girl.

'You're welcome,' she inclined her head abruptly and then turned to Seppo. There was a rapid exchange of information. Seppo turned to his son and snapped out instructions in Finnish. As the boy removed his spectacles and began stripping off his yellow windcheater, Seppo dropped to his knees and began emptying out the contents of his camera bag.

'What does she say?' asked Frank, lost without the language.

Fingers working busily, Seppo didn't bother to look up. 'She says they are worried about one of their people. He didn't make the rendezvous.'

'Do they know what happened? Trouble for us, I mean?'

Seppo shrugged. 'Maybe, maybe not. It makes little difference now – we are committed.'

Frank gestured at the man and woman, at the laundry van. 'These your people too?'

Seppo shook his head. 'Russian Jews. People who got tired of being pushed around. Maybe they're the start of a movement, who knows?' He glanced up. 'Better we don't talk, eh?' He upturned the camera bag and pulled out the inner lining. Three flat packets fell on to the floor. He tossed them to the girl, who slit open each bundle of notes and counted the money swiftly. Then she nodded.

'Thank you. Please –' she turned to Frank and continued in slow English – 'please tell your people that we are growing in numbers. We are not . . . how do you say . . . playing games? And these are not toys.' She pointed at the man's pistol.

'I'll tell them,' promised Frank. The girl thrust the money away and turned to Misha. He had finished reading his mother's letter and now looked excited, determined, close to the tears that came with tangible proof of the proximity of reunion with a mother he had not seen for almost two years. The girl spoke to him quietly and Misha began struggling into Jakko's windcheater.

Frank watched with dawning dismay. Although there was little difference in the boys' ages, their stature differed considerably. The loose windcheater fitted well enough, but the blue slacks flopped over Misha's instep and the white tennis shoes were a clown's size too large.

Seppo was also watching the transformation critically as he stuffed his camera gear back in his bag. 'There is nothing we can do,' he said finally. 'The boy must wear his own shoes. All we can do is hope that no one notices.' He shrugged. 'Who looks at shoes anyway?'

As he was speaking the girl bent down, tucked the trousers to the right length and pinned the material up inside each leg with a couple of safety pins pulled from an inside pocket. Seppo nodded approvingly. 'Good, good.' He glanced at his watch, cracked open the door and glanced down the corridor as Jakko wriggled into Misha's jacket and trousers. Now Seppo tugged Frank aside and spoke softly in his ear. 'You will have to move quickly. Already they are out into the garden. Remember – stay back with the boy, yes?'

Frank nodded. 'Sure – but what about you? Where'll you be?'

'I take Jakko to his mother.'

'Your wife? She's here? In Leningrad?'

'Certainly, she is here. Ten, fifteen minutes, that is all. She is very close.' He sighed impatiently. 'When the boy and I come from our home far to the north, then to Helsinki and then here to Leningrad –' he shaped the route in the air between them – 'she travels alone to Sortavala. Over the top – the northern route – yes?' He shook his finger. 'Only she travels without the papers, the passports, yes? The frontier is very easy. So – now she goes back. With Jakko.'

He saw Frank's look of doubt and laid a hand on his arm. 'Don't look so worried! It has worked before – what could be more natural than for a boy to travel with his mother?'

'And if they're stopped? For papers, passports?'

'If they are stopped, then that too is a little matter. At this time, with the reindeer, there are many hundreds of Finns who cross the frontier without the correct authorizations. The Finns are a very independent people.' The eyes twinkled.

'And if the guide starts counting? When you're away? What if she sees we're one short?'

'So? So she made an error.' He moved again towards the door. 'Come – we are wasting time.'

Frank turned to find Misha standing obediently at his side.

'OK?'

The boy nodded. Frank reached out and gripped Jakko's shoulder. 'Thanks, Jakko.' The boy grinned. Seppo eased open the door, and Frank and Misha hurried down the corridor, past the rope cordon and back into the tiled hallway.

The tour had gone.

Frank glanced swiftly down the empty corridors and felt a moment's panic. They couldn't just disappear! He strode to the far door. Down the steps and into the sunshine just in time to see the last of their group turn down a side path about fifty yards ahead. As they moved to join them the guide appeared around the corner and began to march towards them, gesturing them forward impatiently. For a moment he hoped she would stop and return to the head of her group but she advanced towards them down the gravel path, intent upon delivering a Soviet lecture on punctuality. She stopped a few feet away, huge chest heaving deeply, guide book wagging time with her words. 'You must stay with the group! It is expressly forbidden to wander off on your own, you know that,' she admonished sternly.

Frank nodded contritely. 'I'm sorry, I'm sorry. It's just that there's so much to see. Everything is so beautiful.'

'Yes. We think so. Now – please. You must keep up.' She turned on her flat heel and crunched across the gravel like a battle-tank crossing rough ground.

In Moscow, Igor Bayev tapped the sheets of paper in front of him and glanced up at Mikhail Kostikov with icy disapproval. Kostikov waited nervously, bracing himself for the reprimand that must follow.

'And you told me everything was under control – you told me that yourself, here! In this room!'

'Yes, comrade.'

'Tell me: what effect do you think the death of this . . . this gangster will have upon our nervous Jewish friends? Will they pull out? Eh? Will they abort the mission? Will they panic?' Eyes glittering dangerously, Bayev paused to give weight to a last possibility. 'Will they perhaps *kill* the boy themselves?'

Kostikov looked ahead steadily. 'I do not know, Comrade Direktor,' he admitted miserably.

'Then perhaps you can tell me this, comrade: how do you imagine they will get the boy out of Leningrad – always supposing they decide not to cut his throat to ensure their secrecy?'

'There is the . . . the Leningrad Back Door,' faltered Kostikov.

'What? Speak up, man. I can't hear you –'

'They call it . . . they call it the . . . the Leningrad Back Door. It is a ship – a cruise liner. The MS *Finnstar*.'

: : 20 : : : : : : : : : : : : :

It had begun to rain lightly as the two red and blue coaches splashed through the puddles, crossed the sunken rail tracks beside the mobile cranes and pulled to a halt on the cobbled quay a hundred yards from the moored vastness of the MS *Finnstar*. The coach doors sighed back, the middle-aged Russian guide stepped down and their tour of Leningrad was all but over.

Sitting towards the rear of the second coach, the boy beside him clutching his camera with his face pressed close to the steamy window, Frank watched the debussing critically. As his fellow tourists stepped down into the light drizzle they began tugging on plastic anoraks, adjusting hoods and tying headscarfs, complaining good-naturedly at the damp and unscheduled addition to the itinerary before hurrying over the gleaming cobbles towards the little wooden customs hut set at the bottom of the gangway.

He leaned across Misha and the boy watched him silently. The rain was good: people would hurry, they'd be impatient – and the hoods would help too. He watched again, rubbing his fingers against the smear on the window and peering forward intently, looking for whatever happened to the first passenger to reach the bottom of the gangway, because upon *that* hinged their own chances of success. The window misted over suddenly and Frank rubbed away impatiently.

A woman in a red plastic see-through raincoat stepped up to the wooden hut, said something inaudible to someone unseen standing behind the open hatchway and waited. Frank began counting: . . . five . . . six . . . seven . . . eight. Through the blur of rain on the window he saw a hand reach out and hand over a dark blue booklet. Eight seconds.

They could hack that; that should be easy enough. He tapped Misha on the arm: 'OK. We're going.' He pointed at the hood of Misha's yellow windcheater and the boy pulled it up obediently. They edged their way down the centre of the coach, nodded their thanks to the heavy-faced Russian guide and then joined the gaggle of tourists heading back towards the ship. Towards neutrality. Towards safety. Home base.

With Misha stuck close to his side, Frank walked on nonchalantly. They'd almost made it.

Suddenly the line stopped. There was a hold-up ahead. One of the passengers – Frank recognized him as the same middle-aged, spike-haired American who had deliberately ignored the No Photographs instruction as they drove through the dock complex on the way out – was banging his fist on the wooden sill of the customs shed and pointing angrily up at the side of the ship. Frank groaned: come on, come on – let it go, whatever it is. But the American stepped back, turned to the next passenger waiting in line and began arguing some more. The side door opened and two brown-capped, brown-caped customs officers stepped out into the drizzle and walked round to the American. As the senior of the two civilians began arguing with the American, his younger colleague turned and began sauntering along the waiting line of passengers, glancing into foreign faces with the timeless, impersonal curiosity of the professional.

Frank glanced towards the head of the line as the man came slowly closer, taking his time, his black shoes clipping on the gleaming cobbles of the quayside, the water dripping off the folds of his rain-cape. Come on, move it, muttered Frank, glancing again at the head of the queue. Now the senior of the two customs officers had ordered the American to one side, where, calmly oblivious to the tourist's mounting fury, he was unpacking and then meticulously examining each and every souvenir and personal item in his hand-luggage.

The second customs officer was closer still; then Frank breathed a hidden sigh of relief as one of the Finnish women in front suddenly left the line of waiting passengers and crossed to the man's side. All beams and smiles, she rummaged inside a carrier bag, hauled out a set of colourful Russian wooden dolls and pointed earnestly at a line in her phrase book. The man shook his head impassively and pointed the woman back into line before resuming his slow, methodical pacing.

With a sudden quiver of alarm Frank recognized him as the same man who had taken their passports before they had been allowed to go down to the waiting coaches just a few hours earlier. Pausing a moment only, the man's gaze swept slowly along the line of waiting faces as the queue began to move once more. As he stepped forward, the customs officer looked, not at him, but at the boy at his side. The eyes swept down from the dark hair beneath the hood of the yellow windcheater, down, down, down – and stopped. As Frank watched, as he actually studied the man's face, something changed: that blank look of professional indifference was pushed aside for an instant as the eyes registered something they had been trained to detect. The man glanced at Frank briefly and then turned away and began walking slowly back towards his colleague, the rest of the passengers suddenly forgotten.

He's found what he was looking for – the thought popped unbidden into Frank's mind. He looked quickly at the boy. Misha glanced up and smiled eagerly. Frank smiled back, his mind a million miles away. Christ! What was it? What had the man seen that made him so – he glanced again at the boy and then back at the retreating customs officer as it hit him between the eyes.

They were wearing the same shoes.

They were the same pattern. Different size but same pattern, same style, same colour. Consumer choice of one for the peoples of the glorious Soviet Socialist Republic. Russian shoes on an American boy? He closed his eyes. Oh, Jesus.

He looked at the head of the queue by the hut. Seppo was up there somewhere, near the front. There he was now, stepping up to the wooden hatchway. As Frank watched,

Seppo leant against the wide wooden sill, turned and glanced casually down the length of the queue. Their eyes met briefly and then slid away, as though mutually repelled by the covert nature of their shared, secret knowledge. The second customs officer had walked back now to the head of the queue and was talking quietly to his superior, a hand resting lightly on his arm. They spoke together for a moment as the line shuffled forward beside them. Then the senior of the two men raised his eyes, found Frank and Misha, turned and walked slowly back into the hut.

The line moved on.

Presently the woman in front stepped forward to reclaim her passport. Frank found himself counting helplessly under his breath. Now the woman had packed her passport away in her handbag and was turning to climb heavily up the steep wooden gangway.

'Next.'

It was his turn. Resigned to detection, he stepped forward.

'Your name?'

'Coning. John Albert Coning. United States Passport. I've got the boy with me.'

Four . . . five . . . six . . . – please, no questions. Not to the boy. Please . . . seven . . . eyes watching casually from within the wooden hut; a brown back turning, square fingers running expertly along a line of worn wooden pigeon-holes. The fingers stopped, drew out the precious green and gold passport and riffled through the pages. Seven and a half . . . The officer glanced swiftly at the passport pictures, their lie endorsed by the seal of the American Embassy in Helsinki. Beneath the picture of Frank was the photograph of Jakko they had taken in the hotel bedroom; a Jakko with his hair dyed to Misha's darkness, his features blurred, flared out by their deliberate use of harsh white light. Frank glanced down at the passport reversed on the wooden sill before him and felt his palms go damp. It was obvious; it was plain, plain for all to see; a pathetic bluff dooming itself to failure and him to humiliation and arrest.

He waited there silently, waited for the axe to fall. Seven and three-quarters . . .

The customs officer glanced up and smiled pleasantly. Bang-bang. Exit stamp. He slid the passport on to the wooden sill. 'Thank you, Mr Coning. Next.'

In a daze Frank slipped the passport into his pocket, shepherded the boy up the swaying gangway and dropped down on to the teak decking.

How good it felt beneath his feet.

In Leningrad's Pushkin Hotel, Irena Ryabov had begun packing. Whisked away from the hospital with curt instructions to do and say nothing beyond preparing for the return journey home, she had closed and locked the bedroom door behind her, kicked off her tight shoes and stretched out on the narrow bed, utterly drained. She had lain on the bed staring up at the ceiling for long minutes, her mind an aching, drained place that craved nothing beyond silence. Later, as she began moving round the lonely, empty room, she had begun to worry anew about the boy given into her care, the boy she would never see again. Her worry had grown and, as she packed away Misha's pathetic scattering of possessions, she had started to cry. She was crying now as there came a soft knocking on the bedroom door.

The knocking was unexpected. The last she had seen of the unconscious Kapitan Simonov he was being wheeled down one of the hospital corridors on a metal stretcher.

Brushing the tears away she crossed to the door and opened it apprehensively. Standing in the corridor was a well-dressed civilian in a grey suit. She guessed he was in his early fifties. Judging by the western influence in his dress, he was also important.

'Mrs Ryabov? Mrs Irena Ryabov?'

'Yes?'

'May I come in? I am from the Committee for State Security – but, please, do not be alarmed.'

She nodded tiredly and stepped back into the room. The

man closed the door carefully behind him. 'First, Mrs Ryabov, I am permitted to convey the Party's fullest thanks for your co-operation. We are indeed most grateful –' he peered forward, sharp eyes noting the tears. 'Something is the matter?'

Irena Ryabov brushed a hand impatiently across her eyes. 'It . . . it is nothing, really. The boy . . . I . . .'

'Of course, of course. It is understandable.' He glanced around the room. 'Do you require any assistance? Anything at all?'

Again she shook her head. 'No, no, thank you. I will be perfectly all right in just one moment. I may call my husband, tell him what has happened?'

The man nodded. 'I think so. A short call only – nothing specific, of course.' He paused. 'A car awaits you downstairs when you are ready. The airport at Semipalatinsk is now open. A scheduled flight will be leaving shortly to take you back to that distinguished husband of yours.'

He turned towards the door. 'Oh – one last thing, Mrs Ryabov –'

'Yes?'

'We have spoken to the two doctors . . .' He paused. 'What was it you were saying to the gunman in the consulting room? There at the very end?'

Irena Ryabov felt her stomach turn over. 'I . . . I was . . . I'm afraid I was pleading with him. For the safety of the boy.'

There was a moment's silence as the man seemed to look through into her soul. Then he smiled with a row of expensive gold teeth. 'Ah! Of course – how convincing. Excellent, Mrs Ryabov – excellent. Again, we are grateful for your co-operation.'

Irena Ryabov wondered what he would have said had he known that the boy's camera, and the information and vital secrets that it contained, was now on its way to the Americans.

There was a quick double knocking on the far side of the

high, inlaid doors at the entrance to the PKO committee chamber in the former KGB Headquarters on Moscow's Dzehinsky Square. Marshal Gladky broke off in soft mid-sentence, and he and the other nine members of Protivokoz-micheskaya Oborona looked up expectantly.

The door opened and Genik, Mikhail Kostikov's assistant, hovered uncertainly in the vast doorway, awed by the importance of the meeting he was interrupting and by the very dimensions of the chamber itself. Marshal Gladky, Commander-in-Chief of the National Air Defence Forces, glanced across at Kostikov. 'For you, I believe?' It was the interruption they had all been waiting for.

Kostikov snapped his fingers impatiently, and Genik bustled to his side clutching a sheaf of papers. The room watched silently as Genik laid the papers neatly before his master and then stood back behind his high-backed chair, fingers fluttering at his sides. 'That will be all,' announced Kostikov. Genik backed towards the door, black shoes squeaking on the wooden flooring. When he had gone, Kostikov laid the papers carefully aside and looked around the table at his colleagues.

'You have some information for the Committee?' queried Gladky, scarcely bothering to disguise his dislike for the formidable Head of the KGB's Directorate T.

'I apologize for the interruption, comrades, but it was not . . . unconnected . . . with the matter in hand.' Kostikov paused. 'A report I have just received from Leningrad indicates that the child belonging to the traitor, the scientist Lydia Prolev, has been successfully "rescued" by agents of United States Intelligence, much along the lines we anticipated.'

He smiled thinly. 'It appears the woman may serve some useful purpose after all.' A few of the heavy faces met his with a smile. 'The boy is presently travelling the open route: Leningrad – Helsinki by sea. He is travelling under the protection of an intelligence operative known to our station. The pair are expected to arrive in Washington within the next forty-eight hours.'

The table nodded its approval. Only Marshal Gladky

remained looking down at his hands, a pencil drawing little circles on his notepad. Finally he too looked up. 'You are saying it is now safe to proceed – in the opinion of the Directorate?'

'Yes.'

'There is no further obstacle to the deployment of Proton-Soyuz for offensive tests of Skyshroud? No objections from Intelligence?'

'None. We have led the Americans to the very edge of the cliff. I think they can be trusted to fall over the edge without any more help from us.'

There was a snort of self-satisfied laughter around the table.

*

Irena Ryabov leant back and closed her eyes, her fingers tightly gripping her canvas seat belt as the Aeroflot jet sagged down towards the cluster of low buildings beside Semipalatinsk's concrete airstrip. The aircraft lurched again, buffeted by strong head-winds. Then the noise of the engines sank away to a whisper and they swept in over the perimeter lights to land with a light thump, the buildings, hangars and the long lines of Mikoyan Mig-21s flashing past the window.

Stepping out into the cold wind and climbing cautiously down the steep metal staircase to the ground, Irena Ryabov scanned the knot of winter-coated spectators waiting beyond the chain-link fence. As she watched, one of them suddenly moved to one side and began waving in the short, jerky fashion she immediately recognized. Eduard! She waved back happily, her breath pluming in the cold air, her fears of the flight from Moscow swiftly forgotten as she felt grow within her a love that had only increased during the dangers of their separation.

They came together awkwardly at the edge of the concrete runway, Eduard clasping her tightly in his arms and sweeping her gently off her feet just as he used to do in the old days. She kissed him swiftly on the cheek, confused and a little embarrassed by the amused glances thrown their way by more subdued homecomings. 'Eduard! No, people are watching!'

'Let them! Let them all watch!' But he lowered her quickly enough and stood back, chest heaving. He had been stronger then – and I too was much lighter, she reminded herself, looking fondly into the face of her husband. How old he looks, she thought with sudden dismay; how old and how tired – and how worried beneath the same old smile that had first attracted her to him all those summers ago.

'It is good to have you back, Irena – wonderful! Tell me –' he peered forward anxiously – 'did you have any problems? You said so little on the telephone – and the boy? Did Misha –?'

Irena was nodding happily, glad to be able to bring an end to her husband's miserable uncertainty. 'Everything went perfectly, Eduard. Do not worry so.'

'And you?'

'I *told* you, Eduard: everything was fine.'

'Misha?' Professor Ryabov glanced about and then lowered his voice. 'The camera?'

Irena laid a hand on his arm and steered him round towards the gate that gave on to the airport forecourt. As they walked, the Professor watched her face keenly, hanging on her words.

She smiled. 'I gave the people your message. They heard what I said. They understood – I am certain.'

For once lost for words, Professor Ryabov merely patted his wife's arm several times as they walked towards the gate together. There he showed his pass to the brown-coated sentry, who snapped to attention and smacked his gloved hand across the magazine of his automatic weapon. Irena glanced inquiringly at her husband as they walked out across the tarmac towards their car. 'That's new, Eduard.' She flicked her head back at the guard.

'That?'

'The saluting business. They never used to do that before. No one used to hardly recognize you except within the faculty itself.' She smiled. 'So suddenly everyone else realizes you are a very important, a very brilliant man? I have known that for years!' She hugged his arm warmly as they reached the car. The Professor handed his wife into her seat, closed the door carefully, locked her single suitcase into the boot and climbed behind the wheel. Then, instead of starting the motor, he turned towards her, his face deadly serious.

'Yes,' he said soberly. 'Very important, Irena. Even I am only just beginning to realize how important. You see –?'

He pointed beyond the car window. For the first time Irena Ryabov noticed the new flags fluttering from the masts that stood in a row outside the airport's main entrance, the gangs of workers emptying frozen soil from concrete flower tubs and filling them again with brown earth and fresh flowers. Even the airport building itself was being repainted on the outside. She turned towards her husband, obviously puzzled. 'Eduard? What does it mean? What is happening?'

Professor Ryabov shrugged unhappily. 'There has been – what shall we say? – a few changes in the programme?' He sighed. 'I must have been blind.' He sounded bitter – no, not bitter, she realized suddenly: scared. 'The Proton-Soyuz space launch is scheduled to start in –' he glanced at his watch – 'a little less than thirteen hours' time. Then I am required to supervise the start of Skyshroud tests the day after tomorrow.'

'But you always knew –'

'These tests are offensive, Irena, offensive! Already the place is buzzing with dignitaries, officials, people I have never seen before from the Centre, from the Party – there is even talk within the faculty that Marshal Gladky himself will shortly arrive. And who do you think is at the centre of all this? Who is the architect of this . . . this madness?' He tapped his chest without pride. 'Professor Eduard Ryabov of the Soviet Academy of Sciences.'

'But why? Why do they change? I do not understand why they –'

'Irena – listen to me.' A hand pressed down on her shoulder and he leant closer. 'Tell me: the message, the message about the camera, about what was inside – you are sure the people who took Misha understood? You are sure? There is no room for doubt?'

She shook her head impatiently. 'None. I told him –'

But now her husband's hands were fluttering agitatedly 'You must tell me everything that happened – now, please.'

Irena studied the tired eyes, the deep lines of tension. Then she turned, gazed out of the windscreen and began talking.

When she had finished, 'Thank God. Thank God,' he breathed, sitting back in his seat as though he had just carried a great weight a great distance. 'The boy is safe, and soon they will know what we have been up to. There is still time: soon it will be known, there will be a warning from the powerful Americans, from NATO, perhaps, and then it will be stopped; we will have no choice but to climb down. It *must* be stopped, it *must*!'

His clenched fist pounded on to the top of the dashboard. He turned and smiled awkwardly at his wife. 'I am sorry, Irena, but you will never know what I have been through these last few weeks while these . . . these *clowns* –' he gestured angrily beyond the car windows – 'have been planning their little "demonstration".' He shook his head in disgust and then laid a hand gently on those of his wife. 'From the bottom of my heart, little woman, thank you.'

'Thank me? For what? We are one, you and I, Eduard; we feel the same things.'

He was shaking his head impatiently, burdened with the need to formally recognize his gratitude. 'No, no, Irena: Thank you. For going with the boy when I could tell you so little. For going with such trust. But that business in the hospital? In the consulting room? The man and woman with guns? I had no idea it would be so dangerous. Had I known . . . I am truly ashamed. I never intended to put you at such risk. They did not tell me it would be like that. They said only –'

'Eduard, you are an old woman! I am here beside you, am I not? Am I hurt? Do you see bandages, eh? Do you?' She managed a gesture of airy dismissal that papered over those private moments of quaking fear in the hospital. 'It was nothing – and, anyway, now it is over, forgotten.' Then, abruptly: 'Take me home, Eduard. I would like just to lie with you for a little while – like in the old days, you remember? I would like to lie down and hold you close to me.'

Professor Eduard Ryabov of the Soviet Academy of Sciences, the Soviet Union's leading high-energy physicist, rubbed his nose vigorously, wiped a hand impatiently across his eyes and leant forward to start the motor.

Aboard the MS *Finnstar*, five hours out of Leningrad and now heading west across the Gulf of Finland towards Helsinki, Frank Yates and Misha Prolev were together in Frank's old cabin, the door securely locked from the inside. It was shortly after 11 p.m. A little earlier Frank had ordered supper in their cabin and had taken their trays from the obliging steward at the door. Misha had marvelled incomprehensibly in his native tongue at the sudden choice of dishes placed before him, wolfed down a prawn cocktail, cold salad and three chocolate desserts and then curled down contentedly beneath the thick blankets on the upper berth and gone to sleep. Frank sat below in a single pool of light thrown by the bulkhead reading lamp. He was sitting back, propped by pillows on the bottom bunk while the Russian boy snored gently above.

Frank had a notepad on his knees, a pencil in his hand and a glass of wine balanced safely on the carpet within easy reach, its surface shivering only slightly to the steady, constant beat of the diesels as the ship creamed across smooth seas towards home.

Frank laid his pencil aside in exasperation and frowned at his notes. Then he reached down, took a sip of the chilled wine and replaced the glass carefully on the carpet. He had picked up his pencil once more when he heard the soft knocking on his door.

He swung his stockinged feet down to the floor, hefted the wine bottle in his hand and stepped closer. 'Yes?'

'It's me. Seppo. Seppo Halle,' whispered a voice. Frank released the chain, drew back the bolt and Seppo slipped quietly into the cabin.

'Hello, Seppo. Like some wine?' He lifted the bottle. Seppo nodded readily, crossed to the washbasin and held out a tooth-glass. As Frank poured, 'The boy is OK?'

Frank nodded. 'Had some supper about an hour ago and went straight to bed. Dropped off almost straight away. What can I do for you?'

'I come to arrange the security – for when we arrive in Helsinki. I have asked a few of my people –'

But Frank was shaking his head slowly. 'I don't reckon we'll need any – we'd just be wasting our time.'

'What? Are you mad?'

'No, I don't think so.' Frank crossed to his lower bunk, stooped and waved his notepad at Seppo. 'I've been doing some thinking.'

'What do you mean?'

'I mean: the thing stinks. The boy – the "escape" – all of it.'

'I do not understand,' said Seppo shortly, sipping his wine and watching Frank shrewdly over the rim of his glass. Earlier Frank had placed Seppo at the top of his list of suspects, but he hadn't stayed there long. The thing went farther back than that.

'It was too easy, too pat.' He ran a hand through his hair and sat down on the edge of his bunk. He waved Seppo to the chair and sat forward. 'You've done that trip before, yes?'

Seppo nodded cautiously. 'Several times.'

'How many times?'

'Three times before. Twice like this, as tourist – once as a bona fide guide at the very beginning. Why do you ask?'

Frank held up a hand. 'Bear with me. The routine – for getting back on board ship: much the same each time?'

'Sure. Exactly the same. With the Russians there is a

procedure for everything, no? Why do you – ?'

'You're certain?'

Seppo nodded impatiently. 'Yes, I am certain. Look –'

'OK, Seppo: think carefully. In the past, when the coach pulls up and the people begin to walk back towards the gangway to pick up their passports and come back on board – did that process, roughly speaking, did that take longer, not so long or about the same? Think carefully.'

Seppo thought. Finally 'Longer,' he decided.

'Longer. Much longer? A little longer? How much longer?'

Seppo pursed his lips and swilled the wine around the bottom of his glass. Then he looked up. 'It is difficult. Once it is in the winter. Another time . . . I should say a measurable time longer.' He shrugged. 'So – maybe we were lucky. Maybe they are bored, tired, maybe – but yes, certainly: we come through very quickly.'

'Lucky? Soviet customs control lets you get *lucky*?'

'OK, so it is unlikely: what are *you* saying?'

'On those other times: what was it that took the time? Why did it take so much longer?'

Seppo thought, then he snapped his fingers and pointed at Frank with his glass. 'Because . . . because they ask questions – not just of me, you understand, but of everybody. And they check too. They check the baggage, the cases. Sometimes they even make the confiscations.'

'And this time –?'

'This time? No. No, they did not.' A little light began to dawn.

'And I'll tell you another thing: that second guy, the one who comes out and starts strolling down the line of passengers? He *saw* something, I'm damn' sure he did –' Frank told Seppo about the shoes. 'And what does he do? Does he jump up and down on one spot and start hollerin' for reinforcements? Does he, hell! He just turns round, strolls back to his buddy, tips *him* off and the pair of 'em just pass us through, easy as you please.'

'And you think –'

'I think we were set up. The question is: why?' Frank stood up and glanced quietly over the lip of the upper bunk at the sleeping boy. 'Why?' he repeated softly.

The MS *Finnstar* docked safely at Helsinki at 8 a.m. the next morning.

Frank suddenly leant forward and tapped the taxi driver on the shoulder. 'OK – pull in here.' As the driver swung in to the kerb, Frank turned to Seppo, sitting in the back with Misha. 'You're sure you've got it straight?'

'Yes, yes – it will be all right,' Seppo replied testily. 'I go to the hotel with the boy. We use the stairs; we do not use the lift. We stay in your room –' he held up Frank's bedroom key – 'we wait for you.'

Frank nodded, a hand on the door-handle. It was a measure of their shared suspicion that even the Finn's buoyant optimism had been overlaid by taut silence as both men gnawed on the conviction that they were now merely a small part of something neither fully understood. Consequently they felt naked, vulnerable.

'OK – I'll see you in an hour or so. Just keep your eyes on the boy.' Frank got out, slammed the door and sprinted across the traffic towards one of the big international hotels. He paused on the sidewalk to watch as the taxi that had taken them from the docks slid neatly back into the traffic pattern. As it pulled away, he caught a glimpse of Misha's face pressed tight against the window. 'You'd better know what you're doing,' thought Frank, aware that the boy was now alone with Seppo – alone and unprotected in one of the most accessible transit cities of northern Europe.

He turned abruptly and shouldered his way through the glass swing-doors of the hotel.

It was 11.15 a.m. and the young receptionist was busy booking out the last of the night's guests. Frank picked his way past a mountain of suitcases and waited at the counter, fingers drumming his impatience against the polished wood.

The blonde turned politely towards him. 'Yes?'

'I wish to make a telephone call – person-to-person to the United States. East coast. I'll pay cash for the call.'

'That will be fine.' He jotted down the number on a sheet of hotel notepaper and handed it to the girl. She nodded towards the bank of phone booths set into a discreet corner of the lobby: 'I shall put your call through to number four. It will take just a few minutes.' She glanced at a slim, suntanned wrist. 'You know, of course, that it is not yet 5 a.m. in your country?'

Frank nodded impatiently. 'Sure.'

The girl turned away. Frank crossed to the phone booth and shut himself in. The little box smelt of stale cigarettes. Presently the phone rang once. He swept up the receiver; the line crackled and sang for a moment and then came the operator's 'you're through'.

'General Freeman,' growled the familiar voice. Frank pictured him in that big house of his, rolling over from a deep sleep.

'This is Frank Yates, General. I'm calling from Helsinki. I –'

'Good to hear you, Frank! What's your number? I'll call you right back –'

'Listen, General, I –'

'Hold it, Frank – just give me your number!' ordered the Head of US Air Force Intelligence. Puzzled, Frank did so.

'OK, I'll get back to you. Give me a couple of minutes. No, no – make that half an hour.' The line went dead and Frank was left staring stupidly at the receiver. Now what the hell . . .? He pushed out into the reception lobby, told the girl where she could find him and strode through to the coffee lounge, where he ordered a Danish pastry and black coffee. He sat in a deep leather armchair, his thoughts on the information he must shortly present to General Freeman. He wasn't going to like it, thought Frank. He wasn't going to like it at all . . .

In his home on Beachside Landing General Freeman replaced the receiver, swung his feet down to the carpet and padded over to the window. He pulled back the curtains and stood there for a moment looking down at the gardens gleaming pale and washed flat by the dawn's earliest moments. Frank had called him from Helsinki: that meant he was out, almost certainly with the boy – and that meant that he, General Freeman, was right. He gazed down, conscious of no particular feeling of satisfaction. Then he crossed to his wardrobe and began dressing, the badges and medals on his tunic clinking softly in the silence of the big house as he swung his jacket over his shoulders, picked up his car keys and walked softly across the landing to the spare bedroom. He glanced inside: Lydia Prolev was still asleep. He considered waking her, taking her with him, and decided against it. If he was right, then she was as safe here as anywhere else.

And if he was wrong, asked a little voice?

He closed the door, trod swiftly down the stairs, went through to the garage and slipped behind the wheel of his car.

The roads were empty. Twenty-five minutes later the General's car slid to a halt beneath the concrete canopy of the Pentagon's eastern entrance. The uniformed sentry had been lounging in his glass box yawning, pushing the empty minutes towards the end of his duty. Now he caught sight of the dark blue metal plate with the silver stars and came out of his booth in a hurry. He saluted, leant down, inspected the General's credentials and waved him through to the senior officers' car park. Three minutes after that – having returned the startled salutes of the staff he surprised along the empty corridors with a curt nod – General Freeman was behind his desk and waiting for Frank Yates to come to the phone in a hotel on the other side of the world:

'Frank Yates.' He sounded next door.

'Morning, Frank. How're you doing? Let's hear it: have we got the boy?'

'Yes, General – I've got the boy.'

'He's with you now? In Helsinki?'

'Affirmative. He's out, yes. Alive and unharmed.'

'And you're sure you've got the right person?'

'One hundred per cent, only –'

'Only –?' There was a pause.

'You're not going to like it, General –'

'Try me.'

Frank took a long breath. 'You've been had, General. It's a set-up.' That would set the cat among the pigeons, Frank thought bleakly. He waited for the detonation, the explosion. None came. He pressed the ear-piece a little closer. 'Did you get that? I said you've been had, General. It's a set-up! It's got to be.'

In Washington General Freeman tugged a notepad towards him. 'Go on,' he grunted as the pattern fell into place.

'You hear what I'm saying, General? They *wanted* us to spring that boy, I'm sure of it!'

'Tell me why,' ordered Freeman quietly.

'Why?' demanded Frank incredulously. 'How the hell do I know? I'm just the dumb sonofabitch who –' a cold realization spread within him – 'did you *know* about any of this, General?'

A silence crackled briefly between them, then 'Quit wasting time, Captain. Just tell me why you reckon it was a set-up.'

'You got tape running on this?'

'Sure.'

'OK: it went pretty much as we planned it. We joined the tour, made the RVs right on schedule, picked up the boy, made the switch and began the move back. All that was fine; no problems. Then coming through customs – right at the very end – I'm pretty sure we were detected – I'm damn' sure we were.'

'And?'

'And? And nothing. One guard picks up the idea that we're not quite the innocents we're cracked up to be, right? He passes the word back to his superior and they both turn a blind eye.' He paused.

'Meaning?'

'One guard on his own? That could be carelessness; or a

bribe, maybe. But *two*? That makes it a conspiracy, General! They had to be working to orders! I'm telling you – we were *allowed* through! There's no question in my mind – we didn't out-smart them: we were picked up, fingered yet permitted to come on through, clean as a whistle. Even the friendly said he'd never known it go down so smooth – and our papers? They weren't even glanced at – and this was Leningrad, General! Not some hick border crossing that –'

'OK, you've made your point. When are you coming over?'

'Soon as we can. There's a direct flight due out later this afternoon. If we can pick up clean papers in time we'll be on that; otherwise it'll be first thing in the morning.'

'OK Frank, keep me informed –'

'Just tell me one thing, General: did –?' But he was talking to himself. Frank slammed down the phone and barged out of the booth. That bastard had known – he'd known all along!

Down the steep concrete ramp, past the endless guards with their security checks and the massive steel blast doors, Semipalatinsk's Mission Co-ordination Centre was buzzing with excited speculation. In Control itself, half-a-dozen white-coated scientists and technicians flanked Professor Ryabov, each man glancing frequently from his control console to the bank of television screens built into the wall facing them that linked Semipalatinsk with Launch Control at Tyuratam.

Behind the scientists and technicians, separated by a thick shield of armoured glass from the men who would actually control the Skyshroud mission, were the visitors, the officials, the VIPs. Some standing, some sitting, many smoking nervously, they waited. Most were in military uniform while several wore a uniform of a different kind – the dark lounge suit and red lapel badge of the Party faithful.

Professor Klaus Fuchs stood motionless beside the armoured glass, hands clasped lightly behind his back,

297 :

watching without the slightest movement, without the slightest trace of tension or anxiety as Mission Control moved towards final launch.

Meanwhile, sitting slightly apart from the others behind the thick glass screen, perhaps enjoying the definable isolation that is usually accorded to those of high seniority in any society, Marshal Gladky leant slightly to one side as an aide bent to pass on some tit-bit of information. The Marshal nodded, sat a little straighter in his chair and resumed his study of the silent, disciplined scene before him, retaining it all in his mind to take back to Defence Minister Voskoboy.

No one was surprised that Gladky had chosen to watch the mission from Semipalatinsk rather than Tyuratam. Although the Tyuratam Test Centre on the east coast of the Aral Sea, some nine hundred miles to the west of Semipalatinsk, was responsible for Mission Launch and the physical control of Proton-Soyuz until it was on station, that part of the mission – the launch, the climb through the sky – was now considered routine, passé. It was the space deployment and assembly of Skyshroud, not the hefting of its delicate components into orbit, that offered the real excitement: it was from here that they would get that first glimpse of a world-dominance soon to be secured by this new generation of space battle-stations and by the blackmail threat of new and unimagined terrors yet to be unleashed: Semipalatinsk was where the history would soon be made.

Now the light on top of the blue phone beside one of Professor Ryabov's technicians began to wink urgently.

Fingers pointed from behind the armoured glass and the voices fell suddenly silent as the technician listened briefly, replaced the receiver and then leant across to murmur something to Professor Ryabov. The Professor nodded and turned slowly in his chair until he was facing his gathering of important spectators.

He lifted a hand-microphone and depressed a switch. The noise clicked through the P A system into the spectators' sound proofed gallery. 'Tyuratam Control reports they

: 298

have just passed built-in hold minus five without incident.' He coughed awkwardly, his voice curiously flat and lacking in excitement as history approached. 'In layman's language, comrades, what that means is this: we build into any programme various "abort" positions where we can choose to shut down a launch sequence without damage to that system's components – the rocket, the motors, the manned module, matters of this nature. Tyuratam has just passed the last of these fail-safe positions without incident. We are therefore committed to launch.' He spun round abruptly in his chair as the mouths began opening excitedly behind him.

Professor Ryabov leant forward and studied his pile of papers sightlessly, the same question buzzing around the corners of his brain: why had he heard nothing? Why had there been nothing in the papers, on the BBC's World Service, as he had stipulated? Surely by now *someone* would have examined Misha's camera, realized the importance of those first six frames of camera film – God, Irena had even told them where to look! So what had gone wrong?

'Professor? Professor Ryabov – are you all right?' One of his assistants was tugging urgently on his arm, pointing to the microphone. 'The address system! You forgot to mention launch dialogue!'

'What? Oh, yes – yes. Of course.' He switched on the microphone. 'I will switch to pre-launch dialogue just as soon as – ah!' As he spoke there came a click and the muted howl of static. 'I'll put you through now.' He turned a switch and the voice of some nameless supervisor at Tyuratam filled both control and spectator gallery at Semi-palatinsk:

'. . . T minus one fifty. T minus one fifty. Commence Telemetry warm-up.'

Eyes switched to the bank of six television screens on the far wall. The image on the first two blurred, bar-rolled and then snapped into sharp focus. Now two of the six cameras showed all two hundred and twenty-seven feet of Proton-Soyuz in long-shot, its slim lines still cluttered by the protective embrace of the service gantry. A ragged plume of liquid oxygen trickled clear from a cable-coupling as the camera tilted slowly down the launcher's length to dwell caressingly on the huge, flaring bulk of the strap-on boosters that would fuel the thirty-four giant engines in the first critical moments of thrust before being jettisoned at T plus one hundred and thirty-two seconds.

Ryabov watched, mesmerized by obscenity, sickened by self-loathing. Was this his doing? Was he truly a part of this? Was he about to be *decorated* for what would shortly happen?

The next two screens carried signals transmitted from within the module itself. As he watched, Professor Ryabov saw the three-man crew pressed back in their padded seats, their faces pointing at the sky, their mouths moving soundlessly beneath the gleaming domes of their helmets as they carried out final cabin checks in the re-entry module. Gloved hands, bulky still in the grip of leaden gravity, moved slowly and deliberately over a series of switches set into the bulkhead beside their shoulders. One of the cosmonauts – Ryabov thought it must be Popovich, the commander – pushed the camera abruptly away, the grip of pre-launch tension clearly visible behind the tight smile as he sat on top of sixty million horsepower.

'. . . T minus one hundred and ten. T minus one hundred and ten. Switch to internal power. Service tower away. Away.'

All eyes snapped to the monitors. Power lines fell away, the trickle of oxygen feathered into nothing and slowly, slowly the service tower eased backwards and the arms were lowered until Proton-Soyuz stood alone and erect, a thrusting sliver of burnished metal gleaming in the sunlight.

'. . . T minus forty. T minus forty. Internal power checks now complete –'

Against his will Professor Ryabov felt his eyes drawn to the two television monitors at the bottom of the frame of six, the two he had tried so often and so unsuccessfully in the last few hours to avoid. He did so, despite the fact that they appeared to have nothing whatever to do with what was going on at either of the two space faculties. Both showed scenes of the same dusty high street in some nameless, anonymous village somewhere, anywhere in the Soviet interior. Headscarved peasants – some pushing carts, others carrying bundles, one or two on ancient bicycles – moved in unconscious procession across the implacable eye of the hidden cameras, their slow feet kicking up clouds of hot dust as they made their endless journeys to the fields and back to the hovel-homes lining the roadside. Endless journeys? No, not quite –

'. . . T minus thirty. T minus thirty. Start final range safety commitment. Check, Check, Check.'

Professor Ryabov swallowed and ran his finger around the inside of his tight collar. He glanced again at the television monitors –

'. . . T minus twenty-five. T minus twenty-five. Start liquid oxygen tanking –'

He knew why the cameras were there, why the roads had been closed fifty kilometres around and why over-flying had been strictly forbidden. He had made it his business to find out. He could have told them, could have *screamed* the truth at them, told them that the unmanned, remote cameras were hidden in the backs of specially armoured, heat-proofed and carefully decrepit buses that had been driven into the village and positioned next to the depot twenty-four hours earlier.

'. . . T minus fifteen. T minus fifteen. Radio frequencies cleared and silenced. All clocks running –'

He could have told them the name of the place: Kafiyev-ka. It was the target. Kafiyevka was the living, breathing sacrifice to all their efforts. To all *his* efforts.

Kafiyevka was also populated – and very soon it would cease to exist.

'. . . T minus seven –'

'Six!'

'Five!'

'Four!'

'Three!' His colleagues were on their feet now, chanting in cadence, hands hammering the time on their desks.

'Two!'

'One! Go – go – go!' They pounded, they yelled, they begged, as there was a spurt of orange flame beneath the base of the launcher and Proton-Soyuz rose slowly into the clear air of morning.

Professor Eduard Ryabov did not see the moment of lift-off, the historic start of Proton-Soyuz's journey to its pre-determined position in space. He did not hear the cheering; did not rise from his seat with the others to urge the rocket into the sky.

He sat staring, instead, at another television screen, watching a little girl running across a dusty street, a dog yelping excitedly at her bare heels.

:: WASHINGTON

Thirty, perhaps forty minutes had passed in complete silence with General Freeman tilted back in his chair, his hands linked behind his head as his careful mind explored once more what he had come to think of as his 'evidence': Nicholson, the man he had killed, the man whose death had spawned the first nibble of suspicion; Sam Tolland, the voice of dissent who had been wiped away so neatly; Muratov, the expelled Soviet 'diplomat' who drank champagne on the way to disgrace and exile; the cynicism that had greeted his opening statements before the Nuclear Intelligence Board, and – this above all – a growing inner conviction that he was being led by some unseen hand towards a Russian boy called Misha Prolev.

Freeman leaned forward and depressed the 'rewind' button on the tape-recorder. His conversation with Frank Yates in Helsinki jabbered backwards on the spool. He listened again. '. . . But *two*? That makes it a conspiracy, General!' He stopped the machine and rose to his feet, his thoughts hardening into a sudden need to take the pace of events back into his own hands.

Leaving his office locked behind him, he strode down the

empty, blue-walled corridors, past the framed citations of valour that immortalized a service's dead heroes, and stopped by the elevators. Soon he was showing his pass to the armed and helmeted guard and walking through into USAF INT (OPS) – Intelligence (Operations).

Intelligence works a twenty-four-hour shift. The long, low-ceilinged nerve cell had no windows that might permit electronic penetration and was lit instead by blocks of fluorescent panels that were never extinguished. Now, as Freeman paused at the entrance, he absorbed the mood of busy, dedicated professionalism: teleprinters chattered, phones buzzed with muted urgency and computer print-outs spewed unbidden across the desks of Air Force analysts. The cork-tiled area with its wide metal desks was a place of shirt-sleeves and brimming ashtrays, of white cartons of forgotten coffee, of movement to and from the tactical display at the far end of the room. Officers hurried past with files, teletype clippings and their batches of photographs, too busy, too steeped in the concentration of their calling, to spare the General more than a glance and a nod. He was on their ground now.

He was on their ground – Freeman knew it and he resented their preoccupation not at all. This, as far as he was concerned, was the sharp end, the only end that mattered, the end farthest away from the evasion and cowardice of politics. These were his troops, his soldiers, and beneath his gruff, almost stereotyped exterior, he was proud of every single one of them.

He crossed to a harassed-looking, sandy-haired captain in spectacles seated behind a grey metal desk strewn with large glossy satellite reconnaissance photographs and streamers of SigInt tape. The man glanced up and made to rise.

'General?'

Freeman waved him back to his seat. 'Relax, Captain. You're Liaison Officer, right? Between ourselves, the CIA and NPIC*?'

* NPIC: National Photographic Interpretation Center.

The officer nodded. 'That's correct, sir. I'm on this desk through till 1000.'

Freeman nodded towards the activity behind them. 'What's the word, Captain? You about to request authorization to go to Alert State Yellow?'

He smiled to show he was joking, but Captain Fisher dragged a hand through his hair and did not return the smile. 'It may come to that yet, General – it may yet.' He shook his head in irritation. 'We're getting a lot of traffic right now from Tyuratam. They've notified ABM Verification –'

'Tyuratam?' queried Freeman sharply.

Fisher nodded. 'They've notified ABM Verification that they're about to orbit another one of their "biological" payloads. We've monitored launch signature, but –'

'Hey, Sandy,' called a young lieutenant, 'PhotoInt are holding on nine –'

Captain Fisher reached for the call and turned to Freeman with an apologetic air. 'Sorry, General, I –'

Freeman clapped him on the shoulder. 'That's OK, son. Listen –'

Fisher turned, tapped in the call and spoke into the mouthpiece. 'Hold one moment – yes, General?'

'I want anything, anything you've got by way of an update on that entire area over the last week, five days, you got that? Any damn' thing at all – BigBird, SigInt – if some guy's down there changing his *socks*, I want to know about it.'

'Understood, General. How long do I have?'

Freeman looked up at one of the large clocks set into the top of the tactical display. 'I can give you until 0900.'

Fisher pulled a face. 'I'll get some men on it and see what I can do, General.'

The clock on the wall of Freeman's office showed six minutes to nine when his secretary buzzed through. 'Captain Fisher to see you, General.'

'Show him in.'

Fisher entered carrying a slim black attaché case. He looked trim, taut and efficient. 'I think we might have something for you, General,' he said cautiously, bending to open his case and take out a sheaf of glossy photographs and several pages of typed notes.

'OK, let's take a look.' Freeman led the way to the long table beneath the window. As Captain Fisher began to spread out his findings, sorting the photographs into piles, 'What we've got here falls into two parts: photographic evidence, which is fairly straightforward, and an intelligence profile we've pieced together ourselves from highly selective sources.' He glanced up at the craggy face. 'What I'm saying, General, is that these BigBird pictures speak pretty much for themselves – but our evaluation of this other data I'm about to show you is open to as many interpretations as you've got experts on your staff. It's like trying to nail down a piece of quicksilver.'

'I understand.' General Freeman peered suddenly closer at the top photograph. He tapped the picture abruptly with a thick finger. 'That's the launch site, right? Tyuratam?'

Fisher nodded. The river, the railhead and the new launch complex under construction to the north-west made identification easy. 'I'd like to start there, General. Then I'd like to move on to Semipalatinsk in just a moment. First, take a look at these: all were taken five days ago in a routine BigBird pass.'

He handed Freeman prints showing a long convoy of transporters snaking along a narrow dirt road. 'We weren't looking for anything specific at the time, General, or we'd have gone in on those closer,' explained Fisher apologetically. 'We had to wait till Skyhook brought the pictures back down about twelve hours after these were taken. These two here –' he slid more photographs across to Freeman – 'are just blow-ups of the area caught in the same time-frame. It's the best we could do.'

The General nodded. One shot showed a length of dirt road immediately behind the rear transporter; the other showed one of the transporter loads in close-up. Fisher explained: 'Those heavy transporters almost certainly belong to PVO STRANY – see the swivel-mounting on the canopy bar for the 12.7 mm? That's sort of a trademark of theirs.' He tapped the load on the back of one of the transporters. 'Their cargoes are covered in tarpaulin – that's almost certainly for our benefit – but look here.' He pointed at the picture showing the length of empty dirt road directly behind the convoy. 'See the depth of the track there. That suggests a pretty heavy load.'

'So?'

'The road, General: it's what passes for the main highway between –'

'Semipalatinsk and Tyuratam?'

'You've got it in one.'

'So you people think they're transporting a payload for some kind of rocket to the launch site, is that it?'

But Captain Fisher held up a warning hand. 'We're not that far yet, General. It's pretty easy to channel the facts to fit a particular favourite conclusion, you know? That's one of the problems. But – it could be. It's possible.' He passed Freeman another picture of the same convoy halted outside inner perimeter gates. 'We caught this one on BigBird's return swing ninety minutes later. It shows the same convoy being passed through into the space faculty itself. Now – you see? Usually stores and equipment for the base itself go to either the support staging area down here near the railhead, or to the main support complex. But this baby? She just keeps right on rolling. All this gear was offloaded somewhere north of there – at what we believe are the storage bays that serve the pre-launch staging area. Maybe.'

'And you've no idea what's under those tarpaulins?'

Fisher shook his head sadly. 'Not a one.'

'And the pad itself? At Tyuratam?'

Captain Fisher reached eagerly for some fresh papers. 'That's where it gets really interesting, General: we've run checks through ABM and SALT launch notification procedures. In the last six months we've tracked two notified Kosmos launches – the 213 and the 214 – both tabulated as carrying recoverable biological payloads, only that didn't wash. 213 was almost certainly a Ferret*; 214 was engaged in possible ocean surveillance –'

'What about their orbit?'

Fisher nodded. 'Apogee and perigee check out. 214 was tasked to pass over our Indian Ocean deployments six weeks ago. We've checked with Navy. That mission was after those F-18 Hornet carrier trials that ended over the side.' He pulled a face. 'They should have some good pictures of a few red faces.'

Freeman waved him on impatiently. He'd read that much in the daily intelligence digest.

'What else?'

'Last week Tyuratam logged a late entry with Verification: routine Proton launch with a payload of scientific equipment to measure cosmic rays –'

'Lift-off?'

'Two hours ago,' said Fisher softly.

General Freeman looked up sharply. 'Go on.'

Fisher shook his head. 'The logistics don't fit, General. They must think we've got pretty short memories. They pulled that one back in the mid-sixties with a declared payload of less than a couple of metric tons. There's just no way a mission of that sort justifies the kind of lift capability they're using here with Proton; it's like using a crane to lift a candy bar.'

'So your reading of this . . . this Proton launch?'

'It's a cover,' said Fisher simply. 'Got to be. And for my money it's tied in with whatever was beneath those tarpaulins. Track indentation, weight scales, the timing of their arrival at pre-launch staging – most of all, the power/weight/lift ratio of this Proton launcher – they all fit like they were made for each other.'

There was silence as General Freeman nodded slowly,

---

* Ferret: electronic intelligence satellite.

picked up a handful of photographs and walked back behind his desk. He studied the photographs in silence for perhaps a full minute. When he looked up, 'There's more, General. You want me to go on?' Freeman nodded.

'OK – that's part one I was telling you about – the straight photographic intelligence courtesy the National Reconnaissance Office and NPIC – I'll return to IR interpretation in just one moment.' Freeman nodded again, impressed by the officer's control of both the briefing and the complexities of his subject. Then Captain Fisher made a gentle waving motion with his hands. 'Now we come on to something else altogether: part two – our own evaluation.'

'GIGO?'

Captain Fisher grinned at that. 'GIGO – right: Garbage In, Garbage Out. Your intelligence profile is only as good as your ability to interpret what's put before your eyes.' The smile vanished. 'Our Military Attaché in Moscow included an interesting footnote on yesterday's Daily Sheet. Under "Routine Movements" he included the rumour that Marshal Gladky, C-in-C National Air Defence Forces, is out of town right now. Private aircraft with a flight plan filed with Vnukovo II. Destination rumoured to be –'

'Tyuratam?'

But Captain Fisher shook his head definitely.

'No way, General: Semipalatinsk.'

Freeman smiled and made a beckoning gesture with both hands. 'Keep it coming, Captain – just keep it coming.'

'Yes, sir. Since Proton lift-off there's been a strong build-up in signals traffic between Tyuratam, Semipalatinsk and the *two* satellite tracking ships *Gagarin* and *Komarov*. Both are currently deployed in the Southern Ocean, far down in the south, probably to evade our interception. Tandem deployment like that isn't just unusual, General – it's unprecedented.'

Captain Fisher returned to the table by the window and picked up more photographs. 'Last few pictures, General, then I'm through.' He handed the first to Freeman. 'That's the local airstrip nine miles out from Semipalatinsk. Usually it's a pretty quiet place. So what do you make of these?' A finger rested lightly on a tiny row of aircraft.

Freeman peered closer. 'Looks like a Squadron of 21s.'

'And these, General?' A finger rested lightly on the outline of two larger aircraft parked off the main runway.

Freeman studied in silence, then 'They look like Antanovs. Antanov Cubs,' he said in surprised recognition.

'Right. Heavy troop transporters that can airlift 'em in a hundred at a time.' The finger moved once more across the photograph. 'And these?'

'Tell me.'

'Those little lines on the ground are shadows thrown by flags – here – on these flagpoles – here. We've checked, General: they've never flown flags before, not since we first tied a question mark to the place nine years ago.' He slid forward his final photograph. 'If the flags suggest something important is going on down there, these last two pictures confirm it. This first infra-red was taken of the barracks area at Semipalatinsk one night about nine weeks back – again, we had to dig it out of the files. Note the size of the IR glow around those huts there. Body-warmth analysts put it at a couple of hundred men at most – those huts off to the right there are unoccupied, there's no BG at all.'

He slid a second photograph over the first. 'Now look – this was taken within the last forty-eight hours. Body Glow puts the count at six, maybe seven hundred men, General. Whatever's going on down there, they sure as hell don't want gate-crashers.'

The door closed softly behind Captain Fisher. For long, lonely moments General Freeman sat hunched over his desk in the early morning, re-examining each satellite photograph minutely before reading again the typed, detailed reasoning behind each of Fisher's cautious interpretations: SigInt from Tyuratam; the Proton rocket and its payload; Marshal Vladimir Gladky's visit to Semipalatinsk; the sudden deployment of the two Soviet tracking ships to the Southern Ocean – if ever he had needed proof to place behind personal conviction, then that proof was lying now on his desk. Its arrival was so long-awaited, yet seemed so natural, so *right*, that Freeman was aware only of a tired resignation at the prospect of more struggle as he fought to convince others of what he alone had suspected ever since they first traced the venting of gaseous hydrogen back to Semipalatinsk all those months ago.

Once already he had almost convinced the NIB that he had been right. Very well, now he would convince them again – and General Holt, and the Air Force Director, and the Chairman of the Joint Chiefs of Staff – and the President of the United States himself if it became necessary. He would go the distance. He reached out and pressed the intercom on his desk. 'Janet – is General Holt in yet?'

'I'll check, General.' A moment later, 'No, sir, not yet, He's expected any moment for a meeting with Director McNee.'

Freeman grunted and lifted his finger from the button. Then he gathered Captain Fisher's papers and photographs together and rose abruptly to his feet. 'I'll be with General Holt.'

'But, sir, he . . . .' she began and then stopped. Freeman

was already striding purposefully down the corridor. He knocked briskly on the door of his direct superior, passed swiftly through security and walked into the outer office.

'I'd like a word with the General,' he told the secretary.

'He's not in yet, General Freeman, and quite frankly —'

'I know that. I'll wait,' announced Freeman, sitting in one of his superior's leather chairs, trousers sharply creased, shoes blackly gleaming.

'Yes, sir,' began the girl uncertainly. 'May I ask what it is in connection with? General Holt has a very full —'

'No, you may not. I'll do that myself.'

'Oh.' There was silence, broken shortly by a murmur of voices approaching down the corridor. General Holt swept in, shrugging a dark blue topcoat from around broad shoulders: 'Morning, Cherry —' he began, and then stopped as he turned from the coat rack and saw Freeman rising to his feet.

'Good morning, General,' saluted Freeman formally.

Holt turned slowly, nodding cautiously. 'Clarke — what brings you down this end of the corridor?'

'I'd like a word, sir. In private?' He gestured beyond the closed inner door.

Holt glanced at the clock. 'How long have I got, Cherry?'

'Six minutes, general,' she replied promptly.

Holt shook his head. 'Sorry, Clarke: it'll have to keep. I've got McNee breathing down my neck —'

'It's urgent, General,' announced Freeman flatly, holding his ground. In Freeman's vocabulary there were no degrees of urgency. A matter was either urgent or it wasn't. This one was.

Holt sighed, swallowed his irritation and opened the door. 'Come along in.'

Freeman followed Holt's broad back into the inner office. 'I hear you've given those people on NIB something to think about,' commented Holt as he dropped some papers on to his desk and motioned Freeman to a chair. Freeman grunted non-committally and sat down. The office was similar to his own but larger, better-furnished, more lavishly equipped. General Freeman hardly noticed. His thoughts were elsewhere.

Resting on a glass table beside Brigadier-General Holt's desk was a model of the MX missile set in section amid the controversial Buried Trench Concept. Elevated launch tube poking through a crust of desert scrubland, it was all there – right down to the words 'US Air Force' printed on the flank of the rocket in tiny, neat white lettering. It was a beautiful model, recognized Freeman sourly: a tribute to wishful thinking that used white paint and balsa wood as a substitute for the steel of political will and national ascendancy.

Brigadier-General Holt was watching Freeman shrewdly over the top of his pile of papers. 'Seems Sam Tolland's fall from grace in such an . . . ah . . . abrupt manner upped your personal rating a notch or two.' He unbent a little. 'By which I mean the odds on your predicted downfall over this Hammer obsession of yours aren't quite as steep as they were a few days ago. Now then –' he glanced pointedly at his watch – 'what's on your mind, Clarke? I've got the Director coming by in just a few minutes.'

'You'd better hold those odds until a bit later this afternoon, General,' warned Freeman, holding up Fisher's BigBird pictures.

'This afternoon?'

'This afternoon. I intend to tell the Nuclear Intelligence Board I was wrong,' admitted General Freeman quietly.

Brigadier-General Holt just stared at him as though he had suggested they start eating their medals.

'*Wrong? Wrong* – what the hell are you talking about, Clarke?' he demanded, heavy hands pressed flat among his papers.

General Freeman walked slowly forward. 'I have evidence here, General, that *proves* the Soviet Union is getting ready to deploy their beam weapon in space. Photographic reconnaissance reveals that –'

'Hold it! Wait a minute! Is this some kind of *joke*?' Holt peered forward, thoroughly alarmed. 'You're telling me a beam weapon not only exists – but it's geared now towards *offensive* deployment? In space? It's not a defensive, silo-based system at all?'

General Freeman shook his head. 'I'm not saying the defensive concept has been abandoned – those OTH tests point to that. What I am saying is that offensive, space-based development has been given priority – and that's not an obsession, General, it's a fact of goddam history! Unless we want to see world strategy rewritten around us while we sit here playing with ourselves, we damn' well better sit up and take notice –'

'You don't –'

'Let me finish: you realize, General, an anti-missile system like this isn't even *covered* by SALT?' Freeman held up four angry fingers. 'Just four, General – four of those mothers out there in geostationary orbit and they could knock out every fucking thing we could put in the air between here and Moscow any day they choose! Given that advance, that capability, that *threat*, you think the Soviets are going to sit around and discuss the future of *their* fucking planet with anyone? Do you?'

Holt snorted in derision. Then he picked up Freeman's lengthy submission to the NIB and waved it angrily at its author. 'Let me remind you, General, that what you've got here is about sixty pages of ifs, buts and maybes! Want to know what I think, Freeman?'

'I know what you think –'

'I'll spell it out for you.' He paused, gathered his thoughts and looked up sharply. 'I go along with your critics, frankly: you're a dangerous, volatile over-reactor, Clarke – and you haven't *proved* a damn' thing – that's my personal opinion on this Hammer business of yours. Christ – first you put the credibility of the entire service on the line with some cockamamy theory you can't prove, then you want to go out there, pretty as you please, and say "Hold it, fellers – I was *wrong*"? Shit, General – they'd laugh you out of the fucking building, and the rest of the service would be eating out your ass!'

Holt sat back violently and levelled a finger at his subordinate. 'Well, let me tell you, Freeman – for the record and as a direct order: you start raising that kind of laugh, and those odds on your future will start looking like racing certainties, do you read me, General? Jesus!'

Holt shook his head angrily as Freeman strode to his desk and tossed Fisher's notes and pictures down in front of him. 'The Soviets have a name for it, General: *dezinformatsiya*,' he explained patiently, the muscles on his jaw standing out with the effort of remaining calm. 'They've suckered us along – led us to believe they are working on the defensive role of the weapon, when all the time, all the time we're patting ourselves on the back figuring how more advanced we are than those dumb Soviet peasants –'

'Come on, General! We never suspected they had any such goddam thing until you started in! Why the hell should they decide to make us a present of information like that?'

'How long do you think it would be before we began to get something positive on film?' demanded Freeman as he began to pace Holt's office. 'Two months? Three? Maybe half a year? General, they were trading on a certainty! So what do they do? They feed us the Prolev woman – our one, sole surviving scientist defector, remember? Then they rush around trying to knock her off – only not too hard – just to remind us how vital it is that she testifies before the Board, you with me? Only thing is – what we don't know, what *she* probably doesn't know, is that her information is now way out of date! All she could tell us – hand on heart – is that the Soviet Union is working on a beam weapon *defensive* system with no possible offensive –'

'A month back you told me the Prolev woman wouldn't talk as long as her son was held within the Soviet Union,' said Holt quietly.

Freeman nodded. 'That's clarified now.'

'What do you mean "clarified"?'

'It's ceased to represent a problem. The boy's out.'

'Out?'

'Out. We lifted him over.'

'*Lifted* him? From within the Soviet Union? Nothing came over my desk about that! Are you telling me –'

'There wasn't time –'

'Crap, General! I've told you – Jesus! You just *lifted* the kid?'

'It's academic. The boy's out. He should be arriving in the US about three hours from now. There was minimal risk. I told you, General: *dezinformatsiya* – they practically bought the kid his airline ticket themselves. However –' he tapped the photographs on Holt's desk – 'the real proof's in there.'

Brigadier-General Holt pushed the photographs away without interest.

Freeman watched, astounded.

'You mean that's *it*? You're not even going to check out what I've been saying?'

Holt glanced briefly at the photographs and flicked an eye over Fisher's carefully worded and urgently assembled endorsement of General Freeman's worst fears. Then he tossed the papers aside as though it was a document of passing importance. 'This . . . this assessment makes little difference. Without concrete, incontrovertible evidence I am not going to be party to an ill-advised turn-round in national policy regarding our ICBM programme. Quite simply, I do not believe you have the proof I would need to endorse your recommendation to the agencies involved. Further, I do not believe such proof exists – and without that proof this business stays right here. On my desk.'

'I get it,' said Freeman quietly, 'I really do.' He walked over to the MX missile model and spun round. He tapped the side of the model with a gleaming toe-cap. 'This is all that matters, General, isn't it? This is the big one? Nothing must get in the way to foul up –'

'General, I warn you – your insubordination –'

'Warn me?' spat Freeman. 'Warn *me*, you dumb fuck!' He pushed angrily with the toe of his shoe and the model slid off the glass table and fell on to its side. The wooden missile toppled tiredly on to the carpet and its nose-cone fell off. General Holt, features diffused with rage, rose darkly from behind his desk as Freeman stooped and turned towards him, the wooden missile in one angry hand. 'When the Soviets get that idea of theirs operational, toys like *this* –' he tossed the missile contemptuously across at Holt – 'toys like this won't have a hope in hell. And nor will America!'

'Get out,' hissed Holt. 'Get out of my office, General. As of this date, as of this moment, you're suspended. Do you read me, General? Suspended!'

In Semipalatinsk's crowded Mission Co-ordination Centre there was now nothing to do but wait. They were waiting for dawn to break for the last time over the huddle of shops and warm houses that was Kafiyevka. Without the dawn there would be no light; without light their pictures of what was about to happen to the little town of three thousand people would be of an inferior quality. That, in turn, might make sensory evaluation more difficult afterwards. It was really quite straightforward. And so they waited, slaves to the machines they had created.

Professor Ryabov, still sitting in the centre of the long line of white-coated scientists and technicians in front of the control console, eased the ache in his back and glanced around. The faces of those quietly monitoring the instruments nearby looked lined and strained. They hated the delay, this constant niggling over the details of what might yet go wrong. He watched as Sergei made a minute adjustment to the trim of the space vehicle and wondered suddenly what he would say if he knew that he, Professor Ryabov of the Soviet Academy of Sciences, had spent much of the last few hours willing error, delay and malfunction upon the experimental weapon they had built together.

He rubbed tired eyes, adjusted old-fashioned spectacles and swung round in his chair to look beyond the armoured glass into the stuffy, stale closeness of the spectator's gallery. Only Marshal Gladky appeared quite unmoved by the business of waiting. As Ryabov watched, a portly civilian official in dark, baggy trousers and shirt-sleeves pushed stiffly to his feet and began pacing the narrow confines of the crowded gallery, the sweat staining dark patches beneath each armpit. Ryabov swung back in distaste, his eyes sweeping the monitors automatically. No change. Dawn was still some way off.

The mood inside the Centre had been markedly different fifteen hours earlier as Proton reached swiftly into the cool sky. Then it had all been novel and exciting, a shared moment of history to carry back with them to their Soviets. Now, however, those that remained were left with only the memory of the spectacular moments they had witnessed: of Proton-Soyuz's sudden arrival in orbit; of Kosmonaut Popovich's clear, laconic reports as they duly located Salyut 518 coming up over the shoulder of the moon, waiting for them exactly on station in the endless velvet silence of space, lime-green body gleaming in rich contrast against the kingfisher blue of fragile solar panels spread to the sun like the petals of some luxuriant tropical growth; of Titov's sudden shout of triumph as soft-dock turned to hard-dock and he and Popovich were able to crawl through and equalize cabin pressure between Soyuz and Salyut, their every move watched and monitored by the tracking ship *Gagarin* in the Southern Ocean before being relayed back to Tyuratam for onward transmission to Semipalatinsk.

There had been moments of humour, too, as Titov commenced his long-rehearsed space-walk towards the beam weapon's pre-assembled components in their protected travel-sleeves, the sun's unfiltered rays splashing liquid gold across his tinted visor as he swayed God-high above the earth, tethered to the mother-craft by a thick umbilical carrying telephone, telemetric wires and emergency oxygen supply. Despite all the training, all the mock-ups in the deep-water tank at Zvezdnoy Gorodok, Titov had found it difficult to co-ordinate motor action to weightless components weighing several tons on earth that now offered no resistance to movement or propulsion in any direction. It was an hour before Titov, cursing audibly between each panted breath, and assisted by simultaneous assembly of identical components at Semipalatinsk, had completed the first phase of the assembly. But it had taken a further three space-walks before beam assembly was complete, and by then Titov was exhausted.

Ryabov studied the monitors once more beyond the console's broad bank of red and green lights that had begun now to flash intermittently as the time for ground testing approached. One camera showed the view seen from a remote positioned within Salyut's cupola. It showed the assembled weapon receding slowly down range, inclined with sinister deliberation 23° towards the earth. There had been congratulations when assembly was complete, of course – congratulations and hand-shakes that had left Ryabov quite numb. Skyshroud was out there, assembled, ready. Skyshroud – the defensive anti-missile system he had always pictured sunk deep within a Soviet silo, ready to be deployed only to save the lives of those who lived and worked beneath its strategic shield. Now Ryabov watched, infinitely saddened, while the assembled weapon, his weapon, diminished as the camera-platform Salyut drew silently away.

Viewed like this, suspended, gleaming softly against the darkness of deep space beyond, it looked fragile and incomplete, the whole assemblage linked by a delicate filigree of slender girders that carried no weight but which retained each delicate component in exact, pre-determined relationship one with another: attitude jets that would affect trim, roll and pitch and would be controlled from the panels in front of Ryabov now; the particle injector pioneered all those years ago at Kurchatov, the compensated pulsed power alternator, the lasers that would punch a hole through the upper atmosphere to prevent particle beam dissipation a shaved moment ahead of the particle beam itself, the trigger mechanism surrounded by a lithium blanket . . . Pieced together by brilliance, nursed to life by dedication,

Professor Ryabov's awesome new weapon was just fifty metres long and seven metres wide. In a few moments –

'Professor!' The technician on his left jogged his arm and pointed. 'Look – the dawn! It's coming!'

Ryabov looked. He was right.

Pictures on both cameras hidden in the buses in the village of Kafiyevka in the national *okrug* of Koryak now began to emerge from a milky darkness. Gradually the edges of the squat concrete buildings began to harden into substance as the first rays of morning gave shape and depth to the foreground in front of each camera. Five minutes passed as picture definition grew steadily stronger, lengthening the spectators' depth of field: soon they could see smoke curling from a chimney; now an old woman shambled across a dusty square hitching up her long skirts; now a cart creaked and swayed past the plane trees, the oxen plodding sightlessly between the shafts. At Semipalatinsk, the Mission Co-ordination Centre was utterly silent, each face tight with tension as the seconds fell softly away.

'We have picture definition,' reported one of the surveillance specialists quietly on Ryabov's left. The Professor turned abruptly, startled out of some private trance.

'Geiger, Radiac readings now affirmative,' chimed in another white-coated technician, glancing curiously towards Ryabov, who was sitting motionless before the controls, his hands stretched out before him as, behind them all, the spectators' gallery fell silent, watchful and attentive.

'No change. No change in Skyshroud status,' reported Technical Control.

'Injectors, alternators, MHD affirmative –'

'Lasers and Travel echo,' endorsed Sergei, sitting on Ryabov's immediate right, his eyes fastened on the indicator panel he shared with the Professor, which reflected the beam weapon's state of operational readiness. He glanced sharply across at Ryabov: that last report should have received an acknowledgement, yet the man was still sitting motionless before the firing controls, his eyes locked on some far-away place only he could see.

'Professor?' Sergei glanced round quickly at the gallery and leant over. No one else had noticed anything yet. All eyes were fastened on the bank of monitors. 'Professor Ryabov,' he whispered. 'You all right? You want me to take over?'

The spell was broken and Ryabov turned suddenly towards him, eyes haunted by some inner agony. 'It's . . . it's no good, Sergei.' The voice cracked. 'I can't –'

'What?' hissed the other. 'You must! Go on – they're waiting! We have no choice –' He jerked his head back towards the gallery. A few heads had begun to turn.

'Choice?' murmured Professor Ryabov softly. 'I think –' but Sergei had leant across swiftly and depressed the controls on Ryabov's microphone.

'Going in ten – nine . . .' he snapped. Bent heads turned quickly, startled by the unfamiliar voice, and then turned back hurriedly to their controls as they became caught up in the machinery of the countdown.

'Five – four – three –' chanted Sergei, his eyes on the monitors, finger resting lightly on Ryabov's trigger button as the Professor sat back in frozen immobility as events marched past him remorselessly – 'two –'

There was a sudden whirring, a frantic clattering in the sky above the square in Kafiyevka as the air filled with the clamour of birds taking sudden flight – 'one. Firing now.'

Locked and welded deep within Skyshroud's weightless components, the detonation of the nuclear pellet triggered from Semipalatinsk generated in immeasurable fractions of a second the contained equivalent of a small atomic bomb; a stream of atomic, shredded particles – protons and neutrons that were released, stored, switched and then shot in a single, blinding needle of high energy down through the earth's atmospheric shield towards the target area. Preceded by the laser that bored its path through the dissipating atmosphere, the stream of atomic particles collided angrily with atoms of nitrogen and oxygen to turn the sky itself first red and then deep yellow as the proton beam lanced towards the village.

In Semipalatinsk there was silence. Television monitor

screens of the target area showed no picture. Sensors gave no readings. Sergei leant past Professor Ryabov towards the microphone. 'Report, please,' he ordered quietly, frowning. There was a stirring in the Control Office, then –

'Cameras, audio sensors I'm getting nothing – nothing at all. No readings.'

'Mission Technology?'

'The same.'

'Certain?'

'Absolutely. Detonation took place; the system has functioned perfectly according to this read-out. If there's a problem, it's not up there.'

'Radiation? What are you reading?'

'I have a malfunction with all sensory devices within the target area,' he reported shortly. 'I have no readings – wait one moment.' There was a pause, then 'I have a Roentgen air exposure dose of fourteen point nine. That is a Mammal Reading in excess of fifteen point five. It would be life-destructive.'

'Ah!' seized Sergei. 'If *you* are getting a reading –'

'You misunderstand,' reported the other quietly. 'That reading is at target area plus twenty kilometres. Target area plus twenty.'

There was an awful silence.

Perhaps thirty seconds passed, with each man locked in his own thoughts, Professor Ryabov leaning slightly forward, eyes cast down at his lap, chin resting in the cup of his hand. Then 'We should have pictures any moment now,' reported Technical Operations (Land).

Sergei whirled round, finger stabbing viciously at the microphone. 'From the target area?'

The man shook his head. '*Of* the target area – its periphery. We positioned two TRVs – tracked recording vehicles – beneath overhead shelter ten kilometres downrange. We're moving them forward at this moment.'

All eyes turned once more to the monitors. As they waited, the images suddenly cleared, flickered and then snapped into focus.

The personnel at Semipalatinsk gasped.

They were looking down the throat of a howling, swirling dust-storm. Branches, shrubs and heavy objects flashed and clattered past the camera's unblinking eye. It was six minutes before the worst had passed and they were able to see more clearly.

'Those pictures come from Remote One,' explained the technician without glancing up from his controls. 'Here's Remote Two.' The camera pod atop Remote One panned sharply across a tract of brown, broken ground. It stopped and then panned back to lock on to its mate as an armoured drab-green, flat-topped chassis, three feet high and four feet long, advanced slowly out of a narrow concrete bunker set into the side of a hill, its camera turning, its tracks churning busily. The two TRVs inspected one another implacably and then turned to begin grinding slowly forward up a slight rise to the skyline, their cameras rotating like antennae.

They breasted the rise and the twin cameras tilted forward, sniffing for pictures. They were on a wide, barren plain that stretched emptily before them past acres of scorched, smoking ground towards a horizon shot through with angry yellows and reds. Remote One pushed forward and then stopped suddenly, its camera tilting downwards. What had once been a road was now a littered, debris-strewn battleground. Uprooted trees blocked the way ahead, their branches scorched and ripped bare of leaves. A lorry lay on its side, the cab savagely dented, its paint-work scorched back to bare metal. A piece of raw meat oozed from the driver's cab to mix with a pile of charred cabbages that had been torn from the fields a mile away and carried to this hell of desolation *ten kilometres* from the centre of the target area.

Remote Two swung away, tilted down the crumbling embankment and crabbed steadily on, feeling nothing, seeing everything, questing hungrily. The carcass of a cow came into view, its torn entrails and stiff hoofs pointing the way to where its owner lay face down in the charred and smoking earth, the flames still licking greedily at his mane of white hair, clenched blackened stumps still clutching the animal's rope halter.

The TRVs tracked forward remorselessly towards the devastated centre of the target area among the scorched, flattened ruins on the smoking horizon, their cameras swaying and bumping now as their metal tracks clawed and ground over a pair of gleaming, blackened corpses that choked their path.

Two kilometres from the centre of the target area Remote Two regarded Remote One with proprietary interest.

The paint on Remote One's chassis had begun to bubble.

There was an air of suppressed excitement in the Politburo chamber in Moscow as Marshal Gladky leant forward and the last of the low-level reconnaissance photographs began to circulate slowly around the polished table.

'And these were taken – when?' demanded President Travin. 'How soon after test firing?'

'Ninety minutes, Comrade President,' replied Gladky. 'The sortie was flown on my personal authorization. As a matter of interest, comrades, the aircraft returned scorched back to bare base metal.'

President Travin tapped his pen against the pile of photographs before him. 'Very well. At a recent meeting on this matter, Comrade Voskoboy advocated funding of Skyshroud for major, offensive, pre-emptive deployment. He talked about what he described as a "window of opportunity" looking on to the West which we would be obliged to exploit if we wish to maintain our strategic superiority over the United States. I believe we have now reached a position when further delay, further debate, would be pointless. We wanted to see what it could do –' he tapped the photographs. 'Well, at a price that must never, never be repeated, now we know. In the memory of those who died we must decide, comrades. We must decide now. Today.'

Heads nodded up and down the table.

An aide leant forward to draw the President's attention to another related matter. Travin nodded. 'Ah, yes – security. Minister of Defence?'

'There have been no leaks,' reported Voskoboy emphatically. 'Launch was notified under the existing Soviet/American Verification Agreement and logged as a Proton payload carrying monitoring equipment for near-space evaluation. We have taken the necessary steps to ensure that that is what will be confirmed by US satellite reconnaissance.'

'Comrade Bayev for State Security?'

Heads turned towards the Head of the KGB's First Chief Directorate responsible for Foreign Operations.

'The Americans are about to reach a conclusion which should lead them one hundred and eighty degrees in the wrong direction,' he announced. 'It should prove to be an expensive navigational error. Their Nuclear Intelligence Board will shortly confirm – with, I must admit, a little help from ourselves – that the Soviet Union is committed to particle beam technology with a programme that is wholly defensive in nature.'

There were satisfied murmurs from around the table. Even Travin broke out one of his wintry smiles.

'Our congratulations, Comrade Bayev.' He nodded to include Marshal Gladky. 'Our congratulations to all those involved in the project.' He paused. 'I understand there was some mention of an award to the senior scientist involved in the undertaking?'

'Indeed, Comrade President: Professor Ryabov. You agreed to make the award personally tomorrow. The Order of the Red Banner. The Professor and his wife are to be flown to Moscow in the morning.'

'Very well. Now, comrades – the vote. Do we endorse Marshal Voskoboy's recommendation for immediate funding on a scale that will ensure rapid, offensive deployment – or do we leave that "window" firmly closed? Will you please indicate in the usual manner?'

In his low timbered dasha on the outskirts of the Semipalatinsk space faculty, Professor Eduard Ryabov sat on
alone downstairs. Irena had preceded him up the short
flight of stairs to the bedroom forty minutes ago.

Sitting alone now in the shadows thrown by the single
side light, the Professor switched off the radio and automatically adjusted the waveband away from the forbidden
frequency of Radio Free Europe. He stared sightlessly
across the room: nothing. Not a word. Not a single, solitary
indication that the message had got through. Yet he had
pinned his hopes on that, hidden his fears in that, hidden
them in the microfilm concealed in the back of the boy's
camera long before he had been led solicitously to his car
from Mission Co-ordination Centre, Marshal Gladky's
words of sympathy ringing in his ears as they had all, every
one of them, attributed his slumped, silent withdrawal to
reaction, to strain, to the burdens and tensions of his
brilliant work. How little they knew.

He rose and moved slowly across the dimly lit room, thin
hands reaching out to clutch tightly at the familiar corners
and edges of their furniture as a blind man may search for
his bearings in some strange room. He gripped the edge of
the bookcase with shaking fingers as he stared unseeing at
the rows of ancient, leather-spined books, his world in ruins.
For years he had handed the ultimate responsibility for his
work upwards: towards Klaus Fuchs, towards the State,
towards the Party – always upwards, towards others. It had
not been difficult, he saw now: blinded by the national
habit of obedience, rewarded for loyalty and brilliance,
protected by privilege from the numbing, derisive, transparent inequality of the society he served, Professor Eduard

Ryabov saw with a new and terrifying clarity that he had been working towards a dark and clouded goal. While he had worked for peace in cosy intellectual insularity, men he had trusted without question had been angling for supremacy. For supremacy and, thus, for war. Now, as they stood on the very edge of the ultimate strategic victory, he at least knew that it was over: he could go no further. Despite the attentive plans others had made on his behalf, there could be no escort in the morning, no official limousine to whisk him back to Semipalatinsk where he would witness Skyshroud deployment, no award from the hand of Comrade President Travin in Moscow. He had come to the end.

A tired finger traced an aimless line in and out among the corrugated leather spines. Bitterly, Professor Ryabov found himself wondering which particular piece of scientific brilliance, of moral shortsightedness, had provided the roubles that had made purchase possible. His fingers came to the end of the bookcase and he pushed the heavy velvet curtain gently aside to stare with infinite sadness out at the darkness, seeing nothing.

He realized with a sudden kindling of surprise that his own decision had been taken some hours ago. It was not the absolute, mother-lode certainty that there would be no compromise on this one belated decision that now weighed so heavily upon his mind; for himself, the position was clear beyond prevarication: there would be no more cooperation, no more professional blindness. His attempt to smuggle documentary evidence to the West, to warn America about Soviet intentions via a roll of film in the back of his nephew's camera, had been amateur and romantic, doomed to failure. Now he would take more direct, personal steps to ensure the frustration of the evil men he had faithfully served for so long. That decision came almost as relief, somehow. It was not that which troubled him. It was something else. Someone else.

Irena, his wife.

When it was over and he had gone, she would remain, a

hostage to his conduct, a handy whipping-post for those bent on revenge. He let the curtain fall and returned slowly to his chair by the lamp. Perhaps he could take her with him? He clutched at that idea eagerly for a moment before discarding it once more as impractical. She would be permitted nowhere near the space faculty on such a day, wife or no wife. She had never been there before and had displayed little interest in the detail of his complex work. Besides, the business of passes and permits would frustrate his plans, even as her presence would bind his arms to his sides as the time for action approached.

He paused. For action? Dear God, was he truly contemplating *action* of some kind? At his age? He took off his spectacles and began polishing the lenses absently with a handkerchief as he stared at Irena's empty chair opposite, her neat pile of knitting left on the little oak side-table he had made for her birthday many years ago. Perhaps then he might leave a letter, explain his motives, take steps to remove her from all blame for what was to follow. He shook his head, irritated at such muddled, uncharacteristic thinking, as he replaced his spectacles: such a move would be expected. In any event, a note of that nature would mean little and matter less. Irena Ryabov, wife of the brightest star in the Soviet nuclear crown, would remain an accessory to the greatest of all Soviet sins – national betrayal. He groaned aloud, quietly, bitterly aware just how few options remained open to him. Could she, then, be moved? Could he send her away with relatives or friends until it was all over? That too was impractical. At such a time all movements would be monitored, all access and entry to the locality restricted. Out of long habit Professor Ryabov's thoughts roamed on to examine consequence and conclusion: if she stayed with relatives or friends then she would be found – and they too would be roped in as accessories for the circus of trial and public humiliation that would inevitably follow. Perhaps then she could hide, ride out the patient, remorseless inquiries of the secret police, the KGB? Again he shook his head. Hide? There was nowhere to hide, nowhere to run. Alone, she would be frail and defenceless. Shackled to him by name and marriage, her few years of grace remaining would be hallmarked by the very worst a vengeful State could devise. It was not short of practice. Professor Eduard Ryabov twisted restlessly on his seat: how best, then, to protect the woman he loved?

There was a way.

Lydia Prolev and General Clarke Freeman pushed hurriedly through the bustling concourse at Dulles International Airport and stopped beneath the flight information panel suspended hugely above their heads. As they stared upwards the white lettering flickered and clattered to up-date the visual display. 'There you go, Mrs Prolev – they're down, right on schedule.' Freeman pointed as the word 'landed' began to flash on and off beside Flight US 264 Helsinki.

Lydia hugged the General's arm impulsively. 'Thank you, General,' she managed, close to tears. 'I do not know what to say . . . only – thank you.'

'I'll believe it when I see it,' grunted Freeman as Lydia tugged him towards Arrivals, her eyes shining with excitement. A cluster of non-travellers waited patiently behind wire-mesh barriers. Lydia had to stand on tiptoe to crane over the shoulders of strangers to catch a first glimpse of the son she had not seen for two years. There was a delay lasting no more than a year, then the first of the trans-atlantic passengers began streaming through the opaque doors. Flight-bags banging against hips, bright bags of duty-free clutched in determined hands, there were sudden shouts of welcome; arms were flung wide in greeting as small men were engulfed by big women and battered teddy-bears were squashed between child and grandparent, as harassed businessmen, with one eye on the clock and another on the chauffeurs holding up company identification, pushed – General Freeman tapped Lydia on the arm and pointed silently. 'There,' he said gently. 'Over there.'

Misha.

A slim, dark, tousle-haired boy in spectacles, a gleaming new flight-bag slung proudly across his chest, a plastic inflatable model of a 747 hugged in both arms.

'Misha! Mishinka!' The words bursting from her lips, Lydia Prolev began thrusting her way through those awaiting less momentous reunions. 'Mishinka! Oh, I'm sorry . . . excuse, please – Mishinka!' Still the boy had not seen her, his head turning every which way through the bewildering bombardment of new sights and strange sounds. 'Here! Over here!' she called in Russian. 'Misha!'

He saw her.

Plane forgotten, precious, newly acquired flight-bag a sudden encumbrance, Misha broke into a run and fairly hurled himself across the polished hallway towards his mother, his face lit up like Hallowe'en. How pale, how thin, how *tall* he looked, thought Lydia in a kaleidoscopic whirlwind of emotions as she forced her way heedlessly towards him, bent down and held out her arms. He ran forward – they touched – and she crushed him to her in a cosmic bomb-burst of affection that brought a lump to every waiting throat that witnessed it.

In their little pool of sudden, magical silence, 'Mamma, mamma,' whispered the boy, his excited words muffled against Lydia's cloud of dark hair.

'You did it! You did it! You did it!' She hugged him closer, crying openly now, and rocked him gently to and fro, eyes closed, as the world stood still beyond the circle of her arms.

The crowd nearby had stood back, watching. Some were openly, foolishly crying. A group of emotional Italians began clapping their approval.

Frank grinned down and hefted his flight-bag. Lydia glanced up, saw him and rose to her feet. 'Frank –' She leant forward and kissed his cheek.

This time Frank kissed her, too.

Then he walked forward to meet General Freeman, the smile fading.

'Frank – welcome back, boy. You've done a fine job, fine job! Good to see you!'

There was a significant pause before Frank took the outstretched hand and shook it.

There was a spectators' coffee lounge on the first floor of the terminal building that gave those awaiting flight arrivals the chance of refreshments and the opportunity to look down directly on to the floor of the open concourse below. The tall man lowered his binoculars slowly, paid for his coffee and crossed swiftly to the bank of payphones. He fed coins into the machine, dialled a New York number and the tone rang through. He asked for an extension, then 'This is Ferris in Washington,' he reported, turning to watch the tableau below as Lydia, the boy, General Freeman and Frank Yates turned to walk slowly towards the exit, Lydia's arm around the boy's shoulders.

'The boy has just arrived. Tearful reunion with one and all. He's in. Definitely.'

'Good. We have been notified of no change by the Centre. There is thus to be no physical intervention, is that clear?'

'Perfectly. Do I pull out?'

There was a pause as the other man thought. 'No. You are to stay on station one more day. Call again for further orders at the same time tomorrow. In the meantime, go back to your apartment and stay out of sight. It's almost over.'

'Understood.' Ferris paused. 'There is one more thing –'

'Yes?'

'That general, General Freeman: he's at the airport now – he came with the Prolev woman to meet the boy. He's in civilian clothes, but it's him all right.'

'I don't see the significance. Even American generals, even hawks like Freeman, take time off sometimes.'

Ferris shook his head impatiently. Why did the man in the field have to do *all* the work?

'That Board of his – the Nuclear Intelligence people:

they're supposed to make their decision known some time today. I'd have expected him to be in on that . . .'

There was a short silence. 'You may have a point. Our people will look into it. If it's significant we will reach you at your apartment – same procedure as before. In any event, you are to wait for my call before pulling out.'

'Understood.' Ferris broke the connection.

GEORGETOWN, WASHINGTON

With Lydia and Misha sharing private moments of reunion in the bedroom and Mrs Headley not due back with Louise for another half-hour, Frank Yates and General Freeman were arguing hotly in the lounge as Frank pressed for an explanation that would justify the risks he had taken on behalf of the former Head of USAF Intelligence. Freeman had given him the terse facts of his suspension on the drive from the airport. The news had given Frank little satisfaction. Instead, it merely deepened his own sense of confusion, of betrayal.

The phone started to ring.

'Frank Yates . . . yes, yes. He's right here.' He held out the receiver. 'It's for you, General. Brigadier-General Holt.'

'Tell him I'm a civilian,' growled Freeman. Frank looked doubtful. 'Go on, tell that sonofabitch I'm a civilian!'

'Sir? General Freeman asks me to remind you he's suspended from duty.'

There was a sharp crackle of anger and Frank winced. 'Yes, sir. I'll tell him.' He lowered the phone slowly.

'Well?' snapped Freeman.

'He says to tell you you're unsuspended as from now. You're to get back to the Pentagon right away. Something about BigBird pictures of a place called Kafiyevka.'

'Kafiyevka? Never heard of it,' said Freeman. 'What about it?'

'It's not there any more, General. It's gone – disappeared.'

*

Professor Ryabov lay on his back staring wide-eyed up at the rafters in the darkness above, Irena snoring gently beside him, her profile thrown into soft shadow by the moonlight. He twisted round and glanced at the clock: 4.30 a.m. He rolled back to resume his sightless staring. He was not trying to sleep, because the time for sleeping was gone now: he was trying to marshal his thoughts into some sort of order before taking action to redress the dreadful imbalance he had helped create through his own professional blindness. His mind moved over the options, examining each with minute care before running once more up against the same unavoidable conclusion. Irena. What would happen to Irena after it was all over? He glanced at her sleeping so soundly beside him. He knew what would happen: she would be daubed with the same brush as he; innocent or guilty, she would be forced to share the same fate of disgrace, dishonour and humiliation as they stripped away the trappings of success in their savage hunt for revenge. House, property – the dasha where she slept now – all would go. And then? The camps, perhaps – internal exile at the very least. He shifted restlessly. She was too old, too settled in her ways to face that, he realized bleakly. Better if . . . for the hundredth time he searched for some alternative. There was one and one only: he could back out, he could still change his mind. Nothing was settled, nothing committed. He could drift onwards, a party to the knowledge that his discovery . . . No, no.

Dawn would be here soon

He moved gently on to an elbow and slipped his pillow from beneath his head. He sat up slowly and looked down with love, with pity, at his sleeping wife. 'I love you, my darling,' he whispered huskily. 'I love you.' He leant across, the pillow held out before him, and presently it was done.

He rose from the bed shaking violently, arms aching, panting with exertion and with the horror of what he had done. 'I'm . . . I'm sorry, my darling. So . . . so sorry. But there was . . . there was no other way, don't you see? Don't . . . don't you see?' Stumbling through to the bathroom he tugged on the light above the handbasin and leant forward towards the mirror. Through the bitter pain of self-loathing he watched as the tears began to roll unchecked down seamed cheeks. 'Now . . . now, truly, there is no going back,' he whispered at his reflection, his breath misting against the mirror. A shaking forefinger reached out and slowly traced a woman's name against the glass. Then he brushed it away with slow, deliberate finality, turned off the light and walked back towards the bedroom door. There, on the threshold, he hesitated and peered silently towards the dark, still mound on their marriage bed as though half-expecting Irena to rise from the pillows. But there was nothing. The silent stillness in the bed rebuked him, but there was no sound, nothing beyond the pant of his own breathing and the screaming silence of condemnation inside his own head. 'Forgive me, Irena,' he whispered.

Professor Ryabov crossed to the old chest at the foot of the bed. The ancient hinges creaked protestingly as he opened the lid and lifted out the heavy damask counterpane, which he then unfolded across the width of the bed, eyes flicking involuntarily towards the body of his wife. Slowly and with great care, Professor Ryabov drew the heavy cloth up the length of the double bed until it shrouded the still figure. As the cloth reached her chest, he paused and then leant forward to place a gentle forefinger on the lids of those old, closed eyes. His body began to shake uncontrollably and the room filled with the rack of his sobbing as he leant over, kissed the parted lips in farewell and covered the face with the heavy material.

He turned away and began to dress in the darkness, fumbling with the laces of his shoes in his haste. He struggled into his jacket and turned towards the bedroom door. Then he paused, crossed to his wife's dressing table and picked up the single framed photograph of them standing together, arm in arm, facing the camera one happy summer. Then he closed the door softly behind him and hurried downstairs.

Back in the lounge he crossed to the cold fireplace,

prised the photograph from its frame and placed it carefully in the grate. He turned, irresolute, and then moved towards his wife's desk. Fingers scrabbling in a top drawer, he tugged out the thick pile of letters – his letters to her, written over the years since first they had met, bound together with blue ribbon – and added these to the photograph in the grate. He would leave no trace, he muttered to himself: no trace at all of their privacy, their intimacy, nothing that could be exploited by the men who would soon be stamping their anger into his home with their iron-tipped boots. That, quite suddenly, had become very, very important to the elderly Professor. Quickly now, he began pulling open drawers and cabinets, searching for papers, for letters, for photographs. The family album; the picture of a smiling Misha on the mantelpiece – all went into the pile in the grate. Almost running now in his haste, Ryabov blundered into the kitchen and began tugging open doors and drawers mindlessly, looking, looking, looking, as the voice inside his mind propelled him faster and faster towards the cliff-edge. He tugged at the cutlery drawer. It opened half-way and then jammed. Sobbing with frustration, Professor Ryabov jerked savagely and the drawer shot free. Knives, forks and spoons showered on to the kitchen floor with a crash. Professor Ryabov flung round, tripped on the cutlery and fetched up against the mirror on the wall, eye-to-eye with his own deranged reflection. Eyes wide, sweat-streaked, tie askew, jaw working as the air sawed in his throat, the spectacle of his own degeneration brought him back to his senses. With desperate effort he forced himself back under control. Control. Control is everything, he told his own heaving reflection. Without control you will be lost; without control nothing more is possible; without control all this – Irena's death – all will be for nothing. *Nothing*! He sagged back against the wall, eyes closed. Then he poured water into a glass and drank greedily. He drank again, more slowly this time, rinsed the glass and placed it upside down on the drainer. When he returned to the lounge he was quite composed. He sat in Irena's chair and glanced calmly about him. There seemed to be nothing else. He fumbled for the matches.

Sitting back on aching knees, he watched with eyes infinitely sad as the flames licked fire into the pile of memories. As the flames sent shadows dancing across the darkened walls, he struggled to his feet and crossed to his desk. There was still much to do, much that must be accomplished. He sat down at his desk, cast one more glance at the pile of smoking, burning, browning photographs and letters, and reached towards the telephone with trembling hands that made the receiver rattle on its stand.

Then he paused: they'd trace the call of course – they always did. Twice before this year he had had cause to dial a foreign country on scientific business, and within a matter of hours they had been round, asking their questions, playing back the tape, prying with their stupid minds into his business. He jerked up the receiver almost savagely. Well, let them. What did it matter? He flicked open a little leather book and dialled the operator.

'Yes?' The voice sounded bored, sleepy.

'I wish to place a call to Stockholm. This is Professor Eduard Ryabov. My clearance for such a request comes under Faculty Clearance Two and the call is to be charged against the Faculty, is that understood?'

There was a pause, then 'What is the number?'

'Stockholm 27491. The party's name is Professor Henri Olafsen.'

'One moment.'

Ryabov ran a shaking hand over his forehead and clenched the receiver tightly to his ear. One minute, that was all he needed – just one clear minute, maybe less . . . In some far-off home, the telephone began to ring.

'Operator?' demanded Ryabov sharply. There was silence. They were clear to talk. It was one of the perks of trust, one of the privileges of working at –

'*Ja*?' grumbled a voice. Ryabov remembered with a start that Olafsen would have been asleep too.

'Professor Olafsen? Professor Henri Olafsen of the Stockholm Institute?'

'Yes – who is this, please?'

Ryabov paused, pummelling his brain to remember the words of rusty English the scientific fraternity invariably used when attending the endless international seminars of their calling. 'This is Professor Ryabov. Professor Eduard Ryabov of the Soviet Union. Do you remember? We –'

'Professor Ryabov? Yes, yes – of course I remember. I was honoured to have you at my home here – was it '76? No, no, I recall now. It was –'

'Yes, yes, Professor, I remember too. Please listen carefully – hello? Hello? Can you still hear me?'

'Yes, I can hear you. What is the matter?' The voice sounded puzzled.

'Good. Will you please write down these figures –'

'What?'

'Please! Do as I say, Professor. Time is very short –'

'Wait. I must fetch paper and pencil.' The phone clattered down and Professor Ryabov could hear Olafsen rooting around in the background. Come on . . . come on . . . 'I am ready –'

'Sixty-one twenty north, one hundred and twenty-two forty east. Have you got that?'

'I think so. Sixty-one twenty north, one hundred and twenty-two fifty –'

'One hundred and twenty-two forty! *Forty*!'

'One hundred and twenty-two forty east. Professor, I –'

'Listen to me,' ordered Ryabov urgently, acutely conscious of each wasted second. 'The Semipalatinsk space faculty is engaged in offensive beam weapon development. Within the last two days a prototype test weapon has been launched, assembled and fired from space. Launch was controlled from Tyuratam. Apogee and perigee –'

'Are you serious, Ryabov?' The voice sounded as though it suspected a practical joke. 'A particle beam? Incredible . . . just incredible! Not for one moment –'

'Those figures I gave you are target co-ordinates for a

place called Kafiyevka. Now – listen most carefully: the son of Lydia Prolev, a scientist formerly with me at Semi-palatinsk, was recently permitted to defect to the West –'

'*Permitted* to defect? Professor, are you – ?'

'Yes, yes: permitted! I know what I said,' hurried Ryabov. 'The Prolev boy carried a camera – a gift from me, you understand? The first six frames of that camera film contain –'

'What you are saying, Professor, sounds to me –' The voice stopped suddenly in mid-sentence and Professor Ryabov heard a series of soft, sinister clicks. A sudden cold fear loosened his bowels.

'Hello? Hello? Professor Olafsen – can you hear me?'

Silence. He pushed the telephone away, rose to his feet, swept up his overcoat and hurried outside to the car.

The first rays of morning grazed over the trees to the east. Eduard Ryabov climbed behind the wheel, started the engine and reversed violently down on to the road. Moments later the heavy car was dragging a plume of dust across the face of early morning towards the space faculty at Semi-palatinsk. With Ryabov's foot pressed hard against the floor, the car snaked through sleepy hamlets and raced across deserted, wind-swept crossroads. His mind a welter of half-formed plans, the deep, slow sadness had been pushed temporarily aside by a bleak, bitter anger directed at the State he held responsible. The car swerved suddenly towards a ditch. Ryabov swung the wheel hard and the car slewed back on to the road scattering a shower of gravel towards an old, headscarved woman who stood motionless at the roadside, watching, her feet bound with rags, a gnarled bare arm raised across her eyes as she peered dimly towards the onrushing car, a rusting tin can at her feet holding the day's supply of water. Eduard Ryabov's hands tightened on the wheel as he swept past: rags instead of shoes, a hovel for a home, clothes out of the last century; no running water for miles – yet still his country poured every rouble she couldn't spare into the sophisticated science of mass destruction! And he was a part of the insanity! Had been a part of it. Control – remember, remember, control, muttered Ryabov to himself. As the woman receded in a swirl of dust behind him he saw instead a shuffling column of villagers and a dead man lying sprawled in a field, his head aflame, near a place that had once been named Kafi-yevka.

Half an hour later the first black limousine rolled quietly to a halt outside Professor Ryabov's silent dasha. Leaving the driver behind the wheel, two men got out and strode briskly up the narrow path to the front door. Both carried pistols strapped to their leather coat-belts. One rapped smartly on the door. It swung back. They exchanged glances, loosened the flaps on their holsters and stepped cautiously inside. There was silence. They walked through the hall into the lounge looking carefully about them all the while. 'Professor? Professor Eduard Ryabov?' There was no reply.

The taller of the two sniffed a couple of times, crossed to the fireplace and dropped to one knee to examine the smoking embers of a fire in the hearth. His colleague walked slowly around the lounge and moved towards the kitchen. 'Here – take a look at this,' ordered the man by the hearth, holding up the remains of a badly charred photograph. 'And this – and this –' a finger poked through the ashes. The two KGB officers exchanged glances.

'Look at this lot,' said the man by the kitchen, pointing to the cutlery strewn on the kitchen floor. Without comment both drew their pistols and moved upstairs, the wooden stairs creaking protestingly beneath their cautious weight.

A minute more and they were looking down without compassion at the body of Irena Ryabov. Fastening the flap of his holster the taller of the two men from Internal Investigations tossed the pillow and counterpane aside and glanced up. 'What the hell does this mean, then? You think the old man's gone off his rocker?'

The other shrugged and turned back from an examination of the dressing-table. 'How the hell should I know? But

I'll tell you something –' he bit on the edge of a gold cuff-link and then slipped the pair into an inside pocket with practised ease – 'there's a smell about this I don't like. I don't like it one little bit.' He turned and led the way downstairs. Over his shoulder, his boots clumping on the wooden treads: 'I'm going to call the chief. Let that bastard get out of bed and sort it out. We're out of our depth here, comrade.' He lifted the receiver and started dialling. Then he stopped, swore briefly and dropped the receiver back on its cradle. The line had been disconnected. On his own orders.

It was another four minutes before they had roused the nearest neighbour and placed the call through to District Headquarters. By that time Professor Ryabov was deep inside the space faculty at Semipalatinsk.

Hands clammy with sweat on the black plastic brief-case containing the secret notes, documents and calculations he had taken from his office safe a few minutes ago, Professor Ryabov tried not to hurry. Act normally, he told himself, swallowing nervously as he stepped out on to the neon-lit concrete ramp that led down to the Mission Co-ordination Centre. He repeated his litany: Remember: always, always – control. See how easy it is, he lied to himself, the empty words rattling round a feverish mind: you have made this journey a hundred times before and no one has stopped you. Go on. It will be easy. He forced himself to walk down the ramp, to place one foot in front of another. Good. And again. On he walked, fearing discovery, fearing detection, fearing above all that his courage would not match this moment of greatest need; that he would betray himself and that thus he would betray Irena.

There was a guard ahead now, as he had known there would be, a guard armed with an automatic weapon who was watching impassively beneath a peaked cap as the Professor drew nearer. Ryabov walked on, his steps slowing as his courage ran away through the soles of his shoes at the prospect of confrontation. There was a sudden flurry of movement and Ryabov looked up, fearfully. 'Professor Ryabov –' began the guard, snapping to attention.

Ryabov paused, stopped, almost turned to dart back the way he had come. Somehow he managed a reply. 'Yes? What . . . what do you want?'

The sentry saluted smartly as they came level. 'My comrades and I . . . well, congratulations, Professor, that's all. What you've done . . . what you've achieved for the Motherland – fantastic,' he blurted.

Ryabov felt the cold sweat trickle down to the small of his back. 'You . . . you think so? Thank you. Thank you . . . comrade. That's really . . . most kind,' he managed.

The sentry peered closer. 'Professor? Are you all right?'

'What? Oh yes, yes . . . perfectly.' He walked on down the ramp, round a corner and on past another sentry in a glass-walled booth. Round another corner – still sloping downwards – and then past the heavy steel blast doors. Here he was stopped beside the storeroom and he handed his papers forward for examination. The sentry grinned and handed them back with hardly a glance. With something akin to despair Ryabov realized that to these people he was something of a celebrity.

Into the Mission Co-ordination Centre. Half a dozen technicians were sitting before their controls watching the monitors and making minute adjustments to their equipment before writing up the duty logs in meticulous detail. Others were yawning and making desultory conversation as they whiled away the last of the shift. On the monitors, Ryabov could see that the Soyuz crew were still sleeping, their body-scan readings dipped low into the trough of relaxation. Someone glanced round and there was a brief stirring of interest as the Professor took his seat amid a smattering of applause. He acknowledged this with a taut, stiff smile before the staff fell back into their practised routines, the Professor slotting neatly into the pattern of activity as he pretended to pore over the yellow-edged print-outs that had collected on his desk during his absence.

He sat down to stare blindly at the cards before him, the

thump of his accelerating heart-beat hammering in his ears. He tried to think, to plan clearly, but instead felt only a rising panic of inadequacy. Suddenly he saw that the next phase, the careful and surreptitious re-programming of terminal functionae and the stealthy re-calibrating of acquisition sensors under the very noses of his colleagues, was impossible. The consoles were too well attended, the technicians too alert, too primed with excitement for the morrow to be lulled into inattentiveness. With mounting despair, Professor Ryabov faced failure: concentrating on the problems of physical penetration – problems now solved and behind him – he had given scant thought to the sabotage of the work with which he was most familiar. And it was that which now threatened to defeat him.

Three minutes crept by. Three minutes in which his arms began to shake, his bowels loosened and the voice inside his mind screamed: 'Do something! Any moment now the alarms will go; it will be over! There will be the hand on your shoulder and you will have failed! Do something! Think! Think of Irena, think of her! The woman you loved, the woman you murdered! Was that for nothing? Think of something!'

'Professor Ryabov – may I bring to your attention – Professor? Is everything all right?' One of the duty crew leant forward earnestly, a clipboard of figures held ready for Ryabov's inspection and signature. Leaving his briefcase on the floor by his chair, Ryabov pushed to his feet, the sweat giving his lined face a dull, sickly sheen:

'I . . . I do not feel so good,' he admitted, looking around with confusion.

'Can I –?'

'No, no – it will pass. I . . . I shall be better presently. It is . . . it is an old complaint.' The technician stepped back doubtfully as the Professor walked away: he had to get somewhere he could be alone, where he could think, plan! He walked blindly into the storeroom beside the heavy blast doors, pushed the door closed behind him and sagged back against the wall. Boxes of duplicating paper and stencils,

341 :

cartons of stationery, heavy metal drums of lubricants, a duplicating machine and a heavy stapler set up in a corner – Ryabov dragged a hand across his face as though to wipe away the confusion that surrounded him. He leant against the duplicator and tried desperately to focus his thoughts, to shut off the vivid pictures of his wife's final muffled, thrashing moments. He leant forward, head bowed, and then turned suddenly as the door opened behind him and an armed sentry came into the storeroom. 'Professor? They are saying that you are ill, that you are unwell, comrade. It is best if you follow Standing Instructions yourself: report to sick bay,' suggested the man, not unkindly. He stepped closer and a hand descended on Ryabov's shoulder.

The Professor swung round, the heavy metal staple-gun clutched in one hand, and brought it sweeping round into the side of the man's face in a vicious swipe of deranged energy that bowled the man sideways without a sound. Hat spinning off, he slumped sideways, the Kalashnikov clattering loudly to the floor. Panting heavily, Ryabov dropped the staple-gun and scrambled after the assault rifle, greedy and desperate for the strength it could give him. His fingers closed around the stock. He lifted the heavy, unfamiliar weapon and examined it feverishly. Then he listened, crouched beside the unconscious guard, straining for the sounds that would herald detection. None came.

He rose panting, wiped his hands down the sides of his jacket and moved towards the door, his breath still coming in short, nervous gasps. He paused, breathed deeply – and then stepped out of the storeroom.

He moved silently towards the front of the console beneath the monitors – a portly, untidy little scientist with thinning hair, his face still gleaming with sweat as he blinked in the glare of the lights and clutched the loaded levelled rifle in both hands. First one and then another of the technicians felt something tug at their concentration so that they glanced up to stare in amazement as Professor Ryabov, *their* Professor Ryabov, gestured them from their seats with the muzzle of the Kalashnikov.

'Professor? What on earth do –?'

Ryabov shook his head impatiently. 'Miklov, Radimir
. . . away . . . away from the controls. Step back,' he ordered
with a new and strange strength. 'Do nothing.' His eyes
flicked to the heavy steel doors and the empty corridor
beyond, his words and the barrel of the weapon bringing up
the heads one after another, until all those in the Centre
were standing silent and motionless behind their chairs like
schoolchildren awaiting punishment, their faces washed by
that same look of stunned incomprehension.

Miklov raised his hands and stepped forward slowly.
'Look, Professor – take it easy. What is all this? We're your
friends, remember,' he soothed. 'Put the gun down. You've
been under a great deal of strain, that's all. We've *all* been
under –'

'Stay . . . stay where you are,' ordered Ryabov, stopping
him with a sudden jerk of the gun barrel.

Miklov stopped, then tried again. 'Why, Professor? Why
are you doing this? What can you possibly hope –'

'Why?' demanded Ryabov. 'Why? You want to know
why?' His voice rose. 'Because . . . because it is misguided,
that is *why*. Because it is inhuman! Because . . . because it is
. . . wrong. That is why,' he ended, almost in a whisper.
'Stop!' he commanded suddenly. Just in time he had seen
Miklov's hand come down to the back of the chair and begin
to slide towards the alarm. It didn't need the alarm bells,
the klaxons. All it needed was one shout and the guards
would be tumbling down that corridor in an instant. He
must hurry, otherwise . . . otherwise . . . 'You – Miklov:
you will lead the others through to the spectators' gallery –'

'How can you –?'

'Please – do not argue. Do what I say and it . . . it will
soon be over. It will be over for all of us.'

Miklov turned and began to lead the way between the
empty chairs towards the corridor and side entrance to the
spectators' gallery beyond the steel doors. Professor Ryabov
stopped them beside the storeroom and gestured two men
inside for the unconscious, bleeding guard. As he turned to

watch them bending down for the body another technician lunged forward, stabbed the alarm and slipped back into the cluster of prisoners as the alarm gongs went down. Ryabov swung round, steeling himself to open fire as he searched for the culprit amid the sea of white, scared faces. One of the women started crying. Suddenly Professor Ryabov relaxed, his finger moved away from the trigger. It was done now. And there had been enough killing. The two men backed awkwardly out of the storeroom, the burly weight of the guard hanging head-down between them. The party moved slowly forward and then halted suddenly as Ryabov turned to face the sound he had dreaded, the clatter of steel-tipped boots on concrete.

The young sentry who had congratulated him earlier rounded the corner in a hurry, still struggling with the sling of his rifle. Young he might be – foolish he wasn't. As Professor Ryabov jabbed his Kalashnikov forward nervously, the boy froze and then let his own weapon fall from his hands without a word. It clattered on the concrete. Ryabov nodded his relief, wiped his forehead with a shaking hand and gestured the sentry over with the others. 'With . . . with them . . . good. Now, all of you: in there – quickly.' He herded them inside the spectators' gallery, pulled the door closed and turned the key. Hurrying back into the Centre he glanced fearfully behind him, tossed the rifle aside and rushed over to one of the heavy steel doors, the klaxon filling the corridors with its harsh, strident cough.

Feverish with the need for haste, hands slippery with sweat, he began turning the gleaming spoked wheel that would pull the steel doors closed and lock him, alone, in the Centre. Slowly, inch by grudging inch, the doors began to rumble across the mouth of the empty corridor, sealing Ryabov from the spectators and whatever reinforcements might suddenly arrive around the corner of the corridor. Panting with exertion, muttering a mumble of indistinct prayers under his breath, he spun the gleaming wheel. Then, as the doors drew closer, and the sweat was puddling into his thick eyebrows, he heard the whine of the lift and the crash as the gates snapped back. There was the bark of commands and the clatter of boots on concrete. Three feet to go . . . two . . .

There was a sudden shout. Peering fearfully through the narrowing gap Professor Ryabov saw the first of the guards turn the corner and point. Then his rifle came up, and the first shots crashed out to splash harmlessly against the thick steel doors. Nine inches . . . six . . . three. As the doors came together with a soft, heavy thud, more shots spattered harmlessly against steel plate and whined away down the corridor.

There was a shout, then silence.

He was alone. Professor Ryabov leant back against the closed doors, legs shaking, body quaking with fear and exertion. Looking up, he saw himself reflected in four of the wall monitors and, as he moved around the deserted chamber, the cyclops eye of the camera fixed high on the wall rotated angrily after him, following his every move. He turned and looked across at the spectators' gallery, the need for haste less pressing now. They were all there, pressed against the glass, all watching fearfully for what he would do next through the thick armoured glass, their mouths opening and closing as they shouted lost messages from their world to his.

He hurried over to his chair, a sudden thought filling his mind. He ripped out the microphone connection with the gallery, reached down for the black brief-case and groped feverishly inside. They'd use gas, gas for a certainty; they'd feed it through to him via the air-conditioning: some form of toxin agent – Ricin, maybe even Saxitoxin 'TZ' – something they could use fast and neutralize quickly afterwards. He had thought that far ahead, at least.

Ryabov tipped his papers out of his brief-case and felt inside for his civil defence respirator. He dragged it on over his head and stared impassively into the gallery, infinitely sinister behind the crude, round eye-pieces. He could see the mouths working, shouting at him. He turned away, studied the rows of controls in front of him and forced himself to ignore the claustrophobic restrictions of the gas mask and the wisps of yellow smoke – the trace agent – that had begun to seep from the wall ventings.

Ever fearful of sabotage, theft or even hi-jack of their most precious secrets in space, the Russians had long made it their policy to arm each space vehicle with small explosive charges that could be triggered from the ground. Slowly Ryabov worked his way along the rows of dials as he felt the first of the toxin prickle almost playfully on his wrists and at the bare lobes of his ears. He looked up at the screen: there was Skyshroud, rotating softly in the velvet silence, menacing and earth-pointing as it wheeled high above the world it threatened, its potency already proven.

The prickling was getting worse and there was a tingling numbness now at the edges of his mouth as Ryabov tore his eyes away from the screen and hurried back to the console. Almost immediately his searching eyes found the red plastic cover recessed into the top of the controls. With fingers suddenly, inexplicably clumsy, he broke the seals, slid back the cover and saw a single black handle below: Self Destruct.

Without the slightest hesitation, Ryabov pulled it. Lights began to flash their warning on the control panel as he glanced up at the screen, willing an end to the machine, to the weapon he had helped build.

Nothing appeared to happen.

He was turning away when, suddenly, almost in slow motion, the delicate filigree of slender girders began to peel apart, its fragile, weightless integrity torn from within by the necklace of sealed charges that chopped obediently through its cold heart. Professor Ryabov stood back silently as the work of a lifetime yawed, rolled, turned away and broke slowly into glittering pieces, each expanding from the centre to drift away on a thousand different orbits.

Professor Ryabov was satisfied. He seemed almost oblivious of the swirling eddies of nerve gas as he heaped his papers into careless confusion on the floor, fumbled with his matches – and paused.

He walked slowly back towards the gallery and paused before the armoured glass window, peering through the eye-pieces of his respirator into the shouting mouths, the bulging, silent faces, reaching out to almost touch the angry fists that smashed against the window in an impotency of rage and frustration. If he was looking for an answer, if he was looking for some reason to delay, to change his mind, he did not find it – but when he turned away, finally, he had found, instead, a certain peace.

He returned to his pile of papers and lit a match.

When the flames had died away he kicked the ashes into a swirling cloud and walked back towards the spectators' gallery. They were quieter now and professionally curious as they shook their heads. Why? the mouths demanded. Why did you do it?

Professor Eduard Ryabov shrugged, too weary now to offer reply.

Before the eyes of his horrified audience he now reached up and tore off his respirator. 'I'm coming, Irena,' he said, breathing deeply. 'I'm coming.'

: : 24 : : : : : : : : : : : : : : :

At the exact moment when the extractor fans at Semipalat-insk began to suck out and then scrub clean the poisoned air that swirled around the crumpled, lifeless body of Professor Ryabov, a telephone began to ring in a certain apartment in Washington DC.

Ferris had been reading. He laid the paperback aside and reached for the telephone. This would probably be the recall.

It wasn't.

'There's been an unforeseen development,' reported the voice in New York shortly. 'The boy we talked about earlier left home with a roll of film – a present from his uncle. He must not be permitted to show this film to his new friends. You are therefore authorized to retrieve the film and tidy up whatever loose ends remain in your usual manner, is that clear?'

'How much time do I have?'

'None at all. You are to take action immediately. Nothing clever, nothing complicated – there is no time. Do you understand?'

'I understand.'

'Good. Contact this number when the business is done – and remember: no loose ends.'

In Frank's Georgetown apartment there was a party in progress. High-backed chairs ranged around the dining-room table, they were welcoming Misha to America with an impromptu tea-party. It had been Mrs Headley's idea. Now she patted a napkin to her full lips, pushed her empty plate towards the happy debris in the middle of the table, and rose to her feet. 'Now – just hush up for a minute, you hear?' She flapped her fat arms. 'Now, Louise: what have we forgotten? For our friend here?' she asked theatrically.

'The cake! The cake!' squealed Louise, a hand flying to her mouth as she bounced up and down on the chair, blond hair flying. Frank caught Lydia's eye across the table and smiled. She looked transformed, he decided – lit up from within now that it was all over and she was reunited with her son. Lydia glanced across at Misha and then back at him. 'Thank you,' she mouthed silently above the banter, the laughter. Frank nodded as Lydia leant across to Misha, ruffled his hair for the sixth time and whispered something in Russian as Mrs Headley pushed back her chair and went through the swing doors into the kitchen. There was muffled banging, the sound of drawers opening and closing. Then there was the sudden rasp of a match.

'Frank? Would you fix the lights?' she called, her voice muffled by the swing doors. He rose, turned off the lights and returned to his seat amid hushed, expectant silence.

'Da – da! Here we come!' The doors swung back and Mrs Headley walked carefully into the dining-room, the cake balanced in both hands, its rich chocolate topping ablaze with candles. Louise did some more bouncing up and down, Lydia and Frank clapped, while Misha looked as though he was about to explode with speechless excitement. Mrs Headley placed the cake gently in front of him and stood back, smiling fondly, to watch the awe in the boy's face that was lit by the warmth of a dozen flickering candles.

'I did that,' explained Louise proudly, pointing at the boy's name scrawled in uneven white icing across the cake. 'See? It says Misha! You must blow out the candles – all together!' she insisted as Lydia bent across to translate.

Cheeks huge, Misha blew. The smell of hot wax, a sudden burst of applause and then the lights snapped on again. Mrs Headley handed Misha the long-bladed cake knife and gestured at her masterpiece. 'Well . . . go on. What are you waiting for?'

'No! One moment!' Lydia held up a stern hand and turned to Misha. She rattled something in Russian. They all waited expectantly as the boy gazed mesmerized at his cake. 'Misha! What do you say?' She jogged his arm playfully and everyone laughed. Then the boy looked up at his mother, nodded, and gazed at the ceiling in frowning concentration.

'I . . . I am verr . . . happy to be in this place with all my friend. Thank you,' he concluded triumphantly as the room echoed to more happy clapping.

Generals Holt and Freeman stood over by the window examining in silence the photographs of what had once been the Soviet village of Kafiyevka. Biting across the entire width of the photographs like some gigantic axe-blow was a deep, trench-like scar that sliced impartially across the smoking, levelled ruins of streets, homes and fields.

General Holt tapped the top picture quietly. 'We've notified NSC,* of course: on my authority the Department has sanctioned an SR-71† over-fly mission for ASA‡ downwind of target. We should have the results within five hours.

Freeman grunted. 'That, General, will just confirm the obvious. Don't hold your fire with NSC just because *that* analysis isn't in yet. What we have here, in my view, constitutes the single –' He broke off as there was a hurried knocking on the door. Without waiting for permission to enter, Captain Fisher strode in to Holt's office. He looked pale and shaken, his collar unfastened. He saluted almost as an afterthought.

'What's the meaning of this, Captain?' demanded Holt angrily as he snapped off a return salute and glowered at Fisher.

The Captain swallowed nervously but held his ground. He waved a signal flimsy at the two Generals. 'I think you should see this one, General, right away.'

Holt strode forward, flicked the signal from Fisher's

* NSC: National Security Council.
† SR-71: USAF high-altitude spyplane; speeds of Mach 3 at 100,000 feet.
‡ ASA: Air Sample Analysis.

fingers and studied it silently. A moment's pause, then 'Holy shit,' he breathed.

'Captain?' demanded Freeman. 'What gives?'

'CIA Stockholm station intercepted an open-line telecomm from the Soviet Union to a Professor Olafsen in Stockholm. The call originated from Semipalatinsk. A Professor Eduard Ryabov —'

'Let me see that, General.' Freeman almost tore the signal from Holt's fingers. He read it rapidly and then looked up, eyes blazing, face knifing forward. 'And this is an exact transcript of the call from Ryabov to this . . . this Professor Olafsen?' snapped Freeman.

Captain Fisher nodded. 'That is my information, yes, sir. We monitor all Eastern bloc/Scandinavian telecomms as a matter of routine. Once we'd checked with Olafsen we broke the tape and arranged transcription. The co-ordinates he gives there? The name of that place, Kafiyevka? They all check out, General.'

Holt nodded and pointed at the pictures on his desk. 'We've got that far, Captain.'

Freeman butted in impatiently. 'This last sentence here, Captain: "The Prolev boy carried a camera – a gift from me, you understand? The first six frames of that camera film contain —" and then he stopped. What happened there?'

'The call was intercepted —'

'You mean by *us*, Captain?'

There was the slightest of pauses. 'No, sir. I do not.'

'Jesus!' General Freeman strode to Holt's desk, reached for the phone and began tapping out Frank's home number with urgent fingers. After a few seconds he stopped, broke the connection and tried again. Nothing. 'Come on . . . come on,' he muttered. Then he whirled round. 'Don't just stand there – the camera! It's still with the boy!'

'. . . he says: will he be able to play baseball? American baseball? He has heard much about this game,' translated Lydia, her eyes shining. The cake was disappearing fast now.

Frank grinned and nodded. 'Sure? Why not? Tell you what – I'll teach him myself. Maybe he'll even make professional!' Lydia translated and they all laughed a little at that as Frank reached out for the long-bladed cake knife and cut himself a generous slice of Misha's cake. The doorbell sounded twice as he paused, caught in the act, the cake raised to his mouth.

Mrs Headley took pity on him and waved him back to his seat. 'Don't you move – I'll see to it.' She rose and went out into the hallway.

Frank ate for a moment and then leant forward to mime with his hands across the table for Misha. 'Now – there's this guy with the ball, right? He's called the pitcher. The pitcher.'

'The pitcher,' copied Misha solemnly.

Frank nodded. 'Fine. Now – he throws – pitches – the ball to the guy with the bat; the bats –'

'Frank? Lydia? I . . .' The words sounded small, choked, frightened. Frank stopped and spun round. Mrs Headley was standing in the doorway, a hand clasped to her throat, her eyes wide with sudden fear.

'Mrs Headley? What – ?' Then he saw him.

The man was standing slightly behind Mrs Headley in the gloom of the hallway, a silenced revolver raised to the side of her head.

The cake turned to cardboard in his throat and Frank sat motionless at the table, his hands still before him. The dining-room froze into silence. A quick glance at Lydia: glass raised to her lips, the colour draining from those cheeks as she realized that fate had one last trick to play; Misha looking at his mother, not understanding; Louise staring first at Mrs Headley, then at the revolver, then at him, looking for a lead, for guidance.

'Go forward,' ordered Ferris softly. Mrs Headley stepped slowly into the dining-room and Frank was able to make out the gun more clearly, the black tube of the silencer spoiling the balanced lines of the Smith & Wesson .44. The silencer spelt bad news, he realized – the very worst. The time for pretence was over. He had come to use it.

'Daddy? Why is that man –'

'Sssh, Louise. Quiet now. Just be still.'

Ferris nodded his approval. 'That is good advice. Everyone keep quite still –' he smiled mirthlessly at the children – 'just like in the movies. Stop!' He halted Mrs Headley with a light touch of the gun barrel, and she let out a little squeak of fear. Ferris moved to her side. He was standing now on Frank's left, his side to the service hatch through to the kitchen, the barrel inches away from Mrs Headley's temple, the hammer thumbed back, rearing, poised.

'The camera film: where is it?' demanded Ferris, the gun never wavering. No colourful threats, no wasted words, no self-congratulatory I-suppose-you're-wondering-how-I-did-it? Just straight in: the camera film.

Frank had no idea what he was talking about.

'The camera film?' he echoed stupidly, looking as blank as he felt, hiding the first flicker of hope, of a chance. The gun moved not a fraction.

'The film from the boy's camera, Captain Yates. You know where it is. You will tell me where it is within the next ten seconds.'

There were five of them: himself, Lydia, Mrs Headley and the two children – Louise and Misha. The Smith & Wesson .44 Gold Seal carried six chambered rounds. Frank worked it out for himself. Then he nodded. 'Fair enough. It's in the kitchen. I'll get it.' He placed his hands on the table beside the cake knife and made to rise.

The cold, calm voice stopped him. 'Wait! Where in the kitchen?'

'In the ice-box,' lied Frank, avoiding Lydia's look of frightened incomprehension. They both knew the camera was on Misha's bed in the spare room. The film, presumably, was still in the camera.

'You –' The pistol stretched out softly and touched Mrs Headley on the shoulder. She winced. 'Yes – you, Mrs Headley. Go and fetch it.'

'Fetch . . . fetch it?' she wavered. 'The camera film?'

Ferris nodded patiently, completely at ease. In control.

'Yes. That is what I said. Fetch the camera film. From the ice-box in the kitchen. Bring it to me,' he ordered.

As Mrs Headley moved towards the kitchen, bottom lip quivering, 'It's in a plastic bag. On top of the ice cubes,' said Frank slowly, clearly, aware as he spoke that the words could be sending her to her death. He sat back in his chair, measuring distance, planning his move, plotting the one slim chance he would get. If he was lucky.

The room waited, Misha, Lydia and Louise frozen in their chairs. Frank walked his mind to the ice-box: she's opening the door . . . she's looking up . . . she's reaching for the inner cabinet door . . . she's – thank God! He heard the rustle of a plastic bag being unfolded, the dry clatter of ice cubes being dislodged. Any moment now.

He prayed she wouldn't try and do anything silly, wouldn't try cocking the action, wouldn't try thumbing back the hammer or checking the magazine on the heavy automatic he had hidden there in the days when they had been living here under siege. The hesitant steps began returning across the polished kitchen floor and he gathered himself for the one despairing chance he could give them all . . .

'Daddy –' Louise broke the silence. Ferris turned suddenly towards the girl, the gun moving with him as the doors of the service hatch burst back and Mrs Headley was framed in the hatchway, heavy pistol clutched in both hands, eyes sighting wildly down the barrel as Ferris swung towards her.

She froze, unable to pull the trigger, as Ferris snapped on to the target. Yet even as he turned, so Frank made his move. Mrs Headley had given him the half-second, the fraction of a chance he had been praying for.

Pushing aside his own chair with his left, his right hand swept up the sharp, long-bladed cake knife as he rose to his feet and spun left towards the gunman. There was a blur of movement as Ferris turned to meet him. Frank lunged forward. The knife was through and in, glancing off a raised forearm to sink eagerly through the muscle wall of the man's flat stomach into the soft vitals beyond. Ferris grunted as the blade went in. His legs began to buckle as he lurched forward, the gun arm swinging round. Chairs and crockery went over with a crash as an out-flung arm caught the tablecloth and dragged it to the carpet with them.

Louise began screaming. Then two shots rang out. Mrs Headley's round furrowed uselessly into the ceiling as the heavy automatic kicked high. The shot from the Smith & Wesson thudded silently into the plasterwork an inch to the right of Louise, as Frank twisted his knife arm and jerked viciously, cutting, hunting into the stomach-bag, twisting the knife upwards for the killing stroke as his left arm chopped at the side of the man's head, the knife hand slippery now with blood.

No good. The man was struggling violently, fighting, kicking with desperate strength, bringing the gun hand round. Frank smashed at the silent, sweating face with his left fist, butting his own head against the man's straining, bared teeth. Suddenly, Frank felt a weakening. He prised his fingers loose from their death-grip on the wet handle of the cake knife, wriggled his hand free and lunged with both hands for the gun arm. One more shot into that crowded room . . . With desperate, feral strength he locked his hands on Ferris's wrist, tore the thumb away from the butt and jerked it back savagely until the tendons cracked. A moan of agony broke from the man's smashed lips as Frank ripped the revolver free, tugged back the hammer, rammed the pistol into the man's side and fired twice. He felt the shells thud upwards into the struggling body. The man jumped, arched his back, shuddered – and was still.

For long moments Frank lay panting over the corpse, his daughter's screams dinning in his ears, the sticky dark glue of the man's lifeblood seeping into his torn clothes. Finally 'Lydia?' he panted from the floor. 'Lydia – can you hear me?'

'Frank?' Disbelief, incredulity. He heard a chair scrape back as she began to hurry forward –

'No! Stay back! Get the . . . get the children away. Into a bedroom. Bring a . . . bring a blanket –'

'Are you –?'

'JUST DO IT!' he screamed, the blast of his breath ruffling Ferris's dead hair.

As Lydia hustled the hysterical, sobbing children into the spare bedroom, Frank pushed himself slowly to his feet. He stood there, shoulders heaving, aching in every bone, looking down at the dead man sprawled amid the ruins of their tea party. He lifted his head. Mrs Headley was staring into hell through the hatchway, her eyes huge with the savage terror she had witnessed. Too gone for smiling, Frank nodded his thanks and prised the gun from her trembling fingers. Then he leant back against the wall and waited for the room to stop turning.

Lydia returned with a blanket. They draped it over the butchered man on the floor, stumbled into the lounge and sank on to the sofa, utterly spent.

It was three hours later and General Clarke Freeman was standing before the mirror in his outer office, curbing a fuming impatience as his secretary fussed around him, plucking invisible specks of fluff and lint off an already immaculate uniform.

In those three hours, much had happened. Misha and Louise were now both asleep, sedated and under guard. Frank Yates and Lydia Prolev were in the midst of extensive debriefing, and the last of the security officers had just finished their work in Frank's Georgetown apartment. When they left they used the rear entrance and carried with them the bloody remains of the man called Ferris, the corpse neatly tagged, bagged and labelled. Misha's camera – the one containing Professor Ryabov's vital film – had been whisked away by an earnest, bespectacled technician for process and analysis as the first of a dozen priority calls had been made: to NPIC, to the State Department, to the Chairman of the Joint Chiefs of Staff and to a host of others. Now, as General Freeman's secretary gave his shoulders a final sweep with the clothes brush, the phone rang once more on her desk. She took the call, listened briefly and replaced the receiver. 'Your car's downstairs, General. Ramp 4. General

Holt is waiting for you there. He'd like you to ride to the White House together.'

'I'll bet he would,' thought Freeman grimly. He nodded, swept up his service cap and strode swiftly down the corridor towards the elevators.

General Holt was waiting in the back of the dark blue Air Force limousine, his face in shadow. As Freeman climbed in beside him, Holt pressed the button at his elbow and the glass partition separating driver from passengers sighed smoothly upwards. 'All set for the Chief, General?' asked Holt as the limousine slid forward towards the mouth of the concrete ramp and the daylight beyond, the flags of Holt's appointment fluttering at the bonnet. General Freeman nodded silently, bitterly amused to notice the little signs of nervousness as Holt's fingers drummed softly against a blue-clad knee before darting to adjust the tight knot of his tie and then down again to play with the gleaming clasps of the brief-case on his lap.

'Ryabov's pictures through yet?' asked Freeman idly as the car swept forward, gathering speed towards the Capitol.

'Preliminaries only. Detailed reports should be through within the hour.'

'And when's this conference?'

Holt glanced at an expensive wristwatch. 'For the press? Scheduled for forty minutes from now. They should just make it.'

Freeman nodded and they lapsed into silence as the car sped on. General Freeman waited, knowing it must come soon, knowing that time and the short duration of their journey together were on his side. Finally, it came.

'Clarke,' began Holt. 'That ... er ... that outburst of mine earlier today: in view of later developments I'm prepared to concede I was ... premature, a little hasty. I'd –'

'Premature? Hasty? You were wrong, General – right down the line,' corrected Freeman quietly.

With an eye on the road and the clock unwinding before them, Holt nodded. There was no time for argument; there was time only for compromise, concession – and precious little of that ... 'All right, all right, I was wrong. I admit that. I'd like to hope, however that we can put that behind us now we're going public on this. There are plenty of people out there in the Community only too happy to see the Air Force take a tumble. They don't need to see us feuding among ourselves, Clarke. We'd be handing it to them on a plate. If we could bury our differences –'

'For the good of the service?' mocked Freeman rhetorically as their car swept into M Street and headed towards Rock Creek and Pennsylvania Avenue, the pennants snapping in the wind.

General Holt glanced sharply at Freeman and then nodded. 'For the good of the service,' repeated Holt. 'Yes, that about covers it.'

They drove on in silence, each wrapped in his own thoughts. Then 'And MX? What happens to the missile programme?' asked Freeman.

There was a pause. 'MX, the buried trench concept – all that will have to go back under review. Status on that entire programme will come in for a long, hard look, I promise you.'

'And the Chief? How much does he know about all this? How much has he been told?'

'By the time we get there the President will have the overview. He'll be apprised of the call to Stockholm from that Professor ... Ryabov, and he'll have that first initial intelligence profile from the JCOS's office –'

'Kafiyevka?'

Holt nodded. 'He'll have the word on that, too.'

Their limousine pulled in to the side of the road beside a white sentry post set behind a row of high, spiked railings. Through these railings, beyond a vista of manicured lawns, cedar trees and neatly arranged flower beds, loomed the White House itself. Their Air Force driver wound down his window and handed their papers to the uniformed Secret Service Sergeant in charge of the guard detail. The Sergeant saluted, bent down to peer into the rear of the car and then nodded to a colleague. The high gates clicked open, the car sighed forward and, as the Sergeant lifted the internal phone to warn the White House staff of the Generals' arrival, they drove slowly through the tree-lined grounds towards the ancient powerbase of America itself.

They were met at the sheltered entrance by a young, unsmiling aide in a dark business suit and thick, metal-framed spectacles. He shook hands gravely. 'Will you follow me, please?' Turning, he led the way up a short flight of marble steps and along a thickly carpeted, vaulted-arch corridor, past the China Room and the Diplomatic Reception Room with its South Portico towards the President's Oval Office, the two Generals walking briskly behind him.

The trio crossed the double-doored entrance to the Reception Room and heard the muted stutter of electric typewriters from the staff offices. Along past the kitchens and into the West Wing, with another, shorter length of carpeted corridor interrupted by a series of ornate decorative alcoves. The unsmiling aide stopped before a simple white door. He entered without knocking and Holt and Freeman found themselves in the outer office of the President of the United States. Two secretaries glanced up from their typewriters and smiled pleasantly at the stern-faced Generals. Their escort crossed to one of the desks, leant over and spoke softly into the intercom. Then he straightened, tugged down the sleeves of his jacket until only the merest hint of shirt-cuff was revealed, and gestured to the inner office. 'The Chief of Staff will see you now.'

They went in together.

The President had his back to them, gazing out past the high sweep of elegant bow windows across the lawns towards the Capitol. Between the President and his subordinates stood a heavy oak desk across which had slid the papers that had forged a nation's destiny for two centuries. On that desk now lay a single grey file bearing the highest known security classification within the United States Air Force. They waited.

'Brigadier-General Holt, General Freeman, Mr President,' murmured the aide before withdrawing on silent feet. The door snicked shut behind him and the President turned. Both officers saluted and their commander nodded recognition, the smile that reassured the voting millions conspicuously absent, for there were no votes to be gained here: this was business, the business of ultimate, unvarnished command – business for which once, he recalled, he had hungered. But three years of office had crushed the spring from his step and added lines to the famous face. Looking older now than both men remembered him, the President strode across the Seal of Office woven into the rich carpet at his feet and shook hands. 'General Holt, General Freeman – thank you for coming so promptly. Relax, gentlemen – take a seat. I just want to pick your brains for a moment before I face those . . . those jackals in there.' He gestured wryly towards the press chamber beyond the closed doors and smiled a wintry smile to take the sting out of his words: wars, policies, entire elections were now won or lost by media impact; that too was an unpalatable truth he had been forced to swallow early in a turbulent and accelerated political career.

He waved his officers to two leather chairs and stepped behind his desk. Remaining standing, he hefted the USAF Hammer report Holt and Freeman had put together in such haste two hours earlier and studied the two men in silence for a long moment. 'I am advised immediate and widespread publicity regarding this . . . this development, is the first priority. However, before I go in there, I need the answer to just one question, gentlemen. That question is this: just how serious a threat does this Hammer business pose to our nation? To the western alliance?' He shook his head tiredly. 'I know I can read it for myself, get all the nuances God ever invented from those Agency aides, but I wanted to hear from you people, the men who put it all together. How grave, gentlemen? Brigadier-General Holt?'

Holt leant forward earnestly. 'Extremely grave, Mr President. In my view, the evidence we have placed before you today represents a fundamental shift in the balance of the existing US/Soviet relationship. It cuts clean across all previously agreed and accepted norms of international conduct. If I might be permitted to go further – ?'

He paused and the President nodded impatiently. 'That's what you're here for, General.'

'Very well, Mr President: I believe the development outlined to you today by my own department calls for nothing less than a major and fundamental review of existing US ICBM capability. There should be an immediate –'

'Hold it there a second, General. General Freeman – you go along with that?'

Staggered at the speed, the sheer bold effrontery with which General Holt had pushed him aside to step into *his* shoes as the lone voice of warning, General Freeman could only nod agreement. 'Yes, Mr President. Yes, I do. I go along with that one hundred per cent.'

They talked for several minutes, then a door opened softly behind them. 'Excuse me, Mr President: the Press conference should have started three minutes ago.'

The President nodded and laid the Hammer file aside. 'Fine. How are they, Clyde? What's their mood?'

'I'd say they're intrigued, Mr President. There's the smell of something big in the air. They're not sure what it is yet, but all networks have taken between four and seven minutes' air time on indefinite standby.'

The President turned to his two Generals. 'We'll try not to disappoint them. Just tell me one last thing, gentlemen: when did you start in on this? What first alerted you to this kind of Soviet capability?'

General Holt stepped in quickly. 'It first came to my attention two years ago, Mr President. That's when we intercepted the first technical indicators. Indicators, of course, are one thing – it was the discovery of such a capability that took the time.'

Holt contrived to look both modest and self-effacing. General Freeman watched his efforts with cold contempt. The President made a swift note and came round from behind his desk. 'Gentlemen, you'll join me? Watch from the wings? Could be you'll find it interesting.'

Thirty or forty pressmen and women were clustered in the well of the brightly lit press centre, smoking and talking in low tones in the way of those whose job it is to wait on the whim of others. Television cameras and bright lights were already set up facing the speaker's lectern embossed with the Seal of the President of the United States. A prickle of microphones decorated the top of the lectern, and wires and cables trailed across the floor in apparent confusion.

Brigadier-General Holt and General Freeman waited quietly in the shadows beside the President and his two armed bodyguards. Waiting a moment longer, the aide called Clyde nodded at the President's Press Secretary, who stepped in front of the microphones, leant forward and said simply: 'Ladies and gentlemen: the President of the United States.' There was a scraping of chairs, the press stood and the room fell silent.

The President stepped into view from the side of the narrow, curtained stage, laid his notes beside him on the lectern and glanced at his audience with grave, calculated concern. Taking its cue, the room remained hushed and attentive.

'Ladies and gentlemen of the press, good afternoon.' He paused, drawing in total attention, then 'Foremost among those duties which fall to the holder of this office is the safety and security of our nation.' The cameras turned, the spools of tape revolved busily and the pencils scribbled across clean pages. 'That is a consideration that transcends all others, for without security, other aspects of government, of democracy, become meaningless. That much, I hope, is self-evident.'

The President paused. 'Two years ago I became aware that the Soviet Union was moving towards the development of a capability – I stress the word *capability*, not intention – which, if successful, could alter the very balance of her relationship with the western alliance – a capability that was in complete violation of both clause and spirit of the 1972 Strategic Arms Limitation Talks.

'I address you now, ladies and gentlemen, because I have to tell you that within the last twenty-four hours, an attempt to upset that balance has been made. That it has been thwarted is due to the courage, resource and endeavour of one of my Air Force Generals – Brigadier-General Irwin Holt – whose cogent, urgent reasoning first brought the matter to my attention. The frustration of that attempt by the Soviet Union to alter the status quo raises grave questions about both the nature of our ongoing relationship with the Soviet Union and the necessity to make a swift and appropriate response. It is with this in mind that I wish to reveal to you, for the first time, the following facts . . .'

General Clarke Freeman turned on his heel and walked slowly away.

In the former Headquarters of the KGB on Moscow's Dzehinsky Square, the atmosphere within the PKO meeting beneath the high windows was poisonous.

In the two weeks since the Ryabov débâcle, much had happened. None of it had been good: Igor Bayev, Head of the KGB's First Chief Directorate, had been removed in disgrace the day after Marshal Gladky was called to account for his actions before the Politburo itself; Mikhail Kostikov, First Deputy of Directorate T and the man who had sanctioned Professor Ryabov's visit to Stockholm in 1976, had been summarily dismissed as it became only too evident that the ploy of *dezinformatsiya* had boomeranged viciously on its masters: less than a week after the Soviets had been forced to acknowledge western accusations that they were engaged in offensive space-based beam weapon development in direct contravention of the 1972 SALT agreement, a grave-faced President of the United States had gone on nationwide television to announce the funding of a major, five-year Defense Department programme for particle beam weapon exploratory development.

The whistle had been blown on the start of the very race

the Soviet Union had dreaded and tried so hard to avoid.

Quietly listening to the arguments at the head of the polished table, Marshal Gladky was thus serving now to save, not just the game, but the match itself. He leant forward, and the room fell silent under his grim scrutiny. 'Let me repeat the question, comrades. How long? How long will it be before Minos B is completed, before we can make good the ground lost by another department's ... stupidity?' He glanced towards Kostikov's replacement, and the man looked hurriedly down at his papers.

There was a long silence, as Marshal Gladky raked the row of stern faces with that famous, implacable gaze.

He settled, finally, on an elderly, balding Professor with old-fashioned, round black spectacles. 'Professor? Your opinion would, as always, be highly valued.'

The Professor sighed – perhaps from tiredness, perhaps in belated private recognition that personal integrity and pride had been stripped from his thin shoulders all those years ago in a far-off British courtroom.

'One year, comrade – perhaps two,' murmured Professor Klaus Fuchs.

The following article appeared in the *Daily Telegraph* on 3 October 1978:

AMERICA IN RACE FOR DEATH RAYS

America is reported to be stepping up research into particle beam weapons (death rays) to achieve a new defence against Russian missiles and space-craft by the mid-eighties.

In the wake of intelligence that Russia is pressing ahead in this field the Pentagon has briefed physicists and engineers to complete by December a plan for exploratory development of such weapons, says the Washington magazine *Aviation Week and Space Technology*.

Particle beam weapons would shoot electrons, protons, and neutrons at near the speed of light to destroy targets with high energy concentrations and heat.

In May last year Dr Brown American Defence Secretary expressed some doubt about either America or Russia being near solving the problems involved, but since then some scientists, including Dr Teller, 'father' of the H-bomb, have come to believe big advances have been made.

**More about Penguins
and Pelicans**

For further information about books available from
Penguins please write to Dept EP, Penguin Books Ltd,
Harmondsworth, Middlesex UB7 ODA.

In the U.S.A.: For a complete list of books available from
Penguins in the United States write to Dept CS, Penguin
Books, 625 Madison Avenue, New York, New York 10022.

In Canada: For a complete list of books available from
Penguins in Canada write to Penguin Books Canada Ltd,
2801 John Street, Markham, Ontario L3R 1B4.

In Australia: For a complete list of books available from
Penguins in Australia write to the Marketing Department,
Penguin Books Australia Ltd, P.O. Box 257, Ringwood,
Victoria 3134.

In New Zealand: For a complete list of books available from
Penguins in New Zealand write to the Marketing Department, Penguin Books (N.Z.) Ltd, P.O. Box 4019, Auckland
10.